A. MARIE CANTRELLE

Lifeshaper

For Selina and Azula

And I suppose all my human family members too

1

Kita

Panic crept down my spine. My heart seized and my hands refused to stop shaking.

The door slammed shut on my last day of freedom. I would be killed, I was almost certain. If not killed, then something much, much worse.

I stumbled forward, tripping on the edge my emann. The hem was soaked through with thickly congealing blood, the gorgeous emerald silk drying an ugly brown. As I walked, streaks of crimson followed me.

I wanted to pace, but there was no energy left in my bones. So I dragged myself to my bed and collapsed, my delicate garment ripping.

This room was my sanctuary. My own world in which I, alone, controlled everything. And yet it was now a prison of my own making.

"Goddesses help me," I muttered, but there was no answer from them. There were only my own thoughts.

My own thoughts, and the satiated sighs of the Beast, its thirst slaked on innocent flesh.

The feel of the wet silk against my skin became suddenly unbearable. I forced myself up onto shaky legs and pulled at the fabric. The *emann* ripped, pulling free the rest of the pins, and fell in a heap onto the floor. My delicate leather shoes followed, kicked across the room.

I caught a glimpse of my naked form in the mirror. This image, the normalcy of it, is what finally brought on the tears. And once they started, I could not seem to start. I sank the to the floor, body wracked with sobs so deep that I thought I might throw up.

Sights, sounds, *smells* of the night's events began to creep into my memory. Ran's wide eyes and slack jaw as I watched the sight unfolding in front of him. His accusatory stare as we locked eyes on the ballroom floor. The nauseating, metallic smell of blood that turned my stomach so fiercely it made my vision swim.

No, I thought. *Don't think about it.*

I hugged my knees, feeling the pounding heartbeat as I tried to steady my thoughts. I glanced around the room, looking for something, anything to focus on.

My gaze landed on the fresco painted upon the far wall. It depicted the Goddesses, each with her face contorted in her own aspect. As a child, I had always feared the Goddess of Joy. Her mouth, twisted into a too-wide smile, eyes open so far that they seemed to bulge out of her face. She always gave the impression that she was going to eat me.

Rather, I had always felt drawn to the Goddess of Hope. She had always reminded me of my mother—watching, waiting with a shy smile that encouraged me throughout my childhood, as though she was trying to transmit thoughts of love and optimism. Though I had not been to a temple nor followed the holy texts much at all throughout my life, I found myself praying to her then. Not in any concrete sense, not with words, but with emotion. If she could hope for me, the least I could do is do the same for her, to trust in her.

I got to my feet, legs shaking, feeling slightly like a newborn fawn as I hobbled to the wall. Gingerly, I touched my fingertips to fresco. The plaster came away in a fine powder, the paint chipping slightly.

The events of earlier that night momentarily forgotten, I wondered then how old the fresco was. Was it part of the palace's original construction? Had it been added later?

I was still examining the artwork when the heavy wood doors of my chambers swung open. As the bright light flooded into the dim room, my first thought was, absurdly, my bare skin.

My uncle, the crown prince Ranjali sa Sasun Meloyora, walked solemnly into the room, shutting the door behind him. He still wore his fine black emann, the silk unmarred by gore. The thin silver circlet that had been used to crown him only hours before still gleamed around his temples.

Ran was the perfect picture of royalty. Tall and muscular, with fine, straight black hair that fell in a curtain down to his mid back. His warm tawny skin glowed, even under the circumstances. To say he was handsome wasn't quite right, but he held himself with an easy confidence that attracted women and men alike. His eyes, maybe green, maybe brown, locked to mine, his eyebrows furrowed in concern. His mouth, too wide and very full, was pulled into a worried smirk, completely different from the easy smile he normally wore. He could have been my mother's twin, if she had not been born 20 years before him. We'd grown up together, chasing each other down the halls of the palace as we whooped and laughed. He was the closest thing I'd had to a sibling. Somehow, I feared his disappointment almost as much as I feared my grandfather's punishment.

Holding his gaze, I lowered myself onto a nearby chaise, struggling to still my shaking hands.

"Did he....did he send you to do it?" I asked, trying to keep my voice calm.

"Do what?" he asked.

I gawked at him in disbelief.

"He's going to kill me, Ran."

"No," he replied. "He wouldn't." Ran crossed the room, taking a seat next to me. He placed a hand on my shoulder, but I shrugged it away. He recoiled.

"You know him. He's going to kill me," I repeated.

"He wouldn't. You're family."

"Are you serious? You think that matters here?"

Ran opened his mouth to speak, but then closed it again, sighing.

"Tell me what happened," he finally said, his voice almost a whisper.

"Ran, it doesn't…"

"Just tell me. I'll talk to my father. If you tell me what happened, I can get him to be lenient."

He turned to face me, his eyes pleading.

I buried my face in my hands, my braids spilling over my shoulders.

"I…I think I am losing my mind," I muttered. "I just…I heard this voice. It was so angry and…hungry. It wanted to kill, Ran. And I couldn't do *anything* to stop it. I've never felt so powerless. I've never lost control of my affinity that way. And…I just…" I dug my fingers into my arms, the pain biting as my nails broke skin.

He sighed and rubbed my back.

The events of the evening replayed themselves in my mind. I shut my eyes, trying to push away the images.

"There's nothing you can say to him anyway," I said. "He will take it personally. That's the worst part. That's all he cares about."

"He's not this monstrous person you seem to think," Ran replied. "He can be reasoned with. I'll talk to him. He will see reason. I promise you. Okay? I swear it. He'll understand that it was a mistake." He gave me a wide smile, and his bright optimism broke my heart.

"I trust you," I said, my voice small and broken. And while I did trust that he would do his best, I knew my grandfather. He ruled his empire—and his family—with ruthless efficiency, and I would not be the exception, I felt certain.

Ran drew me into an embrace, which I weakly returned, before striding purposefully toward the door. After one last glance toward me, he knocked on the door and it swung open.

As the door closed and the lock clicked, I got to my feet and meandered to the window. I rested my elbows on the sill, poking my head out into the cool night air. For a short moment, I considered jumping, summoning a huge black bird to catch me and take me away. But I saw the tell-tale pinpricks of lit lanterns that illuminated guard patrols around the perimeter of the palace, and I was so far up that I couldn't be sure I would survive the fall without damage, even if I could scrounge the energy.

As I replayed the day's events, trying to parse what had happened, a nagging feeling caught me. I didn't notice it at first, but how could I? How could I possibly notice the *absence* of a memory? It was like noticing the absence of cold on a scorching summer's day.

But I did notice. There was something missing, a piece I couldn't quite find. I remembered awaking. I remembered breakfast with my mother, watching the guards sparring, and then...nothing at all until just before the Investiture.

Sighing, I looked out across the city. Yor-a—the jewel of the Empire. Just below the hill on which the Imperial Palace rested was the Silk District—home to nobility and stores stocking only the finest artisan goods. With its large, brightly colored houses, all was quiet. Many of the inhabitants had been at the ball; most were probably still sequestered in the palace until my grandfather could decide what to do. Guards patrolled there too, two at a time.

Beyond the inner walls, the Market District was alive with activity. Guards in the market district were more sparse, but civilians were plentiful. Despite the darkness, children were running, exercising their fledgling powers on each other in games I couldn't understand. Little flashes of light erupted from some of their little hands, sparks of lightning chasing friends and siblings. Others flung their hands out, pushing their opponents over with the force of their powers until they all fell. I could not hear them from so far away, but I imagined them laughing and whooping. Parents stood watching, letting the children experiment without getting hurt.

Watching the market children always reminded me of Ran and me growing up. We would run around the rooftop gardens. I would create dozens of small birds to swoop and swarm him. He would yell and run. Sometimes, his feet would slip through the marble floor and he would get stuck, cursing and screaming frustration as he struggled to gain control over his own affinity. Eventually, he became so skilled that any attempt to surprise him with birds or wasps was blocked by walls of solid air and a smug smirk.

The memories created a warmth in my chest that pulled me, for the moment, away from my plight. So I kept looking out, immersing myself, for the moment, in the past.

Merchants in the central bazaar had long since packed up for the night, but still the people strolled the bazaar, none of them aware of the carnage that had taken place up the hill.

Just across the river, a three-tiered pyramid jutted up into the night sky. At the top of the pyramid, the Temple of Hope was perched. I couldn't see into the temple grounds through the walls, but I could just make out the cluster of houses and taverns clinging to the space between the plateau edge and the temple walls.

This city was our city. And on this, the night that I fully expected would be my last, I realized that I hadn't been to most of it. I had rarely left the palace. And while Ran had gone on tours not only throughout the city but to the far corners of the empire, my mother and I had been largely been relegated to life inside the palace walls.

A loud bang on the door startled me from my reveries. In strode a hooded figure, and my pulse quickened. I relaxed a moment later when I realized that it was my mother.

She looked so like her brother, but wore an altogether different expression. Instead of the sad optimism Ran showed, she wore an intense expression of determination: lips pursed, brows furrowed, muscles tensed. A black traveling cloak was draped over the rich purple emann she still wore from the Investiture ceremony. A simple bronze dagger hung from her belt. Her right hand clutched a wrinkled linen shirt, which she tossed in my direction.

I stupidly let it fall.

She let out an exasperated sigh. She hadn't been at the ball, thank the goddesses. She and my grandfather had been mercifully absent. She hadn't seen, but it was clear that she had been told.

"Momma," I muttered. Tears began to well as I approached her.

"Enough of this, Kitania. We need to get you dressed and out of here."

"Wha—?"

She cut me off with a look and went to my wardrobe, rifling through her options before settling on a pair of black woolen riding pants. She thrust them at me and quickly crossed back to the door, leaning against it as she listened. "Get dressed," she repeated, stabbing a finger in the direction of the wardrobe.

"Where are we going?" I asked as I pulled the trousers over my legs.

My mother curtly shook her head and returned to me. She grabbed me by the shoulders, and her gaze fell onto my hair. She took a single braid, running her hands over the small topaz stones—each specially chosen to match my skin tone—woven throughout with thin gold strands.

"We don't have time to take these out," she said. "Anybody who sees this will know you're royalty. Keep yourself covered, do you hear me?"

The expression behind her brown-green eyes roiled like the river rapids, willing me to listen, and I nodded.

"Okay," she said, the tension in her stance relaxing slightly. She shrugged her cloak off and draped it over my shoulders. She pulled the hood over my hair and pat the top of my head reassuringly. "Get some shoes. We are leaving."

I obeyed, digging out a serviceable pair of walking shoes, from the bottom of the wardrobe.

Once I was dressed to her satisfaction, my mother nodded and untied the belt from her waste. She gripped the handle of the dagger, and hugged the sheathed blade to her heart, mouthing a silent prayer before kissing the jeweled pommel. She strapped the belt around my waist and rested her forehead on the top of my head.

"Kita, you need to get out of this palace."

"But—"

"Let me worry about my father. He won't be happy with me, but it will be better than you staying here and waiting for him to execute you. Or worse."

She pulled me into an embrace and held me there, whispering into my ear.

"Getting out of the palace will be the easy part. No one will know you're gone for a while. But after that, you have to make it. You hear me? You *have to make it.*"

"Where will I go?"

"Go to the temple. They'll shield you. They have to. And then, find your father. Okay?"

"My father?" I asked. I blinked in surprise. I had no memory of him. Any attempts to ask my grandfather about him had been met with hostility. My mother rarely spoke of him either. When I was a child, any mention of him brought her to tears. As I got older, all she ever said was that he took her heart with him when he went.

"I don't know where he is," she admitted. " I know he went to the temple when...when he left the palace. He'll have gone. Maybe back to his homeland. The Notasi Tribes roam the coastlines south of the

Empire. I wish I could tell you more, but I don't know where he is. My father made sure of it."

She gripped the handle of the bronze dagger and pulled it close to her heart gently running a finger along the flat of the blade.

"This was Kyr's," she murmured. My father's. "It's a ceremonial piece, he said. He gave it to me during my pregnancy. It's supposed to ensure the wielder's safety." She wasn't talking to me just then, and I wished that I could see into her heart.

She snapped out of her reverie and pushed the dagger into my hands. "Keep this. Use it if you must. It's blunt, but it'll hurt all the same. Do not hesitate. Keep yourself safe. Find Kyr. He'll...he'll know what to do."

She released me and held my gaze again, tears welling in her eyes. She sighed and wiped them away before nodding once more and turning me toward the door.

"Okay," she said, grabbing the polished bronze door handle. "I love you. And..." She trailed off, trying to decide if she should say what was in her mind. "When you find your father, tell him...well, never mind. Just find him. Do you understand?"

She held my gaze, lip slightly quivering, until I nodded.

She swept her cloak from her shoulders and wrapped it around me.

"Wait," I said as she turned toward the door. "In case we don't have another chance. Will you...help Ran for me? He'll need you."

Mother barked a laugh.

"Trust me," she began, pushing the door open, "that boy is the last person who needs help right now. Now let's go."

2

Kita

The moment the door to my apartments closed behind us, any evidence of emotion evaporated from my mother's face, replaced by a mask of indifference.

My mother walked with a purposeful gait, so assured in her posture that her power was not even necessary for much of the way. I walked behind her with my head bowed, trying my best to emulate the way my maidservants walked the palace halls—though in all honesty, I found it difficult to remember, so easily did they melt into the background.

My mother commanded all attention as she strode, and guards and servants alike averted their eyes as she passed. They afforded me no more than a passing glance. It was not until we got down the three flights of stairs, through the east side courtyard, and to the entrance hall that she had to use her power at all.

Just as I was beginning to allow myself to relax, we turned a corner and walked almost directly into a guard. I swallowed hard as I realized that this was no simple palace guard, hired mainly to ensure the servants were kept in line. This was an Imperial Guard, the most elite fighters in the empire, sworn to protect the royal family. Foya, one of the emperor's own.

Her gaze swept across me, and I struggled to steady my breath.

"My princess," she began. On instinct, I opened my mouth to respond, but my mother had better sense.

"What is it?" Mother asked.

Foya's eyes burned into my own, and I glanced down, hoping against all hopes that Mother's illusions would hold.

"I'm sorry, but I must insist you return to your chambers," Foya said. "There has been an incident."

"An incident?"

"Who is this?" Foya asked, gesturing toward me. "I don't recognize her." Her eyes narrowed.

"I wasn't aware you knew each of my maidservants," Mother replied. If she was nervous, she didn't show it. She stood straight, hands clasped together, her eyes narrowed as she put on her most regal voice.

"Well—"

"Foya, please. Leave us." Mother pushed past, but Foya's arm stuck out, grabbing her by the arm.

My eyes widened. I'd never seen a guard put a hand on my mother.

"I will give you two seconds to unhand me," Mother hissed.

"My princess, I apologize," Foya replied, though she did not remove her grasp. "But my orders tonight come from the emperor himself."

Mother paused, glancing from me to Foya. "What is this about?" she asked. She maintained her poise, but I knew her. I could see the subtle twitch in her fingers.

"The ball, my princess. Have you not heard?"

"I did not attend. I have no use for such frivolities."

Foya's grip loosened, and she took a step back, narrowing her eyes as she searched for something in my mother's face.

"There was an...incident," she said. "The emperor has been informed and will be back in the morning. In the meantime, I have been asked

11

to ensure that the family is secured."

Mother scoffed. "Secured? What are you on about? Speak plainly, please."

"Um...my princess, I'm afraid you'll need to return to your room at once."

"This is ridiculous," Mother replied. "You have no authority over me. I am the eldest child of the emperor. Sister to the crown prince. There are two men to whom I will answer, and Ran would have a hard time securing my obedience on most days. So please, step aside. I will go where I please." She tried once more to push past, but Foya stood firm.

"Any business you have can surely wait until morning. Your guard is already waiting at your chamber. Please do not make this difficult, my princess. As I've said, my orders come directly from the emperor. None are to leave their chambers tonight."

The seconds ticked by as my mother considered. Her jaw clenched. She was no warrior, and she knew it. Any attempt to fight would be quickly squashed.

"And you," Foya said, turning to me, "to your quarters. You won't be needed tonight." While she had been almost apologetic speaking to my mother, her command was sharp, making me flinch.

My heart caught in my chest. I had to get out. Getting caught so soon...that would be disastrous. Grandfather would surely punish the audacity, and Mother's as well. We *had* to do this.

"My princess, I must insist." She returned her gaze to Mother, taking her by the hand. *"Please."* There was something else in her voice now. Desperation?

"Well," Mother said quietly. "If you insist on this, then allow me just a moment to speak to my servant. There are things I want brought to my chambers in the morning."

Foya cocked her head, and for a moment I thought she would refuse.

12

But she dipped her head and stepped back, giving us a bit of space.

Mother gripped my wrists, pulling me close.

"You must make it," she whispered. "Do you understand? You *must*. Get to the ziggurat and be careful. You have to convince the High Priestess to host you."

I swallowed. I knew the old laws well. Royalty weren't allowed in the temples, and the priests and priestesses weren't permitted in any of the imperial facilities. I'd have to find away to get around that.

"Find Kyr. It'll be hard, but you can do it. You must."

I nodded, though I felt far from confident.

"Once you're out of my vicinity, the illusion will fade. Stay out of sight. Get out of the palace as fast as you can. Do you understand?"

"Yes, mo—my princess." I lowered my voice and leaned in closer, whispering, "and please look after Ran. He doesn't know the emperor like we do."

I glanced toward Foya, but she didn't appear to be listening.

"Good," Mother said, louder this time, and if she heard what I'd said, she gave no indication. "I want you in my chambers at first light. Make sure you have everything I requested."

"Of course," I dipped my head in what I hoped looked like supplication.

"Let's go, Foya," Mother said, frowning as she strode past the guard.

Foya eyed me one more time, narrowing her eyes. For a moment, I thought that my mother's illusion had failed.

"Get to your chambers," she finally said as she turned on her heels and followed my mother down the corridor.

I waited for several minutes, ensuring that Foya was well and truly gone before continuing on.

The palace was my home. I'd lived there since I was born. And yet, as I turned down hall after hall, I found that I couldn't orient myself. The longer I wandered, the more my heart drummed against my chest.

The quicker I breathed. The more I trembled.

I pressed myself against the wall, trying to steady myself. It was as though I was watching myself from afar, observing my own breakdown.

I forced myself to keep moving.

I found myself at a tight spiral staircase and padded down, hoping I didn't encounter anyone. As I moved downward, voices met my ears, and I grit my teeth.

The entrance hall. I don't know how I got there without realizing, but there I was. The hall was full of nobles, still dressed in their ball finery. They milled about, whispering loudly to each other. Some of them cried. Others screamed at the guards that blocked the front doors.

My stomach clenched. I had to get away, but as I watched the blood-spattered masses, the image of my dance partner's face forced its way to my mind. The way his eyes had widened as his mind caught up to what his body had endured. He was already dead; he just hadn't fully realized it yet.

"My princess!" a soft voice hissed, scattering the memory.

Hazily, I shook my head. My handmaiden, Mina, crouched before me, gripping my hand as she stared up at me.

"What are you doing here?" she muttered, glancing over her shoulder as she ushered me back toward the stairs.

"I…I…"

She placed a finger to my lips.

"My princess, you shouldn't be here. You should go."

"I know," I replied. "It's just…"

"No. You should *go!*" Her eyes pled with mine. "Come. I'll take you."

I jerked my hand away. "I'm not going back to my chambers," I muttered. It was foolish to speak to her. I knew that. But the words spilled forth. "I'm leaving the palace."

Mina stared, mouth open slightly as I tried to slip past.

"Wait," she whispered. "Not that way." She pulled me back against the wall and behind the stairs. I followed as she crept in the dark space, slipping through a door I hadn't noticed before.

"This is a mess," she muttered.

"I know," I replied. "I'm sorry."

"It's not your doing!" she replied.

To this, I had no answer. If she hadn't heard what I'd done, I couldn't tell her. Not unless I wanted to find myself back in my quarters, waiting for death. As we walked through the servant's quarters, I clenched my teeth as I waited for discovery. I didn't know this area of the palace. Even as we made our way through, Mina walked with a confidence I'd never seen in her before. This was her domain.

Every time we heard voices approach, she yanked me down another hall, always out of view.

Eventually, we found ourselves at a small wooden door.

"This is our courtyard. There's a small gate. It leads into the Silk District."

I swallowed hard and cracked open the door. The courtyard was more of a small garden, full of lush vegetation and fragrant blossoms. At the far corner, I could just make out a nondescript wood gate, flanked by two guard.

"By all the goddesses," I murmured as I gently shut the door. "There are guards."

Mina just stared. "I...there's nothing I can do about them," she admitted. "You are strong. Can't you use your affinity?"

I chewed my lip. Of course I could. But...would it obey? And if it would...did I have the energy to maintain it? Though my heart beat a quick rhythm, I could feel the lead in my legs and arms. But I had no choice.

I closed my eyes and envisioned a bird, a great raptor with talons the size of my forearm. Something big enough to withstand anything the guards could throw.

I opened the door a crack and exhaled, and with my breath, my energy flowed out, transformed into a new life. A thin gossamer line between us tugged as the raptor beat its great black wings. It opened its mouth the scream, and in a panic, I willed it to be silent.

Its maw clacked shut as it took off.

The guards noticed, but before they could lift a hand, the bird's claws reached for them, gripping them tight as it flew into the night. Their yells were quickly swallowed by the wind.

Don't hurt them! I commanded as it lifted higher and higher, stretching the line between us so far I thought it would snap. It glided out of view and I ran, legs pumping as I made for the gate. I didn't bother to slow down as I approached, and it splintered as I crashed into it, spilling me out into the Silk District.

I'd made it out. I was free of the palace. I sprinted as far as I could get. My bird, having deposited its prey elsewhere, flew silently over head, watching. Helping me to orient away from the guards that patrolled.

The air was cool, with a light breeze coming down the hill. I wrapped the cloak as tightly as I could as the wind bit through. I was poorly dressed for the chilly air, but running warmed my blood. I couldn't stop. Wouldn't. Not until I made it to the temple, or I collapsed.

Above me, the great black raptor glided noiselessly through the night, its pitch black feathers melting into the sky.

The streets were empty. I passed beautiful, large houses, but the all gates were shut. Even servants were either gone or asleep. I followed my bird blindly, and it did not fail me; as we traversed the wide streets of the upper district, I did not see a patrol.

But just before the streets opened up into the wide open plaza before the middle gate, the bird began to circle. I stopped as I waited for it to make its move, and realized what the problem was.

The large wooden gate was guarded.

Again, I pressed myself into the shadows, thinking while my navigator bird swooped and turned above me.

From what I could see, there were two guards, a man and a woman, standing directly in front of the great wooden gates. The walls themselves were too tall to scale, and any attempt to scramble over would surely be seen.

I needed to get the guards off their post.

A distraction, I thought, pushing the thought toward the shadowy black bird. At once, it swooped down behind a building, leaving me momentarily alone, stretching the thread between us farther and farther until I feared it would break.

There was a large crash, and I stumbled forward as the cord severed.

The guards jumped at the noise, clearly not expecting the night to be any more eventful.

I wondered for just a moment whether they knew about what had happened in the palace, but shook the thought away as they glanced at each other, speaking in harsh tones just far enough away for me to miss the meaning. Moving slowly and carefully, they started toward the noise, hands raised just in case they would need to unleash their affinities.

As soon as they were gone from view, I clutched my cloak around me and ran, legs pumping as fast as they possibly could. I threw myself against the gate, grasping at the wooden bar keeping the gate closed. I threw it to the ground, the clatter no doubt alerting the guards to my location, before pulling at one of the heavy wooden doors. It took all of my weight, but it creaked open.

The gate slammed shut behind me, and I took off again, turning down crowded market streets at random until I was sure that the guards had not followed.

I stopped for a moment, trying to breathe deeply to still my heart.

When I finally took a step, my legs began to shudder. Blackness crept into the edges of my vision, and all the strength left in my lower body gave out.

It was only a moment or two later when my vision came back. My first thought was that I was in my chambers, waking up from a terrible dream. But as I blinked, I saw first the stone roads on which I was lying. My jaw hurt, and I couldn't feel my front teeth.

"You ight?" a voice called from in front of me. I pushed myself up onto my forearms, and came eye to eye with a young woman.

"Y-yes," I muttered as I shifted my legs around and pushed myself to a crouch.

"Ah, be careful!" the woman chided as I tried to stand. She grabbed my arm, her nails digging in as she steadied me.

"Thank you," I mumbled as she helped me to my feet.

"You look a sight," the woman said as her eyes swept up and down my ragged form. Her eyes rested on my braids, and the gems studded throughout.

"I know," I replied. I looked up, trying to find the temple. After a moment of searching, I found the top of the pyramid, just peaking over the small houses and shops cobbled together.

"Ah, wait!" the woman called after me as I started to walk. "You ight? Where you goin?"

"The temple."

"The temple? Someone like you?"

"Yes," I said through clenched teeth.

"Can't go that way! Bridge is over there," she said, pointing left over my shoulder.

"Oh."

I avoided her eyes as I changed course, feeling her gaze on me.

A thought occurred to me, and I asked, "wait, will there be guards patrolling the bridge?"

"This time of night? Course! They gone be there all night. In the mornin', they go and watch from the walls." Her tone of voice indicated that she thought I was a complete idiot.

I stopped walking and turned toward her.

"And is the bridge the only option? Can I cross the river some other way?"

The woman shrugged. "Been havin' rains. River gone be high. No boats gone take you this late. If you trynna avoid guards, you better off waitin' til the mornin'."

"Well, I don't have a choice. I *have* to get there."

She paused for a moment, as though arguing with herself about what to do.

"Well," she sighed. "Come stay wit me tonight."

"I couldn't—"

"Come on," she called, grabbing my arm and dragging me after her. I had no energy to fight her.

She pulled me along, humming to herself as she went. The market district was beginning to quiet down, parents calling their children home for the night.

"Reminds me of my girl," she said over her shoulder. "She neva' wanted to come home at night. Always beggin' to stay out longer."

"Does she still live around here?"

"Oh...well, no," the woman replied. Something changed in her voice, and I suddenly regretted asking.

The woman's home was a small mudbrick structure on a hill that overlooked the river. The entire home was smaller than my apartments, with a small fire in the center of the single room. There was a dying fire in the center of the house, the smoke venting through small windows near the ceiling. There was a woven reed mat next to the fire, along with a small locked chest.

As I stood awkwardly in the corner of the room, shielding my eyes from the smoke, the woman unlocked the chest. She pulled out a second mat and unrolled it, laying it neatly on the opposite side of the fire.

"It were my daughter's," she explained as she ushered me to the mat. "I'm sure it ain't what you used to…" she started, glancing at the gems in my hair.

I gave her a weak smile and said, "It's more than I could have expected. Thank you."

As she stood expectantly, I laid down on the mat, pulling my thin black cloak over my chest. She nodded and went back to her chest, pulling off clothing as she prepared for bed.

I was asleep before she laid down on her mat.

3

Ran

Ran was in awe of his father, in every since of the word. Even after twenty-two years of life, after training in the army, after traveling nearly the entire Melyora Empire, and now after being invested as Crown Prince. After all of that, he still found his father the most impressive, fearsome he'd ever met.

He watched in silence as his father stood at the edge of the rooftop terrace, watching over his domain. The man was utterly leonine in appearance. He was not a handsome man, but his grizzled visage commanded authority. This was the man who brought the southern principalities under imperial control.

He stood with perfect posture, back straight, shoulders back. His skin was a warm bronze, his shiny black hair streaked with white. In the morning breeze, it seemed to flow behind him. Even at this early hour, the man was dressed in the finest linens.

The visage of the man was a sharp contrast to the beauty of the terrace. Water pumped from the river supplied standing pools and nourished cascades of sweet-smelling bird-shaped flowers in oranges, pinks, and yellows. In the humidity of the early morning, the scent of dew on verdant shrubbery wrapped enveloped everything.

21

Emperor Kazin sa Ela Melyora, dressed in his finest linens, didn't match.

And yet, he could be found there every morning, breaking his fast and contemplating.

The emperor turned and fixed his son with a metallic stare.

Ran bowed his head slightly and returned the gaze. Although he had grown taller than his father several years before, he still felt very small in the emperor's presence.

"Ranjali," the emperor said, his voice deep and calm, "explain to me what happened at the ball."

Thoughts raced through Ran's head. He was still unsure of what he had seen, and even after speaking to Kita the night previously, he could hardly believe it. At the same time, there was the relief that his father hadn't been there.

"I—I am not sure, Father," he finally said.

"You're not sure," the emperor echoed.

Ran badly wanted to look away, but didn't dare.

"I mean, I saw this…this giant creature…" he trailed off, reliving the night again in his head.

"Indeed," his father replied. "And this was Kitania's doing." It was not a question.

"Yes," Ran muttered.

"Yes," came the echo.

"Father, she would not do this on purpose. Something has happened to her, I'm…I'm not sure what, but—"

The emperor raised a hand, and Ran stopped talking. The emperor closed the distance between them, placing a hand on his younger child's shoulder, before turning away and returning to the edge of the terrace.

There was a long silence.

"Father, Kita needs our help. We have to help her figure out what

22

happened."

"There are three dead laid out in the ballroom. Young. Barely out of childhood. They were here to try to improve their stations. Perhaps to try and make their case for marriage into the royal family, as though such decisions would ever be left to them. And, of course, celebrate and pledge fealty to you. What am I to tell their parents? Their families?"

"I don't know, but—"

"You don't know." The older man sighed and turned back to his son. "You have a kind heart. That's not a bad thing for an emperor to have. But hard decisions must be made." The emperor clicked his tongue and slowly shook his head. "I had thought your time at the Eastern Fort would have burned away the softness. I thought you would have learned that, sometimes, we must do things we don't want to do."

Ran grit his teeth and rubbed his shoulder. He flexed his tingling fingers and dropped his arm to his side. The last thing he wanted was to be reminded of the Eastern Fort.

"Come here, boy."

Ran obeyed, tentatively making his way to his father's side.

"Look here," the emperor said, pointing down the hill to the Silk District of the city. The district was utterly still. "Our empire is built on their support."

The emperor swept his arm down toward the Market district, and said, "the common people are easy to please. When you struggle to piece together enough coin for food, a full belly is enough to keep you happy. Harvests are plentiful just now. There is little to fear from them." The emperor dropped his arm and turned to face Ran.

"The nobility have higher needs and desires. It is not enough to ensure they can eat. They want to believe that they have influence. And so, if they desire justice, we must give it to them."

Ran flinched.

"Father, what is it exactly that you are suggesting?"

"The person responsible for these deaths must be punished."

"We cannot *kill* Kita!"

The emperor raised an eyebrow and replied, "Be careful, boy." His voice was a hard warning.

Ran ground his teeth. In just a sentence, the crown prince was reduced once more to a mere child.

"Father," he said quietly. "I am asking you for mercy. Kita is our family. She is part of the *royal* family. I am begging you for your mercy. I am certain that she meant no harm."

The emperor interlaced his fingers behind his back.

"And yet, harm was done. You are the crown prince," his father said. "What would you have me do?"

Ran paused, trying to think of a solution that would satisfy his father while sparing Kita's life.

"Well," he began, "the nobility don't know who is responsible for what happened, so—"

"So, what are you suggesting? That we produce a different culprit? Execute an innocent person? Fine. Produce one."

"No, of course not, but…" he trailed off.

"I see," the emperor replied, returning to his position at the edge of the terrace.

"Father, please," Ran whispered. *"Please."*

The tension was thick between them, and Ran badly wished that his father would say something.

Finally, the emperor said, "Kitania is gone."

Ran's heart seemed to stop when he heard it, and he started, "What do you—"

A raised hand cut Ran's sentence short.

"Someone smuggled her out of the palace last night. She is gone. Some of our palace guard reported being swept away by a great black bird. Not only that, the city watch posted at the middle gate reported a commotion last night, followed by a gate breach. She needs to be brought to justice." The emperor turned his head, his gaze glinting, and said, "if you want your mercy, you will have to earn it. Bring. Her. Back."

Ran's eyes went wide as the magnitude of his father's words began to sink in.

"Of course, Father. I will not disappoint you."

"I know, Ranjali. But listen carefully. I want this done discretely. Bring a single guard, no more. I want you to move quickly and quietly. The sooner we can resolve this, the better. The watch who were posted at the middle gate are down with the Imperial Guard. Speak to them. And I am most certain that *Isali*—" he hissed his daughter's name as he said it—"had something to do with this. So, speak to her as well."

"Yes, Father."

"Do not return to this palace without Kitania. Do you understand? My mercy depends upon it. You may go," the emperor said.

Ran bowed his head and turned back toward the stairs leading back down into the palace, wondering whether this had been the emperor's plan all along.

Thoughts swarming, Ran made his way straight to the Imperial Guardchambers. The antechamber was large and sparse, with a large oaken table in the center. Mounted along the walls were a collection of different bladed weapons—lion claw knives, scimitars, and, of course, the black-handled imperial daggers that they all carried.

Evidently, there'd been a fight. The rug under the table was bunched in places, one of the chairs was overturned while another had been shattered against the wall.

Around the table were three members the Imperial Guard—among the most formidable of the Imperial Army, handpicked by the emperor himself and charged with the safety and well-being of the royal family.

They chattered furiously among themselves, making wide gestures as they spoke.

The fourth was seated on one of the few undisturbed chairs, staring at the wall and biting his fingernails.

As the door slammed shut behind Ran, all conversation immediately ceased and each of them stood and bowed.

"My Prince," Ran's own personal guard Sirra muttered. Ran liked Sirra. He was slow to anger, but vicious with a dagger or a well-placed telekinetic blast if he sensed danger. Though he wore his typical impassive expression, Ran knew him well enough to sense the fury hidden behind his eyes.

"Yes, yes, you can all relax," Ran said, waving a dismissive hand.

Ran's eyes fell upon the youngest of the group. Ditan was his his name. He was an Obsidian Islander, a shadowwalker with rich umber skin, a cloud of golden hair shorn on the sides, and eyes the color of the moonlit night. He was younger than the others by years, far closer in age to Ran and Kita then the other Imperial Guard, but the emperor himself had chosen him from the academy. Ran had watched him spar with the others. His command of his affinity was incredible for one so young, with his ability to disappear into the realm of shadows and then strike at an opponent's back utterly breathtaking to watch.

He stood apart from the others, fingers twitching at his sides. It was not difficult to understand his restlessness; he was Kita's personal guard, after all.

Ran sighed and looked over the group of them. "My father tells me you've spoken to a pair of our city watch. Are they here now?

"Yes, My Prince," Sirra replied, dipping his head in another bow.

"I would like to speak to them."

"There is no need, My Prince. We can surely give you any of the information you require," said Sirra.

"Thank you, Sirra, but I would like to talk to them myself. You all stay here." Without waiting for further objections, Ran pushed past the group, and as he opened the door into the next room, they resumed their whispered conversations.

The two city watch sat solemnly at a couch under the window, refusing to speak to each other or even look anywhere but the floor.

Even when Ran entered the room, they said nothing. Just what had Sirra and the rest of the Guard done to them?

Ran quietly sat in an armchair across from the pair, intertwining his fingers as he waited for the customary greeting.

When it didn't come, he gently said, "I have been told that you two witnessed something last night.

The watchmen nodded curtly.

"I would like you to tell me what happened.

"W-we already spoke to the Imperial Guard," one of the patrolmen muttered. The other gave his partner a look that could only be described as incredulous.

"Yes, I am aware," Ran replied, a small smile on his lips.

"We apologize, My Prince, it's just…it's just…"

"I am interested only in what you saw last night," Ran said gently. "Nothing else."

"We were at our post at the middle gate," the first of them, a tall, dark-skinned man began.

"It were quiet," the other patrolman, a smaller, younger man with a sandy brown complexion and bushy black beard, chimed. "Even quieter than normal. Weren't nobody out."

"There was this loud noise. Like…almost like, like—"

"A crash! Or an explosion!"

"We know that we ain't supposed to leave our post. We know that," the beardless guard said. He was sitting up now, thoroughly invested in the story he was telling.

"But it were a quiet night. And there weren't another patrol in that area. So we went to see what it were."

"Both of you?" Ran asked, an eyebrow raised.

"Well, we ain't supposed to leave each other," said the beardless patrolman, as though there were nothing more obvious in the world.

"So, what was the noise then?" Ran asked, setting aside the attitude.

The pair of them shared a look. Ran leaned forward, resting his elbows on his knees.

"A...a bird," said the beardless one.

"Not just a bird," the bearded one said. "A giant bird. Biggest damn bird I ever saw. Huge black thing. Must have been the size of a lion!"

"It had flown into a building," Beardless continued, "crashed straight through. It flailed around a bit and then..."

The pair paused, glancing again at each other.

"What happened then?" Ran asked.

"The bird...was gone. It just evaporated," the bearded guard muttered.

The bird. It was Kita's. There had been too many games as children, too many arguments as adults where he had seen that bird, or some variation of it. It was the creature she manifested perhaps most often.

"Is that all?" Ran asked, leaning back in the armchair.

"Well, no," the bearded patrolman said slowly.

Ran waved a hand at the pair, gesturing for them to continue.

"Just after the bird disappeared, there were another noise. It were the gate, slammin'" explained the bearded gentleman.

"So someone breeched the middle gate last night, then," Ran said with a sigh.

"Y-yes, my prince. We went to check it out but...we ain't see nobody. And we couldn't leave our post again."

The middle gate. Where was she going? It was clear that she was trying to get as far from the palace as she could. But was she leaving the city completely?

Ran rose and thanked the patrolmen before returning to the antechamber.

"Do we have a map of the city?" he asked as the Imperial Guard rose and bowed.

"Of course," Sirra replied. He shot a pointed look at Ditan, rushed forward to the barrel of rolled scrolls. After rummaging through the parchment for a few moments, he emerged with a rolled up parchment, which he quickly opened onto the table. Ran peered over it.

"So the middle gate is here," he muttered, pointing to a spot on the map.

Sirra nodded curtly.

"So that would have taken her into the Market District here...where is she going?"

"If I may, My Prince, any route out of the city would take her across the river."

"Hmm," Ran replied, studying the map. There were three bridges out of the city, but from the middle gate, the closest would put her...at the foot of the temple ziggurat.

It made a certain amount of sense. The temples were independent. They did not get involved in affairs of governance. In turn, rulers and leaders all across the continent vowed not to step foot on temple grounds. This was the way of things, a delicate dance between faith and law.

Kita was royalty. There was a chance they would turn her away. But if she were able to get in and plead her case, perhaps they would shield her.

"She's going to the temple," Ran decided.

He stared at the board, trying to think of a plan. His finger traced the lines of the map off to the southeast. Toward the Eastern Fort just two days' ride past the temple.

Quietly. That was the emperor's mandate. Getting the Eastern

29

regiment involved was a last resort.

Besides, Ran wasn't particularly keen to visit that place after the two years he spent training there.

He cast another glance at the four guards assembled before him. He examined each of them in turn before shaking his head, his mind made up.

"Ditan, with me, please," he said. The youngest of the Guard flinched in surprise as he heard his name.

"My prince!" Sirra objected.

"I know what I am doing, Sirra. I've made my decision. That will be all."

Sirra glared, but bowed his head. Ran understood Sirra's objection. Sirra was personally responsible for his safety. He had years of experience, and had guarded Ran since he was just a boy. But just as Sirra knew him, Ditan would know Kita. Besides, his affinity was too valuable not to use.

"Come, Ditan," Ran said as he turned out of the room.

The young man was quick to obey, and as Ran departed the Imperial Guard chambers, Ditan was close on his heels.

"My Prince, may I ask what you plan to do?" Ditan asked as the two of them headed down the hall, toward the staircase that would lead up to the family's chambers.

Ran stopped and turned to the guard. Ditan was young and wide-eyed, but nervous. He wouldn't meet Ran's eyes, even as the prince addressed him.

"Ditan, I need you to be calm and collected for this. Can you do that?"

Can I do that? Ran added silently to himself.

The young guard nodded. Ran returned the gesture and resumed walking.

"I will tell you everything I am thinking. But first, I want to talk to my sister. That's where we're going now."

Ditan walked obediently behind, moving so silently that Ran had to repeatedly look back to make sure he was still there. Each time he did, Ditan quickly averted his eyes.

When they reached Isa's chambers, a servant ducked inside to announce Ran's presence. Ditan remained outside, instantly falling into his Imperial Guard training. Gone was the timid young man; as he stood outside Isa's chambers, his eyes darted across the hall, checking for threats as his hand rested on the hilt of his dagger.

No wonder the emperor had selected him for the Imperial Guard.

Isa was seated at her antechamber writing desk, her hair loose and flowing over her silk dressing gown. She did not turn when Ran entered, but focused on the letter she was writing.

"Ran, what a surprise," she called, in a tone of voice that indicated that his arrival was anything but.

"Kita is gone," Ran said simply.

"Is that so?" Isa replied, still not bothering to face him.

"She had to have had help. No one saw her leave."

Isa said nothing.

"Isa?"

"What are you here for, Ran?" she asked, finally twisting to face him. Her eyes were hard and piercing, as though she was accusing *him* of something. Inexplicably, he felt the blood rush to his cheeks. Isa often had that effect on him.

"Did you help her?"

"Yes."

"Why?"

She scoffed and turned back to her letter. "Please don't ask me stupid questions, Ranjali. It's rather a waste of both of our time."

Ran strode to her desk and slammed his hand down on the writing surface. A few droplets of ink spilled.

31

"This is serious, Isa," he growled.

She remained unfazed, writing around his hand as she murmured, "Yes, it certainly is."

"I spoke to her last night," Ran muttered. "I told her I would speak on her behalf. I was going to handle things."

"Forgive me if I don't care to put my daughter's fate in your hands."

"Our father is not this evil man you seem to think!"

This, finally, got her attention. She slowly put her quill down and faced him. Her brow was furrowed, and a quiet fury danced behind her eyes, daring him to speak again.

"You don't know the man like I do, Ran," she said, her voice so still it sent a shiver down his spine.

"What does that mean?" he hissed.

"I don't care to educate you."

"You haven't saved her from anything. Do you think he'll just let her go? No, the nobility will want justice. And now it's my responsibility to get it."

Isa stood then, standing almost eye-to-eye with him.

"So what, you're sending people after her?" she asked.

"*I'm* going after her."

Isa recoiled and blinked.

"You?" she whispered. "And you're going to do it? You're going to…to hunt her down?"

"You make me sound like some…I don't know, predator. I am trying to help her, Isa. Father has promised that he will show mercy if I bring her back."

Something in her face changed then. Her eyes softened, her gaze dropped.

"Ran," she whispered. "Don't do this. His promises are meaningless. Do you understand? I need you to understand this. Don't make yourself a part of this."

"It's too late for that, Isa. By helping her escape, you made me a part of this."

She placed her hands on his shoulders. She trembled as her fingers dug into his skin.

"Ran," she said, "I am begging you. I will get on my knees if I must, but *please* just let her go."

He cupped her hands in his. He couldn't remember a time where she had touched him. Maybe when his mother died?

"Where is she going?" he asked gently.

Isa snatched her hands away then, and returned to her seat at the writing desk. She stared out of the window, and said nothing.

"Isa?" he prodded.

"Before she left," Isa muttered, "she asked me to look out for you." She laughed, but it was mirthless and cold. "I told her you didn't need my help, that you would be fine. I didn't imagine then that you would personally go after her. Do you not understand? This is what our father does. He understands how to press at people. He doesn't even need his affinity to do it. How you not see it?"

She leapt to her feet and pushed him bodily away.

Ran stumbled back. He said nothing, but internally he was beginning to question. He had never known his father to be a cruel man. Severe, certainly. Never cruel. But Isa's reaction...

"Be well, Isa," he said softly. "Please trust that I will do everything in my power."

"Just go," she croaked in reply. "I will not tell you where she has gone. If you really thought I would, then you are as stupid as you are naïve."

She always treated him this way, like he was an irritating little boy and not the crown prince. Perhaps it was jealousy; she was the eldest. For 20 years, she'd been the only heir. By law, she should be next in line for the throne. But their father had elected to skip over her. Is that why she hated him so much? It wasn't like it'd been his choice.

He opened his mouth to say something, but thought better of it. Isa was stubborn, and she would not be swayed by him.

He didn't stop as he strode through the door.

Ditan was immediately at his heels. "My prince, what happens now?" he asked.

It was unnerving, how quietly the shadowwalker moved.

"I'm not sure what will happen to Isa. I'm sure my father will want to speak to her himself. We will not be here to see it."

"You have a plan then, my prince?"

Ran turned to find Ditan less than two steps behind him. He jumped slightly, and Ditan took a step back, looking sheepish.

"Yes," Ran said, running a hand through his hair. "I believe I do."

4

Kita

I do not know how long I slept, but when I woke, my hair was half unbraided, my savior dropping the topaz beads into a small leather pouch as she worked. She hummed as she went and politely pat the top of my head as she realized I was awake.

"I know you come from the palace," she explained, though I hadn't asked her anything. "This hair a dead giveaway. Nobody out here gonna have gems braided like this." She clucked her tongue.

"Thank you," I mumbled, but she shrugged.

I pushed myself to a sitting position.

"When we done here, I'll take you to Ezeri's stall. Not Big Ezeri who used to have the stall, mind you,"she clarified, as though I had any idea who she was talking about, "Little Ezeri. He a much better cook. Got the knack for it."

"Ahh," I muttered, "I really must go." The palace would know I was gone. They'd be looking for me.

"Mhmm. Ain't gonna get far without food in your belly. And by the looks of you, they won't be searching for you with me."

I chewed my lip, not knowing what to do. But she was right. If the temple turned me away, I'd have to leave at once. Better to do it with sustenance.

Little Ezeri's nickname turned out to have absolutely nothing to do with the size of the man, who was a hulking beast crammed into a tiny wooden stall. He wore a sullen look on his face as he stirred a gigantic pot of some sort of porridge. As we approached, he grunted a wordless greeting. He eyed me and then my savior, and ladled porridge into two cracked wooden bowls. He stared hard at me for a moment before unearthing several jars. He dug into them with two large fingers, pulling out pinches of nuts and dried fruits, even spices. He sprinkled them delicately into the bowls and pushed them toward us, never losing the scowl on his face.

It was utterly delicious, with the taste of warm spices combined with subtle sweetness from the dried fruits coating my tongue.

Once breakfast was over, I was faced with the seemingly insurmountable task of actually reaching the temple. My savior insisted on accompanying me, though I assured her it wasn't necessary.

"Nonsense," she said. "What kinda host would I be if I turned you out now?"

We approached the bridge. Horses and mules rode past, carrying passengers and carts out of the city. City watch were posted at the end, calmly surveying the scene before them.

"Halt," one of them said as we approached. The heat of their gaze fell upon me, and I looked down. I was suddenly very grateful to be with another person.

"What is your problem?" my savior snapped, jabbing a finger at the watchman's chest.

He took a step back, suddenly caught off guard.

"Ma'am, w-we have orders from the palace to screen all travelers," the watchman explained.

"What for? Honest people, just tryna get by. Those fancy people up the hill ain't got nothing to do with us."

"Wh…what's your purpose, ma'am?" he asked, taking a deep breath as he collected himself.

She exchanged a glance with me and said, "my niece here just got her heart broke. Stupid boy left her high and dry after promising marriage. I'm takin' her to the temple to get herself sorted."

I clasped my hands together and cast my gaze down, trying to look suitably heartbroken, though I didn't really have any experience in the matter.

The watchman stared silently for several agonizing moments. He would see through this ruse, I felt certain.

But, to my surprise, he waved us along. "Be quick about it," he murmered. "There's rumors of a curfew. As if I had nothing better to do tonight."

Breathing a sigh to myself, I stepped onto the bridge.

The river raged high and fast, smashing against the stone arches with the rather unnerving ferocity of late summer. It almost seemed as though the water would carry away the wooden slats, but of course they held.

The ziggurat upon which the Temple of Hope sat was much more massive than I remembered it being. I had passed it upon the rare occasions when I was able to accompany my mother on her travels, but never had I stood at the base, looking up at its entire height. The climb was steep, and there were several times I had to stop and catch my breath, but at last I took the last step and arrived at the plateau of the temple.

"This where I leave you," my savior muttered, taking both of my hands in hers. "The priestesses will take care of you."

I smiled and pulled her into a hug. She patted my back, somewhat awkwardly, before breaking away.

"You didn't have to help me," I said.

She waved my concern away. "You see a girl passin' out in the street, you help. That's just how it is."

I nodded, and just like that, she was gone, shuffling back down the ziggurat.

She was halfway down before I realized I hadn't asked her name.

Before I went further, I turned and looked back over the city. From this angle, it seemed like an entirely different city. Mouth-watering aromas arose from the Market District, highlighting the vibrancy of the area. In contrast, the Silk District seemed almost like a child's playhouse than a living, breathing part of the city.

Though I already longed for my mother, and even for Ran's relentless optimism, and even though it was the only home I had ever had, I had already said my goodbyes to the palace, and everything it represented. It wasn't mine anymore, I told myself. I even almost felt it.

The gates of the temple were manned by a pair of young priestesses. They could not have been older than fourteen or fifteen, and they smiled warmly as I approached. Each wore simple black vestments and held thin wooden walking sticks.

It was all I could do not to collapse in front of them.

"Welcome to our temple," one of the priestesses said. The other pulled at the great oaken door, seemingly her entire weight against it as she swung it open.

"Are you here for worship?" the priestess asked as the other girl ducked inside.

"N-no, not exactly," I said, my voice very quiet.

The priestess turned to me and took my hand.

"You're quite nervous," she said.

"I…I suppose so."

"You have no need to be. Temples are safe from the threats of the outside world."

I didn't quite believe her, not fully. She didn't know my grandfather.

Her face fell slightly as she realized I wasn't reassured.

"Maybe it's best if I take you to see the High Priestess," she said helpfully. "She can assist."

I smiled weakly and nodded.

The High Priestess was not a tall woman, her full height reaching perhaps to the bridge of my nose. Nor was she a particularly old woman—although her long locs were streaked through with gray, her mahogany face was still smooth. Like the younger priestesses who stood behind her, she had a line of small black dots tattooed from ear to ear across her cheekbones. Unlike them, she also had a small gold ring hanging from the center of her nose.

She watched me unmoving, her face stony. I knelt before her, eyes cast down, unsure of what to do. She stood there for several minutes without moving or speaking.

Slowly, I looked up, meeting the High Priestess's eyes. This did not shake her, and she did not avert her gaze.

Finally, she spoke, in a voice that was calm and rich.

"Why have you come to us?" she asked.

"I am seeking asylum," I mumbled.

"Speak up!" she snapped.

"I am seeking asylum!" I said, flinching at the harshness in her voice.

"Hmm," she said. "You *are* scared," she reasoned. "I could tell that from the moment you arrived. Why?"

"I...I..." the words stuck in my throat as the weight of everything that had happened suddenly collapsed around my shoulders.

The High Priestess's face softened slightly, and she slowly approached.

"Calm yourself and speak," she said, more gently this time. As she spoke, the weight upon me began to melt away. My heart beat slowed, and I found myself able to breathe once more.

"The emperor," I began, "is trying to have me killed." My mother's words, her plea to hide my identity still fresh in my mind.

"I see," she said softly.

"I do not aim to impose on your hospitality very long. Just until I can figure out where to go next. Just until I can find…"the words caught in my throat and I was suddenly overwhelmed by the thought of my father. I tried to envision him. Was he a tall man? Was he kind? I struggled to remember *anything* about him at all.

The High Priestess cocked her head, picking up on my hesitation. "Find what?"she asked.

"My father. My mother told me he stayed here for a while. It was a long time ago, but I hoped—"

"That we might remember him."

"Right."

"What is his name?"

" Kyr. He is from south of the imperial border."

The High Priestess's face hardened, and she said, "If Kyr is your father, then you are the princess Kitania."

I jerked a nod.

"You shouldn't be here. The balance between governance and piety is delicate. Your being here could put that into jeopardy."

"Please," I muttered. "Don't turn me away. I have not lied to you. The emperor *is* trying to have me killed. Please." My fingernails dug into the fabric of my pants. My hair swept back and forth along the marble floors as I waited for the High Priestess's response.

She knelt before me, hooked a finger under my chin and gently guided my eyes to hers. Whatever stern stoicism she'd had before was gone, replaced with genuine concern.

"I can feel the truth in your words. And Kyr is a good man. He would want us to help," she muttered.

She took me by the hand and pulled me up. "Come, then," she said. "I'll show you around. I'll have one of the girls track down a messenger. It'll be too far to transmit all the way down to the southern temples, so we'll have to send someone by horse. We'll see if they saw Kyr as he went south. You can stay with us until we hear back. Now, come." She spun on the pads of her feet, her white linen cloak swishing softly against the stone floor.

The Temple of Hope was in every way opposite to the Imperial Palace. As the young priestess guided me through the halls, I saw no elaborate frescoes. No expensive furniture or handmade rugs. Rather, the walls were sleek white marble. The floors were polished, but bare. Furniture was sparse. A chair here, a storage chest there. And yet, it did not feel plain or underdone. Rather, as I walked through the halls, passing young priestesses going about their daily routines, it felt oddly serene.

"Here you are," the High Priestess said as she led me into a small room. Like the rest of the temple that I had seen so far, it was clean, neat, and sparse. In the corner, there was a mat made from woven reeds. A rough blanket was strewn across the top. Sleeping atop the blanket was a skinny cat, a grizzled black mouser with a torn ear. Next to the mat was a small chest, presumably for my meager belongings.

"I have business to attend to. But I will send some of the priestesses. They'll introduce you to Weiran and the others."

"Weiran?"

The High Priestess smirked, but didn't reply.

As she ducked out of the room, I knelt next to the sleeping cat. The Palace had them, of course, though they mostly stayed near the kitchens and food stores.

This one was quite content to ignore me.

I gingerly touched a hand to its forehead and it awoke, affixing one yellow eye on me before stretching, rolling over, and curling itself into a tight ball.

I sighed and opened the chest. I removed my cloak, now dusty and worn at the hem, and carefully folded it before placing it and my bronze dagger inside. Then, in went the pouch of topaz gems.

All of my worldly possessions stowed, I closed the chest with a soft click and sat cross-legged on the floor. Taking a moment, I closed my eyes and just breathed. In and out. In and out.

Let me out, something growled in my ear. My eyes snapped open, but there was no one there.

It was the voice of the beast.

My heart began pounding, quicker and quicker until I thought it might give out. My hands started to shake and my stomach began to turn. I struggled to catch my breath as my throat seemed to constrict.

I didn't notice the door open, nor the young priestess who came in and laid a hand on my shoulder. Almost instantly, my breath returned to normal, and I began to regain my composure.

"Miss, are you alright?" she asked as she gently rubbed my upper back.

"I am now," I responded. "I thought I was dying for a moment."

"Yes, we see that here sometimes," she said.

"What, people dying?" This drew a laugh.

"No, people panicking," the young priestess said. "The people who come to stay here have seen terrible things. But the Goddesses put us in the temples because we can help."

"How?"

The young priestess crouched in front of me, a quizzical look upon her face.

"Miss, that's our power. All the priests and priestesses are the same." She spoke as though it was the most obvious thing she could have ever said. And, I suppose, to her, it was.

"I see," I said, trying to keep the embarrassment out of my voice.

She had the good manners not to mention it. Rather, she said, "If you're ready, Miss, the High Priestess wants me to take you to meet Weiran."

"Who is Weiran?" I asked as I stood and followed her out of the room.

"He leads a group of refugees," she replied as she led me down another hallway, virtually identical to the one from which we came. "We've had quite a few come through in recent months, but never a group this big. He's done good things for them, I think."

"Why does the High Priestess want me to meet him?"

"I don't know for sure, Miss. I expect she thinks you can help each other. He's said to be leading a group south in the coming week or so."

"What do you think about him?"

She stopped walking for just a moment. After a quick hesitation, she started again and said, "I don't know, Miss. I haven't had many conversations with him."

I didn't press her, but her diplomatic silence did not go unnoticed.

In the center of the temple was a large courtyard. A large circular fountain sprung up from the center, splashing cool clear water. The temple had been there for centuries, and to get a fountain spraying water all the way atop the pyramid? It was a marvel.

A large knotted tree grew from the corner of the courtyard, providing shade while its ancient roots wound their way throughout the courtyard.

There were a number of people—some priestesses, some not—enjoying the sunshine.

Under the shade of the enormous tree, two men fought, a ring of refugees watching and cheering. At first, I thought they were just sparring. But as swords bit into flesh, blood sprayed through the air.

As we approached, I realized that the larger of the two men was a priest; I caught glimpses of his facial tattoos as he moved languidly with a pair of matched short swords. His rich brown body was littered with scars—slashes across his back, a thick puncture scar over his chest. He stalked his opponent, stepping effortlessly out of the way any time the other man tried to strike.

The other man was already limping, his left arm hanging uselessly beside him as his blood flowed down his blade and onto the ground, the iron odor wafting through the courtyard.

With a groan, he shifted his sword to his other hand.

The priest barked something in a language I did not understand. His opponent growled and leaped forward. The priest sidestepped and reached around him, hooking his arm under the other man's armpit and pulling sharply.

Time slowed as a loud crack rang through the courtyard.

A second later, the second man screamed, a heartrending shriek that quieted the temple.

A small, stout woman in muddy brown linens pushed through the ring of people. She caught the injured man and slowly lowered him to the ground. She first rubbed her hands roughly over his oozing slash wounds. The injured man hissed as the skin began to knit itself together once more under her fingers. Then, the healer grasped his shoulder with one hand and his upper arm with the other and yanked. He groaned as the shoulder popped back into socket, and the healer dug his fingers deep into his skin. Finally, the healer pat him on his repaired shoulder and shuffled away, wiping her bloody fingers against her linens.

"That," my young priestess said as she jabbed a finger to the injured man, "is Weiran." She tugged my hand as she approached him, weaving through refugees as they dispersed.

As we neared, Weiran glanced up, and my breath caught in my chest.

There are two types of beauty in this world. There is the fragile beauty, the type that you fear will crumble if you touch it. The type of beauty found in ancient ruins, dying flowers, and the frescoes in the Imperial Palace. And then, there's the other kind. The beauty found in dancing flames or violent storms. The kind of beauty you fear will destroy you utterly.

Weiran was beautiful in the second way.

He was tall and lean, with sweat-slick skin like wildflower honey. His hair—the darkest black I have ever seen—was plastered in rings to his face, forcing him to repeatedly push it aside. His almond-shaped amber eyes were rimmed in circles so dark it looked he may have been bruised.

He locked his gaze on mine and in that second, facing my grandfather seemed a more preferable prospect than speaking to this man. And then his gaze slid to someone behind me, and the danger, for the moment, passed. I glanced over my shoulder, but no one was there.

The priest who had just moments before maimed him loomed almost protectively behind. His skin was a rich dark color, and he wore his hair close cropped. He had pulled on a black tunic, and his short swords were now safely sheathed in a black leather scabbard hanging from his belt. His facial tattoos differed from those the priestesses I had met thus far sported, with a line of black dots that began just under his right eye and curved down along his jaw. In addition to the scars I'd seen before, there was also a knotty scar looping around his neck.

"Hello," Weiran said, his voice coarse and breathy. He spoke with a hint of an almost melodic accent that I couldn't immediately place.

"A pleasure to meet you," I replied with a small smile. He didn't return it.

"I don't think we *have* met just yet," he responded.

I blinked, unsure of how to respond.

"Who are you?" he asked, slowly getting to his feet.

"My name is Kita," I replied, extending a hand for him to kiss. An old habit, perhaps.

"Weiran," he said, ignoring my hand.

"The High Priestess has suggested that I speak to you," I explained.

Turning to the other gentleman, I asked, "and what is your name?"

The two shared a smirk. It was disconcerting, watching these two who, just moments before had been locked in the throes of a vicious fight, now seeming the best of friends.

"I do not have one," the larger man said. His voice matched his facial expression, flat and emotionless.

"You…don't have a name?" I repeated, certain that he was perhaps joking.

"Of course not," he replied. "It was taken from me when I was pledged to the temples."

I blinked.

"Have you never been to a temple before?" Weiran asked.

I pressed my lips together. I hadn't asked any of the priestesses their names. It had not occurred to me. But now that he mentioned it, none of them had offered a name, and I had not thought it strange.

"N-no," I muttered. "I never had cause to before."

"Fascinating," Weiran said dryly, a smile playing on his lips.

"Those of us who manifest empathy are brought to the temples," the Priest said calmly. "We give up our names to the Nameless Goddesses and live a life of service."

"But…not at this temple?" I asked.

The Priest blinked slowly and shook his head. "The Temple of Sorrow." He didn't elaborate.

"What are you doing here at this temple?" Weiran asked, interrupting the thought.

I narrowed my eyes.

"We are all fleeing something," he said. "Most of us fleeing war, death. I presume the same is true of you."

"Yes, I suppose so."

He nodded again.

We stood in silence for an uncomfortable amount of time. As we stood, his gaze shifted. I turned to follow, but only the fountain stood behind us.

"So…what is your affinity?" I asked, almost immediately regretting the question.

Weiran's eyes narrowed.

"A rude question to ask someone you've just met," he hissed. The Priest beside him laid a hand on his shoulder.

Again, they shared a look, the meaning of which was lost on me—perhaps they could somehow communicate without words?

I wrung my hands as the heat rushed to my face.

"I apologize," I muttered. "I seem to have a habit of saying the wrong thing."

Weiran softened slightly, and said, "Well, in any case. If the High Priestess sent you to me, it's because you're fleeing the Empire like the rest of us."

I struggled to keep from recoiling at the sentence. Fleeing the Empire? For what? Certainly my grandfather was a cruel man, but yields were prosperous. Food was plentiful. What would people be fleeing from?

"Yes," I said evenly.

"As I thought," he replied, nodding slowly. "Well, it was lovely to meet you, Kita. I am certain we will have many interesting things to discuss in the coming days." He flashed a quick smile, revealing dimples, before pushing past me.

"Do not mind him. He does not sleep much," The Priest said, as though this explained everything about the strange encounter.

"I see," I replied. The Priest bowed his head and wordlessly followed Weiran into the temple, leaving me to wonder exactly what had just happened.

5

Kita

It was naïve of me to believe that I would sleep easily that night. The night before, so deep was my exhaustion that, even despite my savior's meager furnishings, I had fallen straight into sleep almost the instant I nuzzled down into the bedroll.

But my first night at the temple was different. Of course, the day had been tiring. But without extensively using my affinity as I had the night before, I had the energy to toss and turn on the uncomfortable reed mat. The old tomcat had found its way back into the room and purred loudly nearby, content to watch me struggle.

The hard floor beneath me pressed uncomfortably against my ribs as I tried to find a suitable sleeping position.

My eyes had long since adjusted to the darkness, and I stared at the old cat as it licked its paw and wiped its face. After a moment, it stretched and retreated to the darkest corners of the room, where I lost sight of it.

I rolled over to face the door. Flickering light peaked underneath the door, almost mocking my inability to sleep.

Frustrated, I shut my eyes and breathed deep, pulling the scratchy woolen blanket over my head.

I do not recall falling asleep. But when again I opened my eyes, I found myself standing in a river. The water was thick and warm, and when I looked down it was red, staining my legs as it rushed past, the scent of it quickly becoming all-too-familiar.

I turned my attention to the banks of the river. There was no dirt, no trees, no foliage. Nothing but thousands of sun bleached bones stretching to the horizon on either side of the river.

A deep, rumbling laugh erupted behind me. I turned to see the beast before me. It was huge, even bigger than the bear-kin berserkers I'd seen at the army parades. Its body was that of a great black wolf, but broad, with a wide head, short snout, and dozens of sharp teeth. Its legs were thin on long, giving it an otherworldly appearance that was just wrong enough to be unsettling.It grasped some huge sunbleached bone with its front paws, gnawing with glistening black teeth.

In fact, every inch of the beast was black, from thick black fur to solid black eyes and claws.

It stared at me with something like hatred in its eyes as it ate. I stood, unable to move as, sated, it dropped its prey and dipped its head down to the river. It lapped up the blood as though it had not drunk in days and then laughed again as it licked its lips clean. Slowly, it stepped toward me, each paw dripping thick drops into the river as it walked.

It stopped before me and lowered itself into the river with a great splash. The blood flowed thick against my thighs. The beast was so enormous that, even lying in the water, it's eyes were level with mine.

You must let me out of this place, I heard in my mind. *All enemies will fall under my teeth and claws. I will feast.*

I woke then, that strange deep laugh still reverberating through my mind.

Shaking, I sat up. I tried to calm my breathing as best I could, but the image of the beast, lying in that blood river like a dog enjoying a day in a stream, was too much.

49

There was a knock at the door. I couldn't bring myself to stand, but I squeaked out a "y-yes?"

The door creaked open, and I blinked against the light that flooded in.

A large figure walked into the room and kneeled in front of me.

It was the Priest.

I felt my heart rate slow, and I was able to catch my breath.

"Your doing?" I asked.

He nodded.

"You know," he muttered as he lowered himself into a sitting position, "between you and Weiran, the anxiety is so thick I can taste it." He set down a candle, and the light made his tattoos look as though they were dancing.

I felt the blood rush to my cheeks as he said it.

"Sorry," I mumbled.

"Nightmare?" he asked.

I nodded.

"Do you get those a lot?"

"I didn't used to."

"Hmm," he toned. His very presence seemed to have a calming effect, although I wasn't sure if it was him or his affinity.

"So you could…feel my nightmare? From across the temple?"

"Mhmm."

I turned my gaze down, thinking. It wasn't anxiety, it was *terror* I felt in that dream. And this priest had felt that?

"If you felt that," I began, "If you felt what I felt, then how are you so calm now?"

The Priest shrugged.

"It's your fear. Not mine. And…" he paused, thinking. "I do not feel things as strongly as I once did."

"I don't understand."

"No, I suppose you wouldn't."

Changing the subject, I said, "You mentioned Weiran. He didn't seem terribly anxious when I met him before. A bit tightly strung, perhaps, but not anxious."

The Priest shrugged and closed his eyes. "As I said, he does not sleep well. Night troubles him."

"What, is he afraid of the dark?"

This drew a genuine laugh from the Priest.

"No," he replied. "Not the dark."

I waited for him to elaborate, but he didn't.

"Why did you come here?" I asked.

"You seemed to be having a hard time, and I could help."

"No, I mean to the temple. You said you were from the Temple of Sorrow. That's nowhere near here."

"Ah," he sighed. He paused for a long moment before answering. His face remained impassive, but there was a slightly sad look in his eyes.

"You don't have to say," I said quickly. "I know we've just met."

"It's not that I don't trust you," he said simply, "but it's not *just* my story. And I am loathe to hurt people inadvertently."

This made the tale all the more intriguing, but I didn't ask further.

"Will you be alright?" The Priest asked.

"I don't know," I answered truthfully. "A few times the last couple of days, I've felt like I was falling apart. If I hadn't been here, with the priestesses and now with you..."

I didn't know why I was sharing this with him. Maybe he was using his affinity on me. But I didn't care—I needed to say something.

"Is this why you came here?" he asked. "Something that happened to you in the last few days?"

I thought for a moment about refusing to answer, but I found myself nodding.

"I am sorry," he said. "I can tell that you are struggling."

I wrapped my arms around my knees and pulled them to my chest.

"Could you just…make all that stop? Take it all away with your power?"

"I could. But you do not want that."

"Yes, I do. I really do."

He let out a long sigh. "You do not understand what you're asking for. It's easy for me to ease suffering. Easy to reach out when someone is struggling to breathe because they're so afraid. Because those feelings are temporary, usually. To suppress someone's ability to have the feelings in the first place? That would be cruel. Better to learn to manage, I think."

"That seems easy for you to say if you don't feel these things," I muttered.

He shrugged again, and said, "Trust me. I *do* have some experience in this matter. You should try to get some sleep. The High Priestess does not suffer guests who do not work. I'll stay until you drift off."

I gave a humorless laugh, but obediently lay down, pulling the blanket over myself. I didn't think I would easily fall asleep again. But as the Priest sat next to me, a strong sense of calm washed over me, my eyes grew leaden, and slumber claimed me.

This time, I didn't dream.

6

Ran

"I cannot allow it, ma'am. Believe me, it is a kindness."

She crumpled, sobbing and trembling.

Ran straightened and quietly smoothed his clothing.

"Let's go," the prince muttered.

The guards locked the doors to the chamber behind them. Only Sirra followed as Ran continued on.

"My prince, may I speak?" Sirra asked.

Ran sighed. His head had begun to throb, and Kita already had a two-night head start. He'd wanted to leave as soon as he'd spoken to Isa, but patience was required. He had to get into the temple. To do so would require subterfuge.

He wanted nothing more than to get this over with, and he wasn't in the mood for Sirra's protestations. "You may," he replied.

"I do not understand why you insist on taking Ditan with you. I am your guard. I should accompany you."

"I understand your concern, but my mind is made up on this matter. With any luck I'll be back within a few days."

"And if luck is not with you?"

"Then it will be longer. I'll send a message directly to you when

I have news." He gave Sirra a wide smile, trying to project as much confidence as he could muster.

Sirra ground his teeth and said, "Yes, my prince."

The pair walked in silence to the stables, where Ditan waited, chatting with a stable boy. As he noticed Ran and Sirra approach, he stopped and bowed his head.

"Are the horses ready?" Ran asked.

"Yes, my prince," the young stable boy said.

Two white stallions waited. One of them was one of Ran's, a white gelding that nuzzled his shoulder as he approached.

The other was an enormous white draft horse that belonged to Isa, strapped to the carriage holding the dead they would deliver to the temple. The horse was ill-tempered and huge, taller at the shoulder than most men. She'd been gifted the horse when he was just a foal—an offering from some farming family.

He was just as ornery as she was, and they got along swimmingly.

She would not be happy to learn that he had taken her horse, but it was necessary.

"You take the carriage," Ran said, pointing Ditan to the draft. "Are you ready?"

Ditan nodded.

Ran climbed his horse. He shook his hair out and tied it back. He straightened his coat—white, of course—and from the pocket he drew a white linen veil from his pocket and draped it over his face.

"We will make this right," Ran said, more to himself than to anyone in particular.

He glanced over at Ditan. The young shadowwalker had clambered up onto the driver's seat of the carriage and was watching Ran and waiting.

"Let's go, then," Ran said, trying to sound more confident than he felt.

The Silk District was more still than Ran had ever seen. With most of the nobility sequestered in the palace, only servants and guards roamed the streets. The silence was deeply unsettling; it reminded Ran of the time just before summer storms rolled in, when the sky tinged red and the the birds fled.

There were more than two city guards manning the gates that day; after Kita had slipped by, Ran had ordered extra patrols of the area. Mostly for show. It wasn't as though the extra guards would help bring Kita back any sooner, but he had to be shown to be doing something.

As they reached the middle gate, Ran dismounted and approached the guards. Ditan was close on his heels.

"Sorry, but we've strict orders today," one of the guards said as the pair neared. "No one gets through these gates."

Ran swept aside his veil and, sighing, said, "Yes, I'm the one who ordered it."

"Oh, My Prince!" the guard replied, bowing so deeply that Ran thought he might fall over. "We wasn't expecting you."

"I know," Ran said simply. "And I'd very much appreciate it if you didn't announce my presence quite so loudly."

"O-of course, My Prince," the guard said, somewhat more softly this time. The watched Ran and Ditan curiously, taking in their unusual outfits. It was obvious that the guard wanted to inquire, but he refrained.

"I've been told that there's someone here that can send a message for me. Is that so?"

"Yes, My Prince. Ligasi can do it, anywhere in the city." The guard poked a finger in the direction of another guard—a woman around Isa's age, Ran guessed.

The woman—Ligasi—dipped her head as Ran approached, casting her gaze to the ground.

"Hello," Ran said cheerfully.

Ligasi nodded.

"She don't talk, My Prince," the first guard interjected. "Not out loud."

"I see," Ran replied, "but you can send a message for me, correct?" Ligasi nodded again.

"Alright then. I need to send word to the temple. We are accompanying three individuals to be given up to the goddesses for their final rest. We shall need someone to meet us at the ziggurat elevator."

Her eyes widened, and she craned her neck to steal a look at the carriage.

"Please, just send the message."

The woman's cheeks went bright red and she nodded before closing her eyes. She chewed her lip for a moment as they all stood in silence, before her eyes abruptly popped open and she smiled. She nodded once more, clasping her hands together.

"Thank you," Ran said, assuming this meant the message was successfully sent.

Ligasi bowed her head in response. She shifted her eyes to check out the carriage before heading back to her post.

"Ditan, you lead. I want to drive," Ran said as the two of them returned to the horses.

"Of course," came the response. Ran wondered, as he climbed up to the front of the carriage, what Ditan thought of all this. Ditan was a competent fighter and a watchful guard, but Ran truly had no idea how close he had been with Kita. Did she ever tell him of any troubles? Did he know something that Ran did not? Later, a conversation would be in order.

The middle gate opened for them, and they spurred the horses along. The draft horse stamped its feet and snorted, but ultimately it obeyed.

Ran knew the city well, having been taken by his father to every corner of it. But still, every time he crossed from the upper district to the market district, he was taken aback by the stark contrast. The upper district gave the air of privacy; on a normal day, the nobles would remain mostly at their estates. It was rare to see a large crowd, and when there were people out on the streets, they were quiet, demure, speaking softly to each other, wary of others.

The market district was the exact opposite. Even as Ran and Ditan made their way through the middle gate, the district bustled with activity. Children darted across the streets, narrowly missing the horses and carriage wheels. They cackled as they did, playing some game Ran didn't understand.

The adults took little notice of them, walking the markets in the bazaar, shopping or selling their wares. In one stall near the street, a young man, maybe 18 or 19, cooked meat over his bare hands as people lined up to buy. The aroma made Ran's mouth water and his stomach growl. He realized then that he hadn't eaten all morning as they made their preparations to leave the palace.

For a moment, he entertained the idea of stopping to eat, but he quickly dismissed the thought. What kind of person stops a funeral procession to eat? No, completing the procession as planned was the least the pair could do for the dead.

The sun beamed high overhead. Ran longed to remove his coat, which seemed to be drowning him in sweat.

Just a little bit longer, he told himself. *Once we arrive at the temple, we can get changed.*

The procession was generally ignored throughout the entire market district. Though they drew a few odd glances, the people seemed less interested in Ditan and Ran than the goods being sold in market.

Ran was glad of being ignored. The fewer people who knew he was out of the palace, the better. The last thing he wanted was for Kita to learn he was coming and flee; if she left the temple, he truly did not know where she would go.

There was very little traffic on the bridge when they arrived. Most of the farmers and artisans from outside the city limits had arrived with or before the sun, and they would not leave until the day was done. Most of the guards were patrolling the outer walls at this time of day. And so, as they crossed the bridge, they were not stopped, not bothered.

When they arrived at the bottom of the ziggurat, a priestess was waiting for them. She greeted them warmly as they dismounted, smiling widely as she said, "Prince Ranjali!"

Ran froze as she said it; they'd been careful not to mention to anyone that they were going to the temple, except...

Damn. The guard at the gate. Forgot to tell her not to mention us.

"Must say, it's unusual for royalty to accompany the dead this way..." she trailed off.

"Yes, well, it is a quite unusual situation," Ran muttered as he lifted his veil. His sweat-dampened hair stuck uncomfortably to his forehead, and he used the veil to wipe away the moisture.

"Well, follow me," she said cheerily as she turned toward a large opening at the bottom of the pyramid. In the center of the opening was a large raised wooden platform, from which a series of ropes, pullies, and counterweights emerged.

Ran and Ditan led the horses, the larger beast still pulling the carriage, up a large ramp to the wooden platform. Once there, they unhitched the horse from the carriage and a young man led them away to be fed and watered.

"We thank you for bringing them here to us. We will of course give these people the greatest respect." The priestess gave them a small bow and joined the horses, grabbing for a rope to begin the ascent.

Ditan and Ran exchanged a look, and Ran said, "Wait."

"Hmm?" the priestess asked.

"We have made a promise to the families of these souls to accompany them the entire way. We cannot leave them at this stage. And we are tasked with returning the bones once rites are over."

"My Prince, that could take some time," she said slowly. Ran narrowed his eyes at this excuse. His own mother's ritual rites had taken less than half an hour, or so he had been told.

"It is no issue. If the High Priestess does not object, we would happily stay at the temple."

The priestess's smile dropped.

"I am sorry, My Prince, but…"

Ran gave her a small smile. He expected this response. Royalty and religion were not allowed to mix, after all. He cursed himself for not telling the messenger to omit his name. But he was far from giving up.

"I understand. I wasn't even allowed to be here when my mother died. But I've made a promise to others, and I *must* fulfill it."

"But…"

"I know you aren't able to allow me in. But perhaps I could speak to the High Priestess herself. I do not wish to burden you further."

"O-okay. But I must ask that you allow me to speak to her first. Let me take the carriage up. Wait here. We'll be back down once I speak to the High Priestess ." She was speaking more quickly now, eager to get away. She yanked twice on the rope, and the elevator in front of them began to rise.

"My Prince?" Ditan said as the lift rose out of view.

"Yes?"

"Do you think the High Priestess will let us stay?"

"I truly do not know. I certainly hope so."

"And if she doesn't?"

Ran shrugged absently, trying to convey more confidence than he felt. He had never met the High Priestess, but had heard her to be a hard woman.

"Ditan, have you ever been to the temple?"

"Not this one," came Ditan's reply. "The Temple of Joy, up north near the coast. The Obsidian Islands are just off the coast there, and we took a ferry in. My mother brought me. I was sick. She thought I was dying. Burning hot, not eating, not drinking. I was just a child then. I don't really remember."

Ran stopped and turned to Ditan. He'd never had much cause to speak to Ditan before—especially not about his childhood.

"You do not have to speak about this if you would rather not," Ran said, but Ditan just shrugged.

"I survived," came Ditan's wry response. "They bathed me in the fountains. My fever broke the next day. I started eating a bit. Within a week, we were headed back to our village. We were at the temple for every festival after that. But when I went to the Royal Academy, we were far from the closest temple, and I never had the time to take the trip. And when I entered into personal service for the emperor…"

"It is no longer permitted," Ran finished.

Ditan nodded his response.

"Is that upsetting to you?" Ran asked quietly.

"No," Ditan replied, but he didn't look Ran in the eye as he said it.

They stood in awkward silence until the lift returned. Standing in the center was the High Priestess, arms crossed.

"Hello," Ran called cheerily.

The High Priestess stared at them with steely eyes, and said "Why are you here, young prince?"

Ran's smile faltered, but he quickly regained his composure.

"I am sure the priestess spoke to you, but we have come to accompany the dead for…"

"Yes, yes, but why are *you* here? Royals don't come here. It's not permitted."

"Nonetheless, I've vowed to their families to be with them, and I do intend to keep my promise. Will you allow me to stay until the funeral has concluded?"

The High Priestess inspected them carefully, her eyes darting from Ran to Ditan and back.

"No, Prince Ranjali."

Ran flinched. Trying another tactic, he said, "What about my companion here? Will you allow him to stay?"

"My Prince, I cannot leave you unguarded," Ditan hissed quietly.

"No," the High Priestess replied loudly, rendering the point moot. "When funeral rites are finished, we will return your horses, your carriage, and the remaining bones. I do not see any reason for you to stay on temple grounds. It would not be proper."

Ran and the High Priestess stared at each other, the tension thick.

"I simply cannot accept this," Ran finally said. "I have given my word, and I must keep it."

The High Priestess was unmoved. "Then you have made promises that you cannot keep, young prince. This is my domain, not yours. Now, if there is nothing else, I do have business to attend to." She gave him a smirk before tugging on the rope.

Ran watched her rise back up to the top of the temple, his jaw working as he thought of what to do next. Being denied was not entirely unexpected, yet it did not make it any less infuriating.

"My Prince?" Ditan asked quietly.

Ran dismissed the guard's concern with a wave of his hand. He said, "We can't go in, but if I had any doubt before, I am certain now. Kita is here. Can you watch from the shadows? Find Kita, see if you can figure out where she plans to go next?"

"Of course, my prince. But would it not be better to go in and take her now? Between the two of us, our affinities would be especially suited to such a mission."

Ditan was right, of course. It would be a trivial matter for Ditan to steal her away through the shadows. Ran himself could just as easily walk through the walls, if he knew where she was.

But he had a feeling that his father wouldn't consider the mission a success if it resulted in conflict between the crown and the temples.

"Do not enter the temple. Just watch for now. I'll get us a couple of rooms at the inn. Meet me there this evening and we'll restrategize."

"Should we not just return to the palace?" Ditan asked.

Ran considered it. They could be back at the palace within the hour. He could meet with Sirra or his father and come up with a new plan.

But he couldn't afford to return empty handed. His father had tasked him with this mission, and he'd been very clear that any mercy for Kita relied on Ran's success. Besides, staying close to the temple would allow for better observation.

"No, we'll stay here. Go and see what you see."

Ditan dipped his head and stepped into the shadow of the lift, dissolving into the darkness.

7

Kita

I wanted nothing more than a hot bath. Every inch of me seemed to be covered in a fine layer of dust, and wearing the same clothing for so long made my skin itch. In the absence of other options, I stripped, shook out the linen shirt and muslin trousers, and pulled them back on. Feeling slightly better, I draped the blanket over the reed mat and walked out of my little room.

The air outside was cool, biting through my thin shirt. I hugged myself tightly against the early autumn wind. The courtyard was already full of priestesses and refugees, and a glance at the sun indicated that it was nearly midday. I had slept longer than I had thought. I supposed I would owe The Priest a thank you when next I saw him.

I wandered around until I found the dining hall. Breakfast was long since over, and there were only a pair of priestesses cleaning the tables.

"Excuse me?" I called. They turned to me, annoyed that I was interrupting their work.

I gave them a wide smile and asked, "Could I please get some breakfast?"

"No," came the reply.

I blinked at the response. I hadn't expected such a response.

"Sorry?" I called. "Is there no food left?"

"Miss, it's almost midday. We have other duties to attend to. We can't serve you. If you want food, you'll have to see what they have in the kitchens."

Without another word, the two turned back to the tables, attacking stains and spills furiously.

Alright, I thought to myself as I shuffled past them into the kitchens.

The kitchens were stifling hot. The cooks had already started on getting the midday meal together—a stew bubbling over the fireplace.

"Oy! What are you doing 'ere?" one of the cooks—the person in charge, I supposed—screeched. "If you ain't here to help, get out!"

"Sorry," I mumbled, bowing slightly. The cook swatted a hand at me, trying to usher me away.

"I was just hoping for something to eat. I suppose I slept late."

The cook eyed me carefully, hands on her hips.

"I ain't seen you here afore," she said in a tone I suspected she thought was gentle.

"Yes, I only arrived yesterday."

The woman's face softened slightly, and she clucked her tongue.

"Maybe you don't know how things work 'round here?" she asked helpfully.

I shook my head quickly. "No ma'am," I said.

She chewed her lip for a moment before nodding.

"Alright then," she finally said. "Just for today."

She turned on her heel and hooked a finger, indicating for me to follow. She crossed the kitchen to the temple larder, swinging the great doors open.

The larder was full, almost to bursting, with dried meats, breads, cheeses, and other ingredients. My stomach growled at the sight, and I placed a hand over it, trying to quiet the noise.

The cook, graciously, pretended not to notice as she dug through the larder and unearthed a crusty loaf of bread and a soft white cheese.

"'Ere, love. Eat this. And come back when dinner is ready. But tomorrow, be here while we're servin, or you'll get nothin."

I nodded my understanding, took the precious provisions and thanked her profusely as she ushered me out, back into the dining hall. The priestesses thoroughly ignored me as I crossed the room and exited into the courtyard.

I took a quick glance around the greenspace, looking for somewhere to sit while I ate. There were more refugees than I anticipated, maybe 20 of them strewn about the courtyard. The youngest of them was a child, perhaps six or seven years of age, floating cross-legged about a foot above the ground as other children ran around. The oldest of them was maybe my grandfather's age, a man who stood in front of the fountain, watching the others.

The Priest was nowhere to be found, but Weiran sat on a stone bench under the great tree, hunched over and eyes focused on nothing in particular.

I strode over to him and planted myself onto the bench next to him.

He bristled, but I offered him a piece of bread, and he softened slightly.

"Hello," he said through his teeth.

"Hello!" I replied as I took a bite of the bread, trying not to show my unease. He seemed to be looking for someone, or perhaps listening to someone, and he ignored me.

I tried to follow his gaze, but there was nothing but an empty wall before us.

"Are you looking for someone?" I asked between bites.

"No," he responded. He did not elaborate.

"Where is the Priest?" I asked, trying to get him to talk.

"In town."

"Why?"

"I don't see how that's your business." He locked his gaze on mine, and a shiver raced through my body.

"Just trying to make conversation," I mumbled.

"Hmm."

"Why are you so standoffish?"

He frowned and cocked his head, as though listening to someone whispering in his ear. After a few seconds, he turned to me and said, "You're high born. I can hear it in your voice. So now I'm even more curious. Why have you come to this temple?"

I stared at him. As evasive as he was, he had the audacity to ask me about my life? I tore off another piece of bread and chewed it, my jaw popping as I tried to get through the tough crust.

Finally, I said, "I'm here for the same reason as most everyone else. Fleeing the emperor."

"No," he said.

"What?"

"You said you're fleeing the emperor. We're not. We don't know the emperor. We have no business with him. And if we were fleeing him, we wouldn't be coming to the capital, would we? No, I suppose I misled you yesterday. We're not fleeing anything. " The more he spoke, the stronger his accent grew, emphasizing how little he belonged here in this city.

"Then why are you here?"

He shrugged and stood, dusting off his shirt. "Nowhere else to be," he said simply. He gave me a humorless smile. "Now, if you will excuse me, I have business to attend to." He bowed his head slightly in what struck me as an incredibly purposeful gesture before walking away.

I was deeply unnerved by him. Every word he spoke to me seemed designed to cut at me, as though he already knew everything about me and was just humoring me by asking.

I sat in silence, chewing my breakfast, as refugees and priestesses alike went about their daily business. A group of young refugees gathered just in front of the fountain, practicing, as Weiran and the Priest had the day before, combat. I watched curiously as they sparred hand to hand. They did not fight nearly as desperately than the men had the day before, stopping short of causing each other actual harm.

One young woman caught my eye—she had the golden hair and smooth dark skin of the Obsidian Islands, and she seemed to be a shadowwalker. As she fought, she disappeared into the shade of the great tree and, in a blink, reappeared on the other side her opponent, placing the girl into a chokehold.

It reminded me of Ditan, and my heart ached. Ditan was kind, and a good guard. Watching him spar was one of my favorite activities in the palace; the way he fought, striking, disappearing into shadow, and striking again from underneath his opponents' own shadow was utterly hypnotic. I had never seen him lose a fight, even when sparring against the other Imperial Guard. He deserved his position as Imperial Guardsman. He was my friend. If circumstances were different, maybe he could have been more.

And my grandfather was vengeful. Would he punish Ditan for my escape? And what of my mother?

As much as it pained me, I couldn't dwell upon it. If I did, I would fall apart. I had to keep moving forward.

And do what? I had no plan beyond arriving at the temple. I knew no one outside of the city, with the exception of my father. But he had left when I was just a child; I didn't even remember his face, let alone where he was living. One thing I was sure of, however, was that the High Priestess would tire of me eventually.

My breakfast finished, I dusted away the breadcrumbs and decided to take a walk around the temple. It was a beautiful, cloudless day, but suddenly, I was not in the mood to enjoy the sunshine.

Lost in thought, I wandered the halls of the temple, not paying much attention to where I was going. I must have taken an entire lap around the large, square building, before I heard someone calling to me.

"Miss?" a young female voice said. I turned. A bright-eyed young priestess smiled up at me.

"Oh? Yes?"

"The High Priestess would like to talk to you, Miss."

Nodding, I followed as she led me through the sparsely decorated halls.

* * *

When I arrived at the High Priestess's office, she was sitting at her desk, head buried in her hands. She did not react as we walked in.

As I lowered myself into the seat before her, she slowly looked up. She looked weary, her eyelids heavy as she took stock of me.

"You wanted to see me?" I asked.

She sighed deeply and said, "Indeed. I would like you to assist me with something."

"Oh? With what?"

"A funeral."

I leaned back in my chair, eyes wide. Funerals were sacred things, between the priestesses, the dead, and the goddesses. I had genuinely never thought I would see one. As far as I knew, most people never did.

"I don't understand," I said slowly. "Why would you need my help with a funeral?"

"Oh I don't need your help. But I'd like it anyway. Walk with me?" She stood and waited for me to do the same before leading me out the way I'd come.

"You know," she said over her shoulder, "we got an interesting visitor earlier today."

"Is that so?"

"Indeed. Just a day after the princess arrives at our temple, the crown prince arrives."

Ran. He sent Ran after me.

I stopped in my tracks. The High Priestess did not break her stride, and when I broke out of my stupor, I scrambled to catch up.

"Wha….was he looking for me?" I asked in a voice I hoped sound casual. In actuality, I sounded choked.

"He said he was delivering bodies for funeral rites. Quite an unusual task for a prince, isn't it?"

"So, he's here? Is that where you are taking me?"

She whirled around, eyebrows furrowed, a scowl on her face.

"Do not insult me young princess!" she hissed. "I take my duty here seriously. Your prince is not here, nor will he be."

I raised my hands in apology, and she turned back down the hall.

Finally, we reached a chamber I had not seen before. The High Priestess stopped at the door and raised an arm to stop me from going in.

"Prepare yourself, young princess," she warned. "Attending the dead is not an easy task for a newcomer."

I swallowed, and meekly asked, "why did you bring me here?"

She gave a quick smirk before opening the door and shuffling me in.

The room was a large marble chamber, with a great stone table in the center.

Lying on the table were three bodies. The first two were a pair of young women who I did not really recognize. The third, though, stopped me where I stood.

He was my age or a little bit younger. He had been a sweet man, young lord of an estate about a day's ride out of the city. He had asked to dance with me at the ball. He was kind, the type of man my grandfather would have approved of as a husband, if he were a little more politically advantageous. But he had the misfortune of dancing with me at the wrong time.

Their fine, blood-stained emanns were lying in a heap at the foot of the table, as two young priestesses attended the dead, washing away the dried blood from their skin.

As I saw them, a sob caught in my throat, and I fell to my knees. I tried to look away, but couldn't help but look at their faces. They were so serene. Just a few nights previously, they had been lively, excited, terrified. And now calm.

The High Priestess walked to each of the bodies, whispered something I couldn't hear, and gently stroked each cheek like a mother comforting a child. As she did, I saw their wounds. Each of them had been utterly mangled. The boy I had danced with—whose name I now could not remember—was missing his left arm, which was lying next to his body.

Bile rose, and it was all I could do to keep from vomiting. Without a word, I rushed out, still on all fours. The door had barely slammed shut behind me before I began to weep and dry heave simultaneously. Lumps of just eaten bread caught in my throat. My heart thudded heavy in my chest, and I couldn't seem to slow my breathing.

The High Priestess emerged from the room and kneeled beside me, gently rubbing my back as I cried.

"D-d-d-on't m-make me...don't m-m-make me go b-b-ack," I choked out.

"I won't," she said gently.

"Can't you h-help m-me? M-m-make this s-stop?"

"No, young princess. You need to feel this."

This just made me sob harder. My chest felt tight, and I wondered for a moment if I would ever breathe properly again.

The High Priestess hummed a song as she sat with me, and after a while, I was able to get a slow, deep breath.

"Better?" the High Priestess asked, turning to look me in the eye.

I nodded weakly, and she gave me a warm smile.

"I know that was difficult, young princess," she said, "and you may think me cruel. Death is difficult for us all to face. But I couldn't understand why the prince would bring the dead here himself just a day after you arrived." The High Priestess sighed deeply. "When people see they dead for the first time, they feel many different things. My young priestesses cry. Some of them stay in bed for days after, feeling dread at the thought that death will one day come for them. When people bring their loved ones, they feel extreme sorrow, as though part of them has died. I felt those things in you when you saw the dead just now. But you felt something else too—guilt. And that is unusual, I think. Certainly, some feel survivor's guilt, or wonder how they could have done things differently. Your emotions though…well, they're different. So, my dear. I think it's time you tell me what has happened to drive you to the Temple of Hope, yes?"

She waited. She didn't rush me, but continued to rub my back, humming as I slowly caught my breath.

Finally, I gathered myself enough to tell her.

"We began planning the investiture events months ago. As is tradition, most of the responsibility of the planning fell upon Ran. It was his investiture, and it was his job to make the event a success. It was going to be the first time he would be debuted to the nobility of the empire. And it would be a first chance for eligible nobility to try and catch Ran's eye—and mine—for marriage.

"The ceremony itself went perfectly. Ran was his usual confident self as he received his circlet and was officially named Crown Prince of the Empire. Every eye was upon him. I don't know the last time I saw him so happy.

"We moved from the ceremony to the ballroom. The air was filled with traditional music—drums beating and strings strumming as Ran danced with girl after girl. Whole roasted lambs and cows were brought out, and wine flowed. Everyone was happy.

"I heard this voice. It was a low, deep voice, growling at me, screaming, 'Let me out, stupid girl! Let me out!' It was so loud I couldn't understand why the young man dancing with me couldn't hear it.

"But then I saw it. This image in my mind of this creature that had been harassing me. The Beast. And that's all it took. In that instant, the creature manifested, a giant animal, larger than any living being I had ever seen. And as it breathed life for the first time, it *laughed,* this rumbling noise that almost stopped my heart.

"I can't...I can't remember what happened then. But when the thread between me and that beast severed, those three were dead. Throats ripped, stomachs slashed. And Ran! He was spotless. Not a single stain on his clothing—his affinity kept him safe, I suppose. He looked at me as though I had betrayed him. He wasn't angry, not really. He was just...hurt. And he begged me to tell him what happened, but I had nothing to say. I don't know why it happened. And there's an itching in the back of my brain, like this little voice telling me that I *should* know. But whenever I try to focus, that knowledge is just gone."

As I finished telling the story, relief washed over me. Perhaps it was the High Priestess's affinity giving me a reprieve, but for whatever reason, I didn't think so.

"Those young people suffered," the High Priestess said softly. I stiffened, but she did not say it unkindly. "It seems you have suffered as well, young princess. Go back to the courtyard and steel yourself. I have much to consider."

I nodded and stood shakily to my feet, before fleeing this chamber of death.

8

Kita

When Ran and I were 16 years old, his mother, the beloved Empress Sasun died. She was a lovely woman; kind and gentle. She treated me like her own kin, even though we were not related. Despite Mother's disdain for most of the family, she and Sasun had been the best of friends. They were of similar age, had been pregnant together. And really, it was impossible to hate Sasun. Even the emperor treated her with care—she was the only one he was ever kind to, even if they weren't exactly in love.

The mood in the palace had been somber. It was as though all the light in our lives had been extinguished.

Ran begged my grandfather to accompany her to the temple. He wanted to see her delivered to the nameless goddesses himself. My grandfather flatly refused. He asked to be allowed to at least ride with her body to the temple. This request, too, was denied.

So, we watched from the rooftop gardens as the funeral procession slowly rode toward the temple, her veiled carriage pulled by enormous white horses.

The procession made it through the middle gate before Ran broke. He sank slowly to his knees, chest heaving with silent sobs.

My grandfather—heartless wretch—did not show any emotion for his fallen wife. Nor did he comfort his son. In fact, he didn't acknowledge Ran at all. It was my mother who held Ran as he cried, wiping his tears and holding him. It was perhaps the only time I had ever seen her be kind to him.

With that being my only experience with death, I assumed that funerals were somber affairs. But, as I left my room on the morning that the three victims of the Investiture Ball were to be returned to the goddesses, it seemed that most everyone was in a jovial mood.

The High Priestess, the Priest, and a small group of priests and priestesses had left at sunrise. I was grateful that I wasn't asked—or indeed, permitted—to attend. The thought of watching carrion birds pick meat off of human bones made me feel ill.

After breakfast, I wandered into the courtyard, where the remaining priestesses circled the grand water fountain, singing. Their songs were not lamentations, but joyful, high-tempo melodies.

Near the great tree, a figure sat in the grass, huddled in on himself. As I got a bit closer, I realized it was Weiran, rocking back and forth, holding his head in his hands.

"Hey, you alright?" I called.

His head snapped up, eyes darting around. He took deep breaths, one, two, three, and unfolded, stretching his legs and trying to look unbothered.

"I am fine," he said, voice shaking.

To change the subject, I said, "I have never seen anything like this," gesturing toward the singing priestesses.

"No, neither have I," he replied softly. "Did you know them? The dead?" When I raised an eyebrow, he shrugged and explained, "I heard you helped the High Priestesses yesterday."

My head snapped toward him, my mouth open. How had he heard about that? Did he know about the conversation I'd had?

"So you're talking to the High Priestess about me?" I accused.

He raised his hand and slowly shook his head. "No," he replied seriously, "but this place is not that big. I hear things." Under the shade, he looked more tired than usual.

Relaxing, I thought for a moment as to how much to tell him. Finally, I settled on, "no, I didn't know them. I was just helping the High Priestess. At least, I tried. When I saw them..." I trailed off, reliving the moment I first opened the door to the room where the dead were held. I shuddered, and hugged myself to prevent me from trembling.

Weiran watched me intently. "Was that the first time you've seen a corpse?" he asked, not unkindly.

I nodded. Even the dead empress had been swept away before I had the chance to see her.

"Then you are fortunate," he said, his voice still gentle.

"You've seen the dead before, then?" I asked.

He barked a humorless laugh and said, "You ask more personal questions than anyone I have met."

I cast my gaze to the ground and felt my cheeks heat. He was being unfair—he'd asked the question first.

When I looked at him again, he was smiling, but he did not answer my question.

Changing the subject again, I asked, "do you understand any of the songs they are singing?"

He chewed his lip, flexing his fingers and slowly uncurling. "Some," he said. "They're singing in different languages. The ones that are in Avetsi, I understand. They remind me a bit of home. I haven't been to Avetsut in a very long time, so it does make me a bit homesick."

I badly wanted to ask why he had left Avetsut in the first place, but I bit my tongue lest I be accused once more of asking too-personal questions.

Instead, I asked, "what are the songs about?"

"Life, mostly. About the joys we feel while alive. The warmth of the sun, the kiss of a lover, the taste of a favorite meal. They're singing about living."

"A nice sentiment," I said.

He shrugged.

"You disagree?"

"It seems a bit like you're taunting the dead, no? Singing about all the things they no longer have."

"You speak as thought the dead can hear them," I retorted.

"If they can't, then why sing them?" was his reply.

The priestesses concluded their song. As the vestiges of their echoed voices faded, they each bowed low, touching their foreheads to the ground. They rose, and the spell broke. The priestesses returned to the depths of the temple. The refugees began to return to their own routines. I left Weiran under the tree and wandered the temple, helping the priestesses with any duties I could.

* * *

The sun was near setting when the funeral party returned to the temple. The High Priestess gathered everyone to the fountain.

"Tonight, we celebrate. We do not know those dead who we commended to the Goddesses today. We do not know their lives or their stories." At this, I felt the heat of her gaze on me, just for a moment, and glanced around to see if anyone else had noticed. "But it is our duty as priestesses to commit them to the sky, and to perform all of the rites they are owed. As our guests, we invite you to join us this evening."

The Priest had taken up a spot next to Weiran, and they quietly chatted among themselves in Avetsi.

"What are these rites the High Priestesses mentioned?" I asked.

They exchanged a look—Weiran's considerably more annoyed than The Priest's—before turning to face me. The way they seemed to communicate without words made me wonder, not for the first time, if Weiran could read minds. If he could, he gave me no indication.

"The most important have been done," The Priest began. "They have had a sky burial. Next we will feast in their honor. And there is…" he trailed off, his gaze shifting to Weiran.

Weiran looked away.

"There is a ceremonial performance called the Laviba. A battle between the Goddesses and the deathseekers over the souls of the dead," the Priest continued. "I will be the Goddesses's champion tonight."

"I don't understand why," Weiran hissed, arms crossed in front of him.

"The High Priestess asked me," the Priest replied simply, shrugging his broad shoulders.

Weiran's golden eyes flashed in anger, and he stomped off wordlessly.

"I apologize for him," the Priest muttered.

"Why's he so annoyed?"

But the Priest simply sighed and shook his head.

A few of the older girls began to assemble a fire, neatly stacking firewood into a pyramid shape that mirrored the structure of the ziggurat. They placed it in front of the fountain, a good distance away to avoid the spray of water.

Before long, the fire had been lit, and priestesses and refugees alike began to feast.

As I fetched my food and drink—a thick barley beer—I swiveled around the courtyard, looking for Weiran and the Priest. Weiran was sitting in his familiar spot under the tree; the Priest was nowhere to be found.

I made my way to Weiran, the heat of the fire warming my bones as I passed, as I sank down onto the bench beside him. He wasn't eating, wasn't drinking.

"Not hungry?" I asked, raising a mug.

He narrowed his eyes and said, "perhaps you should find someone else to eat with. I don't think I'd be good company right now."

"What's wrong with you? I asked.

He scowled at me, but remained silent.

Just then, the beat of a drum quieted the courtyard.

My attention snapped to the area in front of the bonfire, where one of the oldest priestesses knelt, banging rhythmically on a wide, shallow calfskin drum. Next to her there was a white-haired man I had not yet met, holding a stringed instrument across his lap. He opened his mouth and began to sang.

With a single note, my heart stopped. His voice cut through my very being and I my muscles locked.

"Never trust a siren," my mother had always warned me as a child. "Their songs can lure a faithful man to adultery, or lead a woman to kill her own children." Anything a siren could want could be stolen with a song.

But my fear ebbed away as he sang. Each word—though I did not understand the language—pulled me deeper and deeper into the song.

There, just next to the drummer, was the Priest. He had changed clothes and was wearing white linen trousers. His chest was bare, and white paint adorned his body in an ornate design, swoops and curves and words written in ancient languages. A scabbard was strapped to his back.

He stood motionless for several drumbeats before slowly reaching his right hand up and unsheathing a beautifully ornate steel sword. He spun the blade in fluid circles, his movements controlled and measured. Then, he brought his left hand to meet his right, and when it came away again, each hand gripped a twin shortswords.

As the siren sang, the Priest began to fight, thrusting and parrying as he danced around the fire. The drumbeats sped up and so did the Priest. Each slash was ferocious, as though he were truly trying to kill his invisible opponent.

He moved with a grace and speed that belied his size, and a savagery beyond what I would expect from a ceremonial dance. His movements, along with the siren's rich, deep voice, made me want to cry. I could almost see the deathseekers, their shadowy figures grasping for the Priest as he slashed at them with his blades.

How many times had he performed this ritual? And how many times had he fought, truly fought? The fervor behind his strikes and the scars on his body indicated that he'd fought and injured—maybe even killed—before.

The performance transfixed me.

The drumbeat began to slow. With it, so did the Priest's movements. Finally, he stepped back, jabbed one of the swords backwards, and spun on his heel to—in my mind at least—decapitate the invisible deathseeker with one clean stroke.

The siren ended his song with one last note, and the drum abruptly stopped. The Priest held his final position for a long few seconds before slowly returning his swords to their scabbard and bowing deeply.

The spell was broken, and I was back in the temple courtyard.

I want to play, I heard whispered in my mind.

My heart clenched. No. Not again. Not now.

Let me out, girl. Let me out!

"No!" I said through clenched teeth.

The beast growled its discontent, but said nothing else.

I glanced next to me to see if Weiran had noticed, but his attention was focused on the Priest. The expression on his face was not anger, per se, or ever annoyance, but…hurt.

The Priest approached us. His breath was heavy, and sweat dripped from his face, running the paint on his face.

Before he or I could say anything, Weiran burst into a torrent of Avetsi. He was speaking so quickly that I couldn't parse the different words. His voice was taut, and a vein pulsed in his neck.

The Priest recoiled. He responded, his voice calm and matter-of-fact.

The two went back and forth, Weiran getting more and more worked up as he spoke; the more gently the Priest responded, the more angry he got.

"Weiran, what's wrong?" I asked.

He whirled on me and said something I could not understand. When he realized he was still speaking in Avetsi, he growled his frustration and shot to his feet.

"Kita, I apologize. I think you should excuse us for now," the Priest said. He placed a hand on Weiran's shoulder, but Weiran slapped it away.

"Weiran, let us discuss this later," the Priest said evenly. He didn't seem even remotely bothered by Weiran's outburst.

Weiran blinked and looked from the Priest to me before slowly nodding. "Alright," he said, his voice very small. "I think I had better return to my room for tonight." He swallowed and turned toward the temple. As he walked, he unleashed another torrent of pointed Avetsi, talking to no one in particular.

"I apologize for him," the Priest said, rubbing the back of his neck.

"What was so upsetting for him? He was fine when we spoke earlier."

"Hmm," he sighed, "that is between us. Sorry, Kita. He gets extraordinarily emotional at times. That is really all I can say."

"Must be frustrating for you, if you can sense it."

"It can be tiring, but emotions are part of life. If they bothered me, I would not be able to live."

As I considered his thoughts, I gazed out on the courtyard. In the night sky, the priestesses dined alongside refugees, the two groups intermingling in a way I had not yet seen in my time at the temple. I watched as children—priestess and refugee alike—ran around the fire, chasing each other and barking their laughter. It brought a smile to my face.

"Kita, the High Priestess spoke to me about you," the Priest said softly. My gaze snapped to his, and my jaw dropped open. "Worry not. She refrained from giving me all of the details. But she told me that you knew the dead."

"Is that how Weiran knew? You told him?"

The Priest flinched. "Of course not. She only told me today on our journey to the mountain. If he knew, he found it out some other way."

"Why would she tell you?" I asked through my teeth.

"Because she thinks you need help."

I gave a humorless laugh. "And you're the person that will help me?"

He shrugged. "I am a powerful empath. More powerful than any of the priestesses here, in any case, by far. Perhaps she thinks that is why." He said it matter-of-factually, not remotely bragging.

I thought back to the night he showed up at my chambers to salve my frayed nerves. None of the priestesses had even awoken, as far as I could tell. Yet he had sensed it from across the temple.

He turned his entire body to face me, gently removing his swords and laying the scabbard across his lap. "This is related to your nightmares," he said. It wasn't a question.

I nodded curtly, my mouth tights. I wrung my hands together just thinking the ball and my nightmare.

The beast growled in my ear again. I squeezed my eyes shut. Just as my heart began to race, my breath and heartbeat calmed.

"Thank you," I murmured.

"I was taught to control emotions from the time I was brought to the Temple of Sorrow," he explained. "All emotions, including my own. Perhaps I could help you with that?"

"Perhaps," I sighed. I understood that he was able to shape and control emotions. But could he really help me? Could he help me control the beast? Was the beast even related to my emotions? I wasn't sure.

"You are apprehensive," he noted.

"You don't have to articulate everything I'm feeling," I snapped.

His face did not change.

"Perhaps you should. It could help," he said simply. His face was still expressionless, but I thought I detected a hint of humor in his voice. He stood, bowing his head and gripping his scabbard tightly. "We will begin tomorrow. I will do everything I can to assist you. You have my word."

He gave me a tight smile—as though he didn't know how to do it properly—before retreating into the temple.

I stayed under the shade of the great oak tree, inhaling the scent of burning wood and roasted meat. As I swept my gaze across the courtyard, I locked eyes with the siren. My heart seized as he held my eye. As he opened his mouth to…what? Speak? Sing? Either way, I had no desire to be trapped there.

Pulling my cloak tight against my chest, I spun away.

9

Kita

I sat with my back against the cool stone wall, breathing slowly with my eyes closed.

"What are you feeling right now?" The Priest asked. He sat cross-legged across from me, his posture straight and relaxed. He'd brought me to a cavernous chamber deep in the bowels of the temple. It must have held some ceremonial purpose. There was a simple box-shaped altar in the center, but the room was otherwise empty. I could imagine hundreds of worshipers crammed into to the space on some holy day, or perhaps it was a holdover from days long past.

"Why do you keep asking me things you already know the answer to?" I snapped. For the last few days, every morning went like this. Deep in the guts of the temple, away from prying eyes, he worked with me. The Priest was a natural trainer; even with no experience with an affinity like mine, he seemed adept at working with me. At the very least, he was confident. And, despite my initial skepticism, I *did* feel better after spending my mornings with him.

"Because I'm more interested in your response than the truth," he said simply.

I frowned, petulantly staring him in the eye.

He was unbothered and simply waited for me to respond.

"I guess," I finally began, "I feel alright at the moment. A bit annoyed."

"Why?"

"Because I don't understand why you want me to do this."

"Hmmm. What else?"

"I…" I swallowed. I didn't *want* to talk to him about this, not really. I knew, of course, that the Priest was intimately familiar with everything in my heart. But that didn't mean I was prepared to discuss it with him.

"What else?" he asked again, more gently.

I found myself picking at my fingernails. "I just…feel lost. Everything I thought I was is gone. And my family is trying to kill me. That…" Tears welled in my eyes and I opened them as wide as I could, desperate not to let him see me cry. He might know every emotion I had, but I would not let him see that particular indignity.

The Priest nodded.

"We used to do this as children," The Priest said, "at the Temple of Sorrow. Our trainer would say, 'Know yourself.' He would drill it into us. You are fortunate that I am not as strict as he was."

Sensing an opportunity to change the subject away from me, I asked, "how strict was he?"

The Priest smirked. "A story for another time."

I cursed him in my mind.

"Can we just move on?" I asked.

"As you like. How about birds today?"

I nodded, closing my eyes and preparing to listen to his instructions.

"Think of a bird. A dove. In your mind's eye, imagine the feathers. Imagine the span of its wings. Look at the way its wings flex. Look at its talons. Think of the way it grips its perch. Think of its beak as it opens its mouth and chirps."

I held the bird in my thoughts, examining it from every angle I could.

"Are you ready to release it?"

"Yes."

"Don't. Hold it."

The dove strained against me, longing to be made real.

I held it back easily.

The Priest made me sit there, the strain getting painful the longer we waited. Finally, after an eternity, he said, "Release."

And the dove—black from beak to tail—flew forward, chirping as it circled the ceiling above us. The gossamer thread that connected us strained as it flew higher and higher.

"Good," the Priest said.

The thread snapped, and the bird dissipated into nothingness.

"Lovely," he said, in such a monotone that it made me snort. "How do you feel?"

"Fine. It's just a little bird."

"Alright then. We can do larger birds, and then maybe we will try the Beast."

"What? Today?"

"Do you plan to avoid it forever?"

"You haven't met the Beast," I muttered.

He opened his mouth to speak, but something caught his attention. He cocked his head, his gaze drifting over my shoulder.

"Stay here," he muttered, clambering to his feet. As he loped out of the room, I considered obeying him for a moment, but my curiosity got the better of me. I followed him through the winding corridors of the lower temple, up winding staircases until we emerged outside.

Across the courtyard, the High Priestess locked eyes with him and opened her mouth to speak. For a few fractions of a second, vibrations rumbled through the ground.

The gate exploded inward. The giant red wood crashed into splinters, and the blast flung the heavy stone gateposts through the air, luckily missing any of the refugees. The concussive blast leveled the young priestesses nearest the gate, and dust filled the air, and my lungs. I coughed and sputtered, trying to draw a clear breath.

The noise was, quite literally, *deafening*. The Priest was on his feet, scabbard in hand before I had the chance to react, but although I saw rock crashing to the ground, all I could hear was a tinny whine. Warm liquid dripped from my ear, and as I reached a hand to touch, the pain began to radiate outward through my neck and skull.

I got to my feet, took two steps, and then the ground tilted sideways underneath me. It was all I could do to keep from falling over.

A second blast rang out mere feet away from me. It swept me up, throwing me through the air until I landed with a crash onto one of the stone benches. I felt the crack of breaking bones. A moment later, the pain began to stab at my insides, and tears began to flow. I crumpled to the ground. Even small muscle twitches sent stabbing pains throughout my body. I couldn't get a good breath, and each attempt brought fresh pain.

I lay there, too hurt to force myself to move, too deaf to hear the yells, too blinded by dust and soot to see.

Someone laid a gentle hand on my shoulder. I turned, and just through the haze, I saw golden hair and eyes the color of the starlit night.

"Ditan?" I asked.

He said something, but I couldn't hear over the whining din in my ears. He gingerly took my arm and placed it around his shoulder. I groaned as he started to lift me from the ruined courtyard floor. His heartbeat against my skin was steady and strong, and my eyes felt heavier and heavier with each passing beat.

In the corner of my eye, there was a flash of steel. He jumped back, lying me back down as quickly and gently as he could as a large figure lunged forward carrying a pair of matched short swords.

"Ditan?" I called after him. "Ditan?"

But he was gone into the shadows.

Someone yanked my arm forward, pulling it painfully out of socket as they tried to force me to my feet. I screamed then, sending fresh spasms of pain through my abdomen. I turned my head—it was Weiran. He looked fine—covered in dust, but undamaged by the explosions.

He yelled something, but I couldn't hear him, couldn't respond.

He turned his head abruptly, and I followed his gaze.

Through the haze, I could see a number of people, dressed all in black—the black uniforms of the Imperial Army.

I don't know why my mind went to the night of the ball then. Maybe it was the sight of bodies strewn across the courtyard, or maybe it was the reminder of the imperial presence. But the image of the Beast came unbidden to the forefront of my mind, and I was far too weak to stop it.

It ripped its way from my mind to reality with a shriek that I could not hear. If anything, it seemed bigger, more ferocious, more *hungry* than I remembered. It stood on its double jointed hind legs, long tail sweeping back and forth as it lifted its giant head to the air, sniffing like a dog.

Please don't hurt anyone, I thought, though I had very little faith I could make it do what I wanted.

But, to my surprise, the beast turned to face me, and something in its demeanor changed. It still looked as ferocious, as dangerous as before. But as I watched it bound forward toward the soldiers, I quite simply *knew* that my request had been accepted.

As it strained against me, stealing what little energy I had left, my vision began to blur. And then, I saw nothing at all.

The first thing I noticed when I regained consciousness was the squat little healer standing over me. As I blinked away the darkness, she prodded at my ribs. To my surprise, most of the pain was gone.

I tried to sit up, but she slammed me down with a surprising amount of force.

"Be still," she snapped, her voice clear and stern.

I was lying on a rough cot. The stone walls of the room told me I was probably somewhere in the temple, but I did not recognize it. My tunic had been torn asunder, gathered in a heap underneath me.

"Whoareyou" I muttered.

"The person saving your life," the healer replied.

"I'm fine," I whispered.

"You are now," she replied. "Your ribs had pierced your lungs. You are very lucky that Weiran got you here when he did."

I turned my head. Weiran was standing behind her. His arms were crossed, and his gaze was far away. I wondered what was on his mind. The circles under his eyes seemed darker than ever, and every few moments, he gave a curt nod or shook his head.

"Who're you talking to?" I murmured.

Suddenly, his eyes snapped to focus and his mouth tightened. He did not reply to my question.

"Alright. I've healed what I can. Your body will do the rest," the healer I supposed said. "Lie still, y'hear me? I'll be back after I attend to the others."

"Mmmmk…."I said.

The door swung open. I strained to see—there were three men, two refugees, each flanking The Priest as they tried to lead him in. Each step pulled a yelp from The Priest's lips. There was a knife lodged in his chest, all the way to the hilt.

I tried to sit up, but my body was weak, and my muscles gave out.

Weiran lept away from his perch, and in only a step or two, he was at the Priest's side, helping to guide him gently to a mat on the floor.

"What happened?" Weiran demanded. His voice was high pitched and frantic.

"He was fighting someone," one of the refugees said as he stepped away. "One of the bombers? I don't know. It was a shadowwalker. He couldn't keep up. Slipped into the shadows before the Priest could strike back. Fucking imperials!"

"Shadowwalker? Imperials?" I muttered. *Ditan?* No one acknowledged me.

"Hey, how are you feeling?" Weiran said, his voice tender. He sank to the ground at the Priest's side. The healer placed a soft hand on his shoulder.

"Weiran," the healer said, his voice gentle, "when we move that knife, I got seconds before he bleeds out. The knife's in his heart. I can't promise that I can save him."

"Just heal the wound," Weiran snapped.

"I'll do my best, but..."

"Just. Heal. The wound."

"Okay," she said evenly. Then help me. Remove the knife. Then apply as much pressure as you can."

He gave a curt nod. With one hand, he held the Priest's. With the other, he grasped the handle of the knife and pulled sharply, freeing the blade with a wet *slorp*.

The Priest's breath quickened, as though his lungs refused to fill. Blood spurted, and Weiran pressed hard against the wound. The healer put his hand on either side of Weiran's and pushed his power into the Priest's body.

"Weiran," The Priest called, his voice low and raspy. "If I die..."

"Stop. You know you will be fine."

"No! Just let me...let me...."

Perhaps remembering that the rest of us were in the room, Weiran switched to Avetsi.

"Please!" the Priest replied. "I do not want to keep coming back.

Please!"

Another curt Avetsi phrase.

The Priest let out a strange noise—a choked sob, and then a sigh. His eyes glazed and then stared, unblinking, at the ceiling as his fingers relaxed and his arm fell to the side.

"Shit," the healer spat. "I'm sorry Weiran. I did what I could but—"

I felt the tears began to well.

"Fix the heart," Weiran said.

"But—"

"Just do it!" he yelled, his voice tight. He swallowed and added, "Please."

The healer stared at him for a moment, her mouth gaping, eyebrow raised in question, before nodding curtly.

A long moment elapsed.

"Okay," the healer finally said. "The heart's fixed, I can feel it. But what does it matter if…"

Weiran slowly turned his head toward the healer, her eyes wide and teeth clenched.

"Be ready," he hissed. "He will be uncontrollable."

"He's dead," the healer pointed out.

But before Weiran had the chance to reply, I felt it.

It wasn't just sadness. It was a deep, dark despair, the likes of which made me want to die. It wasn't just anger. It was a deep, dark fury that made me want to kill. Myself? Someone else? That, I didn't know.

I gripped the edge of the cot so hard my fingers turned my fingers white. I resisted the urge to leap to my feet, resisted the urge to find the nearest blunt object to swing or throw.

A sob escaped my lips as the full weight of my emotions came over me.

"Oh!" the healer gasped. "Oh!" She sank to her knees and bent her head to wail.

"Stop it!" Weiran yelled at the corpse in front of him, perhaps louder than he needed to.

There was a sharp gasp, a shallow wheeze, and the Priest opened his eyes.

He gripped Weiran's arm, clawing so deeply that he left deep scratches. His eyes went wide as he pushed himself up to a sitting position. He glanced around the room, back and forth and back and forth, the whites of his eyes bloodshot and stretched. He was like a wild horse cornered.

"What?" I sobbed.

Weiran barked something at the Priest, in that melodic language I wished in that moment that I could understand.

The Priest replied, and the two fell into an easy conversation. The Priest's voice lost its shakiness as he began to settle into deep, even breaths.

The intense despair began to subside, and I was able to breathe— something I hadn't realized I had stopped doing.

The healer sat on her heels for a moment, wiping her eyes on her tunic.

"Okay?" Weiran asked, his voice soft and gentle as he lightly caressed the Priest's hand.

"Yes," replied the newly revived man. He closed his eyes and his breathing slowed into a rhythm.

Weiran sank back against the wall and let out a deep breath. All the color had gone from his face, and his lips held a tinge of blue. He raised a shaky hand to his face to rub his eyes. He looked as though he could collapse at any moment.

"Please," he said, his voice small and hoarse, "leave us."

The refugees nodded and obeyed. The healer was more hesitant, but after a sharp look from Weiran, she too left the room.

Weiran got to his feet. His legs trembled like he was a newborn foal.

He staggered over to my cot and collapsed to the floor, landing on the hard stone with a groan.

"I think," he said through his teeth, "it's time that we spoke."

"You're a deathseeker," I blurted.

His eyes flashed hot and he clenched a fist.

"Do *not* call me that," he hissed. "I am no god. No vengeful spirit. I'm just a man."

"A man who just brought a dead man back to life," I pointed out.

"Let's talk about *you*," he countered. "I saw that...that thing. That—"

"Beast," I finished.

Weiran sighed and said, "Yes. You set it on the Imperial Army. And you know what's so interesting about that?" He sat forward, his eyes boring into mine. "From what I heard, only the royal family themselves have dominion over reality. That's the story, isn't it? The worldmakers, they call themselves. It's all shit, of course. The worldmakers haven't existed in centuries. And yet, here you are. So who are you, really?"

"It seems we both have things we'd rather not discuss," I muttered.

"Fine," Weiran snapped. "Yes. I am what the old stories call a deathseeker. It's a stupid, stupid name. I don't seek out the dead. I don't battle the Goddesses for their souls."

He breathed a deep sigh, and for a long moment we sat together in silence, avoiding each other's eyes. Finally, he said, "Have you ever been to the sea?"

I blinked at the change in subject.

"What does this have to do with—" I started.

"Have you been to the sea?" he cut in. He stared with an intensity that reminded me why I feared him when I first laid eyes upon him.

I shook my head.

"The city where I grew up was on the coast. I suppose the city is all that's left of the principality of Avetsut. It's all imperial now," he muttered. "Down at the docks, fishermen would go out on their reed boats with these gossamer fishing nets. They were so fine that only water could pass through. I would watch the fishermen as they tossed those nets overboard. And I would watch as they hauled the nets up, full to bursting with fish. Crabs. Snakes. Rocks. Those nets would drag everything from the depths."

He paused, wringing his still-trembling hands.

"My affinity is like those fine gossamer nets. The dead, they...they get caught by my power. Except I can't....I can't figure out how to get them out. They find me. They attach themselves to me. Even right now they're all around us. Trying to talk to me. No, not talk. Scream. " He grimaced and buried his face in his hands. "They are *incessant*. And if I ignore them? They wait until I sleep and *show me*."

"Show you?"

"Every night, I dream. Not pleasant dreams. I don't dream of love or family or adventure. I dream of death and decay and slaughter. They show me how they died. And I can assure you, it's never old age. I've seen men slaughtered with swords. Entire villages burnt to the ground. The worst are the berserkers—they tear people apart, limb from limb. These people scream at me for vengeance. For what the Empire has done to them. And they deserve their vengeance."

"What are you talking about?"

"Are you really so blind, Kita? Perhaps it's because you have never left this city. Perhaps it's because you think that running away from the emperor is enough. No, these people scream because the Empire killed them. And I intend to help them find their rest."

"Surely you exaggerate," I said, though I didn't fully believe my own words. My grandfather had always proven to be a cruel man. His punishments of both me and my mother were fierce when he thought we had stepped out of line. But to unleash the berserkers? That seemed excessive for anything but extensive unrest.

"Are these soldiers then?" I asked.

He laughed, but there was no humor in it. "Soldiers? Is that what you believe? Is that the lie you've been sold? That the Empire is defeating its enemies in glorious battle?"

I said nothing. That *was* what I had always been taught. The further one traveled from the capital, the more other kingdoms and principalities sent their forces to claim our land. Our military strength was our protection.

"What, precisely, are you insinuating, then?" I asked.

"I insinuate nothing. I am telling you that those dead souls who scream for vengeance in the night are not soldiers. They are women and children. They are merchants and farmers. They're all citizens. That's what the Empire does—it fights its own citizens."

"Why did you come to this city?" I asked pointedly.

He waved my question away. "Bombing a temple. A temple! The one institution that is supposed to be safe from imperial control. That is what this empire is," he spat. "Innocent people. This is not new."

I recoiled at the venom in his voice.

"I watched you bring the Priest back to life. He was dead. And you restored him to life," I finally said, trying to keep my voice gentle.

He nodded, slowly, but still wouldn't look at me.

"Then can't you bring back the others who died?"

"Sometimes, if things are just right. If a body is not too badly damaged. If I have enough energy. Sometimes, I can pluck a soul from my net and return them to their vessel. But I've tried so many times, and failed the vast majority. It takes a lot from me. It's a hard thing, not just physically but..."

He closed his eyes, and a tear rolled down his cheek. Some of the color was beginning to return to his face, though the dark circles rimming his eyes were blacker than I had ever seen them.

"That wasn't the first time you brought him back, was it? He said—"

"No, it wasn't," he interrupted, but he didn't care to elaborate, and I didn't dare push him.

"Now, it's your turn," he said, finally looking me in the eye as he wiped away his tears. "Who are you? A royal?"

I swallowed and said, "Yes."

He nodded, the expression on his face unreadable, and asked, "how does a royal end up at a temple?"

"My grandfather—the emperor—was going to have me executed," I explained. No need to give him the full details. Not now. Maybe not ever.

"Did you deserve execution?" His stare was so intense that I badly wanted to look away.

"He would certainly say so," I replied. The unsaid words hung heavy between us, but he didn't press it.

"Is that why they bombed this place?" he asked. His voice was even, but his eyes were full of fury.

"Ran wouldn't bomb a temple."

"The crown prince Ranjali," Weiran mused. "Is he who they sent after you? If so, evidently he would. Evidently he did."

The image of Ditan, frantically dragging me from the rubble. Was he there on Ran's order? Ran wouldn't do something like this. It wasn't in his nature. But...

"This is your family," Weiran whispered sadly. "This is what they do."

The sentence weighed thick in the air between us, until finally Weiran got to his feet—a bit steadier than he had been before.

"What now?" I asked.

"For now, I think it's best you get rest. Your body is still trying to heal itself. And I...I need some rest myself.

He gave one more longing glance at the sleeping Priest before slowly shuffling away from the room.

10

Ran

To say that Yor-a was in disarray was severely underplaying the situation. Word spread quickly about the attack at the temple. Rumors flew, and within hours, the entire Market District was alight.

Ran had been at the inn when the bombing happened. While Ditan had gone to scout ahead, he'd waited, wringing his hands as patrons and innkeepers screamed and fled.

And now, as Ran and Ditan fled down the ziggurat steps, hundreds, maybe thousands of civilians flooded the area surrounding the ziggurat base, trying to break the city watch's ranks.

They had to leave the area. There were too many people. The chaos was too intense. Kita would be safe within the temple walls. Or at least, Ran hoped she would be.

The pair slipped down to the stables at the base of the temple, collecting their horses before taking the path behind the ziggurat. Getting to the palace would be difficult with the mass of angry—no, violent—citizens. And anyway, the emperor's mandate was clear. If Ran wanted mercy for Kita, it would be given only if she was returned. He couldn't go back without her.

They pushed the horses hard, galloping away from the city to create some distance.

"This is a mess," Ran muttered, calmly stroking the neck of Isa's white draft horse—Kourivan, as he'd taken to calling it. It was a fitting name; "stubborn one," in the old tongue.

Ditan sat silently astride his own mount, waiting.

"Why would the army have done this? It makes no sense. Father said he wanted Kita captured quietly. Why send the army?" Ran asked as they cleared the cacophony of the city.

"Perhaps he grew impatient?" Ditan replied, though his voice lacked any sense of conviction.

"Perhaps." But Ran had never known his father to be impatient. Decisive, certainly. But impatient? "And you're sure you saw soldiers?"

"I'm not sure, my prince. It looked that way, but things happened quickly, and it was difficult to see through the smoke and dust. They certainly seemed to be wearing the imperial blacks." He paused, glancing toward the ground before adding, "Kita was there. I saw her. I had her in my grasp, but a priest attacked before I could bring her out. I failed. My apologies, my prince." Ditan gripped his horse's reins, prodding the beast forward and refusing to catch Ran's eyes.

"Deathseekers take us," Ran hissed. "This should have been simple." Kourivan shook his head and pressed onward.

This bombing was a new complication. He'd not been told of any plans his father may have had, but that didn't mean the emperor didn't have them. The man was known to be thoughtful, and there were many times when he'd kept Ran away from the council room. If he hadn't seen the advantage to telling Ran, he wouldn't have told him.

The High Priestess would protect Kita. In the meantime, he needed to figure out what was going on. Returning to the palace without her was not an option—his father had made that very clear. So, he did the only thing he could think to do.

The Eastern Fort. It was the last place Ran wanted to be, but the best place to find answers about what was going on. The Commandant was a vile woman, but she had the emperor's trust. It was the closest imperial outpost; at the very least, he could wait out the chaos until the city watch got the Market District under controlm.

Ditan was content to ride in silence. Ran was grateful.

They rode for most of the day, sticking to the path. They road was empty, leaving them alone with the sounds of squawking birds and rustling leaves.

The first time Ran had made this trip, he'd felt nervous, but proud. He'd taken trips around the Empire with his father, of course—months-long journeys to the Vayanshan Mountains in the north, voyages by sea to Avetsut. They had traveled many times to various forts and castles.

But once his mother died, his father had decided it was time for him to get a proper military training. Oh, Ran had been swordfighting since he was a child, and working with a tutor on a near-daily basis in the use of his affinity. But a keen military mind needed honing away from the palace, and so the emperor had demanded Ran be trained as an officer at the Eastern Fort. Of course, Ran would outrank everyone there, but the emperor was very specific—while there, Ran was not the heir to the Empire. He was just Ranjali Melyora.

That first journey to the Eastern Fort had taken nearly a week. The weather had been poor, and his carriage had moved slowly. Each night, his personal guard—five guards deep with Sirra at the lead—had insisted on setting extensive perimeters before they could bed for the night.

He had been so excited, so proud that his father thought him fit to one day lead the Empire's military campaigns.

But that was before he met the Commandant.

The sun fell beneath the tree line, casting long shadows across the path. Ditan seemed to instinctively seek the shade out, his horse drifting off the path.

"Let's stop before we lose the last of the light," Ran called.

Kourivan pawed at the ground as they dismounted. Ran stroked the horse's mane, and it nibbled at the collar of his shirt.

"Shall I go hunting?" Ditan asked as he hitched his horse.

"Fresh meat is always appreciated," Ran said with a tired smile.

Ditan nodded, briefly touched the hilt of his sword, and dissolved into the darkness. Ran couldn't be sure, but he thought he detected a small smirk on the guard's lips.

It was a strange feeling. At once, Ran felt at once entirely alone and keenly watched. Such was the nature of having a shadowwalker nearby. Ditan seemed entirely comfortable in the shadow realm—Telombraj, the shadowwalkers called it—moving through it without hesitation; at times, he seemed more at ease in shadows than in the realm of reality.

As Ran began to remove their blankets from he horses, the hairs on the back of his neck prickled. Was Ditan truly hunting? Or was he just watching, unseen?

He had stopped them in a good spot; defensible, clear sightlines into the forest. A small clearing where they could take turns sleeping. Ran effortlessly fell into the process of camp-making; a holdover from his days at the Eastern Fort. After two years of sleeping on dirt or, if he was lucky, the lumpy cots at the fort, his soft bed at the Imperial Palace had taken time to feel like home again. This, the road, was almost more familiar.

An animal shriek nearby signaled Ditan's return from the world of the shadows. Just a moment later, he was back at their campsite, a rabbit in his fist.

Ran gestured toward the center of the clearing. Before long, a fire roared between them, the rabbit slowly roasting.

Ran flexed the fingers on his right hand. His arm itched fiercely.

Memories flooded in, but he didn't care to relive them.

"Where were you trained, again?" Ran asked, trying to take his mind off his own thoughts.

Ditan blinked, and said, "oh, the, uh, the Cala Imperial Academy to the northwest, near the sea."

Ran couldn't help but laugh. His mother was from Cala. "I see. What was it like?"

Ditan eyed the prince suspiciously. "It was...much like any other imperial training, I would imagine. I started there as a child, so it's what I knew. They taught me to fight. Taught me to use the shadows to my advantage. There were other shadowwalkers, so I had a lot of practice. We were taught imperial history. We were taught our letters and numbers. It was the best education I could have hoped for as a poor boy. But reading and history were not my strongest subjects."

"Fighting?"

"Indeed. I transferred to the capital a few years ago." He paused, poking at the rabbit with a stick. "I learned more there than I thought I would. We had do to things that..." he trailed off and swallowed.

He didn't need to finish the sentence. Ran knew. The Imperial Barracks had an unassuming name, but it was where the most elite soldiers trained. Those who would become Imperial Guard, assassins, or spies. The kind of people who would need to kill without hesitation.

Traitors and enemy spies spent their final days at the Barracks. The worst of them faced the most inexperienced of students.

"I trained at the Eastern Fort for about two years," Ran said. "My father thought it best to get military training, since I'll be taking control over our armed forces when I become emperor. I grew up with tutors, swordmasters, and the finest affinity trainers in the empire. So I thought the Eastern Fort would be similar."

"And was it?"

Ran barked a humorless laugh. "It was not. My father put me under the direct command of the Commandant, and she was not happy about it. Her exact words to me were that she 'had better things to do than to babysit a spoiled princeling.'"

Ditan smirked.

Ran sighed. The Commandant had sized him up quickly and decided that he was not up to her standards. He was soft, well-fed. He had never known a day's discomfort, let alone strife.

She'd made it her mission to change that.

In her mind, she was a kingmaker. She was shaping him to be the kind of emperor that could withstand anything. She withheld food. Forced him to spend extended periods of time on the road with his unit—they hated him for that at first, though he'd won them over eventually. But the worst was what she called 'torture training.'

"You are a high profile target," she had said. "If you are ever captured, our enemies will make you beg the goddesses for release. They won't kill you; you're too valuable. Instead, they will pry any secrets they can from you, through whatever means they can. You must learn to withstand them."

She'd sat him in a chair, up in the fort's tower. He'd been alone with her as she circled him, pacing like a wild animal sizing up its prey. He'd wanted nothing more than to put space between himself and her.

As though reading his mind, she'd said, "if you use your affinity, this will be worse for you." She'd said it calmly, but in her voice there was a touch of malice that warned him away from even considering the possibility.

Finally, she'd placed a hand on his shoulder, and he finally learned what her affinity was. At first, the muscles in his shoulder twitched and tingled. Then, they contracted, all at once, straining against each other so hard he had thought they would tear. And then they did, ripping away from ligaments as sparks of static jumped from her fingers.

His screams rang through the stone halls of the fort, but no one came to his aid.

Only when his shoulder was mangled would she call the healer in to repair the damage. And then, she would do it again, over, and over, and over. Some days, he'd have a reprieve. Sometimes, he'd go weeks without being called back to her tower. Other times, he'd be there every night for a week or more.

One time, he couldn't take it anymore. Instinct took over, and his shoulder went intangible, her hand slipping through. She'd fallen, and he'd known from the instant she scrambled to her feet that he had erred. She'd left him there, his shoulder muscles torn and useless, and returned with someone he did not recognize, a young woman, barely out of childhood. The woman had been unsure, but with some prodding from the Commandant she'd fixed him with a stare and his mind caught fire.

She'd probed the recesses of mind, gently and deftly, until she found his deepest fears and insecurities. She found the death of his mother, how he'd quite literally stumbled across her lifeless body one day while searching for her in her chambers. She replayed that memory in his mind, over and over, as the Commandant had his body healed once more in preparation for more electricity. He'd scarcely noticed that the pain had gone until she started again.

It was perhaps the darkest night of his life.

He'd spent so long in that tiny room that he thought for a while that the Commandant was trying to kill him, or to get him to kill himself. And finally, when she had beaten him down thoroughly, both physically and emotionally, he simply had to make it stop. He'd reached out with his own affinity then, felt the air in both his tormentors' lungs, and turned it solid.

He'd sucked in deep breaths free from pain for the first time in weeks as they struggled. He could have killed them, their faces turning grayish blue as they clawed at their chests and throats. It was the young woman—still a girl really, forced into this torture as much as he had been—who brought him back to himself as she reached feebly for him.

He'd released them then, expecting the Commandant to find new ways to punish him for his rebellion. Instead, she'd risen shakily to her feet, brushed off the dust from her uniform, and smiled.

That was the last day of his torture. She'd allowed him to rejoin the troops, and he did not interact closely with her further. He'd spent the rest of his days at the fort trying his best to forget everything that had been done to him. He'd drowned himself in alcohol, searched for anyone in the fort that could ease his mind, either through their affinities or through their bodies.

Ran did not share this with Ditan. How could he? He hadn't even told his father. He wasn't even sure his father didn't know. In the darkest corners of his mind, he wondered if perhaps his father had commanded it.

"Get some sleep, Ditan," he finally said as he picked his share of the rabbit clean. "I'll take the first watch."

The shadowwalker did not argue. In minutes, Ditan's breathing slowed to a deep, even rhythm.

Once Ran was sure Ditan was asleep, whatever barrier, whatever dam he'd built within broke. He collapsed in on himself, burying his head in his hands as tears streamed down his face.

11

Kita

For a moment, strolling through the foliage outside the remaining courtyard walls lifted the weight of what had happened.

I was stronger. Still a bit sore, but ambulatory at least. My ribs were still sore, my muscles weak. Given how broken I had been, I found myself thanking the Goddesses that the healer was nearby when the walls came crashing down.

I snuck a glance at the Priest as he leaned down to examine some of the lushly colored plants spilling out of their beds. If he felt anything from his death and subsequent and resurrection, he didn't show it. He moved with his usual stoic grace.

"What exactly are you looking for?" I asked. My voice was still gravelly and sore.

He pointed to a nondescript green plant with large, curled leaves. "Ibama weed. Chew that, and it'll help with your beast, I think. At least, I've seen it help others with their affinities. I had hoped to have more time here before we left you, but now…" he sighed deeply. "On the road things are more difficult. It'll be a salve on difficult days."

He harvested as much of the plant as we found there, stuffing the leaves into a bag at his hip.

Satisfied that he had gotten what he had come for, he lowered himself to the ground, groaning as he sat against the wall.

Perhaps he was more tired than I had thought.

I bit my lip as I sat beside him. It was hard to look at him, and impossible to forget what I had seen.

"Ask," he grunted, sensing my feelings if not my thoughts.

"Are you alright?"

He slowly turned his head to look at me. His chest was bare, and the knife wound had healed to a gnarled scar directly over his heart. The offending weapon was in his bag, the hilt jutting from between the greenery.

"My wounds are healed," he said simply.

"Right, but...you were..." I trailed off, too uncomfortable to say the word.

"Dead," he said helpfully.

"But surely that must be upsetting," I replied.

He shrugged. "Dying is easy," he said. "Being dragged back to life is the difficulty."

I waited for him to elaborate, but he didn't feel the need. Instead, he closed his eyes and breathed deeply, in and out, as the afternoon sun beamed down on us both.

"May I ask you a question?" I asked.

"I suppose," he responded, not opening his eyes.

"All of those scars. I had assumed you'd been wounded. But you were killed, weren't you?"

"Yes," he replied. "Four times now." He said it simply, as though discussing the weather.

But four times? How could anyone, even someone as unflappable as him, be so calm about staring down his own mortality and losing?

"May I ask how?"

"One day, you will learn not to ask such personal questions," he said, though his tone of voice didn't indicate a rebuke.

"Apologies," I muttered, sinking against the wall as much as I could.

He allowed me to stew for several moments before finally, he said, "I was at the Temple of Sorrow. It's where I was raised and trained as a peacekeeper. They don't have those here, so close to the palace, but we were tasked with helping the people in the villages out beyond the old borders. We ran afoul of beserkers."

Beserkers. The Empire's elite warriors, able to embody the fiercest of animals. Bears, lions, jaguars. The emperor reserved them for suppressing skirmishes. It didn't make sense for them to be anywhere near a Temple.

"Why were they there?" I asked.

"You would need to ask the emperor, I suppose," he replied, his voice cool. "Our entire Peacekeeper squad was killed. I was fortunate, I suppose, that Weiran was hiding in the village there. I was the only one whose body was whole enough to bring back."

He was so matter-of-fact, talking about his own death. I couldn't understand how he could discuss it without even the slightest pain.

"The second time," he said, interrupting my thoughts, "I drowned. We were fording the river near the Kyori Mountan Pass. We didn't know that the border had moved by then. An Imperial patrol refused to let us through the pass. Weiran was furious, but there wasn't anything he could do. We turned around back across the river. I slipped. I am a good swimmer. But when you're swept under by river currents, you're helpless. I have no desire to drown again; that feeling of helplessness as you try desperately to hold your breath. Eventually the pain is too much and your lungs take over." He laughed, humorlessly, and added, "A stupid accident."

He shook his head, shuddering.

"The third time," he started. His hand drifted to his neck, where a corded scar wrapped around his throat. "The Imperial Army hanged me as a traitor. They came across our camp out west. They'd had reports of rebel saboteurs in the area and decided not to take chances with us. I fought, but I took a spear right here." He laid a hand against a small, circular scar in the center of his chest. "They had a healer fix the damage and then they strung me up. That was not so bad. They broke my neck properly, so I didn't feel it much."

He took the knife that had been lodged in his heart from his bag and turned it, closely examining it from tip to pommel. The sun glinted off its edge, right into my eyes, but I couldn't look away.

"An imperial blade," he said simply. "I suppose they've killed me again."

With one smooth motion, he flipped the blade and offered it to me, hilt first.

As I took it from him and inspected it myself, I knew he was right. I had seen blades just like it almost every day in the palace. The Imperial seal was pressed into the guard.

"I don't understand why they would attack a temple," I mumbled.

"Neither do I," said the Priest, his voice still perfectly even.

The stillness in his voice was finally too much for me to ignore, and I said, "is this not upsetting to you? How can you be so calm?"

"Nothing upsets me anymore," he said. "Things simply are what they are."

I furrowed my brow. He was lying. He had asked, no, pled with Weiran the night before. It was the only time I had ever heard any sort of emotion in his voice, but it had been there.

"That is untrue," I said, laying the knife down across my lap. "You were upset when you were dying. I heard it in your voice."

His eyebrows knit together.

"What do you mean?" he asked. "I...I don't remember much, truth be told."

I hesitated. I didn't know if he truly did not remember or was just trying to avoid the subject.

"You asked Weiran to let you go. You begged him. You wanted...I think you wanted him to let you die. And then when you came back..." The memory of that deep despair washed over me, and it was as though I was experiencing it again. It was more than sadness; it was hopelessness. It was the essence of tragedy itself. I hoped I would never have to experience it again.

"Oh," he said, and I thought I detected a slight hint of something in his voice. I fixed my gaze on him, but he avoided my eyes. "I...I am sorry you had to be here for that," he said. "I don't remember coming back. I never do. But Weiran tells me that I...that I lash out. I apologize." He bowed his head slightly, still avoiding my eyes.

"What was it?" I asked. "What could make you feel that way?"

"I don't know," he said. "As I said, I don't remember. I don't remember ever feeling that deeply before. But..." he hesitated, and I thought he might change the subject. "Kita, I don't want to die, if that's what you think. I would very much like to stay on this plane for as long as I can. But there's something you must understand. When I was three years old, I was sold to the Temple of Sorrow. I didn't get the choice to become a priest; it was foisted upon me. My name was stolen from me and I was devoted to the Goddess of Sorrow. And every time I've died, Weiran has brought me back because he thinks I have some role to fulfill. I've never gotten to choose anything for myself, not really. And when he brings me back....I'm not the same."

"What do you mean?"

"It's like....I retreat further into my power and away from myself. I get stronger and stronger, more able to sense and bend others' emotions. I can tell you where everyone in the temple is, I can tell you that the High Priestess is crying at the fountain. I can tell you that Weiran is *finally* sleeping. Peacefully, for once. I can tell you who has died, because I don't feel them anymore. I can tell you that your prince was in the area, but he has gone now."

I blinked. He knew about Ran, then?

"I can feel all these things," he continued, ignoring the chill I felt along my spine, "but my own emotions are….just gone. Perhaps they're still there, buried deep within me, but I don't feel them, not really. It's like…it's like being surrounded by people yelling. Everyone else is so loud that I can't hear myself. This is what death has done to me. And every time he brings me back, I lose myself a bit more."

I sighed, and for a moment contemplated giving the man a hug; he seemed as though he could use one.

But he sensed my feelings and waved them away. "I do not need your pity, Kita. But I will be glad to leave this city and return to the road. Things are simpler there, and there are fewer people."

Something bothered me about what he was telling me, but I couldn't quite figure out what it was.

An uncomfortable silence hung between us. Neither of us would look the other in the eye. The knife rested uncomfortably on my lap, and I pushed it aside. It clattered to the hard stone floor, and he took it.

"I think perhaps I'll get some more rest," the Priest finally said. "Healing is hard work. Perhaps it would be best if you did the same."

I nodded, and realized that I was still very tired indeed.

I returned to my makeshift quarters—thankfully on the side of the temple that had not been damaged—and lay down on my bedroll. The ornery black cat had returned, either unbothered by the bombing or too stubborn to leave. As I pulled the thin blanket up to my shoulders, it occurred to me that perhaps The Priest was making me tired, some use of his power I had not considered. But I didn't have the energy to fight.

12

Kita

The young priestess who led me down the hall did not tell me where she was taking me. She did not exchange pleasantries. She did not speak at all. It was hard to blame her, but I found myself wishing she would say *something*, if even to cry or curse the goddesses, just so that I could soothe her.

She kept her gaze turned down as we walked, as though she were trying desperately to avoid the world.

Finally, she stopped and opened the door to what was, I realized, the High Priestess's quarters.

The High Priestess sat solemnly at her desk, chin propped up against her fist. Her eyes were red and puffy, and her mouth tightly drawn. Darkness around her eyes showed her weariness. She still wore her stained garments, covered in dried blood and a thick layer of white dust. She seemed unhurt, aside from a few cuts and scrapes on her face.

To her right stood the Priest. He stood solemn and still, in a clean black tunic and trousers. He wore his twin swords sheathed on his left hip, and his intertwined fingers resting on the hilts. Only the slight movement of his eyes as I entered the room betrayed that he was made of flesh and not stone.

In contrast, Weiran was fidgety, unable to contain his restless energy. He bounced his leg rapidly, and repeatedly cracked the bones in his fingers as he waited. He seemed to be entirely recovered from the bombing, and his eyes were bright and clear.

He'd slept, evidently.

As I shuffled in, he fixed me with an icy glare. I stopped, struck by a thought I had not considered previously.

Weiran was a deathseeker. I had watched him snatch the Priest's soul away from the Goddesses' grip and return it to his lifeless form. Could the opposite be true? Could he pull a still living spirit and return it to the Goddesses?

My heart began to pound, and I half expected one of the empaths to calm me, but they didn't. Instead, they just watched as I stood, clutching at my chest. Weiran kept me locked with his gaze.

"Please sit, young princess," the High Priestess said, her voice jagged.

I did as she said, remembering as I did my old governess's stern voice as Ran and I ran up and down the palace stairs.

"How are you?" I asked gingerly.

The High Priestess blinked at the question, as though it hadn't occurred to her that someone would ask.

"Heartbroken," she said, her voice strained and cracking. "I lost several girls. Some hadn't even been marked yet." She clicked her tongue and shook her head.

"May the goddesses protect them," I said softly.

The High Priestess sighed and nodded almost imperceptibly.

I sank into the chair opposite. The way they all were staring at me, eyes sharp and accusatory, reminded me of my grandfather's face.

It made me wish desperately that I was a shadowwalker, that I could slip away unseen into the darkness.

"Kita," Weiran said, snapping me back to the room.

I tried to meet his gaze, but his eyes were still so fiery that I looked away.

"First, I want to extend my apologies that you were hurt while under my care. Weiran tells me your injuries were quite serious."

"The healer did fine work," I muttered.

As though I had said nothing, she continued, "That said, there is something we must discuss. It is a rule amongst the temples to separate our faith from the governance of the empire and other powers. To protect us and the people who rely on these temples. To stay out of the petty squabbles between kingdoms and principalities. This has been the way for centuries."

"I know," I said softly.

"But I saw you at our gates. Desperate. Terrified. And against better judgment, I allowed you safe quarter. And now—" she stopped, burying her face in her hands.

"What are you saying?" I asked.

"You cannot stay here, not any longer. I…" The High Priestess trailed off.

I recoiled. I could not fault her, but it wounded nonetheless; where could I go? I didn't know anyone else. Had barely even left the capital. I didn't know how to respond. I knew that I hadn't done anything wrong, logically I knew that. But listening to the pain in her voice, could I say she was wrong? My being there had put everyone at the temple at risk. And this bombing…had it happened because of me? Had more people died simply because I was there?

My heart began to pound and I looked to the Priest for help. He gave me a small nod, and calm washed over me. I exhaled deeply and folded my hands in my lap. Calmly and clearly, I said, "Where am I supposed to go?"

"Where are you supposed to go?" the High Priestess repeated, her voice raised. "Where are you supposed to go? I am sorry for you, truly

I am. I wish that circumstances were different. Your father told us he would travel back to his homeland once he left us. Perhaps he's still there. I do not know. But I'm sorry; you cannot stay."

I sat back in my chair, processing this information. Of course, I knew that I would not have stayed at the temple forever. But I thought I would have more time to plan. To gather information, to process everything that had happened.

Weiran stepped forward, clasping his hands in an effort to stop fidgeting. He started, "This empire has shown that there is nothing it will not do, no line it will not cross. Innocents have died, not only here but across the far reaches. Your family has ripped these lands apart. Stolen independent principalities, and destroyed peaceful nations. We came here to petition the emperor for peace. We know now that this will not happen. This bombing, this needless loss of innocent life...it is just too much. There were children!"

He smacked his hands down on the desk. I jumped at the noise.

"You are complicit in this," he said softly.

I stared down at the floor, my eyes tracing the lines in the white marble.

"I have done nothing," I whispered.

"This is your family. They are the ones who have done this. They are the ones who have *been* doing this. While you stood on high, up on the hill, looking down on your people, eating fatted lambs, drinking fine wines, dancing and relaxing, people have died. They have told me their stories. They rage as they are caught in their suffering. You have done nothing, and that is precisely the problem."

"What would you have me say?" I muttered. "I didn't know." My vision began to blur as tears welled.

"You didn't know," he repeated. "I believe you. Perhaps you didn't care to. It doesn't matter. What matters now is what we're going to do about it. I am angry, and I am tired. My people feel the same."

"What are you saying?" I asked, finally mustering the courage to look him in the eye. His gaze was still intense, but though he was looking in my direction, his eyes seemed focused on something far away. Perhaps more of his lost souls.

"There are no words that this Emperor will respond to. No pleas that he will consider. His people suffer and die and he does not care, because suffering is his intent. We intended to petition him, but I see now. Trying to talk to him will lead us nowhere. Talking is not something I am interested in anymore. We are going to fight."

"Fight?" I parroted. "You plan to fight the largest army the world has known? With a few refugees?"

"And perhaps a wayward princess," the Priest chimed in.

My head swiveled toward him, my jaw slack.

"Excuse me?" I asked, my voice higher than I intended.

He simply smiled serenely and nodded toward Weiran.

"Kita, think on this. I know this is your family. But you ran from the palace for a reason. You know that the emperor and the crown prince will hunt you. They have shown that they are willing to kill you. If they weren't, they would not have bombed the temple. You very nearly died."

His words were harsh, but could I really argue? The sharp pains in my ribs, the blood dripping from my ears. The labored breaths I took as I struggled to get air. All of those things were real. I could have died, if not for the healer's quick action. And Ran...

Ran had always been good. He was so optimistic, naively so. I never thought him to be like his father. What had changed, so abruptly? He had promised to try to help me. So *why* was he trying to kill me?

"I...I don't want to be a part of this," I said. "I'll go. I'll find my father. But leave me out of this, please."

"And you know where he is?" Weiran asked.

My cheeks warmed. "Somewhere down south," I said softly.

"South?" he repeated. "South near Avetsut? Out past the outer reaches? To the jungles? The savannah? Where?"

"I don't know," I snapped.

He nodded. "As it happens, our immediate plan is to travel south. To my homeland."

I swallowed. I'd known he planned to travel south—the Priest had told me as much. But now, everything had changed. Nothing made sense. South was where I needed to be, but with these people? These… what? Revolutionaries? Traitors?

"Come with us," he said. "At least as far as Avetsut. If you do that, you have my word that I will do what I can to help you find your father."

He turned toward the Priest, who added, "and I will do my best to help you regain control over your affinity."

I chewed the inside of my cheek as I considered it. I had to leave the temple. I had nowhere to go. Weiran's help was as good an offer as I could hope for. And yet I could not shake the feeling that there was a great deal he wasn't sharing.

"I am no fighter," I protested. "And even if I was, I cannot fight my family."

Weiran raised his hands and shook his head. "I am not asking you to. I am simply asking you to accompany us. See the damage your family has done first hand. Perhaps you'll change your mind. Perhaps you won't. But I promise you that after we arrive at Avetsut, I'll personally accompany you as we make inquiries about your father. He would have had to stop there if he went further south, and you'll need someone who speaks the language to help you."

I searched his face for some hint as to his plans. He wouldn't tell me more than he wanted me to know. I knew that. I couldn't understand *why* he wanted me to go with them if he didn't care if I joined him. But despite how animated he was in his mannerisms, he was still adept at hiding his thoughts.

He smiled, and I shuddered as a chill raced down my spine.

"Alright," I said gingerly. "I'll go with you. But I want no part of this fight."

"Of course," he said. "As I said, that is your decision to make." He took my hand, helping me to my feet.

"You should gather your things. Eat well. Get some rest tonight. We will leave tomorrow at first light. The road south is well-traveled, but dangerous. There will be imperial patrols. We will spend a great deal of time off the path. Be prepared."

"I'll go to the market shortly," the Priest said. "Am I correct in assuming you haven't spent much time on the road?"

I didn't answer. I hadn't spent *any* time on the road. I had no idea what to buy or how to ready myself for a long journey.

"I-I can pay," I stuttered, but the Priest waved me off.

"Save your coin," he said. "We may have need of it later."

As I left the High Priestess's quarters, I thought of Ran, and with each moment I thought of him, my heart shattered into smaller pieces. He had always been my best friend, more a brother to me than an uncle. But there was a gulf between us now, and I found myself hoping against all hopes that I would never see him again.

13

Ran

Ran sat astride his horse, just off the path, hidden in the brush. The Eastern Fort loomed ahead, imposing and grand. A patrol had gone out and returned in the time they sat watching, and yet Ran couldn't bring himself to drive his horse forward.

Ditan had the courtesy not to speak, standing silently beside the prince, holding his own horse's reins as he waited.

"By the goddesses," Ran muttered. With a groan he dismounted, handing the reins to his guard as he straightened his clothing.

"What would you have me do, my prince?" Ditan asked softly.

"I think it might be best for you to tether your horse back out of view. Can you follow from the shadows? I think it would be ideal if the Commandant thinks I'm alone."

"Are you certain, my prince?"

"For now. But be prepared." Ran absently rubbed at his shoulder.

"Yes, my prince." Ditan dipped his head. He obediently tethered his horse and then dissolved into the shadows.

Ran felt the familiar prickle at the back of his neck that he always got when Ditan watched him from shadows. It was a comfort, knowing that someone was there, silently watching as he faced down the terror of the Eastern Fort.

Breathe, Ran. You are in command. Breathe.

Sighing, he pushed through the thick brush and onto the horsepath, the huge white stallion tossing its head behind him as he led it along. He had barely taken a step when a horn blasted out, announcing his arrival.

A lump formed in the back of his throat, but he forced it down and pushed forward.

"Halt!" a voice called from atop the fort gates.

Ran obeyed, interlacing his fingers in front of him as he waited. His hair fell into his face as he did, but he didn't dare move it. Best not to provoke a reaction.

After several long seconds of standing still, the great wooden gates swung open. A single soldier strode out as others gathered at the entrance.

Ran's nerves calmed slightly as the soldier approached.

"My prince," the soldier, a stout young man with near-black skin and shorn hair, said as he bowed his head.

Ran's face broke into a wide smile.

"Obaye!" the prince shouted, pulling the man into an embrace. "You're still here?"

"It's good to see you Ran," Obaye laughed. "What are you doing here? Last time I saw you, you swore you'd never return."

Ran shuddered, pushed the hair from his face, and sighed. "Yes, I did say that," he muttered. "As much as I enjoy seeing you, and—" he paused to gesture at the assembled crowd—"what looks to be the rest of the squadron, I am here on official business. I need to speak to the Commandant."

Obaye's smile faded. "Must be serious indeed," he said.

Ran flexed the fingers on his left hand. How much did Obaye know about what had happened to him? Ran had certainly never spoken of it to anyone. Still, in the nights on the road, when he sought comfort in the arms of anyone who would have him…they must have had some inkling.

"It is," Ran said, his tone measured. "Where is she?"

Obaye sighed and replied, "not here. She left with a small squad about a week and a half ago."

Bile rose in Ran's throat.

"The bombers?" he asked, his mouth dry.

Obaye blinked. "Nah, they ain't here either. They left on orders maybe a day or two before she did. A shame! They would have wanted to see you."

Ran chewed the inside of his cheek as Obaye spoke. More than anything, he had hoped that his friend would tell him that the bombers were still there, that they had never left. It would have been lovely to meet with some of his old friends, to chat and pretend that the temple bombing hadn't happened, if only for a moment.

"Do you know where they've all gone?" Ran asked, trying to keep his voice even.

Obaye barked a laugh and replied, "Of course not! I have been promoted a bit since we last spoke, but not nearly high enough to know the Commandant's movements.

Ran smiled and inspected his old friend. Obaye had not changed much in the two years since last they had spoken, not on the surface. He still wore his wry smile and casual stance. But there were *some* differences. His uniform was, as always, immaculate, but the once black linen had faded into a dark gray. And just above his left hip there was a wide slash that has been messily stitched.

Obaye caught him looking.

"It was a skirmish up north. Slashed me to the bone. Still have the scar. Fucking Kayasi. We were patrolling out near the outer reaches. They ambushed us." He shook his head, crossing his arms as he remembered. "It was a nightmare. Three dead. Some sort of coordinated attack."

"Not hard to coordinate if you're all reading each other's minds," Ran pointed out.

"Yeah, I guess. In any case the Commandant recalled us after that. New strategy." Obaye shrugged.

"When was that?"

"A year back. Leg ached nonstop throughout the summer rains."

The pair laughed, and Obaye ushered him toward the gate.

The soldiers at the gate swarmed them almost immediately. Some were some of Ran's old squad, excited at the return of an unexpected old friend. Others were relatively new recruits, eager to catch a glimpse of the famed prince. Ran greeted them all warmly.

For a moment, it was like the good times. The evenings after training was over, when all the soldiers ate together. The survival training nights, when they would go out into the forest and sleep under the stars. He hadn't always hated being at the Eastern Fort, not at first.

After chatting for several minutes, Obaye pulled him away from the throng.

"We sent out the message. Apparently they were nearby. The Commandant is riding hard to get back before nightfall.

Ran rubbed a hand through his hair, sending it cascading in a black curtain down his back. He wondered what Ditan was thinking. Was it best to wait at the fort, leaving Ditan watching from the shadows? Or would it be better to reconvene, to have a discussion about the best move?

No. He was the crown prince. He needed to be decisive.

"Of course," he said with a smile, hoping that his tone was sufficiently warm.

Obaye broke into laughter and slapped Ran on the back, ushering him deeper into the camp. "Come Ran. I'm sure you're tired and hungry from being on the road. We'll get you fed."

Ran was well into his meal when Obaye asked, "So, how have things been out in the capital? I can only imagine you dressed in your finery, eating fine foods, drinking fine wines. Wooing women? They'll have you married before year's end, at the chagrin of everyone here, I'm sure."

For just a moment, the tiniest fraction of a second, Ran hesitated, freezing mid-chew before resuming, hoping Obaye wouldn't notice.

He did and mumbled, "We don't have to talk about your palace life if you don't want."

"No, no, it's alright. It's just far less glamorous and far more tedious than you might think. Meetings mostly, with my father, his advisors. Important, certainly, but not terribly interesting."

"I don't know, Ran. It must be far more exciting than the military life. Waiting, training, waiting, marching, waiting. The occasional skirmish. Waiting. Maddening." He shook his head and took a swig of his ale.

It was certainly true. It *was* a lot of waiting. But he hadn't minded all that, the simplicity of life. The ease of falling into his training. True, Ran had been ecstatic on the day his term at the fort was over, and had never desired to return. But Obaye had never been forced to endure torture at the hands of the Commandant, nor had anyone else that he knew of.

Maybe, if life had gone a different way, if Ran had been born to a different father, maybe then military life would have suited him.

Ran breathed a deep sigh and finished his food in silence. Obaye, perhaps sensing something wrong, filled the silence easily with tales of his travels. It was nice to forget everything that had happened as he listened to his friend speak.

After finishing their midday meal, Obaye took him around the fort, introducing him to those who had moved in in the two years since

Ran had left. Ran politely spoke to them all, though their names slid from his mind almost immediately after they were spoken.

For the much of the rest of the day, Ran walked the fort, talking to soldiers and waiting. The longer the day dragged by, the tighter the knot in his belly became. It felt as though there was a fire, burning away at his insides.

A horn sounded—two blasts.

"Commandant returning!" someone called from the top of the wall.

For a moment, Ran thought he might faint. He wanted to retreat any way he could, to press himself against the rock wall of the fort, anything to not be seen. But he forced himself to approach the gates, positioning himself just off the path so that she would see him immediately.

The gate began to swing open. The scrape of wood on rock sent his heart racing.

As soon as the gate fully opened, almost as though she had timed it perfectly, the Commandant thundered in, standing in her stirrups. Her horse was well-lathered, its eyes bulging out of the sockets.

Behind her, a giant of a woman rode a giant of a horse.

The pair of them noticed him and dismounted, passing their reigns on to a young, relatively new soldier.

The Commandant looked smaller, slightly more frail than Ran remembered. She was a head shorter than him, with tawny skin and medium brown hair that had been lightened by the sun's harsh gaze. As always, she wore it tied tightly back in a knot. She was thin, but wore her uniform in a manner that projected power. And it wasn't just her affinity, the static that emanated from her when someone wandered too close. It was the way she carried herself, as though even the prince himself could not trouble her. She was covered with long-healed scars, some of them new since Ran had seen her last.

Her companion loomed even larger off her horse, if it were possible.

She was so tall that she could rest her elbows on the Commandant's head, if she liked. From her dress—animal skin breeches and a second pelt draped across her shoulders—she was not military. She had rich golden brown skin and a wild tangle of hair nearly the same color, if a little lighter. Her eyes—a vibrant yellow—betrayed her nature. They were feral and feline in their ferocity.

She was a beserker—lionkin, if Ran were to guess. This was not good news; the beserkers were dangerous creatures fueled by rage and animal instinct. They were almost impossible to control once unleashed. If beserkers were nearby, authorization would have had to come from very high command.

"My Prince," the Commandant called, bowing her head in an exaggerated motion. Her voice dripped with sickly sweetness.

"Commandant Hasit," Ran mumbled.

"Of course we rode ahead when we got your message," the Commandant said as she walked toward Ran. The beserker followed close behind. Though she could kill the Commandant with ease, there was absolutely no doubt about who was in control.

"I hope you will introduce me," Ran said, inclining his head toward the beserker. He tried to keep his heart and voice steady as the woman looked him up and down.

"Do I scare you, little prince?" the beserker asked. Ran had expected her voice to be gravely and deep, but it was surprisingly warm and soft. Disarming, even.

The Commandant smiled widely as she locked her sharp green eyes on Ran.

Ran swallowed. "Well, there is certainly a reason we employ your kin in the most extreme situations," he said in the most measured tone he could manage.

The beserker barked a laugh, a sharp noise that jolted Ran to the core. Ran allowed himself to breathe again.

"My prince, allow me to introduce Lady Akatian Kansuin," the Commandant said.

"A pleasure to meet you, Lady Akatian," Ran said with a smile.

"Please call me Aka, my prince. We are not so concerned with titles in the south."

"Aka, then," Ran said, though his heart still pounded.

"It is clear that you have something urgent to discuss," the Commandant cut in. "I'll head to my office, and we can talk in private."

Before Ran could say anything, she pushed past him, the static clinging to his skin and raising the hairs on his arm.

Breathe, he told himself.

Ran waited for several moments before making his way to the tower. Once confident that no one was following him, he slipped inside the tower door and waited.

She was gone, already in her closed office, and Ran muttered, "Ditan."

"Yes, my prince," came the reply as Ditan came through the shadows cast by the torchlight.

"First impressions?"

"Difficult to say at this stage. Shall I go ahead and watch?"

"Yes. We'll reconvene later."

Ditan dipped his head and was gone once more.

Ran tightly grasped his left hand to stop it from trembling as he began the climb to the top of the tower. With each step, he longed to stop, to return to the palace.

But he had to know what had happened, and he still had to find Kita.

So he forced himself to take a step, and another, and another, until he arrived at the Commandant's personal chambers.

The Commandant sat at her desk, fingers tented in front of her face. As Ran entered, she gestured toward a chair in front of her.

"I must say," she began, watching him as he walked slowly to the seat, "I did not anticipate a visit. Kazin has not sent word."

The use of his father's given name was a challenge. She stared hard at him as she waited for him to react.

He refused to take her bait.

"Well, I had no intention to be here," he replied, a bit more viciously than perhaps he intended. He sat back and cocked his head, watching her closely for a reaction.

She gave none.

"And yet, here you are."

Ran swallowed. He wasn't sure how much to reveal. As he sank into his chair, he settled on, "The emperor has given me leave to do what I must."

"And what is that?"

"Not your concern."

She narrowed her eyes.

"Then do tell what it is you need. The Eastern Fort is always at the service of the Empire."

"Where is the bomb squad?" Ran asked as innocuously as he could. "It would have been nice to see them."

"Uh-huh," she replied, her voice and expression flat. "They've been reassigned to the north to address the skirmishes up there. By now they ought to be..." she trailed off, thinking. "...probably near the Temple of Anger by now? But if that's all you needed, I could have saved you the trip if you had only sent us a message."

Ran watched her carefully. She made him so uneasy, but if he was going to learn anything from her, he'd have to remain as stoic as possible.

"Has word of the Temple of Hope reached this far?" he probed.

The Commandant sat back in her chair, tilting her head. She sighed and said, "Our messenger received a call about terrorists bombing the Temple. I am awaiting further orders regarding the matter. Have you anything to add?"

Terrorists?

"There is some evidence to suggest that the perpetrators were Imperial Army," Ran said flatly.

"Excuse me?" the Commandant replied. "And what, this is…an interrogation?"

Ran did not reply, allowing her to draw her own conclusions.

"Allow me to save you some time. We had a supply run scheduled to arrive here at the fort several weeks ago. It didn't arrive. Myself, Aka, and a small contingent rode out to investigate. Do you know what we found, my prince?" She almost spat his title. "We found the camp where our soldiers had stopped for the night, just a few days out from where they started. The soldiers were all dead. The supplies and coin were missing. The conscripts they were bringing? Gone. And a few days after that? The temple is bombed. Certainly doesn't seem to be coincidental to me. If the emperor has concerns I am more than happy to ride to Yor-a to discuss them with him."

She fixed him with a glare that suggested that she wanted nothing more than for him to disappear.

On one hand, her words, were they true, were a relief. He hadn't wanted to believe that the army—his army—could be responsible for the destruction he had seen. It hadn't made sense.

But terrorists, impersonating the army…that was a bigger problem.

Still, it wasn't *his* problem, not directly. Not yet.

Leave it, he told himself. *Get Kita. Let Father handle this.* But it ate away at him.

"If you are quite finished accusing my men of these heinous acts, I would like to get some rest. I've been riding all day and would like to decompress. I'm sure we can arrange lodging for you for the evening. I'm sure you'll want to get back on the road in the morning."

It wasn't a suggestion, really. She wanted him gone. The look in her eye combined with the sparks jumping around her fingertips told him how serious she was.

If she was telling the truth, guards would be swarming the temple to investigate. Kita would have to move on. But he had no way of knowing where she would go next, and so no heading.

"I think I'll stay a few days," he said with a smile. "I have other reasons for being here."

"What reasons?" she asked through gritted teeth.

But he just smiled and left her to stew.

14

Kita

Naked and shivering, I slowly lowered myself into the cold stream. I felt the sting of dozens of eyes on me and pushed the thought from my mind as I sank down to my neck. Using my fingernails, I started the arduous process of scraping the dirt from my skin as I positioned myself away from the crowd.

As my ragged, tangled curls unfurled around me, dread crept down my spine, and I shivered, though whether from that or the cold, I could not quite tell. Gulping down three quick breaths, I closed my eyes and dropped myself down beneath the surface.

A moment later, I surfaced, the breeze biting at my wet skin.

"Hope herself," I muttered as began to rake my fingers through ends of my hair, trying to delicately tease out the tangles.

As trembles wracked through my body, I longed for the near-boiling heat of baths in my personal chambers. I had not truly appreciated the relaxing heat, the soft soaps and fragrant oils, until I had lost them.

My hair felt rough in my hands, nothing like the soft, luscious curls I remembered.

For a moment, I felt as though I might cry. Though, a stream would be the perfect place to do it unseen.

I sighed, and returned to my hair. Easier to do that than grapple with useless memories. Better to do that than to catch anyone's eye.

When I was satisfied that my hair was suitably detangled, and that I was as clean as I could be, I turned.

To my surprise and relief, no one seemed to have any interest in me at all. Most of the group—Weiran's refugees, who numbered more than I had thought—were bathing themselves, chatting amongst themselves as they washed away the dirt of the road and the temple. Others stood in the shallow edges, scraping dirty clothes against rocks. Still others tended the few horses that the group had managed to scrounge.

I dragged myself to a relatively empty section of the shore. My clothing had been collected for washing. I hugged my knees to my chest, allowing my hair to fan out over my nudity.

"This long hair is a bad idea," a voice called. My head snapped around to find The Priest standing behind me, his face dispassionate.

"Could you…" I started. If I was not already feeling self-conscious, I certainly was now.

He shrugged and turned away, but did not leave.

"You really should cut it," he said.

"Why?" I muttered.

"It'll get you killed in a fight."

I furrowed my brow. Hair would get me killed? I clicked my tongue in disbelief.

"Get dressed," he said. It wasn't a request.

"My clothing is being washed," I hissed.

"Hmm," the Priest intoned. "I'll be right back."

I didn't acknowledge him, and I didn't hear him leave, but a moment later, a folded set of black breeches, a simple black tunic, and a pair of hunting boots fell in a heap next to me, along with clean underclothes. I glanced up toward him, but he had politely turned his back to me.

With a groan, I pushed myself to my feet and pulled the breeches on—they were a bit tight, but would work. The tunic was loose, flowing around me with every move.

"Here," the Priest said as I got the boots on. I looked up to see him handing me a knife, handle first. As I took it, I recognized it, with revulsion, as the knife that had, just days earlier, been embedded in his chest. It was clean now, but the ornately carved dark wood handle was so evident.

"It's the only spare I've got," he said, reading my thoughts. No, not my thoughts.

Trembling, I grasped the knife in my right hand. It fit neatly in my grasp. I thought the carving would feel rough and course, but it was well-worn and comfortable.

"Have you wielded a knife before?" he asked.

I thought of the brass dagger my mother had given me. It was ornamental—blunt—and in any case, I'd never had cause to brandish it. I shook my head.

"I thought not."

Though his tone was as calm as ever, I resented it anyway. I pursed my lips and gripped the knife firmly.

"What are you trying to accomplish here?" I asked.

"Attack me," he said.

I gaped at him and parroted his words back. "Attack you?"

"Do it," he said. "You're armed. I am not." He held his hands out wide in front of him, showing that the scabbard that normally hung around his waist was not there.

"I...don't want to hurt you," I said, but even as I did I knew how ridiculous it sounded. I had no fight training. The Priest had a multitude. But still, it seemed unfair.

This drew a laugh from him, a loud bark that I had not expected. My face burned.

"Kita. Do it. I promised to teach you."

"Yes, to help me control my power, not to fight!"

"The two are the same," he said simply with a shrug.

I swapped the knife to the other hand before returning to my right. That was better.

I locked eyes with the Priest and, feeling foolish, ran at him.

He stood, relaxed, as I charged at him, waiting until the knife was only inches away from his chest. He made his move, side stepping me with ease. His arm shot out, grabbing at my hair. He twisted his hand in the damp curls and pulled hard, snapping my head back.

My grip on the knife loosened, and, with his other hand, he twisted it from my grasp and aimed it squarely at my throat.

"And that is why this long hair will get you killed," he said simply.

I will KILL him, a voice growled in my ear. The beast, I knew. I swallowed, hard, trying to push it away.

The Priest sensed it, or sensed something, at least. He released me, flipping the knife so that its hilt faced me.

I snatched it, too roughly, and it bit into the flesh of his hand.

He didn't react as blood welled and dripped to the ground.

Yes, I will drink his blood until there is none left, the beast whispered, almost seductively.

"Hmm," the Priest intoned. "Is this your affinity that you're grappling with?"

I opened my mouth, but words would not come as I desperately tried to keep the beast inside.

The Priest watched my face, wordless, as he sensed my anguish. He did not try to help me, did not try to calm me as he had when I'd woken him with my nightmares. He just watched.

The beast groaned, perhaps in frustration in my efforts to reign in it.

Let me out! it said, but it wasn't a command. It was a longing. It was begging, I realized. And this brought me some measure of satisfaction, though I could not say why.

A moment later, it quieted completely.

"Fascinating," the Priest muttered, and I was shocked to see that his eyes were wide—an expression of genuine emotion that I had not seen in him before.

Whatever hint of emotion was there passed quickly.

"You could have helped me," I muttered.

"Is that what they do in the palace?" he asked. "When you struggle with something, people jump to your rescue?" There was no malice in his words, but they stung all the same.

He sensed my hurt feelings and placed a hand gingerly on my shoulder, giving it an awkward pat.

I smiled and turned my attention to our company. None were looking in our direction.

"Kita, be careful with them," the Priest said. His voice had taken on a strange tone that I couldn't identify.

I turned to him, but his face was as stoic as ever.

"They hate me," I said softly.

The Priest shook his head.

"They hate the Empire," he pointed out. "They don't know you. And Weiran—" he abruptly stopped talking, as though realizing he was saying more than he meant to. He smiled weakly, but said nothing more.

"Will you introduce me to some of our companions?" I asked.

"Hmm," he intoned. "I will put some thought into who would be best for you to meet. And I'll speak to Weiran about it."

At mention of Weiran's name, I frowned. I didn't understand why Weiran's opinion on the matter should have any bearing on it.

"Kita," the Priest warned. "You have to remember. Weiran has led these people across the Empire. They look to him. He knows each of them, knows their loss. *Feels* their loss. They trust him."

"More than they trust you?"

He shrugged. "They cannot lie to me. They cannot fool me, and they know it. And this unnerves them. They *don't* trust me."

This struck me as deeply odd. Everything I had come to know about the Priest was that he was a good man, despite his odd lack of emotion. He seemed to want the best for people. Weiran, in contrast, was so volatile. It didn't make sense to me.

But he would know better than me, I supposed.

"Where is Weiran, anyway?" I asked, scanning the shores of the stream. He was nowhere that I could see.

The Priest did not answer.

I sank down to a sitting position, running my fingers through my hair.

"You really should cut it," The Priest said.

I snapped my head toward him, but he was already walking away.

I scowled. Logically, I knew he was right. But as I clutched the damp waves in one hand and the knife in the other, all I could remember was my mother, sitting behind me as she brushed my hair. I was royalty. Royalty simply did not cut their hair. And though I had left the palace, perhaps never to return, I couldn't bring myself to part with that part of myself. So, I gingerly placed the knife in front of me and began to braid my hair.

I fumbled over the wet locks. Normally, my maidservants styled my hair after washes, their nimble fingers working quickly and efficiently. I had never considered it a particularly difficult task, but when they finished, every strand of hair was neatly encased in their elaborate styles.

I was not nearly as capable. Though I was able to fashion a messy braid, unruly curls popped through. I wound the long braid into a knot, but it took me several tries before I could get it to stay.

I sighed in frustration as I grabbed my new dagger. I pushed myself to my feet. As I turned back toward the horses, I stopped.

Someone was watching me.

She was a small, lithe woman. She had red-brown skin with eyes such a delicate blue that they almost seemed to contain the entire sky. Her golden hair exploded in a soft halo of curls around her head, save for three fine braids along the right side. The shadowwalker I'd seen sparring at the temple.

Slowly, I tucked the knife into my waistband.

"Hello," I said slowly with a brief wave.

The woman nodded in reply.

"What is your name?" I asked, taking a step toward her.

She took a step back, unsure.

We stood there, locked in each others' gaze for several heartbeats before finally she said, "Nokinan."

I smiled, trying to project as much warmth as possible, and said, "A please to meet you, Nokinan. My name is Kita."

Again, we stood in silence, and I desperately wanted her to say something.

Finally, she said, "You from the capital?"

My smile faltered for just a moment, but if she noticed, she gave no indication.

"Yes," I said.

"Hmmm," she said. If I thought was this the beginning of a conversation, I was mistaken, as she simply nodded and walked away. I watched her as she walked to a nearby tree, where two young children were huddled. She whispered something to them and they glanced in my direction. When they caught me looking, their gazes snapped away. I made a note to talk to the Priest about Nokinan and her family later.

The sun began to slide past the horizon, and I—and others—started to get ready for bed. I returned to my horse and pulled off a moth-eaten blanket given to me by the High Priestess before we left the temple.

The horse nuzzled my ear as I scanned the area, trying to find a place to set up for the evening. My first instinct was to find Weiran and the Priest, but they were nowhere I could see.

As daylight faded, a chill ran through me. It would be a cool evening, especially with wet hair. There were already a few fires blazing, but I didn't have the courage or energy to ingratiate myself with new people.

Nokinan and the two children with her were in the process of laying out bedrolls. I pasted on a smile and approached.

"Would you mind if I camp here for the night?"

"Not at all," Nokinan replied. The boys watched curiously as I sat nearby—just close enough to feel the warmth of the fire.

If I would have expected them to speak to me, I was once again mistaken.

I did not sleep well that night. The ground was deeply uncomfortable, and I was not tired enough to overcome my discomfort. Each time I began to doze, the wind would shift or foliage would crinkle, and I would find myself wide awake again.

I am not sure how long I was lying there when an inhuman shriek pierced the night.

I bolted upright, swinging my head back and forth. Many of the refugees had not woken. Those who had simply blinked sleepily and turned over.

Again, the scream rang out. I had never heard anything like it, but it was not, I decided, inhuman at all. No, the anguish and despair I heard was all too human.

I began to push myself to my feet, but I caught Nokinan's gaze. She sharply shook her head and gestured for me to sit.

I obeyed.

The younger of the two boys was still asleep, limbs splayed in a manner only comfortable for small children. The older, however, had awoken and crawled to Nokinan's lap.

"It's alright, Nedya," she said, her eyes locked on mine. She gently stroked the back of his head.

The screaming stopped.

"What was that noise?" I asked.

Nokinan ignored my question.

"Auntie, can you tell me a story?" the child—evidently called Nedya—mumbled groggily.

"Of course," Nokinan replied, still holding my gaze. "Which story would you like?"

"Mmmm," the child thought, nuzzling into her chest, "Tell me about the deathseekers!"

I raised an eyebrow. Certainly all the traditional stories would be too frightening for a child. But the boy seemed excited—this was a story he had heard before. How curious. Was Nokinan's different from the tales I remembered?

"Ahhh, the deathseekers. As you wish.

"Before there was this world, there was Telombraj. In those days, it was the realm of the Nameless ones. It was a place of shadow, yes. But it was also a place of power. And for millennia, they lived there in peace. But eventually, they grew bored."

"Bored? But they're gods!"

"Well, you get bored after an hour on the road!" Nokinan laughed, tickling the boy's stomach.

The child collapsed into a sleepy fit of laughter.

"So, in their boredom, they created life."

"Humans?"

"Animals at first. But the animals couldn't live in Telombraj. It was too dark. There were no plants—they don't grow in Telombraj. So they made a new world, full of light and vegetation, and they put their new creatures there. But they wanted more. So they pushed themselves further and created humanity. To their new people, they gave aspects of themselves, each goddess giving up a piece. Joy. Wrath. Hope. Any emotion we can feel was given to us by one of them. They finished by blessing us with affinities, so that we could shape the world in the manner that best suited us. In those days, there were no shadowwalkers or worldmakers. There were no sirens or beast tamers. There were only those who could mold the earth and her elements. And for a time, all was well."

By this time, I was wholly invested in the tale. I had heard the story of creation before, of course. My mother would regale me as a young child about the goddesses and their whims. But there were enough differences in the way Nokinan told it to make it new.

"But what about the deathseekers?"

"Patience, my love. It is said that, at first, humans did not die. They lived eternally, just as the Nameless did. But the earth couldn't bear it. Children were born, they grew, consuming plant and animal alike until there was almost nothing left. So the goddesses decided that their creatures would be reclaimed after a while. In this way, life was a cycle. The goddesses gave up aspects of themselves to humanity, who died and were returned to the goddesses.

" The goddesses were powerful. But they did not understand their creations, not really. They did not realize that there would be those afraid of death. Afraid of returning to Telombraj. And they did not realize that, with each new generation, their creatures were changing and growing. They did not foresee what would come next. The deathseekers arose; not quite gods, but more than humans had ever been. And they refused to let their loved ones go. They had the ability to capture souls, to return them to their rightful place on this plane. The goddesses could not abide it; the earth could not bear the weight of all of humanity, and they could not bear being opposed. So, they fought. There was a vicious war, goddesses killing their own creations, their children! Stealing their souls away so that the deathseekers could not claim them. In the end, they were too powerful, and they prevailed over humanity and the deathseekers."

I perked at this statement. By now, Nokinan's telling was entirely different than anything I had heard as a child. My mother had always spoken of deathseekers in a hushed tone. Allpowerful demons, borne from whatever had spawned the goddesses, with only one goal—to steal human life.

"The goddesses were not willing to forgive their creations easily. They created new beings—worldmakers. Those with the ability to hold dominion over others. To shape and change reality itself. They positioned these new creatures to subjugate the rest—a punishment for their foolish rebellion. And they stripped their creatures of the ability to visit Telombraj, all except a select few who could travel between two worlds. Messengers who would bring word of the humans' activity to the goddesses. Shadowwalkers. But I, just like my ancestors, have been to Telombraj. I have seen the shadow plane. The goddesses are not there any longer. No one knows where they have gone, or why. All that remains of them are those who worship them, those who revile them, and those who travel still to their realm."

The boy had fallen asleep, snoring softly in Nokinan's arms. She knew, and did not care. Her eyes were locked on mine as she finished her story, though I couldn't understand why.

As I settled back down for the night, pulling my thin blanket over my shoulders, I couldn't help but think of her story. I had been wrong about deathseekers, that was abundantly clear. Weiran wasn't some otherworldly demon. But I couldn't shake the feeling that there was something strange about him that I still did not know. Something that Nokinan did.

139

I shivered. There was no doubt in my mind that the story she told was as much for me as for the boy.

15

Kita

I dreamt.

I say I dreamt, but it was not a dream, not really. It was as real as the waking world.

I found myself in an unfortunately familiar landscape. I walked along a white riverbank, small bones crunching under my feet. Warm, thick, blood lapped against the shore, but did not stain my stark white emann. The sky itself was gray, the air sticky and hot.

Downriver, I could just make out a great mound in the midst of the river. As I walked closer, I saw that it was the beast, lying on its side, facing away from me. Its huge form heaved as the cascade of blood flowed over its black fur.

I stepped into the river. My emann flowed behind me, the unstained white fabric a stark contrast to the gore all around.

As it sensed my approach, its ear twitched, and it rolled over to face me. It stood and stretched like a cat before lowering its head to mine and sniffing me. A deep rumble erupted from its throat.

My heart felt as though it would hammer its way out of my chest.

The beast shook its fur out, flecks of blood flying in all directions. None landed on me.

It stared at me for several long breaths. It stood, completely still, but something rippled along its skin, and the beast was gone.

In its place, there was a man, or some approximation of a man. He was very tall.While the bloody river pushed against my waist as I walked, it rose only to his knees. His skin, hair, and even his eyes were all pitch black, his locs falling all the way past his hips, the edges just touching the surface of the river.

His face was ever so slightly *wrong*. His eyes were slightly too far apart, his nose sharp and long. His black lips curled over long, shiny, black fangs.

Again, a deep rumble rose from his chest, and I stopped where I was, unwilling to get any closer. I didn't notice anything about him change perceptibly, but everything that had unsettled me about his face shifted into a more human-like visage.

"You," he growled, his voice as deep and dark as a summer storm, "you are a cruel god."

I blinked in surprise.

Overhead, a large black bird circled, shrieking as it passed.

"I am no god," I said, my voice so clear that it didn't sound like mine.

"What else should we call you?" the beast asked. He didn't move, but was suddenly closer to me. His face was shifting again, as though he was moving quickly, despite standing stock still.

"You made us. We are as you command us," he purred. "We only do as you will."

I balked at this. He circled me, that strange rumbling hum now so loud that I felt it. I felt very much like a rat being stalked by a cat.

"You murdered people. Innocent people. You ripped out their throats as I watched," I explained.

He was suddenly in front of me again. His eyes narrowed.

"So you are cruel *and* a fool," he said. His words were harsh, but his tone of voice was not. He was not angry. He was…resigned. In that moment, I was overcome by the urge to embrace him.

Something rippled across his skin, and he was truly a beast once more. We locked eyes for a long moment, and it—he—dipped his head into the river to drink before padding off downstream. I watched as he walked until he disappeared around a bend in the river.

I woke, my heart hammering in my chest. I felt as though I would vomit.

The Priest was standing over me, hand outstretched. He wore an expression of slight surprise as he withdrew his hand and stepped back. He straightened and gave me a weak smile. The sky was still ink-dark.

"What is it?" I grumbled, aggressively wiping the sleep from my eyes. The dream hadn't yet left me, and I was not in the mood to be bothered.

"Let's go," he said.

"No," I growled, pulling the blanket up.

"We must get on the road. Let's go."

I tried to ignore him, but he yanked the blanket away.

"Kita, training. Let's go."

I sighed, perhaps more dramatically than necessary.

I stood, but before I could speak or walk, the beast's voice rang through my head.

Let me out! Please.

I swallowed and followed the Priest to the horses, where Weiran was waiting, already astride. He nodded as we approached, his eyes full of sad weariness. He didn't speak as the Priest and I saddled up, and we all rode in silence as the sun began to peek above the horizon.

The two men didn't speak, and I was grateful. The previous night's dream still weighed heavily on me, the image of the beast and his humanoid form still vivid. I wasn't sure where we were going, nor what we were going to do once we got there, but it seemed the least of my worries.

After riding for a while along the horsepath, we diverted into the woods. The Priest led us to a clearing, where the three of us dismounted and ate a small breakfast.

Weiran and the Priest didn't speak to one another as we ate, but they moved in concert with each other, passing things among themselves as though they knew the other's thoughts.

Once we finished our breakfast, the Priest rose and gestured for me to do the same. Weiran remained with the horses, watching with rapt attention.

"What is on your mind?" I asked as the Priest stood across from me, staring without saying a word.

He smirked and said, "so much about us is tied up in the way we feel. Some people are more controlled by their emotions than others."

"And what? I'm one of those people?"

"I think so," he said simply.

I frowned.

"Tell me about your affinity," the Priest said. "How does it work?"

"If you don't know how it works, how do you plan to help me?"

"That's why I'm asking," he replied, as though he was speaking to a small child.

Now awake and fed, I resisted the urge to snap back with a snarky remark.

"Is it like the worldmakers in the stories?" Weiran asked, an edge of sarcasm evident in his voice.

"Are you like the deathseekers in the stories?" I snapped back over my shoulder. My patience did not stretch *that* far.

I thought this would anger him, but he chuckled.

"Kita," the Priest said, bringing me back to the moment.

"Alright," I grumbled. I stretched my fingers, trying not to think of my dream. "I'm not a worldmaker. I'm…I don't know what you would call me. A lifeshaper? It's simple enough. I envision the being I'd like to create, put my energy into it, and there it is. The being is connected to me, I can communicate with it. It's tethered to me."

"Hmm, yes I know all of this already" the Priest intoned, tapping the hilts of his swords. "Can you tell me about the creature? The beast?"

At mention of him, the beast growled in my ear.

"What can I say? I don't have control over him."

"Why is that?"

"How should I know?" I snapped.

The Priest's face showed no reaction, but still, I felt bad, like I had done something wrong.

"Let me ask a different way. Was the ball the first time you created him?"

I turned my attention to Weiran and felt myself grow warm. For some reason, I had hoped that Weiran wouldn't know about that. But seeing how he watched, with no change in expression, it was clear that he knew exactly the Priest was talking about.

"Yes," I said quietly.

"And it wasn't intentional," the Priest replied. It wasn't a question, but I answered it anyway.

"No. And that had never happened to me before."

"And he returned at the temple bombing."

"Yes."

"A situation in which you were in quite a lot of danger," the Priest said thoughtfully.

"I suppose so."

The Priest nodded. He unearthed his small lionclaw knife from the small scabbard strapped to his chest and spun it as he thought. The movement was captivating; each time I thought he would cut himself, his finger moved deftly aside. Finally, he caught the spinning blade and gripped it in his fist.

"If you were going to fight, what would you create to be your champion?" he asked.

I blinked at the change in subject.

"Don't think too much. Just do it. What is your first instinct?"

I became keenly aware of the eyes on me and suddenly wished I was lying on the uncomfortable dirt, the ratty old blanket pulled to my chin.

"Go ahead," the Priest said gently.

Sighing, I closed my eyes. A champion. My first thought was the stories my mother had told me, about the old wars. The times when honor dictated fighting with swords, not affinities. I'd never seen pictures of them—all the paintings of those warriors had been destroyed at the beginning of the Melyora dynasty—but my mother had a way of carving the images firmly in my mind.

The warrior I pictured wore scaled leather armor, with a brass sword brandished above his head. He wore a leather helm, with long, dark warrior's locs spilling down his back. His black eyes were wide and bloodshot, his mouth open in a terrifying shout.

Once I held the image firmly in my mind, I let out the breath I had been holding and released him into the world.

I had never created a human before. I'd never felt the reason to try. So it didn't occur to me that his clothing would not emerge with him.

The warrior stood, naked and poised to pounce. His eyes—like the rest of him, pitch black—darted around, assessing the situation. Before I could speak, he leapt forward, crashing bodily into the Priest. In the same movement, he wrenched the Priest's scabbard free from his hip. As the Priest steadied himself, my warrior stepped back, coldly unsheathing the twin swords.

I glanced back toward Weiran. His faint smile had faded, and he watched with rapt attention, leaning forward as though he would spring into the fight at any moment.

I turned my attention back to the Priest and my warrior. My energy was already fading quickly, so I hoped he would let me release the warrior soon.

The Priest regained his balance and raised his hands in surrender. My warrior glanced to me and I gave him a small nod. He sheathed the swords, but stubbornly refused to drop them.

"May I ask you a question?" the Priest asked, directing his attention at the warrior himself.

Again, the warrior looked to me. I nodded.

"Speak," the warrior growled. His voice had a deep, rough timbre that reminded me of a landslide.

The Priest took one step forward. "I can't comprehend you. Your emotions…they…they're slippery. I can't get a grip on them."

"Where is your question?"

"You are like no creature I've ever encountered. I want to know more about your very nature!"

"I fight. That is all. I am as my maker created me."

I froze. His words were so familiar.

"I see," the Priest said, narrowing his eyes. "Then, shall we fight?"

The warrior smiled, black teeth gleaming in the sunlight. "It is the only way I know."

"Keep the swords. You'll certainly need them."

The warrior barked a laugh and, without waiting, launched himself forward, freeing his stolen swords and swinging them in a huge arc toward the Priest.

The Priest was not caught off guard. He stepped aside, easily dodging the attack. My warrior spun on him, but again, the Priest dodged. For several minutes, the two sparred—my warrior attacking, the Priest avoiding. The longer the fight continued, the more the gossamer thread connecting the warrior and me drained my reserves, until my eyelids began to grow heavy, my legs unsteady.

The Priest noticed. One last time, he stepped out of the way of the warrior's attack. This time, he spun on his heel and struck out with the lionclaw knife, burying it deep in the warrior's throat.

A yelp of pain escaped my lips. Thick black blood spurted from the warrior's wound, but as he moaned and dropped to his knees, his pain was my own. He looked to me, his creator, silently begging me to do something, to save him. I heard his thoughts as clearly as if he were speaking as he pleaded, *Help me!*

But what could I do?

I, too, fell to my knees as the life flowed from him. Though his eyes were entirely black, the life drained from them nonetheless. He gasped one last breath and went still, staring blankly at me as he died, his body fading into nothing.

My vision blurred and went dark.

"Hey," a gentle voice called. My eyes fluttered open. The Priest crouched over me, pressing a damp cloth to my forehead. "Are you alright?"

"Y-yes," I muttered. My hand flew to my throat. I was, of course, uninjured, but the vestiges of pain still radiated through my body. How long had I lay there, feeling every bit of my creation's death?

The beast writhed, full of ire, deep in my chest.

"Weiran, the herbs," the Priest called over his shoulder.

Weiran obediently pushed forward, rummaging in his bag until he produced some of the plants we had picked back at the temple. He pushed them into my hands and watched expectantly.

"It will help," the Priest said. "Quickly, now."

I glanced from the Priest to Weiran and back, suddenly reluctant. Did I really want to erase the last of my newest creation? It felt wrong, like a mother abandoning her child.

"It *does* help," Weiran whispered. "Immensely."

I sighed and nibbled at the small green leaves.

The taste was perfumey, the texture somehow slimy, but almost immediately the beast quieted.

"Use it sparingly," the Priest said as he helped me to sit up. "We won't be able to replenish our stores until we get to Avetsut, if they have it."

"I…I never felt anything like that before. I guess…I guess no one has ever killed one of my creatures before."

"I must admit that I didn't anticipate that. Your affinity is infinitely fascinating."

"And powerful," Weiran added, his voice almost wistful. "Either the empire does not know what it has lost with you, or it knows very well, and that's why it wants you dead. You are a threat to the emperor himself, aren't you?"

"Of course not!" I snapped.

But images of the ball came flooding back. The young man who asked me to dance, now nothing but bones. If only Ditan had been there, he could have spirited people away from the Beast's gaping maw. But he hadn't been.

Why hadn't he been? Why was everything from earlier that day so difficult to remember, while the ball itself was so clear?

"Kita," the Priest said, bringing me back to present. "Whatever it is you're thinking about, let it go."

"You don't understand," I murmured, hugging myself so tight my fingers tingled.

"He may not, but I do," Weiran replied. "I understand being haunted. Let it go, if you can."

I glanced up at him. He wore a somber expression and refused to meet my gaze.

"Hmm," I replied. "What a pair we are. Life. Death."

"Suppose so," he sighed. He turned away and said, "Let's go. The sun is high. We need to join the others on the road.

The Priest mustered a weak smile and pulled me to my feet. He rested his hand on my back as I walked.

I was far from steady, but I forced myself to the horses. I tried to mount my beast, but the Priest shook his head sharply and took my hand.

"Don't be foolish. We don't need you falling. With me."

It seemed prudent not to argue.

16

Ran

Ditan stood quietly in the corner of the room, arms crossed. The Commandant had set aside a room in the barracks for the visiting prince. The privacy allowed them to keep Ditan's existence a secret, and the shadowwalker had immediately gotten to work spying through the camp.

"This is getting frustrating," Ran sighed as he lounged back on his cot. "How could there still be nothing?" It had been days, and despite all of Ditan's best efforts, he hadn't found even a whisper about what had happened at the temple.

"Perhaps it's time to consider moving on," Ditan replied.

"Move on where? There's nothing to go on. We can't go back home, not yet." Ran furrowed his brow. It wasn't just that he didn't want to fail. It wasn't that he feared his father's ire—he didn't, not really. But failure meant Kita's life, and that he could not take.

Ditan glanced down at his feet and muttered, "I want us to find Kita too."

"Your Princess, you mean," Ran said with a wry smile.

Ditan fidgeted and cast his gaze to the ground. "What about the camp that was hit?" Ditan asked, changing the subject. "That may be

151

worth inquiring about."

Ran sat up. "The camp," he echoed. "I am not sure it's related." He let out a deep sigh. "But it's all we have. I'll head out and talk to our lionkin friend." Ditan clicked his tongue, but Ran ignored it, continuing, "Maybe you should look around the Commandant's quarters. If there's nothing there, find the messenger and follow her."

"Yes, my prince," Ditan murmured before fading back into the shadows.

Ran found Aka in the first place he looked—the mess hall. When she saw him, she broke into a broad smile and waved him over. The hall was full of soldiers he didn't recognize—a squad returning from assignment, he supposed. They must have gotten back to the fort some time in the night.

"Bring your prince some breakfast!" she yelled to no one in particular.

Ran smirked. Despite his initial misgivings, he had found her to be jovial, pleasant, and almost impossible to dislike.

"How are you, Aka?"

She gave a thumbs up. "I am well. I will be better when I can leave this place." When she saw his face, she added, "It's not that I don't enjoy your company, but I would prefer to be back south."

"Your family?"

"Ah, Prince Ran. There are some things we don't discuss," she warned. She smiled as she said it, but her yellow-brown eyes flashed with annoyance.

"Apologies."

Someone appeared with a plate of stewed meat and flatbread. Another soldier was right behind with a mug of barley beer.

Aka watched as he tore off a strip of bread and dipped it in the stew.

"Not as good as the food at the palace, is it?" she asked.

"I would never presume to insult the cooking. I've been on kitchen

RAN

duty too often." He popped the bread into his mouth and chewed. It was true that the palace had a great deal more spice than the fort did, but anything was better than dried meats and fruit of the road.

"Ahaha! You amuse me, princeling. Tell me. Do you have a wife?"

Ran choked at the sudden change in subject. Aka laughed as he fell into a coughing fit. By the time he could finally draw breath again, his chest and throat were sore. He took a long drink and once he finally caught his breath, he sputtered, "N-no wife."

The curtness of his response made Aka laugh harder, and he smoothed his hair back to try and regain some sense of composure.

"No, I am not married. I've had lovers before, but the right match has yet to be struck."

"Ah yes, you seem the type to have many lovers."

Ran's cheeks burned, but he refused to give her further ammunition. Especially not at the fort, where several of those lovers were stationed.

"Have you been in love, Prince Ran?" she asked with a wry smile.

"Love is not a luxury afforded to royalty," Ran replied. His mother and father certainly hadn't loved each other, though they were kind enough to one another. He'd never had a partner himself, though he'd spent many a night in the arms of the other soldiers. That had been a coping mechanism, not love.

"Hmm. I suppose not," she replied, more quietly this time.

"Where is all this coming from?" Ran asked. "Why do you care?"

Aka shrugged. It seemed to him that there was something she wanted to say, but whatever it was, she kept it to herself.

Ran took the opportunity to change the subject. "Aka, may I ask you something?"

"You may always ask."

"Can you tell me about the supply camp?"

"Oh, that? There is not much to tell, princeling. A skirmish, some stolen supplies. This is not something to concern yourself with." She

153

shoveled the last of her stew into her mouth and drained her beer.

"That may be, but I wish to know more about it," he said.

Aka locked eyes with him, as though searching for something. Then, she shrugged. "As I say, there is not much to tell. We got there too late for me to get any scent trails; animals had picked over many of the corpses. Someone ambushed the camp and stole the supplies. They took the conscripts. They even stole the soldiers' uniforms."

"Why would they steal uniforms?"

"Yes, that is a curious question, isn't it? Perhaps they wished to humiliate. It would not be the first time that such things have been done. Now, I regret that I must leave you. The Commandant needs me today."

"For what?"

Aka shrugged. "You must speak to her if you want to know these things, Prince Ran."

He closed his eyes and nodded. Aka clapped him hard on the shoulder as she left, and he watched as she threw open the mess hall door and disappeared into the sunlight.

When Ran finished his breakfast and entered the courtyard, Obaye was waiting for him. The young soldier refused to meet Ran's gaze, shifting his weight uncomfortably from side to side.

"What is it?" Ran asked directly.

Obaye rubbed the back of his neck. "I...I've been ordered to confine you to your quarters."

Ran raised an eyebrow. "The Commandant?" he asked.

Obaye nodded.

"She say why?"

"No, and I didn't ask. Ran, you know what she's like. You don't go around questioning her. You just obey."

"She has no control over me," Ran replied, pushing past.

Obaye grabbed his arm. "She has control over *me*. And the rest of us. Don't make this difficult. Just go to your room for the rest of the day, and all will be well."

Ran narrowed his eyes. Whatever she was doing, she didn't want him to know about it. So, naturally, he had to find out.

Obaye lifted his gaze, pleading with his eyes.

"Obaye, release me," Ran said in a low voice. "I am here on my own business and she cannot interfere."

"Think about us!" Obaye snapped.

Ran stared at his friend. Obaye looked away once more, absently scratching at his thigh, where the fabric in his trousers had been resewn. Ran's instinct was to pull his friend into an embrace, to reassure him that all would be well.

But that was a lie, and he knew it. The Commandant knew him, knew him better than he was comfortable with. She knew that he was close to his former companions, his friends. She knew he would not want to see them harmed.

And he knew that she did not make idle threats.

But whatever she wanted to keep him away from, it could be the only link he had to the temple. To Kita. And he was not the same soft-hearted boy that she had known. She herself had made sure of it.

Now is the time to prove it, he thought as he grit his teeth.

And so, Ran looked at his friend and said, "Release me. I am your Crown Prince, and I will not be told where I may or may not go."

The look Obaye gave him broke his heart, but he kept his face still as Obaye stood back. He turned toward the Commandant's tower, and did not look back.

As soon as he shut the tower door behind him, he started to shake. He gripped one hand with the other, hoping to still his trembling fingers, if nothing else.

Ditan appeared, waiting patiently for Ran to acknowledge him before starting, "My prince, there's a witness."

"They're speaking to a witness? And she's hiding that? Why?"

"They're..." He trailed off, casting his gaze down. "My prince, they have the High Priestess."

A pained, muffled cry echoed down the stairs, setting Ran's teeth on edge. He raced up the stairs, taking the steps two at a time, and phased through the door.

Inside, the High Priestess sat at a small table. A large golden lioness stood behind her, licking gore from its lips. As he looked a bit closer, he realized that the High Priestess was holding her mangled arm to her chest. She was desperately trying not to show emotion, but the pain on her face was evident.

The Commandant stood before her, watching dispassionately.

Ran couldn't believe it. "By all the goddesses, what has happened here?" he demanded, his voice shaking with rage.

The Commandant's head snapped toward him, her mouth twisted in a scornful frown. "You should not be here," she growled.

"I will not be told where I may go," Ran replied. The two of them locked eyes and he was determined to stare her down. He was tired of her posturing, tired of feeling so powerless under her gaze.

"We are doing as we were ordered to do," the Commandant said slowly, as though she were talking to a very stupid child. "We have been tasked with finding out how a temple right outside our capital city was bombed."

"You will leave me to speak to this witness myself," Ran replied. He was surprised at how calm he sounded—he certainly did not feel it.

Sparks began to gather around the Commandant's fingertips. For a moment, he thought she would strike him. Perhaps she planned to. But before she could, Ditan was there, hooking an arm under her armpit and around her throat. In his other hand, he held a dagger to her throat, pressing the point to the flesh.

"You will not harm the prince," Ditan said. He, too, was eerily calm.

The Commandant swallowed hard, the point of the dagger drawing a single drop of blood. "So. You've brought a shadowwalker with you. Clever."

Ditan looked to Ran, waiting for an order.

"Remove this woman from my presence. Ensure she does not bother me before I am done here. And bring us a healer too."

Where Ditan brought her, Ran couldn't be sure. Perhaps to the realm of shadow, where sane men were driven to madness. He didn't really want to know. But in a second, Ditan and the Commandant were both gone, leaving the prince alone with the High Priestess and the beserker.

Aka—still in lion form—seemed content to watch. The High Priestess eyed her wearily, still clutching her mangled arm.

"Aka, you should leave us," Ran said quietly.

The lion turned its great head toward him and blinked before padding to the door. Her bones creaked and snapped as her form shifted until she stood as a woman once more. She turned the knob, gave him a wink, and padded naked out of the room, the door softly clicking behind her.

Ran sank into a chair opposite the High Priestess. She shot at him a look so venomous that it was a wonder he didn't dissolve.

"My lady," Ran said gently, "what did they do to you?"

She thrust her arm forward. Ran grimaced as he saw it. It was more than just bite marks—it was as though Aka had gnawed on her arm. It was a wonder that he hadn't heard any more screaming.

"You have my most sincere apologies. The moment I was alerted to what was happening, I came to stop it."

"Things were fine until the day that you royals showed up at my temple," she hissed. "Since then, I've lost my home. I've lost some of my girls. And now, after I come here to help you figure out why this has happened, your people do this to me. I've told you what I know, and you've had a beserker destroy my arm. This is an utter outrage. There are reasons why the temples don't get involved with your petty politics. But what are we supposed to do when you set us in opposition?"

Ran listened calmly, but inside he raged. This was beyond anything he had imagined. She had to sense his anger, but perhaps she didn't care.

"My lady, I know the power you hold. And I know you can tell if I am lying to you. Please believe me when I say that we did not bomb your temple. The people here were supposed to figure out what happened. I will have them dealt with. I will have you healed. And I will make sure the temple is rebuilt. This is all I can offer you."

She was silent for a long moment as she considered both his words and emotions.

"You will do these things because they must be done," she said. "It does not assuage your guilt. Perhaps you didn't bomb the temple. But it is your responsibility all the same." She shook her head.

Ran sighed, building the confidence to ask his real question. "I am looking for my niece. Kitania. Kita. I know she was at the temple. When Ditan last saw her, she was unconscious and injured. Is she—" His voice cracked as he finally confronted the thought he had not allowed himself to think before. "Is she alive?"

The High Priestess hugged her arm close as she narrowed her eyes, looking for something in him.

"She was afraid of you," the High Priestess replied.

"Of me?" Ran asked, incredulous. "My lady, you have a false impression of me. I have only been trying to help save her life."

The High Priestess stared. She was grappling with something. Was Kita so afraid of the emperor, that she thought he would or *could* compel Ran to harm her? His heart sank at the thought. Kita, the person in the world he was closest to, was afraid of him.

"She lives. Her wounds were severe, but the healers saved her. She left the temple with the rest."

"Please, my lady. Tell me where she went."

"If I tell you this, I want your assurances that you and your Empire will leave us alone. You will rebuild the temple, and then you will leave us be."

Ran paused. This was a dangerous discussion; he wasn't the emperor. His father had, thus far, respected the traditional separation between the empire and the temples, but he could always decide otherwise. Ran wasn't the emperor yet, and his father was still in good health. But he needed this information. On the other hand, she would know if he lied.

So he decided to tell the truth. "My lady, I cannot speak for my father. Only myself. I have no quarrel with the temples. I recognize that my actions in the past have infringed upon you. I can assure you that I will not interfere with temple business. I can promise that I will speak to my father about the issue. That is all I can do."

He waited. She thought for a long moment, slowly looking him up and down as she considered.

"She went south. Searching for her father in his native lands."

Her father. Ran knew next to nothing about the man. Isa didn't speak of him often, and Kita never. Ran searched through his memory banks. Where was he from? Somewhere beyond the borders, but beyond that, Ran had no idea.

In any case, Kita would have to travel through Avetsut to get there. It was a start.

Behind him, there was the soft sound of footsteps against the hard stone floor, followed by the wretching of someone being shadowsick.

Ran turned just in time to watch a rather green-faced young man empty the contents of his stomach as Ditan smirked behind him. Ran rolled his eyes and turned back to face the High Priestess. Her face was was quickly turning grey.

"Quickly!" Ran barked. He pushed his chair away from the table and nodded in the High Priestess's direction. The young healer, beginning to regain his bearings, stumbled forward.

Ran walked out with long, purposeful strides. Ditan, as ever, followed silently behind. As they reached the courtyard door, Ditan laid a hand on Ran's shoulder.

"Wait. My prince, we cannot leave her here. Not with them."

The statement hit Ran hard. He whirled around, and Ditan staggered back.

"Do you really thing I would do that?" Ran asked through gritted teeth.

To Ran's surprise, Ditan gave him a shy smile. "I had the utmost faith in you, my prince," he said.

Ran narrowed his eyes, but let it go.

"Find Obaye," he said, turning back to the door. "Bring him to our quarters." He pushed the door open, flooding the entry with sunlight, and added, "have him walk. We don't need him getting sick."

Ran didn't have to wait long. Only a few moments after he sat down in the chambers he'd co-opted, the door opened and Obaye and Ditan strode in.

The air in the room was thick and tense. Obaye refused to meet Ran's gaze, hugging himself and shifting from foot to foot.

"You wanted to see me?"he asked through gritted teeth.

"Obaye, enough of this. I'm getting you away from here."

"Am I supposed to be grateful? The rest of us will suffer."

"You will watch your tongue," Ditan hissed, raising his dagger.

Ran raised a hand to ward Ditan away, and the guard stood down.

Obaye, to his credit, was uncowed. "Ran, you've sentenced us all. The Commandant will be furious. Perhaps you've left this place behind, but these people are my family. Unlike you, I don't have anyone else."

Ran swallowed, but he wouldn't allow himself to waver. "You will say your goodbyes. You are leaving this place. You will accompany the High Priestess wherever she would like to go. Take another soldier with you. Someone you can trust. When you're done, you'll transfer to the capital. You'll be free of her."

"No."

"Excuse me?"

"Your little errand must be important. So I'll go. But I'll come back here when I'm finished."

"You would disobey your prince?" Ditan asked, raising his dagger once more. "You could be flogged for that. Imprisoned. Even killed."

Obaye locked eyes with the prince, waiting for him to make a decision.

Ran wanted to force the issue. It would be good for Obaye to leave. The detail in the capital would be a promotion. Anything would be better than being stuck under the Commandant's reign. And allowing Obaye to defy him would set a precedent that Ran could not abide. But...Obaye was his friend. And his anger was not unwarranted.

"As you wish," Ran said. Without another word, he turned to his desk and began to write. When he was done, he yanked at a chain around his throat, producing a lapiz lazuli cylinder seal. He rolled it into the shallow dish in which he had poured his ink and then rolled the impression onto the bottom of the letter. Once the ink dried, he carefully folded the paper and passed it to Obaye.

"Treat her well. She has been through an ordeal."

Obaye stared as Ran carefully wiped the ink from the seal and replaced it under his color. Then, he stormed out.

Ditan eased as the door shut behind him.

"Did I do the right thing? Allowing him to dictate like that?" Ran asked, his voice very small.

Ditan shrugged. "I do not know, my prince. As long as the High Priestess is escorted safely, does it matter what happens next?"

Ran leaned back in his chair and sighed.

"I don't know," he replied as he pulled another leaf of paper.

* * *

The sun was on the verge of rising when Ran slipped from his quarters. Most of the fort was still asleep, save for a few guards posted on the walls. It was easy to stay just out of sight until he reached the gates. He was not in the mood to talk to anyone, and preferred to leave without explaining his next move.

Ran glanced around. Above, a pair of guards chatted as they patrolled. He waited for them to pass before slipping noiselessly through the massive oak gate. Once on the other side, he hugged the walls until he could disappear into the woods.

Ditan waited with the horses. Ran gave him a nod and the pair mounted, trudging through the forest until the Eastern Fort was nothing but a quickly fading memory.

Ran allowed himself to breathe, and to think. But they had been on the road for less than an hour when the sound of hoof beats filled the air.

Ran tensed, shooting a look at Ditan. The pair pulled off the road, watching quietly as an enormous horse and rider came into view.

"Lovely princeling!" Aka shouted as she reined in the horse beside their hiding place.

"Are you following us?" Ran demanded.

Ditan quietly drew his dagger.

"Yes!" she laughed. "I was hoping to travel with you."

Ran stared, incredulous. After what they had seen her do, she *dared* to act as though nothing had happened?

"Are you quite finished torturing witnesses?" he snapped.

Aka's smile faltered, and she dismounted her horse.

"Do not approach the prince," Ditan warned.

Aka threw her hands up. "You wound me, princeling. I serve the emperor as I am bound to do. I have no choice in the matter."

"And yet, you have evidently abandoned your post. So are you under orders now?"

She adjusted the lion pelt on her shoulders.

"You know, the old worldmakers had true power. The power to bend reality. To bind families for generations."

Ran was familiar with the old stories. In one such tale, a child empress was coerced into using her affinity to bind all the beserkers—called skinshapers, then—to the Melyora family. Even once the child died, the bond remained strong. As new generations rose, none of whom possessing the same level of power, that connection remained.

He hadn't held much stock in those old stories. Most of them, he found, were exaggerated to explain the ways of the world. So, what was Aka suggesting? That that particular tale was true?

"I...I had hoped to ask your leave to visit my family," she muttered.

Ran glanced at Ditan, who sharply shook his head.

"Your family is in the south, I presume?" Ran asked.

"Yes, in the savannas. My children are there."

"My prince, this is unwise," Ditan hissed.

Ran nodded, but he already felt himself faltering. "You will accompany us" he said, fixing Aka with as authoritative a look as he could muster. "If you assist us in our aims, then you have my leave to see your family."

She frowned. He'd thought it a generous gesture, but the way she tensed as he said it gave him pause.

"My sincere hope," she began, her voice bitter and low, "is that someone finds a way to free my kind from these obligations. Until then, I will do as you ask, as I have always served the Melyora family. And perhaps it was naive of me to think you could let me go."

The Meloyra family. Not the empire. Curious wording, Ran thought, but he decided against questioning her further.

"Come then," he said.

17

Kita

I fell into an easy routine; each morning at first light, the Priest woke me and we rode ahead of the group. Some days, Weiran accompanied us. Sometimes, Nokinan. Given that the only other shadowwalker I knew was Ditan, I expected her to be as adept a fighter as him. She wasn't. Ditan was quick and ruthless with a blade. He used his affinity strategically, forcing his opponents into shadow with strong, decisive strikes, giving himself the advantage until he could deliver a decisive blow.

Nokinan was clearly not trained in combat. With a blade in her hand, she couldn't do much more than swing wildly. Instead, she spent most of her time in the shadows, waiting until the moment presented itself to surprise her enemy.

Other days, we were alone. These were the days the Priest seemed to enjoy the most. He devoted his time to studying my creatures, not only in their fighting but in their very nature.

But no matter who was with us, the morning passed much the same; We found a clearing, and we fought. I created the most fearsome warriors I could conjure, each of them increasingly savage.

The Priest fought them each with vicious excitement, reveling in his sword dance. It was fascinating to watch; this was a man who had, since childhood, been trained to kill at in service of the goddesses. Each movement was fluid and practiced. It was like violent theater.

Though he still remained composed and stoic, it was clear that he was enjoying himself. He carried himself lightly, his footfalls barely producing noise. Each time he bested one of my warriors, he would barely rest before demanding another bout.

He was careful not to kill them. I couldn't stomach the thought of going through another creation's death, and he was kind enough to not put me through the pain. But he was skilled enough to incapacitate, slicing through tendon and bone until my warriors could not continue. Then, I would sever the bond between us and watch the creature disappear.

Once I was too spent to create anything else, we caught up with the group, by then on the road themselves. We walked for the entire day, and by the time the sun began to crawl toward the horizon, we made camp. My exhaustion was so deep that even the Beast remained quiet.

It got to the point where I could sleep anywhere, in any position.

But the peaceful oblivion of sleep did not last long on this particular night.

* * *

An anguished wail roused me. It was the sort of sudden wake-up that leaves you unsure of the time, date, or year. We'd been on the road for three weeks, and I'd thought we'd left this strange noise behind.

It was moonless night, and the sky was inky dark. The fire had died down, though there was enough light to see Nokinan asleep nearby, the boys snuggled into her chest.

I wiped my eyes and looked around camp. Just as I'd noticed before, those who had woken seemed unconcerned.

But this time, Nokinan wasn't awake to warn me off.

I pushed myself to my feet. I swayed as I stood, exhaustion clinging to me like humidity on a post-monsoon evening.

I followed the sound of the screaming. With each step, the light behind me faded. I opened my eyes as wide as I could, as though somehow I could will myself to see further.

The screams cut off. I paused, listening. For a moment, I heard nothing but the sounds of the forest around me—the light breeze flowing through branches. Insects and small animals called, either oblivious or indifferent to everything else going on.

I considered returning to our camp, but curiosity won out in the end. I swallowed, and kept walking in the direction where the noise had been. I wouldn't allow myself to entertain the idea that I was going to get myself lost.

Another noise caught my attention, and I paused to listen. It was a halting, repeating pattern that I couldn't, at first, identify.

Assured that I was walking in the right direction, I pushed forward. Through the thicket of trees, I could make out a dim light, like the last vestiges of a campfire. Once I got a little bit closer, I recognized the sound—sobs. Terrible, hysterical sobs.

I pushed through the last of the trees into a small clearing, and froze.

The Priest was seated at the fire. In his lap lay Weiran, crying. As he sobbed, The Priest gently massaged the nape of his neck, displaying a tenderness I had never seen in him.

The Priest must have known I was there. If he looked up, he would surely see me. But he didn't.

Weiran didn't seem aware of anything at all beyond the two of them. As he cried, he grasped the Priest's free hand, squeezing so hard that both their arms shook.

How maddening it must be, shouldering the burdens of the dead, even in sleep. Perhaps it should not have surprised me that he suffered so much. But, perhaps inexplicably, it did. The image of him sobbing this way ran so counter to the way I saw him. And as I watched the Priest lay a gentle kiss on the top of his head, I wondered how he could possible allow someone he clearly loved to suffer so.

As quietly as I could, I turned and returned to camp, but despite my aching muscles and tiredness, I slept poorly.

I found myself hovering somewhere between sleep and wakefulness when a sharp whisper cut through my fog.

As usual, the Priest stood over me, muttering my name. Though every muscle screamed at me to relax, I grasped his hand and dragged myself up, nearly pulling him down on top of me.

"Take all your things," he said as I reached up toward the canopy, slowly rotating my torso to stretch out my tight back muscles.

"Why?" I replied with a yawn.

He gave a casual glance over his shoulder.

"Weiran and I have business nearby. I thought you might like to come."

Something in his tone gave me pause. Though his voice was as stoic as always, there was a hint of hesitation.

"What sort of business do you mean?" I asked, trying to maintain a similarly relaxed tone of voice.

He didn't reply, and I suppose I didn't expect him to.

I raised an eyebrow as I gathered my bedroll and followed him to the horses. The now familiar black stallion butted its head against my shoulder as I approached, looking for a treat. I dug through the pack on his side, but there was nothing for him.

"Sorry my boy," I muttered as I pat his neck.

Too tired to worry about neatly packing, I scrunched the bedroll into a ball at thrust it into the saddlebag.

The air was wet and warm, the scent of sea air heavy on the wind. We were nearing the coast, drawing nearer to Avetsut, and to my new life. What would my father be like? Would he want me? Did he have an entirely new life, a new wife, new children?

The sun was directly overhead, peeking through the canopy, when a shout ripped me from my reverie.

My head snapped up just in time to see Weiran fall from his horse. The Priest reigned his beast in and leapt off, rushing forward.

"*Korek-tsa!*" Weiran growled as he pulled himself up from the muck. His face and hair were covered with mud, but he seemed otherwise unharmed. A string of what I could only assume was Avetsi profanities ensued as he paced aside the horses.

After a few seconds of this, the Priest blocked his path. Weiran tried to push back, but the Priest pulled him into an embrace. The pair stood there, locked in each others' arms, for quite some time, my presence utterly irrelevant.

Finally, they separated and returned to the horses. Neither of them looked at me as they started down the trail.

We arrived at a small village nestled between two roads. There were the familiar mud homes that I had seen every day in the capital, alongside larger buildings fashioned from wood. It was utterly unremarkable, at least visually.

The changed entirely when Weiran dismounted his horse.

Some of the villagers fled indoors. Others rushed Weiran and the Priest, jabbering excitedly in Avetsi as Weiran grimaced. The circles under his eyes were especially dark, and he looked as though he wanted nothing more than to curl up near a fire, but he patiently chatted to them, waving the Priest away.

The Priest handed the horse's reins to a villager and nodded at me. I followed him across town.

As we walked, a strange song began to play. I couldn't place the instrument—maybe it was a voice—but it seemed to lift and twist with the wind itself. It did not just hit me, but it penetrated my very soul.

There was nothing, in that moment, that I wanted more than to listen to that song for the rest of my days.

The Priest seemed unmoved, and I could not understand why he kept walking, why he wouldn't just stop and listen. When he noticed that I had stopped, he pulled me along gently, barely listening to the music.

As he pushed open the door to the tavern, the music intensified, soaring to a volume that enveloped my being.

I found myself moving forward, following the sound.

Abruptly, the music stopped, and the spell it held over me was broken.

Blinking, I glanced around the tavern and locked eyes with a rather surprised-looking young man.

My heart began to pound as I remembered where I had seen that silvery blonde hair before. It was the siren I had seen at the temple. He wore an expression of surprise, as though he hadn't expected us, or perhaps he had been simply been so lost in his music that he hadn't immediately noticed us come in.

The Priest strode over and reached out a hand and said, "Good to see you again, Tsavi."

Tsavi. The name struck me as distinctly Avetsi, but sirens were indigenous to the north, near the mountains.

"It's about time you got here," the siren replied. His accent was just as puzzling as his name, some strange amalgamation of Weiran's Avetsi lilt and something else I couldn't place.

"Ah, well. We can only move at the speed of a crowd," the Priest replied.

Tsavi's eyes met mine. "Ah. I remember you," he replied. "You were at the temple, yes?"

I nodded curtly. His eyes narrowed.

"You've a strange song. Chaotic. Discordant. Why is that?"

The Priest cleared his throat, and I silently thanked him.

Tsavi seemed reluctant to take his eyes off me, but said, "Events are falling into place. Weiran will be pleased."

"Good."

"Are you going to properly introduce me to your companion?"

The Priest turned to me, silently asking with his eyes. I gave him a quick nod.

"This is Lady Kita. She hails from the capital."

"Ah," Tsavi replied with a sly smile, "a long way from home, then."

"Not as long as you, I would imagine," I replied.

He shrugged and said, "I've been traveling most of my life. No place is home, not really."

"That sounds rather sad."

"Maybe at first. Now, I like being on the road. Even better on the sea." He closed his eyes and breathed deeply. "Nothing like the ocean air."

"I've never seen the sea," I admitted.

Tsavi's gaze jumped to the Priest, who just shrugged.

"A travesty. You must spend some time on the water. Nothing like it."

"I imagine the music must carry nicely over the water," I said, trying to remain casual

His smile faltered for just a second. "Yes, as I'm seducing maidens to their deaths at sea," he said with a touch of annoyance.

I lowered my eyes in deference. I hadn't mean to offend, but if I were to say that I hadn't been thinking of that old rumor when I said it, it would be a lie.

"I'm sorry," Tsavi murmured to my surprise. "Let us change the subject, yes? In the Vayanshan Mountains, you cannot really say you've met someone until you share a meal. So, if you'll allow me just a moment, I'll talk to Lanaiya in the kitchens." He flashed a wide smile, the kind of smile that warms your soul, and rose.

As he left the table, I turned to the Priest and asked, "Why did you and Weiran bring me here?"

"Patience, little princess," the Priest replied, his voice and face infuriatingly calm. "Just eat. Get to know Tsavi. He's a good man." His lips tightened slightly in what I nearly took for a smile.

"Are you trying to marry me off?"

He rolled his eyes. "Only a royal would think of such things. You must change your mindset. Enjoy life, as much as you can."

I scoffed. "You and Weiran are planning a coup. If you get what you want, there will be blood and more death than I care to see. And you're talking about enjoying life?"

He shrugged, and for an instant I thought he would continue with his annoyingly enigmatic ways. Instead, he replied, "Enjoy things until you can't."

Still annoyingly vague, but sincere.

Tsavi returned to the table, still smiling brightly. A short while later, a small, red headed woman approached with a large platter of a fragrant stew and warm, doughy flatbread. She set it on the table before us and rushed away before I could even say thank you.

Tsavi tore off a piece of bread and passed it to me. I scooped a bit of the stew and shoved it into my mouth. Goat, warm and spicy and more delicious than anything I'd had since I left the palace.

Tsavi seemed content to watch me eat, but I couldn't bother to be self-conscious.

"There we are," he said as he finally took a bite himself, "we are officially acquainted."

"If only I could meet everyone this way," I said between bites.

He laughed.

The Priest took a piece of bread, but Tsavi sucked his teeth. "Eating before your boy? He'll be disappointed."

"I am hungry and he may be some time. I'm not waiting."

Tsavi barked a laugh.

We were nearly finished eating when the tavern door slammed open. The tavern owner—Lanaiya, Tsavi had called her—shouted a curse in Avetsi as Weiran stumbled in.

"You want something to eat?" the Priest asked calmly.

Weiran shot him a fiery look and said, "I am tired. Exhausted, actually. I am going to sleep."

I expected him to approach the tavern owner to arrange payment, but he just exchanged a look with her and stalked off to the stairs.

"Are you going to follow?" Tsavi asked, his eyebrow raised.

"I'm going to finish eating," the Priest replied. Nonetheless, it seemed to me that he ate a bit more quickly than usual.

Once finished, he quietly rose, nodded to Tsavi, and followed Weiran upstairs.

Tsavi leaned forward, resting his chin on his fist, eyes slightly downcast. He said, "When you're ready, I can speak to Lanaiya and arrange your room.

I smiled in reply. I *was* tired. But I looked at him, this strange creature, and something about the way he looked at me made me say, "I'd rather stay up for a bit."

He broke into a wide grin that made him look like a mischievous little boy.

"In that case," he began, "you should dance with me."

I narrowed my eyes and looked around the empty, rather quiet tavern.

"Are you going to sing?" I asked nervously.

He scoffed. "If I do, you'll weep. Hardly a fun night. No, no, Lanaiya will play for us. She may not look it, but she plays a marvelous lestri."

He was right about one thing; she really didn't look the type. But as though she had heard us, she appeared with a strange stringed instrument I recognized from Tsavi's lament at the funeral—he'd evidently been counting on me deciding to stay. Seeing it hit me with a pang of sadness as I remembered the circumstances surrounding my first experience with it.

Lanaiya started to play. She was not as good as Tsavi had been—I didn't really expect that she would be—but she slapped her hand against the wooden base as she played, giving the tune a jaunty feel.

Tsavi grabbed me by the hands and pulled me to my feet. I wasn't expecting to be dragged away so quickly, and I stumbled against his chest. His heart beat strong against my own chest, seeming to mirror the tempo of the song—was that another feature of his affinity?

He wrapped his arm around my waist, and I tried to follow as he led. Dancing with him brought back memories of the ball, of the nameless young man who died in my arms. My breath caught in my chest and I froze.

"Are you alright?" he whispered in my ear.

I didn't know what to say. I didn't want to talk about what had happened; I wanted one person in my life to be unburdened by what had happened because of me. So, instead, I said, "Could you just… could you sing for me?"

"Ahhh," he replied. He seemed to understand something, though I couldn't figure out what he thought he knew. He started to hum, very quietly, drumming his fingers against my back as he coaxed me into swaying with him.

I focused in on his voice. It didn't match what Lanaiya was playing, but I didn't care. His voice cut through me, easing my worries and filling my mind with images of the sea.

Once I was able to breathe again, he stopped, offering a smile as he led me around the empty tavern.

"Thanks," I murmured.

"People don't ask me to sing very often," he admitted as we swayed and spun around the floor. "They fear what will happen. They think I'll steal their wills away." He snorted and shook his head. "All nonsense, of course. My song can ease fears, can paint a picture, perhaps even comfort the grieving with images of their loved ones. But control? That's beyond me."

Something in the tone of his voice told me he was trying to assuage my own fears.

"So, what is Yor-a like? I've never been," he said, changing the subject.

"That's not true," I pointed out. "You were at the temple. I saw you."

"The temple, not the capital. I thought about crossing the river and exploring. But there were too many guards for my liking."

"Hmm," I replied. I wasn't sure how much to tell him. Weiran had reacted poorly when he found out who I was. If Tsavi learned my past, how would he react? Finally, I settled on, "It was my home. It's all I knew, really."

"It seems a nice enough place, but living under the emperor's gaze?" He clicked his tongue.

He raised his arm, leading me into a twirl.

"How does someone born in the mountains wind up on the sea?" I asked.

He sighed. "That is a painful story."

I cast my eyes to my feet. "You don't need to tell it if you don't want."

"Another time," he said, and I thought I could detect a hint of sadness in his voice. "You know," he said, changing the subject, "I must apologize."

"For what?" I asked nervously.

"I saw you at the funeral. I should have introduced myself. It was rude of me not to." His voice was velvet-smooth.

"Probably better that you didn't. I wasn't having a good day."

"Better now?" he asked.

"Yes, I think so. Time and distance, I suppose."

Lanaiya's tune wound down. Tsavi spun me once more and we slowed to a stop.

He let me go, running a hand through his silvery blonde hair. He had been so self assured before, but now he shifted uncomfortably from side to side, not meeting my gaze.

I opened my mouth to say that I would go to bed. But then I thought of what the Priest had told me—Enjoy things until you can't. So I leaned in, firmly gripped his face, and kissed him.

He flinched at first, but quickly relaxed.

"Ah!" Lanaiya screeched. "Out of here!"

Tsavi and I exchanged a look and I wordlessly followed him upstairs.

His room was small and warmly furnished with a bed, chair, and basin. He was apparently traveling light, with only a small pack sitting on the chair.

As soon as the door was closed, I kissed him again, hard. Hungrily. He pushed me—playfully, but forcefully—onto the bed, and pinned my hands back above my head. I moaned softly as he moved down to my neck, to the bit of collar bone showing beneath my shirt.

I freed a wrist and slid my hand up his shirt. His body was hard and muscular—befitting the life of a seafarer, I supposed.

He pulled away just long enough to pull the shirt over his head, I pulled away his belt and he was on me again, touching my face, brushing his hands through my hair, tracing the curves of my body as he undressed me.

He pinned me again, and I strained against him.

"I'll stop if you want," he breathed into my ear. "I'll stop."

"You will not," I hissed, nipping his earlobe with my teeth.

For a moment, just an instant, it was like before I had left the castle. He was on top of me, but I was in power. I was in control. This man would do what I asked, because I was his princess and he had no choice. And he did as I asked. He did not stop.

Later, we lay together, Tsavi moments away from sleep, me tangled up with him, my chest on his back. I gently scratched his scalp, drawing a sleepy moan. He was so fair that his skin had bruised and reddened in places.

It had been a good night, to say the least. He was a good lover, so attuned to my body that it was as though he could see into my mind. But I had already decided it would be the last. I enjoyed Tsavi's company, but all I could think as I lay there with him was Ditan. All the coy flirtation that had never gone further, despite spending almost all our time together. We could have had a night like this, but we never did. Perhaps he was too shy, or I was too concerned with my grandfather's opinions, but there was just so much regret.

Besides, there was an unsettling thought building in the back of my mind, an irritating itch that I couldn't seem to scratch. I couldn't shake the feeling that maybe I was getting attached only because of the sweet songs he sang, the hum of his voice. Despite his arguments to the contrary, I'd heard stories of sirens ensnaring minds. Perhaps those tales were indeed just tales, but how could I know? I'd just met him.

Tsavi began to sing a sleepy tune, a breathless, wordless song that made me think, once more, of the sea.

* * *

The sun had not yet risen when the door to Tsavi's room opened with a slam, jarring me from my sleep. I wiped my eyes and leaned over Tsavi's somehow still sleeping frame.

Weiran stood in the doorway with a lantern raised to perfectly illuminate a venomous glare.

"Wake him," he said simply, seemingly unsurprised to see me.

I glared back defiantly. He was mistaken If he thought I would respond to that type of order.

Weiran rolled his eyes and surged forward, roughly shaking Tsavi while shouting at him in Avetsi.

"Wha?" Tsavi groaned as he rolled over. In his startled panic, he fell from the bed in a heap.

"We have to move. Now," Weiran said tersely.

"Now?" Tsavi complained as he pushed himself up.

"Yes. Get dressed and let's go. We don't have time to wait." And Weiran was gone, closing the door behind him.

"Alright, alright," the siren replied, running a hand through his ruffled silvery hair. In moments, he was dressed, and I was alone.

18

Kita

Three huge black birds circled above my head, squawking as they chased one another through the sky. I watched them, breathing evenly as each bird pulled against me.

Someone on the town gate shouted, "Riders incoming!" The threads snapped and the birds fluttered into nothingness.

I rose from the dirt and dusted off my trousers as three horses thundered in, the gate slamming shut behind them. The first two horses bore the Priest and Weiran. The third was a white horse with no rider, but something slung across its back. At first, I thought it was a deer, bleeding deep, dark red onto the animal's hide.

"Get the healer, quick!" Weiran snapped, pointing at some townsperson. "Get him inside."

The Priest ran to the white horse's side and roughly pulled what I had thought was a deer free.

It wasn't a deer at all, but a person, covered in a putrid mix of mud and blood so thick that it wasn't until I got close that I saw the flashes of silvery hair underneath. "Tsavi!" I shouted, running to his side. His eyes were closed. Was he breathing? I couldn't tell.

"Kita, move," Weiran warned, his eyes ablaze. He shoved me aside as the Priest carried Tsavi forward, holding him like a mother holds a sleeping child. They brought him to the inn, to the room he had been staying in, and lay him on the bed.

"Is he—?"

"Shit," Weiran interrupted, his gaze softening as he turned back to Tsavi's still form. "Shit!" His eyes floated upward—to one of his unseen ghosts, I suppose—and he shook his head slowly.

The town's healer—a girl no older than fourteen or so—appeared and knelt beside Tsavi. She grasped his chin and turned his head.

"Nothing I can do for him," she said gruffly as she got to her feet.

"Bring him back," I said softly.

Weiran's gaze shifted to me, full of fire that made me want to retreat.

"No," he replied.

I blinked. Had I misheard? He had the affinity for just this situation. And he just…wasn't going to use it?

The Priest stepped forward and laid a hand on my shoulder.

"What?" I snapped. Something moved in my chest—the Beast, stirring for the first time in a long while.

"There's no time. We have to get on the road tomorrow. If I bring him back I'll be out for days."

"So what? Why such urgency? You can save him. You can—"

"I said no!" He whirled on me, his beautiful face twisted in anger. "You spend one night with him and think that you know him. Let me assure you very plainly that you do not."

With each step he took toward me, the Beast growled a bit louder.

An unpleasant thought forced its way into my mind. I could unleash it. I could have it intimidate Weiran—force him to do what I wanted. When confronted with his own mortality, he would surely stand down.

The Priest positioned himself between the two of us.

"Perhaps it would be better, Weiran," he said, his voice still frustratingly still.

Weiran's eyebrows flew up.

"After all the times you've hated me for bringing you back?" he hissed. Realizing that he'd said more than he meant, he stepped back, folding his arms.

"You brought me back because it was necessary. That's what you always said." He paused, fixing Weiran with a stare that told me that necessity *wasn't* the only reason. "Your plans hinge on Tsavi's affinity. He's too powerful to waste."

This was maddening. Talking about Tsavi like he was a tool to be used, and not a human being.

"Plans can change," Weiran said softly, but even I could sense at that stage that he had already changed his mind.

He knelt down at Tsavi's side and paused, thinking. He nodded to the healer, who got to work searching for whatever bodily damage he'd sustained.

And then Weiran turned to me, a strange smile on his lips.

It was all I could do to hold his gaze.

"If I do this, then I want your word that you will help us," he said.

My mouth dropped open. He could not seriously expect me to go along with his mad plans, to position myself in opposition to my own family. Could he?

"If his life is so important to you," he said, "then you owe me for it. Wrangling his soul back into bonds it's already shed is not an easy thing. And he may not forgive me for it. So I want your assurance that you will pledge yourself to our cause. That is my price."

"Weiran," the Priest started, but Weiran waved him off.

"Fine," I said through gritted teeth. "But if I should meet up with Ran or any of my family, I will not fight them. Don't ask that of me."

"As you say," he said.

I could not believe myself. I couldn't join his foolish coup attempts. I shouldn't be entertaining this. But Tsavi...

Weiran placed a hand on Tsavi's forehead and closed his eyes, breathing a deep sigh.

"Keep him calm as we do this," he said to the Priest. "If he's anything like you when you come back, he could drive us all to madness, or worse."

The color began to drain from Weiran's face, as his face contorted into something like pain. I hadn't noticed that before, when he'd returned the Priest to life. His hands trembled, his body swaying, until finally, there was a wet, squelching gasp.

Tsavi turned onto his side and vomited blood and viscera onto the bed and floor.

Weiran collapsed beside him, and the Priest wordlessly helped him to his feet. Weiran fixed me with one last fiery look and the Priest took him away, leaving me alone with Tsavi.

"When...is this? Is this now?" he croaked. His voice was rough, missing all the melodic tones it had had the night before.

I debated what to tell him. I had no idea what he had experienced on the other side of death. I didn't know how to soften that blow for him.

"I'm here," I whispered.

He blinked slowly, and rubbed his eyes.

"Kita?" he asked, blinking again. "I can't...I can't?"

"Take things slowly," I replied, reaching for his hand.

He flinched at my touch.

"Why is everything so blurry?" he asked, rubbing his eyes so roughly I thought he would hurt himself. "Why can't I see?"

"A price is paid," the Priest said. "Kita, you should go. Let me speak to him."

"No."

"Yes. There are some things the living aren't meant to know. You shouldn't hear these things."

I stared at him, daring him to remove me, but he didn't engage. He simply stood, silently, until my resistance melted away, and I acquiesced.

* * *

Time moved strangely. Minutes seemed to inch forward at a glacial pace, but when I looked up, the sun had begun to set.

The door swung open and the Priest stood in the doorway. He wore a grim expression, and when he noticed me watching, he sighed and pushed past.

"Tsavi?" I called as I gingerly walked into the room.

Tsavi sat up, covered in dried mud, blood, and vomit, gripping the sheets on the bed so hard this his knuckles were white. He turned his head toward me. There was a slight cloudiness to his eyes.

"Are you alright?" I asked as I sat on the bed beside him.

"I can't see properly," he said. "Death has stolen that from me. Everything is fuzzy."

He fixed his gaze on me, tears forming in his eyes as he desperately tried to focus.

"The Priest told me that returning to life robbed him of his emotions. I suppose it takes different things from different people," I explained.

"Oh, I feel. I feel intensely. I want to cry. I want to scream. I feel...stuck here. I was..." He trailed off, shaking his head.

"What happened? How did you...how did you die?"

Tsavi sighed. "It was so long ago."

"It was this morning," I reminded him.

This seemed to surprise him. He clasped his hands together. As he looked down, he seemed to realize how dirty he was, and started to scrape the mud away with his fingernails. He dug so deep into his skin that I thought he would cut himself.

"We split up to watch the camp. I was going to run distraction while Weiran and the Priest hit the supplies. I don't know what happened on their end, but I got ambushed. They had a knife to my throat before I could sing a word. By time Weiran and the Priest got to me, the imperials had gone and I was there, choking on my own blood. And then things get a bit fuzzy."

I so desperately wanted to know more, to probe him about the things he experienced in death. But I refrained.

"I should have come with you," I said softly.

He scoffed and waved me away. "This is not your fight." He managed a weak smile.

"It is now, I suppose," I replied.

"Hmm?"

I paused. If he didn't know what Weiran had said, the deal we had struck, I didn't want to be the one to tell him.

In any case, he changed the subject. "I didn't know what Weiran was," he said. "Not really. I never asked. Sun and sea! A deathseeker!"

"It's fortunate that he was there to bring you back," I said evenly.

"Fortunate," he repeated sadly.

"Are you feeling okay? Do you need to rest?"

He swung his legs out from under the sheets.

"Not before I bathe," he grunted.

I chuckled.

Tsavi got to his feet and stopped, arms spread wide as he swayed. I offered a hand to help steady him, but he refused it, shuffling slowly toward the back of the inn. He held his hands out in front of him as he walked, doing his best to avoid walking into any obstacles.

While he bathed, I got a pot of boiling water from the kitchen and some towels and went to work cleaning away the grime from Tsavi's bedroom. It was strangely meditative, scrubbing away at the dark stains until they gradually came free.

When I was satisfied that the stains on the floor were gone, I pulled the sheets from the bed and dropped them into the pot to soak before returning the pot to the kitchens. The kitchen maid stared hard at me and ripped the sheets from the pot.

"No!" she screeched. "Cold water!" She tutted and shook her head before dragging the sheets out back.

* * *

That night, there was a knock at my door. When I opened it, I was somewhat surprised to see Weiran. He kept his gaze cast low, wringing his hands as he stood. His lips were still tinged blue, his eyes rimmed black with sleepiness.

"What is it you want?" I demanded. He flinched.

"I came to say…" he stopped, running a hand through his thick black curls. "Will you come and take a ride with me?"

I crossed my arms. "Is this a demand? My payment?"

"No, no. I just…I want to show you something. To explain myself."

I narrowed my eyes. I didn't understand him. One moment he was demanding absurd things from me. The next, he was acting…contrite?

"Look, I am sorry," he said. "Truly. I wish I could explain to you the things that were going through my head in that moment. Thankfully, cooler heads prevailed."

I willed him to look me in the eye, so that I could show him how it felt to be powerless under my gaze, but he wouldn't look up.

"Fine. Show me what you need to show me."

He perked up slightly, though he still wouldn't meet my eye, and shuffled away, out of the inn, to the stables.

The Priest was there to meet us, two horses already saddled and pawing at the ground.

"I'll stay with Tsavi," he murmured as I mounted up. I flashed him a weak smile and he shot a look that I couldn't interpret at Weiran.

Weiran ignored it and clicked his tongue, urging his horse forward.

The night was dark, the moon half full. But Weiran galloped ahead, his horse surefooted through the forest.

After riding for a while, Weiran slowed. We seemed to be in the middle of the forest path, nothing identifiable about it that I could see, but he was sure. He dismounted, hitching his horse to a tree just off the path.

I followed.

Weiran pulled a small lantern from his horse's saddle along with a flint and steel from his pack. Once my horse was safely hitched, he lit the lantern, put a finger to his lips, and beckoned me follow.

He walked as surely as he rode, turning at odd places in a pattern I couldn't discern, until we came upon a small clearing.

The metallic smell of blood clung to the air. As the light from Weiran's lantern passed over the clearing, I could make out the dark outline of legs and arms. My stomach churned as my mind cast back to the day the temple was bombed.

"Sun and sea, it wasn't supposed to be like this," he muttered. "It was just a supply run. We were going to steal supplies, that's it. We didn't know."

"How many?" I asked.

He shrugged, stepping closer.

I followed behind and realized that the lifeless forms I saw were children, each shackled together. There were four of them, three boys and a girl, each lying in a pool of blood.

"Why?" I asked, my voice trembling.

"I could guess. Imperials only take children they deem useful. Strong affinities. Everyone else they would have killed."

I knelt down, reaching a hand to the girl. She had to have been no older than ten.

The beast growled as it started to writhe within me.

"We didn't know there would be children. The Priest and I were north of here, attacking the supply line. Tsavi was here to raid their camp. We knew they'd leave someone to guard the camp, but we didn't know there would be children. By the time we realized and got over here, the children were dead and Tsavi was lying in the mud, bleeding out."

"Are they here still?"

He rubbed his eyes. In the dim lamplight, I couldn't quite tell whether he had been crying.

"Her name is Miari. She doesn't understand what's happened. She wants her mother."

He quietly lowered the lantern, placing it on the forest floor. He knelt over the little girl's body, his trembling hands moving to her shoulder.

"All I could think when Tsavi died, when I saw him standing over his own body, was that we had to move, quickly. And that we would need powerful allies. But I should not have put you in that position. I am sorry." His voice cracked as he spoke.

I will avenge, the Beast hissed. I took a deep breath, and he quieted.

"This affinity is an affliction for you," I said quietly.

He sighed as he stood, lantern in hand. "Yes, it does feel that way most of the time," he admitted. But he gave me a weak smile nonetheless.

"I must know, Weiran. Did Tsavi hear you barter with his life?" I asked.

Weiran cringed, but replied, "yes, he did. But you can ask him yourself. He understands. He's been in this fight longer than any of us. You don't know him. You met him yesterday. But you should be careful. He has more bitterness toward the empire than perhaps anyone I've met. It's best you don't get closer than you are." He ran

187

a hand through his mess of curls and said, "Look. I won't compel you to join us, not if you truly don't wish to. But I won't lie to you either. Neutrality is no option here. Not when there are children like this—"he gestured to the babies lying before us, flies buzzing around their faces—"being taken and killed."

Weiran's words gave me pause. I didn't know much about Tsavi's past; he'd been uninterested in discussing it. But I suddenly wanted very badly to hear what he had called a long, sad story.

I resolved to speak to him the next day.

"Come on then,"Weiran said softly. "We both need the rest."

We had just mounted the horses once more when a song started, ringing out loud and clearly through the night.

There wasn't a discernible tune, and there was no way, as far away as we were, that we should have ever heard it. It penetrated my soul, coaxing me, no, pulling me forward. The horses snorted and followed the voice.

It was Tsavi's voice, that much was obvious. But there was something sinister in it, a dark edge I had not heard before.

Tears welled in my eyes, but I couldn't take my hands off my horse's reins.

I tried to call to Weiran, but my voice caught in my throat.

When we got back to the town, the gates had been battered down. In the town center, Tsavi and the Priest stood. While the Priest was his usual stoic self, Tsavi looked positively unhinged. His hair blew wildly in the wind, his eyes, though cloudy, were ablaze with fury. He was half naked, wearing only clean linen pants. His new scars almost shone in the dim light of the moon. As his mouth moved, spittle flew. He was singing so loudly that it seemed to be a scream.

Surrounding them were a small squad of imperial soldiers, each standing still with tears running down their faces. A crowd of townspeople gathered around.

188

Tsavi's song compelled us forward, forced us to dismount and step through the soldiers' ranks and join our friends.

"Tsavi," I managed to croak out, but he shot a venomous look and my teeth clacked shut.

There were words to his song now, words in a tongue unlike any I had ever heard. My mother had told me stories of the siren's songs before, how they had their own private language that could drive a man to madness. Maybe there was something to those stories after all.

I slowly sank to my knees as if pushed down by an invisible force. Weiran and the Priest followed suit. I lifted my eyes, forced by Tsavi's song to bear witness.

The first of the soldiers freed a dagger from his scabbard. It was hard to see in the night, but I imagined it was the same type that had killed the Priest. The knife traveled upward, shaking as the soldier tried to stop.

Tsavi's song was too strong.

The soldier plunged the blade into his own chest. He gurgled as blood fell from his lips and he collapsed, dead.

The next soldier drew a dagger.

"Pleeeeeaase," the soldier managed to squeak, but he, too, fell to Tsavi's song. One by one, each of the soldiers did the same, until all of them lay dead in the circle.

Tsavi gasped, and as the song broke so did his hold over us. I fell forward, sobbing wildly into the mud.

Someone pulled me up roughly. Tsavi. His cloudy eyes locked onto me, and there was hatred in them. Not directed toward me, I didn't think, but still sharp and cutting. Without speaking another word, he disappeared back into the inn. The townspeople dissipated, leaving Weiran, the Priest, and me outside with the dead.

19

Kita

The first tendrils of morning light illuminated my small room, pulling me from the oblivion of slumber. I laid there for several moments, allowing myself to revel in the rough cushion. For just that moment, it was like being in my old apartments in the palace. No sleeping on the ground, no worrying about coups and death or even the beast.

Then I remembered what had happened the night before, and my pleasant mood soured.

I dragged myself from underneath the quilts and to the washbasin. I almost didn't recognize the figure staring back at me in the mirror; I didn't wear road-weariness well. My eyes looked sunken, with dark circles I had come to associate with Weiran. I scowled at myself, but there wasn't much I could do but wash my face and drag fingers through my tangled curls. Fighting with my hair, I was beginning to see the utility in cutting it, but I refused to give the Priest the satisfaction.

Sighing, I went downstairs. Lanaiya caught my eye and nodded as I walked into the main area of the tavern. She, too, had been transfixed by Tsavi's actions the night before. As I walked, trembling, back into the tavern, she took one look at my face and dropped a room key into my hand.

"*Friko?*" she said as I sat at a random table. When I shrugged and shook my head, she said, "*friko*...eh...food? Food?"

I smiled and nodded.

She beamed, delighted that we had understood each other, and I made sure to commit that particular Avetsi word to memory.

I ate with a strange mix of relief and trepidation. It was nice to be alone for the moment, to savor the meal. I wasn't used to Avetsi food, the peppery flavors that contrasted so sharply with the rich tastes of the palace, but it was a comfort nonetheless. On the other hand, knowing that Tsavi was just upstairs after what he had done, made me restless. Beyond that, I kept thinking back to the ball, and that kind boy I had danced with. I too, had killed people with my affinity. It had been horrific, and they hadn't deserved it. So, how could I possibly feel such disgust, such rancor toward him? How was that fair?

"Good morning," a flat voice said. The Priest slid into the seat across from me, his arms folded.

I nodded at him. I didn't really want to talk to him, not yet. But, as always, he was intuitive enough not to ask me to.

"Shall we practice today?" he asked. "I'd love to have a look at your beast, if you wouldn't mind."

I bristled as the beast stirred within me, perking up at mention of him.

"Don't," I warned.

The Priest was unmoved. "I think we will need it in the days to come," he said.

"He's dangerous," I hissed. More quietly, I added, "I don't want to hurt anyone."

The Priest shrugged. "All the more reason to practice. How can you ever expect to control it if you don't work on it?"

I quietly shoved another bite of food into my mouth. The entire exchange reminded me of one of my childhood tutors, who would flash an annoyingly vacant smile whenever asking me to do something I did not want to do.

The beast stirred, straining against me as he sensed an opportunity to be released.

"Fine," I hissed, hoping to pacify the both of them.

* * *

We rode a ways out of town; for this, I was grateful. I was unsure of whether or I would be able to control the beast at all, especially when there were other people around. The Priest took me to a small clearing. A spring bubbled across the edge, cool water making its way toward the sea.

"Alright then. Let's see him," the Priest said once we had both dismounted.

I shifted from one foot to another. So soon?

Let me out, the beast demanded, clawing at my very being like a cat at a closed door.

"You're alright," the Priest muttered. I looked up at him in confusion, and realized that I was hyperventilating. I focused, steadying my breathing, and nodded.

"Okay," I muttered, closing my eyes. I didn't have to work especially hard to visualize him, to give him shape in my mind. He already existed, fully formed. I just had to unlatch whatever barrier I had constructed within, and he bounded forward, let loose in the clearing.

He seemed even larger than I remembered, towering even over the Priest, shaking his great head in the breeze.

"Don't hurt anyone," I begged as he ran, but he didn't seem to be paying any attention to me at all. I had expected aggression, for him to turn on the Priest, but he seemed content to just lope around. He approached the spring and drank, closing his eyes in pleasure before flopping down in the middle of it.

I didn't understand. He was acting like a puppy.

"Magnificent," the Priest said under his breath. His normally stoic expression was gone, replaced by wide-eyed wonder. Slowly, he approached the beast, hand outstretched, as though he was going to pet him.

"*Do not touch me,*" the beast growled. His mouth didn't move—and in any case, he didn't have the facial structure for human speech—but the Priest shuddered, clearly receiving the message. He raised both hands in supplication and dipped his head.

I strode forward, stepping in front of the Priest.

The beast lowered his head like a chastened dog.

"I don't understand you," I said with a touch of annoyance. "You are a murderer. I watched you kill people—innocent people. And now you behave like this?"

The beast stood, raising himself to his full height, and fixed his great black eyes on me.

"*I am as you made me,*" he said simply.

"So you blame me? For your actions? Why would I do that? Why would I create you? Why would I have you do those things?" My energy was quickly fading, but I didn't care. I straightened my spine and stared him down, almost daring him to respond. I half expected anger, the rage I had felt from him at the ball and in the days following.

But it didn't come.

"*You misunderstand me. I do not blame; I just explain. You are a cruel god,*" he said, quietly and with a touch of sadness. "*I am as you made me, and I know no other way to make you understand.*"

And he flopped down once more, resting his chin in the spring.

My vision started to swim. I tried to steady myself, but the earth beneath me seemed to lurch, and I fell forward, the gossamer string between me and beast snapped.

The Priest caught me and helped me down. He brought me a skin of water, remaining annoyingly silent as he lifted it to my lips.

"So, did you get what you wanted?" I asked bitterly between sips.

He sat beside me and sighed. "It is a beautiful creation," he said. "More than any of your warriors that I've fought, your beast seems… real. Like a fully formed, sentient being."

I said nothing. What was there to say about something like that? If it was a sentient being, then surely it had control over its own actions. But, despite his words, the beast certainly seemed to place a great deal of blame at my feet, and I couldn't find it in myself to disagree.

"It called you a god. Curious wording."

I scoffed, but he persisted.

"You are a god, aren't you? To them, at least. If the goddesses created us, and you created the beast, then it makes sense he would think you divine."

"A god would know what they were doing," I retorted.

The Priest just shrugged. "I've been in service of the goddesses since I was a child. In all the scripture I was ever taught, 'knowing what you are doing' was never a requirement for godhood."

Despite myself, I chuckled.

Once he was satisfied that I would not keel over the second I took a step, he helped me to my feet and said, "come on. We have to get back."

Obediently, I mounted my horse. I barely remembered the ride back—I was too busy thinking of my beast and his words. You are a cruel god. The same words he'd spoken in my dream.

* * *

The village seemed a great deal more populated than it had been when we left. As I looked around, I realized that the refugees from the temple had arrived. Nokinan's boys ran screeching in the center of town, playing with the town's children. At the tavern, Weiran and Nokinan waited to greet us. As we arrived, Weiran and the Priest shared a meaningful look and a cryptic nod.

"We're going to move tomorrow. Tsavi will brief you," Weiran said quietly as I dismounted. Before I could ask further questions, he was pulled away, talking to some of the many townspeople still clamoring for his attention.

I bristled. I hadn't talked to Tsavi, and I wasn't ready to. But Weiran had spoken with a finality that indicated that the matter was closed, and in any case, he was gone before I could protest.

The Priest laid a hand on my shoulder for a moment before breaking off to follow Weiran.

Nokinan fixed me with a quiet stare. I couldn't tell what she was thinking, and she made me uneasy. She stood, unmoving, as I shuffled around her, breathing a sigh as the door shut behind me.

But my peace was not to last. Tsavi sat waiting at a table near by. As I walked in, his clouded gaze shifted to mine, and he asked, "Kita?" His voice was strained, and his eyes were rimmed with red.

I slid into the seat across from him. I didn't know what to say, and he didn't seem to either. We sat in awkward silence for a long while, until finally I mustered the courage to speak.

"Weiran says you have information for me," I said.

He cleared his throat, swallowed, and nodded. "Uh…ye-yeah. I just got here a few days ago. I've been down in Avetsut for a few weeks now, watching and talking to people in the city. From what we can tell, the Empire's grip on it has loosened in the last few months. They're basically using Avetsi guards to hold it, with a few high ranking officials keeping the troops in line. They're able to do this because they have the support of the Triumvirate—the three princes whose families have historically held the principality."

"Because the Empire is shifting its focus north," I said. I had heard talk of the strategy in the palace from Ran, who had been excited to be included in strategy meetings.

"R..right," Tsavi said, eyes narrowing. "We think we can exploit that. There's talk of unrest among the people. They're displeased with the Triumvirate, who they feel has sold the principality to the Melyora Empire for their own wealth. One of the princes, the so-called 'yellow prince,' appears to be most easily swayed. So, when we get to town, he's agreed to have an audience with Weiran. We want to be ready for that by loosening the military control of the city. To do that, we need to infiltrate the imperial outpost and remove the officers. Then, the Avetsi guards will turn to the Triumvirate."

"And Weiran hopes to use diplomacy to sway them to his cause."

"*Our* cause," Tsavi corrected. "And I don't know his plans with the Triumvirate. I only know what I need to. That's how he operates."

"So I've learned," I muttered. "So, what does that mean for me? I already told him I'm not willing to kill for this...this coup of his."

Tsavi looked down at his hands splayed across the table. "I wish those guards had not shown up here last night," he muttered. "It would have been better for you not to see that."

I barked a mirthless laugh before I could stop myself. "You forced men to take their own lives. And you forced us to watch. It would have been better for you not to do it!"

He smacked his hand down on the table. "I did not lie to you. I never had that kind of power before. Never. It was like...all my anger, all my bitterness at this empire and what they did to me just flowed from my lips, and I was powerless to stop it. It was...terrifying. Feeling so strong, so powerful, like there is no limit to what you can do. In that moment, I wanted them all dead for what they had done. Not to me, but to those children. They deserved justice. But it was like my affinity just...exploded. I could do anything—I could make them do anything. And I don't even think I really meant to, or perhaps that's just what I told myself after. I don't know. I was a songweaver. A simple songweaver. Now, I'm truly a siren."

I placed a hand on his, and he looked up.

"I've felt some of what you say," I replied. "That feeling that your affinity could destroy the world, if you let it. All I can say is...don't let it."

He swallowed once more and pulled his hand free, and I feared for a moment that I had said something to offend him. But he took my hand and laid a gentle kiss on it.

"You and I will just be focused on distraction," he muttered. I blinked at the change in topic, and he continued, "We'll create a diversion, and while the soldiers are focused on us, Nokinan and the Priest will strike. The plan is to try and carry out the entire thing without bloodshed. The Avetsi soldiers are mostly innocent in all this, and we'll need them on our side. They've no love for the empire."

I nodded, willing the beast to be cooperative.

He smiled weakly and got to his feet.

"Wait," I said as he turned to leave. He shifted his gaze to mine, and I continued, "will you dance with me?" I am not sure why I asked him; the thought of what he had done turned my stomach, and the sight was burned into my memory. And yet, he seemed so broken, so lost.

And anyway, I felt a strange kinship with him; hadn't my beast done the same? To innocents, no less? How could I judge him?

He broke into a wide grin for just a second before it faded. Slowly, he shook his head. But as he reached the stairs to head back upstairs he turned back and said, "if we win tomorrow, we'll dance all night."

20

Kita

I crouched down at the corner of the stone outer wall, peering quietly around the bend. The wall was solid and extended all the way into the sea. Waves crashed against it, as though trying to drag the entire encampment into the black water.

The moon overhead was heavy and bright, just over half full. Its position was perfect; even with the beast's black fur, there was enough light that he would be visible.

"Whatever it is you're going to do, now is the time," Tsavi whispered. His breath was hot on the back of my neck, and a chill shuddered through my body.

I glanced back at him, giving him a smile that I hoped was reassuring. In truth, my stomach was clenched.

This wasn't the life I had ever imagined. Even on days when I dreamed of escaping the palace, my ambitions only ever extended as far as the family I might marry into. Perhaps, if things had gone differently, I might have been married off to an Avetsi prince, and been in the exact same place.

A soft touch on my shoulder pulled me from my memories and hypotheticals.

"And you?" I asked.

Tsavi avoided my eyes. I didn't need The Priest's empathic affinity to understand how he felt. He didn't trust himself. By all the goddesses, I wasn't sure I trusted myself. The beast had obeyed my wishes the day before, but would he tonight?

I turned back. Where were Nokinan and the Priest now? Were they in the shadows, watching and waiting? Were they already moving through the fort? I didn't hear anything that would give me a hint either way.

"Alright," I muttered, more to the beast than to Tsavi or myself. Closing my eyes, I unlocked the door within myself that kept the beast at bay.

Tsavi gasped behind me and muttered something in his mother tongue.

My eyes snapped open to see the beast, somehow even larger than before. He seemed a bit more feline, not necessarily in appearance but in demeanor. He seemed to smirk at Tsavi's disbelief, shaking out his fur and reaching forward for a stretch.

"Distract them. Menace them but by all the goddesses, do not hurt anyone," I hissed.

"I am as you make me," he replied. His voice—if it could be called a voice—was quiet, but it penetrated deeply, almost like Tsavi's singing.

The cord connecting us stretched as the beast leaped effortlessly to the top of the wall. It threw its head back and released a snarling, otherworldly howl that reverberated through my body.

My energy quickly began to deplete. My edges of my vision started to blacken, and I swayed as the beast hopped down into the fort.

For a second, there was silence, followed by screaming. A bell started to clang. There were flashes of what looked like fire, and the smell of singed fur wafted toward us.

I grit my teeth as I realized that I was afraid. Not for myself, but for my beast. I didn't feel any pain, like I had when the Priest had sparred with my warrior, but I worried nonetheless.

I gripped the stone so hard that tiny bits of it splintered off underneath my fingernails.

"Don't let them hurt you," I muttered, as though trying to reassure the beast.

That familiar deep rumble of a laugh was his response.

"Are you alright?" Tsavi whispered.

I turned my head to respond, but the ground shifted beneath my feet and I fell forward, smacking my face against the wall.

Tsavi propped me up with a groan, wrapping his body around mine as I sat, holding my head in my hands as the line between the beast and me strained. Blood filled my mouth; I had bitten my tongue.

Tsavi rested his head on my shoulder and hummed, a clear, low note that vibrated through my body. My vision cleared, and the gossamer thread thickened as energy flowed into my limbs. I blinked and nodded, urging him to keep humming as the beast ran through the fort.

More blasts of light. I felt them, tiny pinpricks against my face and chest, but there was no pain. Smiling, I willed the beast forward. I couldn't see what he was doing, but I felt his elation, his joy at being free. He was savoring the moment, and a pang of guilt washed over me. How could I have deprived him of this for so long?

"How much longer?" I asked through grit teeth, but Tsavi kept humming, and I made a decision. As long as he kept going, so would I.

I rested my forehead against the wall, taking deep breaths as I focused on maintaining the connection between myself and the beast.

A strong vibration rattled through the wall. I glanced back at Tsavi, but he looked as confused as I felt.

There was a loud crash, the sound of stone smashing.

Tsavi was quick to his feet, and he yanked me clear just as the wall in front of us tumbled into pieces, his humming stopping as he saved us both.

At once, my energy almost completely dissipated. I had just enough time to see the beast bound through the rubble and into the waves, pursued by soldiers hurling balls of fire, rock, lightning, metal, desperately trying to exterminate him.

The thread snapped, and my vision went black.

* * *

Hands hooked under my arms, dragging me away.

I blinked. I was slumped, astride a horse. Someone held me up with one arm, steering the horse with the other.

I blinked again. The moon shone bright and uncaring overhead.

My eyes fluttered and shut once more.

Someone led me, stumbling, into a small wooden building. Maybe it was our inn. Maybe it was somewhere else. I couldn't tell.

My eyes sprung open. I was lying in a bed, burning. Someone had tucked thick fur blankets under my chin. I tried to kick them away, but succeeded only in tangling myself further.

"Peace," someone whispered nearby. I managed to turn my head to find the Priest sitting in a chair across the room.

"Will you unwrap me, please?" I asked through gritted teeth.

Wordlessly, he rose and freed me from my fur prison. At once, I felt as though I could breathe.

"What...what happened?" I asked, wiping sweat from my brow.

"Well, broadly speaking, our plan succeeded. We captured our targets. Your distraction worked beautifully. We all reconvened to celebrate, but Tsavi was standing over you, trying to wake you. He couldn't shake you out of it."

I blinked, remembering the vague recollections of being brought to this place, wherever I was.

"How long has it been?"

"Better part of two days. I thought you might die. You were so cold."

I gawked at him. His face was, as usual, completely calm, but his voice betrayed a touch of relief. But death? Had I really been so close?

"I suppose I pushed it too far," I muttered. I mentally examined my body, traveling down my spine, feeling the brush of the my tunic against my skin. I moved each finger and each toe. Whatever had happened before, I felt fine.

"I'm glad you didn't die," the Priest said simply, and I couldn't help but smile.

I stood, a little unsteady, and stretched, reaching to the ceiling. I slowly moved my head from side to side.

"Where are the others?" I asked.

"Most of the refugees are going to stay here, make new lives. Some will go to Avetsut, I'm sure. Weiran, Nokinan, and Tsavi have already ridden ahead to the city. Right about now I think they're probably at the Cliffside Palace, speaking to the Yellow Prince. When you're up to it, you and I will ride to meet them."

I nodded slowly, absently dragging fingers through the ends of my hair. A knot tightened in my belly. The palace, my mother, Ran. They all felt so far away, so long ago. Now that I was so close to Avetsut, the future seemed so uncertain, but what I knew for sure was that my former life was over. I wouldn't see my mother again. I wouldn't see Ditan or Ran or anyone else that I had ever been close to.

Throughout the long journey from Yor-a, I had stopped myself from thinking about it.

At some point, I realized, I had stopped thinking of myself as a wayward princess. But what did that make me?

The Priest watched dispassionately.

"Let's," I started. I stopped, swallowing hard, before continuing, "let's just go."

He flashed a tight smile and nodded.

* * *

I hadn't thought much about the moment I would reach Avetsut. It had always seemed so distant, like a fleeting daydream. Weiran had rarely spoken of it, and I had never been, so I expected nothing.

And here I was, looking over the city from the clifftop, and I didn't know what to think.

The city was enormous, far larger than Yor-a. It stretched from the cliffside to the coast, and sprawled so far in either direction that I couldn't make out an end. Unlike the capital, with its neatly delineated districts and dark mud and reed houses, Avetsut seemed to have been cobbled together as more people moved into the area. I counted at least three or four marketplaces, small painted homes crowded around. To the far south, I thought I could make out a large, purple and white complex that could have been a palace, and another—this one painted plainly but covered in centuries worth of vines and greenery—close to the harbor.

The harbor itself was dotted with small reed fishing boats. I could just make out the sheen of the nets catching the light. Docks and warehouses lined the area, and workers darted in and out.

Near the center of the city was a large amphitheater. At the moment, it was empty, but I envisioned plays and concerts, attracting all of the city's most art-inclined citizens. It would be able to hold hundreds, if not thousands. All those people, jostling to see and hear. It must be a place that valued performance.

To our right, just a ways down the horsepath, was another palace.

From looking at it, I could see why its denizen was called the Yellow Prince. From where we were, most of the palace was obscured by walls, but the top floors of the palace were painted—freshly, it seemed—in a bright yellow that would have to be highly visible from just about anywhere in the city. I imagined what it must look like at sunrise, and vowed to wake early to see it for myself.

I turned to face the Priest, who stared stony-faced at the city below. "It's incredible," I whispered.

He just shrugged. "Let's hope so," he muttered. Before I could ask what he meant, he clicked his tongue and led his horse toward the palace on the cliffside.

As we neared the palace walls, a guard raised a hand, and both our horses stopped, heads drooping slightly.

"*Pareté!*" the guard called.

The Priest raised his hands in surrender and replied in Avetsi. The two exchanged a few sentences, and the guard barked at someone within the confines of the gates. We waited for a short while— a moment or two at most—before a servant darted out, muttered something in the guard's ear, and disappeared again into the safety of the compound.

The guard lowered his hand—though not his gaze—and the horses shook off their spell. I rubbed my mare's neck, assuring her that all was well, and urged her forward.

The grounds within the gates were verdant and alive with beautiful flowers, enormous blooms of orange, red, and yes, even yellow.

Weiran, Tsavi, and Nokinan awaited us at the palace doors, stood in a line to the side with others I didn't recognize. They'd washed and were clothed in fine, richly colored linens. Weiran had even had a haircut, his unruly curls short and tamed. Without his hair to hide them, his eyes blazed even brighter.

I tried to catch Tsavi's gaze, but for some reason, he seemed determined not to look in my direction.

On the other side, there was a line of what I assumed to be servants, each dressed in surprisingly colorful linens. At the Imperial Palace, the servants melted into the background of every room; they were ever-present, but hardly noticed. But here, the servants were only delineated by the simplicity of their attire, not the color.

And out in front, was the Yellow Prince.

As with the city itself, I'd had no expectations of the man. His name had come up in my days at the Imperial Palace; he had even been floated, at times, as a potential husband for me. But I knew nothing about him.

He was a man of about 35 or 40 with the same bronze complexion as Weiran. His hair was cropped—utterly unlike any royal of the Imperial Family. His face was unremarkable. He wasn't especially tall or attractive, but he was adorned in gold jewelry, from several gold hoops through his ears, a bar through his septum, and small rings through each eyebrow. Despite the heat, he wore a heavy purple cloak that had been embroidered with what I suspected was actual gold. As we approached, he gave us a diplomatic smile, revealing small emeralds drilled into his eyeteeth.

A servant boy—couldn't have been more than 13 or 14—stepped forward and said, "You stand in the company of the Most Illustrious Prince Dahv Entslor, Lord of the Cliffs and Shadows."

I looked to the Priest for a hint as to how to proceed. When he raised a fist to his chest and bent at the waist, I followed suit. A quick glance at the servants and guests lined outside showed no inkling that this was the wrong thing to do, so I allowed myself to relax.

The prince spread his hands in welcome, revealing a bare chest adorned with more gold piercings and a large, twisting tattoo. As he began to speak, the servant boy translated for him.

"My honored guests, I welcome you to my home. Please allow

yourself to feel at peace here."

I combed through my memories, trying to recall the correct form of address for the Avetsi princes, but if that information ever existed in my mind, I couldn't find it.

"Thank you for your hospitality, my prince," I settled on, hoping that the Priest would translate diplomatically.

I needn't have worried. The Yellow Prince merely smiled politely as the Prince translated my greeting and continued on.

"My servants are at your disposal. Please do not hesitate to ask for anything you need. I understand you have been on the road for some time, so please take tonight to relax and have a hot bath. I'll have dinner sent to your quarters. I do hope you will join me for a meal tomorrow."

Before we could respond, the Yellow Prince turned to his servants, smile suddenly wiped from his face, and nodded once, curtly. He turned on his heel and disappeared into the palace.

The servants immediately rushed forward. Stable boys took our horses, and a pair of handmaidens—twins, or at the least sisters—strode to me and bowed. The servant boy who had translated for the prince followed sheepishly.

"Hello, my lady," he said, his voice suddenly soft and quiet. "We will attend to you. If you have any needs, please tell me directly so that I may relay them."

"I'm a bit surprised to find someone who speaks my mother tongue," I told him with a smile.

His cheeks reddened, and he looked away. "It's…it's my affinity, my lady. I know many, many tongues."

"A useful affinity indeed," I smiled. "You must be quite an important person in the palace, indeed."

He chewed the inside of his cheek, perhaps to try and keep his composure, but a slight grin broke through anyway.

Unlike my childhood home, with its cavernous corridors and muted frescoes, the Cliffside Palace was full of labyrinthine that seemed to twist and turn almost at random. In contrast to the warm colors outside, the interior of the palace were richer, deep blues and greens punctuated with ornate paintings and statues.

Finally, we reached my chambers. The servants pushed open the great wooden doors to reveal a space that was utterly unlike anything else I had seen in the palace. The entire space was muted in color, with beautiful frescoes of the goddesses adorning the walls—a surprise, given that, to my knowledge, the Avetsi didn't worship them. There was a sitting room, with a large wooden desk stocked with paper and ink. Through an interior door was the bedroom, with a large bed occupying the middle of the room and ornate quilts enticing me to sleep. There was a huge window that looked out upon a private courtyard, with more of those enormous red and orange blooms. This botanical haven was the only hint that I was in Avetsut and not back in the palace that had been my home.

To the side, there was a washroom, with a large porcelain tub already full of steaming water.

"The prince likes to host his guests from the capital here. Is this to your liking, my lady?" the servant boy asked.

"It is," I replied.

I sat at the desk and faced them. The twins stood demurely, hands folded, waiting for orders, but somehow, it felt odd to give them.

"What are your names?" I asked.

As the boy relayed my message, the girls looked at each other and back to me.

"I am Kodritse. My sister is Malen," the boy translated for them. The girls kept their gazes to the floor.

"And you?" I asked, turning to the boy.

"Oh, Tesyel," he replied with a bright smile.

Almost immediately, I took a liking to the three of them. The girls helped me undress—something that now seemed so frivolous when I was perfectly capable of undressing myself—and helped me into the steaming water. Tesyel remained in the corner of the room, eyes politely averted, to translate as the girls ensured I was comfortable.

One of the girls—Kodritse, I think—sat in a high chair behind the tub, a small basin full of hot water in her lap. She pulled my curls into the hot water and scrubbed them gently, using her fingers to comb out tangles without pulling.

At first, the girls worked without speaking. But after a few gentle questions from me, they opened up, spilling tales of their childhood in the city. Tesyel was their cousin, I learned, and the three of them had been under the care of the girls' mother until they were selected for service at the Cliffside Palace—a rarity for children with such humble blood. They'd been there for years, and they had attended dignitaries from the Avetsi principality, southern Notasi tribes, and even queens and kings from across the sea. Once they got talking, they were impossible to stop, and I closed my eyes and sighed in pleasure as their words washed over me. At a certain point, it didn't matter what they were saying, just the gentle intonation of the three of them speaking was enough to lull me into a deep calm.

The three scarcely seemed to notice that I had stopped responding. When the girls were finished bathing me, they roused me from my stupor to wrap me in a thick, warm robe. They led me to the bedroom and sat me in a chair facing the grand courtyard window and ran combs through my hair, carefully detangling it and massaging fragrant oils into my scalp. Satisfied that their work was complete, they wrapped a soft towel around my hair and tied it in a pile on the top of my head.

"We will take our leave now, if there is nothing else you require," Tesyel said with a bow.

I smiled and nodded.

The three of them were nearly to the chamber door when a thought occurred to me.

"Oh, wait!" I called.

The three turned, an expectant look plastered on each of their faces.

"Could you please send for Tsavi? I'd like to speak with him."

Tesyel translated, and the three exchanged a look and a brief word in Avetsi.

"Of course, my lady," Tesyel finally said, though he had lost his cheery smile.

* * *

I wrung my hands as I waited. Why had he refused to look at me before? The thought rattled annoyingly through my mind, and I couldn't stand it.

I walked to the window and leaned out. The night air was cool and damp, and the sea breeze tugged at me.

I hoisted myself over the window sill and sat waiting.

There was a knock on my chamber door.

"Enter," I called.

"You wanted to see me?" Tsavi's voice floated through the room. He poked his head into the room, as though not quite sure if he wanted to come in. He breathed a sigh and shuffled into the room, head down, and joined me at the window.

I paused. Suddenly, I wasn't at all sure how to talk to him. I hoped he would be the one to break the silence, but he seemed content to stand in silence.

"Have I...have I done something?" I finally asked, my voice a bit quieter than intended.

Tsavi sighed and hung his head. "I am angry at myself," he admitted.

"Why?"

"Because I was a fool. I should have known better."

"Meaning?"

He turned to face me, his pale, clouded blue eyes searching mine. It was like he was searching for something in my gaze, or perhaps he was trying to force his eyes to focus.

Finally, his eyebrows knit together as he said, "You're the missing princess. I should have fucking known. Kita. Short for Kitania?"

My jaw hung slack as realization dawned over me.

"I just assumed you were named for her. Lots of girls in the capital were. But when I saw your affinity…when I saw what you did a the base yesterday, I understood. Sun and sea, I thought the stories were lies."

"What stories?" I asked, teeth gritted.

"About the investiture ball."

I froze. He'd heard about the ball?

As if guessing my thought, he continued, "Oh, I'm sure the emperor did his best to quash the rumors. But people talk, and I make it a point to know what's happening. And when I saw that creature, I knew."

So he knew. Who I was, what I had done. The way he looked at me now, with such disdain. Heat rose in my chest.

"I didn't mean for that to happen," I muttered. But why was I trying to explain myself to him? He had murdered people in the worst possible way, forcing them to take their own lives. And yet, he sat there in judgment of me?

"It doesn't matter," he replied. He clasped his hands together and leaned forward. "Whatever you did, whatever the truth is. That doesn't matter. Don't you see? What matters is that you are Meloyra blood. You lived this wondrous life of bounty while out in the Empire, children were stolen from—" his voice caught in his throat, and I realized that he was crying. "Children were stolen from their homes.

210

Their families. I was stolen from my home. My father, murdered for trying to protect me. Pressed into service for an empire I hated. I was a child! Thirteen years old, forced to kill until I couldn't take it anymore. We stole land my people lived on for centuries for the benefit of you and your family. Eventually I deserted. But where did that leave me? Aboard a coastal ship, pressed into service again. Forced to—" he stopped, and this time, he didn't continue. He trembled so fiercely that I could feel it through the windowsill.

"I—I didn't know about that," I whispered, but I could hear how flimsy it sounded. I tried to lay a hand on his shoulder, but he batted my hand, and my response, away.

"I believe you," he said bitterly. "And I believe that you never meant harm. But it doesn't matter what you meant, or what you knew. It matters what I know. And I can't reconcile this, Kita."

I folded my hands in my lap and lowered my head. Tsavi's pain was palpable, almost physical.

"When…when I was dead," he started, his voice entirely too timid, "I saw myself murder you. Not with my words, not with my song. With my hands. With my rage. I couldn't understand why, when I saw it. But now, I think I do." He sighed and leaned his head out into the night air, closing his eyes as the breeze lifted his hair. "I did enjoy the night we shared. I wish we could have had more dances," he said quietly. "And if things were different, maybe…" he trailed off and sighed once more. "It doesn't matter. Weiran trusts you. The Priest trusts you. I trust their judgment. But please, do not call for me again."

I stared at him, trying to think of something to say. But there are some pains that words do nothing to salve, and it was clear how much I had hurt him, just by keeping silent.

"You can't help the family you were born into," he said softly, "and perhaps you being with us now is you trying to make amends. I applaud you for that, if that is indeed your aim. But there are things I can't forgive," he said, turning to leave, "no matter how unfair it might be."

21

Kita

I sipped my tea politely, glancing around the room. Weiran looked to be in a good mood, chatting jovially as he shoveled food into his mouth.

The dining room, like most of the palace, was brightly colored. The walls had been painted with bright orange and yellow pigments. The rug that ran under the table was lush and a dark purple. The table itself was a wood I'd never seen before, with a gorgeous purple tone that complimented the rug. The chairs had been upholstered with green dyed fabrics, and the tableware glittered gold.

The Yellow Prince sat to my left at the head of the table. Unlike the rest of the room, he did not eat—he sat, chin resting on his clasped hands, watching with polite interest as conversation floated through the room.

Nokinan sat directly beside me; she poked at her breakfast with her fork, not meeting anyone's gaze.

"How are the boys? Will they be joining you here?" I asked with a polite smile.

She scowled.

"No," she snapped. She grimaced, perhaps realizing her tone was a tad sharp, and added, "they'll stay in the village. They'll be safe there." She stared down at the table, her breathing a tad too quick and shallow.

"Well, I do hope you'll be able to visit them soon," I replied.

To my surprise, she looked down, tears forming in her eyes. "I had hoped to help them, when their affinities first manifest," she said, "The older boy is around the age I was when I first visited *Telombraj*."

"I'm sure you've prepared them well," I tried to reassure.

"It was terrifying the first time. I just…got unstuck from this realm, found myself in a world seemingly made of shadow. Couldn't figure out how to get back." She had a faraway look in her eye, like she wasn't really speaking to me. So, I said nothing. I wasn't sure what would help her, and the last thing I wanted was to say the wrong thing.

With Tsavi at odds with me, I didn't want to make more enemies.

"My lady, the prince is speaking to you," Tesyel muttered in my ear. I glanced up sharply to find that the Yellow Prince's eyes were locked firmly on mine.

"Oh, I apologize," I said, straightening. I took another sip of tea and forced a smile. "Tesyel, can you repeat?"

"He says, 'I have met many women from the capital, but none so lovely as you.'"

I pasted on a smile. This was nothing I had not encountered before from suitors visiting the Imperial Palace.

"I appreciate your hospitality, and thank you for your kind words," I replied. More than anything, I wanted to be elsewhere—anywhere elsewhere. But Weiran had asked me to attend breakfast, and I would do as he asked.

"Have you been to Avetsut before?" Tesyel's demeanor was completely different than it had been the night before. He was reserved, and he refused to look up to meet my gaze.

"I have not had the pleasure," I replied. I hoped my short responses would deter the man, but, of course, they did not.

"Ah, well you must allow me to show you the city. We can take a ride later in the day, if you like."

I took another sip.

Tesyel discretely tapped me on the shoulder and pointed. Weiran had taken notice of the Yellow Prince's interest. His eyes burned into the side of the prince's skull, but Prince Dahv took no notice.

"Your Excellence, have you had the opportunity to confer with the other princes?" Tesyal translated for Weiran.

Prince Dahv's expression shifted abruptly into an annoyed scowl.

"So eager to speak of official matters. The day is early. Let us enjoy our meal."

Weiran did not back down. "This cannot wait!" he exclaimed.

I stared at him, open-mouthed. If anyone had ever spoken to me that way when I lived at the palace, they would be beaten.

Dahv shrugged the outburst off and returned his attention to me.

"My lady, did you know this petulant child—" he jerked his finger in Weiran's direction—"used to run around these halls as a boy?"

My eyes flit from the prince to Weiran, who stared down at his plate like he was being chastened. And I suppose he was.

I pasted on my most diplomatic grin and replied, "No, I didn't." In fact, I knew very little about Weiran's life. He'd never mentioned anything about his childhood, and by the expression pasted on his face, he wanted nothing less than for me to be told about it.

"Yes, yes. His family were healers here for generations. His grandmother pulled me screaming into this world! We thought for sure he would follow the family path." The prince clicked his tongue and slowly shook his head.

"I see," I said politely. Why was he telling me this?

"His father and sister served here for many years, tending the gardens. Greenthumbs, you see. Gone now, of course. Left to tend new gardens, as it were."

"She doesn't need to know about them," Weiran muttered.

The Yellow Prince dismissed him with a wave.

"You see? This boy—a child of servants—thinks he can direct me."

I said nothing as Weiran seethed. The Priest laid a hand on his shoulder, but Weiran shrugged it off.

"I have done what I promised. We have removed the Imperial officers and—"

"And what? You think this is a solution to anything? That the Empire will release its grasp on our beloved land? No. They will retaliate."

"Weiran. Don't," the Priest hissed as Weiran opened his mouth to speak once more.

The pair exchanged a long look, and Weiran finally seemed to come to some decision.

"I apologize for my insolence," he said quietly. "I only ask for a public audience."

"A public audience has not been given in many years. Things have changed in your absence, young Weiran."

"For all my family has done for you and yours, this is all I ask."

It pained him to be so subordinate. He wore it plainly on his face, in the way he carried his body. The Weiran I had come to know was so clearly in control of himself, in control of everyone around us. This version of Weiran was alien. It was almost uncomfortable to watch.

"A public audience? What is that, exactly?" I asked. As Tesyel translated, Weiran shot a venomous glare, but I pretended not to see. I had lived my life surrounded by capricious fools like this Yellow Prince, and though I certainly didn't care for him, I thought I could handle him.

"Ahhh, my lady. It is a uniquely Avetsi tradition," came the reply. "In certain circumstances, the three princes hold court in front of the entire city. Citizens come to hear arguments, to witness the settlement of disputes. It is our way of listening to the people."

"It sounds rather noble," I said, lifting my teacup to my lips as I fixed my gaze on him. It was utterly transparent, what I was doing, but he didn't seem to notice. "The emperor would never dare—too afraid to listen to his people. He surrounds himself with sycophants and does as he pleases. Disgraceful, and the reason I left the Capital. Avetsut seems...much more enlightened." I did my best to pour as much flattery into my words as possible.

"Enlightened indeed! We govern for our people by listening to our people. It is our way."

Weiran's eye twitched.

"I would love to see one of these public audiences," I said. "I think it would—"

"Then you will have it!"he said, smacking his hand against the table. "You will have your public audience, and then you and I can discuss your thoughts about it—in private, of course." A lecherous smile spread across his face, the emeralds in his teeth catching the light.

My stomach clinched. I swallowed hard and, in the most enthusiastic voice I could muster, said, "Wonderful!"

Weiran blinked in surprise and, judging by the expression he wore, disbelief.

The Yellow Prince sat back, his eyes twinkling, and chuckled as he took a sip of his drink.

* * *

Kodritse and Malen greeted me with wide smiles and an abundance of energy. I eyed them with suspicion as they dragged me to the bedroom and pointed wildly at the bed.

"Goddesses all..." I muttered as I approached. A length of fine white silk laid across the bed. It was an emann. Boldly embroidered golden leaves and blooms twisted their way across the fabric. The entire piece shimmered in the late morning light.

I gingerly touched it; it was a work of art, made by someone highly skilled. A piece fit for royalty.

"You all just had this here?" I asked. To my surprise, the words caught in my throat as I stared at this well-crafted reminder of home.

"The prince was told of your arrival ahead of time. There are weavers in the bazaars that can create almost any clothing someone could ask for," Tesyel said. "I believe the prince would like to show you off. This is to be worn at the public audience."

I frowned. It was a beautiful emann, and, if adorned correctly, it would look stunning against my sun-darkened skin. But there would be no mistaking me in it; anyone who saw me would know I was from Yor-a, and would know I was highborn. Would it be that much of a stretch to assume I was the lost princess? Would word of the ball have made it this far south?

It didn't matter, I quickly realized. Weiran, for reasons he had not deigned to mention to me, wanted this public audience. I had gotten it for him, and my presence would be required. So, I would wear this emann and trust in whatever plan Weiran had created.

"I know you'll dress me to perfection," I said to the girls.

They glanced at each other and broke into wide smiles, nodding enthusiastically.

I strode to my window, looking out at the courtyard. The flowers were the size of my head, and so very vibrant. Perhaps Weiran's sister had designed this garden. I hadn't even known that he *had* a sister. Though, in some ways, I had come to view him as a friend, it was clear that I really didn't know him at all.

The thought was troubling, but I pushed it away.

"Should we go down into the city?" I asked, affecting a smile as I spun around.

The twins blinked in surprise, but Tesyel nodded.

"Have you been down to the Shadow Bazaar?" he asked. "You could buy anything there, you know."

I shrugged. "I haven't seen any of the city yet. But really, it's information I need."

"Information?" Tesyel repeated.

"I'm...I'm looking for my father," I admitted. I don't know why I decided to tell him this. He was a stranger, a member of the Yellow Prince's household. But he seemed a sweet child. Eager for...something.

"Is he here? In the city?" he asked.

"No, I don't think so. I am hoping that someone will know where I can find him."

Tesyel shrugged. "We can try," he offered hopefully.

I dug through my belongings, groping around until I found the pouch of topaz beads.

"I don't have coin," I started as I opened the pouch, running my fingers over the cool, faceted surfaces. "Only these." I dumped the pouch onto the silk, the brown gems glittering in the sunlight.

All three of them stopped and stared.

Kodritse muttered something, and Tesyel swatted her arm in response.

"What?" I asked.

"Is this...are these real gems?"

"Of course!" I said.

"Put that away," Tesyel whispered, shoveling the gems back into their pouch.

I frowned. "What are you doing?" I asked.

"My lady, you cannot bring these to the Bazaar."

"Why?"

"Because! This...this is too much." He took one of the small beads

219

and held it up to the light. "This will buy anything you need. Leave the rest."

He had a strained, desperate look on his face. So, rather than argue, I did as he suggested, and returned most of the gems to their pouch.

"Alright, we'll just take these," I said, holding up three of the smallest stones I could find.

Tesyel didn't look satisfied, but he nodded. "Information then?"

"Information," I said.

"This...this is a dangerous thing to seek, my lady."

"Nonetheless, it's what I need. I need to know about the Notasi Tribes. Have you heard of them?"

He furrowed his brow, but nodded. "Their people come here often, selling old relics. Someone will know of them."

* * *

I thought the Bazaar would be similar to the market district of the Capital. Nothing could be further from the truth. The market district was small, and mainly agricultural. The Shadow Bazaar seemed to stretch as far as I could see, with vendors selling goods of all sorts. And it was only one of several bazaars, from what I could tell.

Tesyel darted into the crowd, zipping past people with a focus I had not seen from him before. It was all I could do to keep up.

Eventually, he led me to a side street, and for a moment I wondered if he was leading me into some sort of trap. He quickly glanced over his shoulder—left, then right—and grabbed my wrist, pulling me into a nondescript wooden door.

Inside was a small, mostly bare shop. A few trinkets hung from bent hooks in the walls; nothing of much value. A gaunt, bored-looking woman leaned across the counter, eyes focused on nothing in particular.

Tesyel launched into a torrent of Avetsi. I tried to look as though I was engaged with the conversation, like the barrage of percussive syllables meant something to me.

The shopkeeper slowly blinked, seeming to notice us for the first time. She rolled her eyes and drummed her fingers against the counter. When Tesyel finished speaking she fixed him with a look of annoyance and tried to shoo him away.

"Give her a gem," Tesyel whispered.

Obediently, I fished in my pack and unearthed one of the topazes, placing it gently on the counter.

The woman stared at the stone, jaw hanging slack. She leaned in close, so close that her nose nearly touched the topaz. Gingerly, she tapped at it with a finger, rolling it along the counter.

I had no idea what she was trying to ascertain, but, apparently satisfied, she swept the gem into her other hand and pocketed it.

In a slow, choppy cadence, she began to speak. Tesyel watched her with rapt attention, occasionally asking a question. It was everything I could do not to interject.

Finally, she stopped talking and waved us away. Tesyel flashed a wide smile and pulled me back outside.

"What did she say?" I muttered as he led me back to the Bazaar.

"When we return to the palace," he sang. His chipperness was almost irritating, but I obeyed.

He eased his pace as we melted back into the crowd of the Bazaar.

"Wait," I said as he strolled past the myriad booths.

He turned, an eyebrow raised, and I asked, "Do you want anything? Or do you think your cousins might?"

His cheeks burned red as he averted his gaze.

"N-no, my lady," he muttered, rubbing his arm. "It's forbidden."

I wanted to protest, but he rushed off before I could, forcing me to follow or be swallowed by the sea of people.

As we made our way back to the cliffside, I watched the bazaar. As I observed, it struck me just how…desperate the people seemed. At home—no, the capital was not my home anymore, I reminded myself—the market district held a relaxed atmosphere; people sold their wares as shoppers strolled by. Sometimes, they closed early in the day, content to attend other business or travel out to the farmlands.

Here, the pulsating masses swarmed the stalls, shoving coin, if they had it, or any valuables they possessed into sellers' eager hands. And the stalls hawking luxuries—gorgeous silks, beaded jewels, kohls and lip stains—were mostly passed over in favor of those selling fish and grains. People pushed past each other, screaming, even crying when stores ran dry.

I asked Tesyel about it, when we arrived back in my apartments.

He responded with a head tilt. "What do you mean, my lady?" he asked. "The people are hungry." He said it as if it were the most obvious thing anyone could have ever asked.

"Perhaps I just don't understand the value of money," I offered tentatively.

He just sighed. "Is a full belly not the most valuable thing there could be?"he asked, and I conceded the point.

"And the information we bought?" I asked.

He rushed to the door and put his ear to it, listening intently for several seconds.

"Okay then," he breathed as he turned back to me. "The Notasi are nomadic. They move often, never settling at one place, so it's hard to nail them down."

"But your contact knows where they are?" I asked, rubbing my hands together.

Tesyel moved his head back and forth. "As I said, the Notasi come here often. Unfortunately, the last trading party just left a few weeks ago. They won't be back for months. But she heard from them that they're uncovered some relics—very, very valuable relics, according to her. Apparently the next trading party will be very large, with a great deal to trade."

"Okay?" I replied. I cared about nothing so little as I cared about relics.

"It means they won't be here for some time, but they *will* be in the same place until their relics are secured."

"And she knows this place?"

"Well, vaguely. The Notasi are protective of their secrets, but she said that she knows it to be near Oryn-Tal. She said something about an outpost that is supposedly the last stop before reaching the city, but she didn't know the name of it."

Oryn-Tal. The City That Looks Upon the Desert. I searched through my memory for some information. It was a city in the far south—one of the free cities, as Avetsut once was. Beyond that, I knew very little. Not even its location; just a general idea.

But it was a start.

I pulled the boy into an embrace. He stiffened, but I held him. I feared if I let him go, the tears would start.

He softened, and melted into my arms, squeezing with all his body weight in the way that only children can.

* * *

I found myself wandering the halls of the palace, not searching for anything in particular. The Cliffside Palace was labyrinthine, with halls melting into each other, each turn leading to a new corridor with drastic changes in wall color, artwork, and even feel of the floor under my feet.

I heard something. Someone, speaking—no, arguing. My curiosity getting the better of me, I followed the sound to a nondescript door. Opening it, I found myself in an interior courtyard, enormous orange and yellow blooms swaying slightly in the wind.

Weiran sat cross-legged in the center of the courtyard. His eyes were squeezed shut, his hands clapped over his ears as he spoke. He switched back and forth between the Imperial tongue and Avetsi, and I got the sense that he was talking to multiple people, but he spoke so quickly that even when speaking Imperial, I could only make out a few words here and there.

Moving quietly, I sank to the ground beside him.

"Reach into my pack," he said through gritted teeth, and I realized he was talking to me. I did as he asked, digging into the small bag lying on the ground in front of him and pulling out a handful of mostly dried herbs.

Without looking, he snatched them from my hands and shoved them into his mouth, chewing so quickly that streams of green juice ran down his chin. His trembling stopped, breathing slowed, and finally sighed and dropped his hands.

"Is it...is it nice to be home?" I ventured, trying to distract him from whatever torment had claimed him.

"This place is not my home," he whispered. "And in case you are entertaining any fond thoughts of my family and the Yellow Prince, allow me to clarify. My mother is missing, taken for her skills as a healer by the Empire. I have no idea whether she lives or dies. I looked for her during my time in the Empire. But with nowhere to begin, I have no idea. My sister and father are dead, though the Yellow Prince pretends otherwise. I keep my affinity close, so he couldn't know that I know, but my sister has been with me for some time. A simple fever claimed them, if you can believe it. If my mother had been here, they would have lived. She was very skilled. Most healers can heal injuries, but treating illnesses is another matter. Mother could have saved them, if she wasn't traded away by the Yellow Prince."

"I'm sorry to hear that, Weiran. Truly."

He glanced at me, his amber eyes full of sadness and rage.

"It doesn't matter," he said, looking away. "We've got our public audience, which is the only thing I needed from this wretched man. We don't need to deal with him past tomorrow."

I knew better than to ask what his next steps were. Instead, I said, "things are coming to an end, then."

He blinked in surprise. "No," he said, "not an end. A beginning. Years of planning are about to come to fruition, and you're going to be a part of it."

"For me, I meant. This is where we part ways, isn't it?"

He turned away. "Is that what you want? Truly?"

"I have been honest, Weiran. I have to find my father. You knew this. I may have a lead now, and I have to follow it."

He nodded and replied, "I know. But it was worth asking." He clapped me on the back, fixing me with a smile that seemed oddly sad.

"The Priest tells me our mission was a success," I said.

Weiran's lips curled into a smile. "Oh yes," he said. "The Empire underestimates us. When they took the principality, they killed the most senior officers in our army. But they left the rest of the power structure intact. It is a strategy that has worked for them elsewhere. Kill the head, replace it with your own. The men will fall in line. And for a long time, they did. But they do not know the spirit of the Avetsi people. We will not be kept under imperial rule forever." As he spoke, his gaze seemed to shift. It was as though he was speaking not just to me, but the entire city.

"So you got what you wanted. The Avetsi military will support your cause?"

He chuckled. "Just wait until tomorrow. Everything will come into sharp focus. I promise you."

A bit unsteadily, he got to his feet, brushing away the dirt and slinging his pack across his shoulder.

"Tomorrow, then," I said. And then he was gone, leaving me alone among the blooms.

22

Ran

Being in Avetsut brought back so many memories.

Not memories of Avetsut; the city was still somewhat of a mystery to him. But as he sat on a dock of the Avetsi Bay, water lapping against his toes, he thought of his mother.

She'd taken him to visit her hometown of Cala, a city to the northwest of Yor-a. He'd been just a boy then, beginning to come into his affinity, and she sat with him on the docks, watching the ships roll in and out. She'd held him tight as the gulls squawked overhead. Every few minutes, a bird would swoop down, spearing a fish before climbing into the sky once more.

He'd been scared of the ocean then. It felt so big, so hungry as the waves crashed against docks and cliffs and sands, swallowing whatever it could.

She'd hugged him to her and whispered, "we may not be worldmakers like your ancestors, but that doesn't mean we have to fear. Come." She'd taken him into her arms and walked to the edge of the dock. He yelped as she stuck one foot over the edge, burying his face in her chest, waiting for the ocean to swallow them.

But the water didn't take them. As he'd tentatively opened an eye, he gasped as he realized that they were walking on the surface.

"Do you want to try?" she asked, ruffling his hair.

But he'd been too scared.

That was then. Now? The ocean was his. It belonged to him. It could not harm him. It couldn't drag him underneath. He could simply force it to spit him back out. There was nothing there to fear.

The wind picked up, tearing at his hair. He liked this city. He liked the sea. He liked the bazaars. He liked the people, their earnestness; their spirit.

And he liked the anonymity. Sitting there in the morning sun, he could almost forget his purpose.

Almost.

"Hello, lovely prince," Aka's voice called, cutting through his reverie. He rubbed his eyes and turned to face her.

As angry as he'd been at the Eastern Fort, his malice toward her had melted. She was too amiable. And besides, it was hard to fault her for what she had done at the Eastern Fort. Like Obaye, Aka had been at the mercy of the Commandant.

"Anything?" he asked.

The beserker flopped down beside him and shook her head.

"Don't worry about it," she said. "If she was traveling with a group as we suspect, it might have taken them a long time to get here, even if they had a head start.

"I'm not worried," he lied. They'd been in the city for over a week, and none of their searching had materialized anything. Try as he might, he couldn't quite shake his dread.

"As you say," Aka replied, dipping her head.

"You've spent some time in this city, haven't you?" he asked.

"Indeed. Hard not to, when you travel between the empire and the lands to the south."

"Perhaps there's someone you know, then. Someone who would

have intimate knowledge of all the goings on."

Aka stretched her arms high above her head and sighed. "This is a big city, princeling. There is much to know. Hard to focus on what might be important. Maybe you could petition one of the princes? They're loyal to the empire."

"Nominally, at least," he muttered. He didn't trust the princes, not really. When the empire took Avetsut, they hadn't fought. They'd capitulated without bloodshed. Certainly, it was a decision that aligned with the empire's interests, but Ran's father had seen the move for what it was—self interest. The emperor didn't trust them, and neither did Ran, especially not when he was in the city alone.

"Then what would you suggest?" Aka asked.

Ran hesitated. He found himself missing Ditan's company. The shadowwalker was gone, searching the city in his own way. Ran felt his absence acutely. Even when Ditan observed him from the shadows, Ran always sensed his presence. He hadn't realized just how comforting that was until now, when he didn't feel it.

Now, despite sitting shoulder to shoulder with Aka, he felt alone.

What would his father say, if he were there? Did his father even *know* he was there? He'd sent word with a messenger in one of the crossroads towns they'd passed through, but he hadn't waited for word to come back.

Ran clasped his hands together. He had to find Kita. He had to bring her home. There was no other option. But Avetsut was so big, and he had no idea how to search it.

"Perhaps you should allow yourself some grace," Aka said, perhaps sensing his apprehension. "You are attempting something very difficult. To find one woman in a city this large, when you know nothing of her plans? Trust yourself. Trust your shadowwalker. Allow yourself to breathe."

Ran sighed. He didn't really want to talk about it. "Can you tell me how you came into the service of my family?" he asked, changing the subject.

Aka's face turned stony, and she crossed her arms.

"I already told you," she said. "My kind has served the Melyora family for generations. We were cursed by a worldmaker."

"Yes, you told me that already," he said. It was still so hard to believe. The worldmakers...beings with the ability to shape reality. He'd always had doubts that they'd actually existed. If they had, why was there still such conflict in the world? Starvation? Drought? Why hadn't they solved it?

Yet Aka certainly believed herself to be bound by them.

"Then what more is there to say?" she replied.

"I mean...that was so long ago," he said. "How are *you* forced into this?"

"I do not know how the worldmakers' affinity worked. All I know is that I have always felt called to Yor-a. From the time I was just a cub, I was pulled in that direction. We all feel it at some point, that call. My parents tried to stop me. They understood what I did not. If they could only prevent me from going, perhaps they could delay my servitude. But the pull grows strong, you see. I left home and wandered north until I reached Yor-a. And do you know, they were waiting for me?"

"For you, specifically?"

"For me, or my kind. I barely spoke to them before they brought me before the emperor himself. Imagine that! Being a young thing, having left home for the first time, and you get brought before the most powerful person in your world." Her voice was harsh; bitter. "That was many years ago. Before your father was even born."

Ran balked. She didn't look that old to him, though he'd heard that the beserkers aged differently than most other people.

"It's better now than it was. In those days, I could scarcely leave the palace. I always had to be under the emperor's feet. I know it's your home, but I despise that place. Too closed up, too...civilized. I prefer the fields."

"And...your children?"

The corners of her lips twitched. "Three of them. Two boys and a girl. Your father was kind to me when he was crowned. He let me go home. I finally had freedom again. But when I got there, my parents were dead. My pride was so different than it had been when I left. New leaders. Friends gone, trapped in their own servitude. I didn't really recognize it. I was lucky, though."

"What, you found love?"

She barked a laugh. "I thought so at the time. I had my children at least. The boys will be off with their own prides now." She hung her head, clasping her hands together. "If the emperor calls them, they'll be compelled to come. So far, he hasn't, as far as I know. My service has been enough. My greatest hope is that they can live their lives unencumbered by this curse. But my parents had that same hope for me and my siblings, and we see how that turned out. My siblings, all killed in military action. And me, forced into allegiance to an empire I care nothing about."

Ran swallowed. "I am sorry to hear that," he said. "I never knew about this...compulsion. I swear it."

Aka sighed and leaned back, staring up at the clear blue sky.

"You fail to understand, lovely prince. It doesn't matter what you knew. It doesn't matter what your father knew. This is just the way of the world. This is the curse our people bear. And do you know what? We live anyway. We love anyway. Even knowing our children will be born into the same bondage, we have them anyway. Does that make us fools?" She turned to him, her eyes wide and earnest.

"I have no interest in forcing your compliance," Ran said. "I don't want to be the kind of emperor that has to force his subjects to follow."

Aka snorted. "You say this now. Kazin said it too. He wasn't always the hard man he is now. But like him, you understand little. I did not leave the Eastern Fort because I wished to, though I was, in the end, happy to do so."

"Then why?"

"Because the safety of the Meloyra heir is paramount. Whatever orders the emperor gave me—to follow the will of the Eastern Fort Commandant—I was drawn to you, young princeling. Not because I wished to be. But because that is the way of the world. That is the way the worldmakers made it. I am compelled to ensure your safety. So, you see, it matters little what you say. It matters little that you are a good man—and after traveling with you a while, I do believe you are. But your assurances mean nothing to me. In this matter, you are as powerless as I am. Do you see now?"

Ran ground his teeth, but did not answer.

Aka laughed, a loud bark of laugh. "Come now, Ran. Stop stressing yourself. Your princess will show herself. And do not worry about me. I understand how my life works."

"Wait," Ran replied, a thought crossing his mind. "If you are so compelled to follow me, to follow my family, is there some way to sense her? If it is as you say, and you are forced to follow the Melyora, can't you follow her?"

Aka cocked her head. "I don't think it works that way, lovely prince. At least..." she trailed off, closing her eyes and lying back into the wood of the dock. For several moments, she was quiet, breathing in and out.

"I feel you, Ran," she finally muttered. "Strongly. You are a blazing fire, roaring right in front of my face. But..." She trailed off, the cool sea air hanging between them. "But I think, perhaps, she is near."

Ran got to his feet, wiping his hands on his trousers. Kita was close. He would recover her. Everything would be as it should.

"Will you walk with me?" Ran asked, holding a hand out to Aka.

"Where?" she asked.

In response, he took her hand, helping her to her feet.

With a smile, he turned to the bay, and took a step he'd been too afraid to make with his mother.

23

Kita

It had been quite some time since I had felt so regal. Kodritse and Malen wound the white silk emann as though they did it every day, twisting and folding the fabric so expertly that they hardly needed pins to keep it in place. They braided my hair with great care, fingers moving so quickly that it was like having a team of servants working. Though we refrained from adding jewels, the finished style was elegant, noble, and exceedingly imperial.

They produced a number of bangles, slipping them onto my wrists and ankles so that every movement I made produced little tinkles of noise.

"These belong to the prince. They were his mother's," Tesyel said as he inspected them. "They'll be gifted to his wife, once the emperor sees fit to find him one."

"I didn't know such a match was under the emperor's purview," I murmured. This was a lie, of course. I knew very well how very interested my grandfather was in cementing the bond between capital and the Avetsi isthmus.

There was a knock on the door. Before I could respond, Tesyel was there, poking his head out. There were hushed whispers, and Tesyel shut the door once more.

"My lady, your presence has been requested by Lord Weiran," he said.

The girls followed close behind as Tesyel led me through the twisting corridors until I found myself in the front courtyard.

Weiran was sharply dressed in the Avetsi style. He wore fine black trousers with a long, loose-fitted, emerald green linen shirt. Behind him, roaming among the flowers, was the Priest, who had swapped his worn vestments with new black linens.

There was another man there, a soldier by the look of him, who spoke in a rapid string of Avetsi as Weiran nodded along.

When they noticed me, Weiran broke into a wide smile and bounded over.

"Kita!" he called, clapping me on the back. "Good of you to come."

"Who is this?" I replied, nodding toward the soldier, who was shifting his weight from side to side, evidently uncomfortable at my intrusion.

"Ah, not to worry," Weiran said, his fingers digging into my shoulder. "*Maesi tsa,* Tesyel. You can leave us now," he said, turning toward the young interpreter.

Tesyel glanced at me, unsure, but I gave him a reassuring smile and he quietly returned to the palace, the girls following close behind.

"Kita, allow me to introduce the new Lord Commander of the Avetsi Guard. Hiran Liage."

I dipped my head politely, and the soldier waited for Weiran to translate before taking my hand and planting a gentle kiss upon it.

"Commander Liage will be at the public audience; there were just a few logistics left to handle." He spoke a few more words, and the Lord Commander turned on his heels and headed down the long drive toward the city.

"What is it that you want?" I asked once the soldier had disappeared from view.

"This is a momentous day," he replied.

I raised an eyebrow. A nonanswer. I'm not sure why I would expect anything different.

"Care to elaborate?" I asked. "Why is this so important anyway?"

"Today is the culmination of years of work and planning."

"Most of which you have not deigned to share," I muttered.

He ignored me and continued. "Kita, everything is falling into place. You've played your part beautifully, and I can only thank you."

I glanced at the Priest, who wore his typical stony face. He locked eyes with me for just a moment before returning to the flowers.

"Well, I do appreciate you having allowed me to travel with you. I'll miss you all as I journey forward."

"Yes, you'll want to move on, of course. I heard you took the boy into the city to ask around. I wish you would have asked me first."

My eyes narrowed. "I didn't see that it was your business, Weiran."

My annoyance did nothing to dent his smile, though I detected a spark in his eyes.

"Did you think about the fact that you're a fugitive in a city where you do not speak the language, flashing jewels that clearly mark you as an important person? You're fortunate that nothing happened. The boy led you well. He likes you. What if he didn't?"

I grit my teeth. He was probably right, but that didn't make it any less annoying.

"What did you find out?" he asked.

"I have a direction. Nothing more."

"Indeed." Weiran smirked and turned away, joining the Priest near the flowers. He examined a bloom carefully, lifting it to his nose and inhaling its scent as he continued, "I think the boy is probably trustworthy. He's a good lad. He wants to do well in this world."

"Is this all you wanted?" I asked, crossing my arms. "Because I'm sure there are many things I could be doing."

"There are just a few things I wished to tell you before we make our final preparations. First, I ask that, no matter what you see on the stage, you remain calm. There are a great many things riding on the success of this public audience. Everyone is necessary, especially you. There may be things you don't understand, but I ask you to trust me. Trust us."

"How can I when you won't tell me anything?"

Again, he ignored my protest and continued, "Secondly, I have some information of my own to give you. The crown prince has been spotted in the city. You're still being hunted. I would refrain from leaving the palace unless you're with us."

My heart clenched. Ran was here?

"Was he…" I swallowed. "Was he alone?"

"No," Weiran replied. "He's been seen talking to a beserker. Hmm. Imagine that."

What? A beserker? This didn't make sense. Why?

Over the course of my travels, I had allowed myself to forget about Ran. I had imagined that I was safe from him, from my grandfather. I knew going home was not an option, but I had thought that I could escape. But he was here? He had managed to track me down?

"I…" I trailed off, not sure what to say. My thoughts were twisting, and just the mention of Ran was sending me into a spiral. My heart pounded. The beast began to stir. Flashes from the ball forced their way into my mind. I thought I had put those thoughts away, but the face of the boy who had asked me to dance was suddenly as vivid as it had been the night of the ball. The ground beneath me began to churn.

"Kita." The Priest's monotone voice broke through. I hadn't noticed him approach, but he placed a hand on my shoulder and said, "breathe. You're safe."

I looked up at him and nodded, forcing air into my lungs. As he whispered words of encouragement, I nodded, shaking out my hands and feet.

Weiran watched with mild interest, apparently unperturbed. His face was unreadable. I wanted him to say something, to acknowledge anything, but he did not.

A few moments later, three carriages pulled up to the front doors of the palace, each pulled by black horses dressed in jeweled harnesses. The doors to the palace swung open, and the Yellow Prince strode out, followed by Nokinan, Tsavi, and others I did not recognize.

The Yellow Prince smiled broadly as he saw me. He took me by the hand and led me to the front carriage. Weiran was quick to join us. The Yellow Prince's grin faltered slightly, but he did not protest.

He spoke politely as we rode down the cliffside road—or, at least, Weiran translated everything politely. I responded with pleasantries of my own, staring out the window as the horses pulled us along.

The carriages moved slowly. The streets were filled with people, none of whom seemed interested in moving for the horses.

"Are all of these people headed for the public audience?" I asked.

"Many of them, yes," Weiran replied.

"How long has it been?"

Weiran barely concealed his irritation as he translated, "seven or eight years. Evidently the practice stopped once the Empire took control."

* * *

The amphitheater was far larger in person than it appeared from the top of the cliffs. Hundreds of Avetsi were already there, with more and more arriving by the moment.

The Yellow Prince offered his arm, and I took it, trying desperately not to search the crowds. If Weiran was right and Ran was in town, it seemed likely that he would be in attendance.

I walked arm in arm with the Yellow Prince, listening vaguely as he spoke, until we climbed the steps to the stage.

Already waiting were two ornately dressed men seated on what appeared to be stone thrones. One of them was around the Yellow Prince's age or perhaps a bit older, wearing a fine purple cape and golden jewelry adorning his body. The other was a young man, barely out of childhood. He was dressed a bit more sedately in black and white linens and a single gold ring through his eyebrow.

"Good afternoon my lady," the younger man said with a smile. I was about to introduce myself when the Yellow Prince ushered me toward the third stone throne. He lowered himself into the seat and pat the armrest. Obediently, I took up position next to him.

Weiran and the others remained downstairs in front of the stage. I watched intently as Weiran whispered furiously first into Tsavi's ear and then into Nokinan's. Nokinan nodded and dissolved into the closest shadow, while Tsavi turned and watched the crowd.

"I'll translate for you," a voice in my ear muttered.

I jumped at the Priest's sudden appearance. I hadn't noticed him come up onto the stage.

"How is this going to work?" I muttered.

"In a moment, one of the princes will call the audience to order. Then Weiran will be allowed to speak."

"What does he hope to accomplish?"

"By the end of the day, if all goes well, Avetsut will declare its independence."

I blinked. He hoped to be that persuasive?

The Yellow Prince rose and stepped forward. He rose an arm and called out, his voice ringing through the amphitheater.

"Citizens of our beloved city," the Priest translated, "we gather together today to engage in one of our city's most treasured traditions. The public audience."

He stared down at Weiran and beckoned him up.

Weiran bowed, the picture of meekness as he climbed. Tsavi slid around the wall of the stage, quietly moving out of sight as Weiran turned to face the gathered masses.

Whispers rippled through the crowd as Weiran smirked and began to speak.

"My people," the Priest translated, "this city, this principality. This is my home. There is nothing in this life that means more to me than this place. This is why I wanted to speak to you. Ever since the Empire has taken control of our city, our people have gone hungry. Our children have been conscripted. All the while, the princes have grown fat on our suffering. Look at them. Look at them!"

I nervously glanced at the princes. To my horror, they watched dispassionately, evidently unbothered by his words.

Gooseflesh rose on the back of my neck as realization creeped over me.

"What is this?" I hissed at the Priest, but he did not acknowledge me.

"These sycophants have allowed the empire to take our city with no resistance, handing over control of our city guard, of our farms, of our money. Handing over control of our home. Of you!"

The crowd watched with rapt attention, scarcely making a sound as they watched.

"The Empire and these fools have underestimated us," Weiran continued. He waved a hand behind him and from the shadows, Nokinan appeared, imperial officers on each arm. She disappeared again and returned with more soldiers, until the area in front of the princes was full of officers captured from the fort a few nights before.

"What is he doing?" I demanded.

"Kita, please," he replied, his teeth gritted. "Don't make things more difficult."

"What are you talking about?"

A glint of light caught my eye, and my head snapped forward in time to see Weiran raise a familiar tiger claw knife.

I tried to rush forward, but my legs would not obey. It was then I realized that a low, droning voice was singing a single clear note.

"I am sorry about this," the Priest muttered.

Before I could respond or protest, the breath caught in my chest. It was as though I was being dragged underwater and suddenly all the nerves, all the worries I had felt were gone. All the emotions that had been building were sucked away, leaving only my body standing still on the stage.

I watched as Weiran dragged the first officer forward. The man was ragged, his face wet with tears. Weiran raised the knife and lowered it to the man's throat, and the officer slumped forward, twitching for a moment and then lying still. The crowd erupted into screams. Some shrieks of horror, many more cheers.

Each of the officers was dispatched in turn. Weiran's hand and sleeve dripped with gore, and I watched on, unperturbed.

Around the ampitheater, some of the Avetsi Guard drew weapons, but they were few. The rest of the guard were too quick, and they easily dispatched the dissenters.

My mind, sluggish though it was in that moment, began to put together what was happening. A coup. An actual coup. No wonder Weiran had been so giddy.

Tsavi's voice shifted. He maintained the note rooting me to my spot, but somehow seemed to add an additional song on top of it, his voice layering in on itself. The first of the princes—the older prince in the purple robes—rose from his seat and walked dreamily forward, a smile on his face.

The expression on Weiran's face had changed. His eyes blazed, his mouth was twisted into a sneer. It occurred to me that I should be afraid, but I wasn't.

Weiran grabbed the prince's arm and dragged him forward, to the very edge of the stage. He snarled, "These men have made a mockery of us. They have committed the greatest of treasons, and they will be punished." Then he lifted the knife to the prince's throat and slashed, pushing the prince's body out into the crowd as they bayed for blood.

The young princeling was next, and though he walked smoothly forward, his eyes darted furiously around, as though he was hoping someone could save him. I could do nothing but watch as he, too, was cast into the crowd.

The Yellow Prince was last, and Weiran stared hard at the man who had been our host. His disdain for the man had been clear, but it had become evident that it was more than contempt. He truly, truly hated this man. He lifted the knife slowly, allowed it to bite into Yellow Prince's flesh, and whispered something into his ears before ending the triumvirate for good.

The crowd was raucous by now; those in the front rushed forward, trying to rip the clothing and jewelry from the princes' bodies. It occurred to me that some of this reaction could be Tsavi's doing, though I had no way of knowing for sure.

"This city is ours, and I assure you that I will not allow us to be taken advantage of any longer. I will protect us from the Empire. This is my promise to you. But we are not finished yet."

Weiran turned toward us. His hair was mussed, his face and tunic spattered with blood. His eyes blazed still, but there was something else in his face that I couldn't quite decipher.

The Priest laid a gently hand on my shoulder and lightly pushed me forward. I followed his lead, walking toward the front of the stage.

Rationally, I knew that something was wrong, but I couldn't bring myself to care.

"This woman is Kitania sa Isali Melyora. Fourth in line to the Imperial Throne, and—"the Priest abruptly stopped translating.

I turned to face him, and for perhaps the first time since I had known him, there was emotion on his face. Confusion, combined with something else—surprise? How curious, that our positions had switched. Was this how he felt all the time?

He muttered something to Weiran, but Weiran did not acknowledge him. Instead, he grabbed me painfully by the forearm and hauled me forward.

For a moment, he turned, locking eyes with mine. I knew then what he was going to do, but I couldn't have stopped him if I wanted to, not with the Priest and Tsavi both working against me. And with the Priest's influence, I truly didn't want to.

He raised the knife to my throat. He hesitated, swallowing hard as he looked me in the eye.

"You have done us a great service," he whispered, and then the knife bit, cold and deep into my flesh. "Thank you."

He jerked the knife free. I didn't even feel the pain as hot blood spurted from the wound, choking me as it flowed back into my lungs.

All the strength evaporated from my legs and I felt myself falling. He caught me and lowered me gently to the ground.

"Kita!" I heard, or I thought I heard, and I looked out to the crowd. Someone was running toward the stage, and I tried to focus my eyes, but the harder I looked, the more darkness seemed to creep into my vision.

Someone appeared abruptly in front of the running man. He crashed into the sudden figure, but before they hit the ground, they were gone, leaving nothing but shadow.

My eyelids grew heavy, and though I tried, I couldn't keep them open any more. I sputtered and coughed, took one more ragged breath, and then...

Nothing.

24

Ran

Ran crashed to the ground, the weight of another person crushing the breath from his lungs. His instinctively flung the body aside, struggling to draw air.

He groaned and pushed himself up, only to realize that he couldn't see.

He blinked as his eyes slowly adjusted to the darkness.

The darkness? It was the midday. He turned to look at the person who had hit him, but he was suddenly alone.

"By all the goddesses," he muttered as he looked around. The ground was slick and shiny black. His hand slipped as he tried to push himself up, painfully wrenching his shoulder.

"Ditan?" he shouted, but the darkness seemed to swallow his voice.

He carefully got to his feet and scanned the environment. In the distance, there were enormous structures that looked almost like buildings, though they were made of the same slick black material as the ground and slightly shone in the dim light.

"Ditan!" he screamed, so loud that it hurt his voice.

As he listened for a response, he realized that he heard voices. They were quiet, as though they were talking loudly far away. He strained to listen, but he couldn't make out what was being said.

He tried to put the whispers out of his mind as he walked. There was no way to mark time; though it was as bright as a full moonlit night, there were no moon or stars overhead.

He walked, and walked, and walked, and yet the strange obsidian cityspace in the distance did not seem to get any closer.

"Don't wander," a feminine voice muttered close to his ear.

He threw up his hands, turning the air around him solid, but as he turned, there was no one there.

"I'm the only one who knows where you are," the voice said, but again, there was no one there when he turned.

He slid into a fighter's stance, listening intently, but all he could hear were the distant voices.

"Listen carefully, *my prince*," the voice spat.

Ran spun, and this time, there was a young woman standing before him, her golden hair almost shining in the darkness. She wore an expression of pure malice, and he recognized her as the shadowwalker who had produced the imperial officers at the public audience.

"If you get lost, there will be no one to find you. This place is not meant for people like you. It will drive men to madness. So, by all means, if you wish to lose your mind and wander Telombraj for the rest of your pathetic life, then walk."

Ran grit his teeth as wrath welled within him.

"You and your group of terrorists murdered my niece," he said, surprising himself with how calm he sounded. "I will kill every one of you."

The shadowwalker frowned and crossed her arms. "The era of the Melyora is coming to an end," she said.

They were going to kill him, he realized. They had murdered Kita in front of a crowd, and they would do the same to him. He was a fool. He had been so single-minded on finding Kita that nothing else had mattered. And now, the future of the empire itself was in question.

Isa was still alive, he reassured himself. There was still an heir. And there was still a chance he could get out of this.

But not by doing what he was told.

He closed his eyes and reached with his affinity, allowing himself to feel the air as it traveled into her lungs. He clenched his fists, and solidified the oxygen as she breathed it.

His eyes snapped open as her expression changed from one of triumph to confusion and then terror. Her chest spasmed as she tried to breathe and instead choked on solid air. He stared directly into her eyes, watching closely as her eyes flit wildly from side to side. She reached for him, but he as she reached for him, he stepped around her grasp. Her eyelids fluttered and she fell to her knees, scratching at her throat.

He would have killed her. It made sense to kill her. If they didn't have her, they couldn't reach him, and there was a chance that Ditan would find him, no matter how remote that chance was. But as he watched the life begin to drain from her eyes, he noticed just how young she looked. Suddenly, she wasn't a confident, capable shadowwalker, but a scared young woman, younger than him or Kita by a few years at least.

He thought of the Commandant, and her twisted smile when he had almost killed her the same way.

"By all the goddesses," he muttered as he relaxed his grip.

She sputtered a cough and gulped down air as fast as she could, crawling shakily away from him as she stared at him, wide eyed and terrified.

He met her gaze with as much fierceness as he could muster and kneeled over her.

"I am going to kill you all," he said, his voice steely. "You'll die, choking on your own breath. And I assure you that it will be a mercy compared to what my father will do."

He stood over her, his heart racing.

She disappeared.

"By all the goddesses," he muttered to himself. "What a fool you are, Ranjali."

Ran fell to his knees. Tears welled in his eyes. Tears for Kita, tears for himself.

And those damnable voices, whispering, screaming, always just out of his audible range. Glimpses of light and movement pulled a the very corners of his vision, but each time he moved his head, there was nothing there.

He remembered his mother. She was the kindest of them all. When his affinity first manifested, and he would slip through the floors, she would be there to comfort him, and then to teach.

As he sat there in the darkness, heart pounding, voices boring into his very being, he tried to focus on the things she had taught him.

"Reach out with your hands and touch the ground. Focus on the feel of it. Reach deeper. Focus on the tiny particles and push them aside. They will respond to you."

He reached his fingers into the stone and gently swirled his fingers. The rock liquefied under his touch, soothing his battered nerves. He closed his eyes, meditating on the feeling of the fluid stone, and listened, trying to parse the voices.

At first, he couldn't make anything out. But the longer he listened, the more individual words stood out. He realized that they were mostly speaking Avetsi. He wasn't fluent enough to understand, but it was still a small comfort. Dozens, maybe hundreds of Avetsi voices, lapping over each other like water flowing over a cliff, splashing chaos on the rocks below. He thought that, maybe, after a while, he could tune them out.

He slipped his hand free and flexed his fingers. He was confident in his fighting skills, but Kita had a far more powerful affinity than his, and she had been killed with no effort.

They had a siren. He'd heard the notes, been riled with the crowd. He'd bayed for blood with the rest of them, despite the insanity of it all. So, if this siren returned, that's where he'd need to strike first.

But if he stayed where he was, he had no chance. He had to get far enough away so that their shadowwalker couldn't find him. Hope not to get hopelessly lost himself. Simple enough.

He sighed and got up, surveying the land in front of him. The strange obsidian city loomed large. If he walked toward it, there was a chance.

Onward he went.

25

Kita

Describing my death is somewhat like trying to describe love to someone who has never experienced emotion. There was nothing, the complete cesession of sight, smell, or touch. I had nothing to perceive with, so I didn't.

And yet, there was everything. Every thought I had ever had, every memory. Everything that had ever happened to me, or even things that might have been, all happening at once. All happening not at all.

Each thread of my life, woven together in a strange tapestry.

I pulled a thread and saw—but did not see—my father. He was a plain looking man, with smooth dark skin and a thick scar over his left eye, which was missing. His hands were rough, but held me—a baby, hands grasping and flailing—gently to his breast, cooing softly as he bounced me.

I searched for any hint of myself in him. Maybe there was the shape of my smile, maybe the glint in his eye. My mother stood before him, biting her fingernails as she watched.

"This is not right," she said. "I'll come with you."

"And what will that accomplish?" he replied. His voice was deep and soothing, with a hint of a strange accent I couldn't place. "You know the man. He'll hunt us down."

"He has another heir. He doesn't need me anymore."

"You think that matters to him?"

My mother sighed and wrapped her arms around herself. "No," she admitted.

"Let me do this for you," he murmured. He reached for her with one arm, balancing me with the other, pulling his family close. "I'll go, and you and Kita will have a good life. I don't see another option."

My mother buried her head in his chest and sobbed.

I released the thread and selected another.

This time, it was a future that might have been—my wedding day. Ran presided—my grandfather did not attend—as I approached the altar dressed in the customary purple emann. My husband took his place behind me, fastening a ceremonial golden necklace around my throat. He was the Avetsi prince of the harbor, the young man who Weiran had murdered.

My mother moved with me to Avetsut. She was happier in the palace, and my husband was kind enough. He taught me the language, and I bore him three sons. Two took after their father, commanding the seas with their thoughts. The third had an affinity I had never before seen—divining an object's history with a touch. He was my youngest, but from the day his power manifested, my mother fell into depression, deeper and deeper until, one day, she just left. We searched for her, but never found her again.

I released the thread. Was my mother destined for misery in every possible instance of my life?

And what of me? I heard-but-did-not-hear. It was the familiar, guttural growl of the beast. So he had been dragged to this place, this afterlife, with me?

"What of you?" I asked.

I am as you made me. But why did you make me?

"Well, I certainly did not mean to."

Then why?

I thought of answering him, but knew it was fruitless. He was no different from me, really. Just like me, he yearned to know about himself. And I yearned to know about him.

I searched through the threads, looking for...what? Some instance of him?

I stood over the outer courtyard, watching the Imperial Guard spar. One one side of their makeshift arena, Ran's guard Sirra readied himself, crouching down to stretch out his legs. On the other end, Ditan stared ahead, shaking out his arms.

They picked up blunted daggers. Ditan ran a finger along the blade and glanced up, nodding curtly. The sun was high overhead, the shadows scarce. He'd have to fight in the light.

As though there were some unseen signal, the pair launched themselves at each other. Ditan ducked as Sirra slashed. The movement gave Ditan just enough shadow to step in and vanish.

There was a tense second as Sirra circled, dagger raised, and Ditan reappeared just behind him, evidently finding enough of a sliver of darkness.

Sirra spun around and flung his hand up, blasting Ditan off his feet into the courtyard wall, but before he landed, he was gone again.

Ditan didn't wait this time, materializing crouched in the shadow of Sirra's outstretched dagger. He surged forward, driving his shoulder into the older man's sternum.

Sirra fell, but was not yet beaten. He raised his hand once more, catching Ditan and lifting him into the air. With no purchase and no shadow, Ditan was trapped there, waiting.

"You're learning, pup," Sirra growled as he pushed himself to his feet. "These midday sparring lessons are getting tougher on my old bones."

Sirra walked slowly toward him, turning the young shadowwalker to face him.

Ditan's chest heaved. Sirra opened his mouth, perhaps to taunt or perhaps to teach, and Ditan took the opportunity to fling his previously hidden dagger at the older man.

Sirra easily deflected the attack with a twitch of his fingers, but the distraction was enough to break his hold. Ditan landed and scrambled back toward the wall, slipping into the shadow of a hanging light.

"Good!" Sirra laughed. He pulled his knife close, and spun slowly in place, watching and listening.

He took a step backward, creating enough of a shadow for Ditan to emerge underfoot and sweep his legs.

Sirra grunted as he fell forward, smashing his face into the ground.

Ditan pressed his knee into Sirra's back, a sly smirk on his face as the older man barked a choked laugh.

* * *

We left the sparring ground, heading back toward my apartments. As we turned down an empty corridor, I pulled him into an embrace.

"That was impressive!" I said.

He blinked in surprise, standing stiff for a second before relaxing into the hug.

"Thank you, my princess," he muttered, looking down at the ground. Though he tried to hide it, the slight smile on his face was evident.

"I'd rather watch you spar than to go to this ball," I admitted, turning down the hall.

Ditan chuckled. "I don't know. The servants and guards are abuzz with excitement. I think it could be fun."

I sighed and slowly shook my head. "If you went, you'd know. These types of events are tedious. Politely dancing and chatting. And since it's all to celebrate Ran, I can't even sneak away with him to complain. It's all a bit maddening."

Ditan shrugged. "I should like to see such an event," he admitted.

An idea formed in my mind. I gently pulled on his arm, stopping him in his tracks. "Accompany me then," I said.

He raised an eyebrow and cast his gaze down. "It would be improper, my princess," he said quietly.

"No, I expect it. Command it, even. I need my personal guard, don't I?" I flashed him a bright smile.

He snuck a glance at me and quickly looked away once I caught his eye. "If...if you insist, my princess," he said.

My grasp on the thread loosened slightly. I didn't remember this happening. Ditan at the ball? He hadn't been there. And I had asked him? None of this made sense to me. Was this the start of a possible future then? Or was this what had actually happened?

I smiled brightly all the way back to my apartments, my step a bit more lively than usual. As we arrived, Ditan took up his customary spot just outside the door. It was fascinating to watch him shift into observation mode. His deep blue eyes, once shy, were suddenly alert, shifting back and forth across the hall. He stood casually with a hand on the hilt of his dagger. He seemed more comfortable with his hand on a blade, far more at ease than when I engaged him in conversation.

I tried to imagine what he would be like on the dance floor, moving me through the space as nobility and royalty stared at us, but I couldn't picture him in that setting.

My handmaidens ushered me to my bedroom, where they descended on me, braiding my hair, weaving in the topaz gems.

As I floated in the nothingness of death, it occurred to me that I had no memory of *any* of this. Everything after the sparring match was just...gone. It all seemed familiar, but despite the fact that it had happened only a few months prior, it seemed far away; there were only glimpses of emotion, nothing else.

The great wooden doors of my apartments swung open. My head snapped to the sound, my eyes narrow at the intrusion. I was just about to open my mouth to complain when I realized who it was.

The handmaidens all shuffled back to the wall, heads bowed in supplication, as the emperor strode in.

He wore an expression of barely contained fury. He raised a hand and jerked a finger toward the door. The handmaidens wordlessly shuffled out.

"Grandfather," I said, an eyebrow raised. What was he doing there?

"Do you think," he started, his voice gravely and dark, "that there is anything you could do in this palace that I would not know about?"

"I don't understand," I replied. And I didn't. What was he on about?

"I have long worried that you would follow in your whore mother's footsteps."

I balked. My first instinct was to shout, to defend my mother from this strange slight, but I knew better.

"Or perhaps you follow from your common father," he growled. "It matters not. I see now. I was too lenient with your mother. I will not allow you to embarrass this family."

"Grandfather, you know I live only for this family," I replied.

He raised a hand to quiet me.

"You will be silent, and you will listen."

I bowed, clasping my hands together nervously.

"I have been told that you have asked your guard to the ball."

I said nothing, trying to conceal the surprise. I hadn't noticed anyone in the hall. Did he have a messenger spying on me?

"My guard accompanies me everywhere," I said evenly.

"Do not try to fool me, child!" he erupted. "You *know* that I have

255

been arranging a beneficial marriage. The last thing this family—no, this empire—needs is for you to whelp a bastard child. So, I can see that I must be more firm with you."

"As you say, Grandfather," I muttered. I kept my gaze low, smart enough to know not to look him in the eye.

"Do not just placate me, child. You will do as you're told. That is the end of the matter."

"Yes sir," I whispered, staring hard at the ground. Tears were beginning to well in my eyes, but I blinked them away, desperate for him not to see me cry.

"Good," he said. I chanced a glance up at him and instantly wished I hadn't. The expression he wore was almost predatory. "I will see you at the Investiture. I expect that you will behave exactly as you should."

"Of course, Grandfather," I replied, and then he was gone, leaving me alone.

A deep rumbling vibration ripped through the stone floor and walls. An inhuman roar sounded from the hallway.

Like a fool, I leaped to my feet and flung the door open.

"Ditan?" I called.

"Get back!" he screamed, his voice sharp and loud.

I moved to obey, but a shadow out in the corner of the corridor caught my eye.

Though I didn't recognize it at the time, the clarity of life and death told me it was the beast, though he looked different than I remembered; my beast was a deep, inky black from tooth to tail. This beast seemed more organic; its fur was a deep brown, its eyes yellow and slitted, like a serpent's.

"What is that?" I shrieked.

"Get BACK!" Ditan shouted once more, and then he was gone into the shadows for an instant before reappearing under the beast's feet. He thrust his dagger upward, sinking it deep into the creature's chest.

The beast shrieked and reared up on its hind legs. Ditan wrenched his dagger free, but before he could move away, the beast swatted him, lifting him bodily from his feet and slamming him into the wall. Ditan crumpled to the floor, clutching at his chest.

"No!" I screamed.

The beast turned its great wide head, fixing me with a cold, dark stare. Without shifting its gaze, it opened its jaws, its yellow fangs dripping with saliva, and launched itself toward Ditan's battered form.

I tried to reach out with my affinity, but my mind was blank, and in any case, the monster moved too quickly.

Ditan screamed as the beast closed its jaws around his chest. It was a raw, primal noise that rooted me to the spot. Blood spurted from his lips. The beast shook him once, twice, and dropped him in a heap.

The screaming stopped. The beast raised its great head and licked its lips, content in its violence.

There was another scream then, and it took my several seconds to realize that it was coming from my lips, a savage noise that tore at my throat.

Someone hooked a finger under my chin and gently pushed my head up.

It was my grandfather.

I blinked, still screaming, heart pounding. He shushed me as though he was calming a crying baby.

I tried to speak, but I couldn't stop screaming.

"Look now, girl," he said, waving an arm.

I reluctantly followed his gesture and realized that I was back in my room, holding myself on the bedroom floor.

"I...I..."

"Yes, I know," he murmured. "I want you to hold on to that image. That terror. I want you to think on it the next time you get it into your mind to act out."

It wasn't real. It wasn't real. My grandfather, the bastard. He'd done this.

"Di-Ditan?" I croaked.

My grandfather clicked his tongue. "Have you not learned, girl?"

"No, no, wait," I said, grasping at his hands. "I've learned. I have."

"Good. Then I won't have to teach the boy the same lesson."

I held his gaze, his meaning clear.

"N…no," I whispered. "Please leave him be."

"Well, that depends entirely on you. Do as you're told."

My grandfather straightened, dusting his shirt. He flashed me a venomous smile and disappeared through my bedroom door.

I fell to the floor and curled in on myself, sobbing so hard that my face glistened with tears and snot. My body convulsed as strands of hair ripped free from the roots.

"My princess!" a soft voice called. I hadn't noticed the door open, but Mina, my handmaiden was by my side, frantically wiping my face. She knelt before me and helped me up, rubbing a hand in my hair in a gesture she probably thought comforting.

Her eyes fluttered gently as she crouched. A hand flew to her mouth as her eyes snapped open.

"No!" she muttered. "Oh, my princess, what a horrible thing. I hope you don't mind me saying so, but the emperor is *not* a nice man!"

It was almost funny, looking back now. Of course he wasn't a nice man. He never had been. And yet, it was also strangely sweet. He could have her tongue for saying such a thing, and he'd already proven that his spies infested the palace walls.

Mina nodded her head, seeming to come to some decision, and returned to my side, rubbing my back as she dried my tears.

"I can't do much, my princess," she said. "I am not the most powerful. But…if you'd like. I can try and help you forget this evil thing," she said. "Maybe it will bring you some peace."

I slowly turned my head. I'd stopped crying; by then, all I could do was just stare straight ahead. I nodded almost imperceptibly and allowed my gaze to fall to the floor.

What a broken, pathetic creature I was. This was what my grandfather did, not only to me, but to the empire. Reality was as he decided it should be. He was no worldmaker, but he imagined himself as someone for whom reality was no issue. And his vision for the world was filled with terror.

Mina lowered her head, resting her forehead on mine. Her eyes fluttered once more.

I let out a long sigh as everything that had happened—asking Ditan to the ball, my grandfather's ire, the terrible creature—flew further and further away. At first, it all seemed like a distant dream. Then, it seemed like the very world around me was beginning to fade, until I melted into the handmaiden's arms and drifted off into sleep.

So this is what happened. This was why I didn't remember.

And yet, I was born, the beast reminded me. And yet he was. So, I did not release the thread just yet.

* * *

I watched with a strange sense of anxiety as Ran strode solemnly up the aisle. Scores of nobles, hand chosen by the emperor, lined the great hall, dressed in elaborate emann. Ran stared straight ahead, intent on his role in the ceremony.

I stood beside my mother. She, too, wore an anxious expression, which I attributed to the complexity of the situation. This could have been her; it should have been. She was the eldest child of the emperor, but because of my parentage, Grandfather had removed her from the line of succession.

She never spoke of the matter, but growing up I'd always catch the way she looked at Ran. The longing glances, the envy toward the life she should have had.

I couldn't identify the source of my own anxiety, but it was strong as Ran approached. The hall was completely silent as he sank into the imperial throne, and my grandfather took his place before him.

"Ranjali sa Sasun Melyora," my grandfather's booming voice echoed through the hall. "This evening, you become the crown prince of our glorious empire. With this title, you take on the responsibility for the prosperity of all her people. It is a grave responsibility, and not one to be undertaken lightly. Do you understand?"

"I do," Ran replied, his voice clear and determined. My grandfather smiled—it was the warmest smile I'd ever seen from him—and placed both hands on Ran's shoulders.

"Sasun would be proud of you," he muttered.

At mention of his mother, Ran bit his lip and looked down. He refused to let the emotion show, but I didn't need to be a priestess to feel it. I knew him well enough.

My grandfather turned back to the crowd and continued the ceremony, but I couldn't focus. There was a strange, impending sense of doom in my chest. It was like a swarm of arrows flying through the air, coming straight for me, but I couldn't figure out who'd shot them.

As I walked arm-in-arm with Ran toward the ballroom, the feeling grew.

"Are you alright?" he asked in a hushed tone.

"I..." I didn't know what to tell him, so I settled on, "Of course. Enjoy the ball. It's your night."

He didn't look convinced, but he took me at my word. As we entered the ballroom, the mouthwatering scents of roasted lamb hit us. The finest musicians in the empire plied their craft, filling the air with a jovial atmosphere.

And yet, the feeling of dread grew. Why?

Two young women approached and, in an instant, Ran's concern was wiped away as he allowed them to carry him off.

I was left alone. My mother and grandfather were not in attendance. Mother never liked these sorts of events, and Grandfather? Who knew. Probably off visiting his concubines.

I knew no one there except Ran.

"Excuse me, my princess," a voice called, breaking me away from my thoughts. It was a young nobleman. I'd seen him in the city a few times; he always seemed pleasant enough.

I pasted on a smile and replied, "yes?"

"Would you allow me to lead you in a dance?"

In truth, I there was nothing I would rather do less. But I offered my hand, and he took it.

He was too shy to talk much as we danced, which allowed my mind to wander. I wanted nothing more than to return to my bed and sleep. Perhaps that would ease this damn feeling.

"I have wanted to approach you before, you know," he said.

"Hmm," I replied, hoping he would stop talking.

"I've seen you in the city. Just last week, in fact."

"Is that so?" I said flatly.

"Indeed. I had made up my mind to come and speak to you, but your shadowwalker guard did not seem inclined to allow conversation," he laughed.

I opened my mouth to reply, but before I could, I froze in place.

Ditan. Ditan should have been there. Why wasn't he?

It was as though a dam in my mind had been chipped, just enough, and just in the right spot. All the memories of the day came flooding through.

And that horrible illusion, with the enormous, deadly beast.

My heart pounded as I pulled myself away from my suitor. I wanted to run, but that beast was in my mind, in my soul. There was nowhere I could go to get away from its terrible gaze.

And then it tore its way out of my mind and into the room. Towering and black, saliva dripping from its dark fangs. And just as it had done in my memory, it threw itself at the closest person—the boy who had asked me to dance—and closed its jaws around his chest. He didn't even scream, just gurgled pathetically as it dropped him in a heap to the floor.

I dropped the thread. Suddenly, I did not want to see anymore.

Except...

There was another thread that caught my attention. Despite my reservations, I pulled at it.

There I was on the stage, Weiran standing before me with knife raised. My face was still, as though I were watching the clouds go by, rather than facing down my death.

He cut my throat and I stumbled forward, blood spraying the crowd before me as they screamed. The mass of people pulsed like a living organism, shouting in words I could not understand. Were they outraged at Weiran for what he had done? Were they voicing their support? I could not tell.

I watched the light flicker and fade from my own eyes as Ran darted forward, reaching for me.

Someone appeared from nothing in front of him—a shadowwalker. Nokinan. A second later, they were both gone, and I died once more.

I released the thread.

I wasn't upset, not really. There didn't seem to be much point in it.

26

Kita

I could have floated in nothingness—and everything—with the beast for eternity.

Why do you not name me? the beast asked. *Why am I always 'the beast' to you?*

I hadn't considered it. He had always been the beast in my mind. In fact, none of the creatures I had ever made had ever been named.

Of course, I'd never had the kind of relationship I had with the beast.

"How do you see yourself?" I asked him.

A strange question, the beast replied.

"How so?"

I am as you made me, came the familiar, yet no less irritating, reply.

"But part of living is to explore your own self. Your own sense of being."

He hesitated for a moment, as if the thought had never occurred to him before.

I do not know my 'sense of being,' he said. *I do not think you gave me that.*

It was a profoundly sad thing, not to have a sense of being, I thought. Though he didn't seem upset about it at all; it was simply an alien concept to him. And finally, I understood what he had been trying to tell me all along. He was as I made him, and that was all. He was just an extension of my imagination, and though he was sentient, he was ultimately nothing more than the qualities I had imposed upon him.

No wonder he'd once called me a cruel god.

"I don't know how to imbue you with a sense of being," I told him. "I think that's something you need to develop on your own. But maybe giving you a name would be a start."

I paused, allowing his essence to wash over my own. I imagined it was similar to motherhood; growing a life, giving it a name and releasing it out into the world. He was my child, in a way, grown in my mind instead of my body.

"If you don't know who you are," I began, "then who do you want to be?"

The beast was quiet for a moment. *I...I have enjoyed being a protector. I think that is who I wish to be.*

A protector. The role I had given him—although inadvertently—at the temple.

"Zentouran," I said, feeling the name as much as saying it. An old name—no, a plea, to the goddesses, really. "Please protect." A prayer to protect a child, repurposed to give meaning to the first of a new species.

Zentouran, he repeated.

"Do you like it?" I asked, suddenly nervous. I badly wanted him to approve.

Something shifted. It wasn't something that could be seen, or even felt, but it was there. *He* had changed.

Zentouran. My name. And his voice seemed almost to crack.

And he was not the only one changed by his naming. We settled into one another, our essences entwined. And yet there was a separation I hadn't felt from him since the day he was first made.

Time does not exist in death. And so it was that we floated there, together. Pulling at threads. Observing every possible iteration of my life. For eternity. For an instant.

Until.

A force pulled at me, as though someone had slung a rope around my hips and dragged me away.

The dark nothingness of death shimmered and faded away, giving way to a soft white light. Zentouran stirred with a groan, like a cat being woken prematurely from a nap.

The light slowly diffused, and I blinked to try and get my eyes to focus.

Wait. I blinked?

I allowed my gaze to travel down to realize that I had form. My hands were as I remembered, my arms. I was wearing the white emann I had died in, and it was wet and sticky with blood.

I touched my fingers to my throat and touched wet, meaty flesh. Horror creeped in as I pushed my hands further into the wound, all the way to my windpipe.

Noise started to creep in. A cacophony of voices, screaming and crying.

I was surrounded by others, many of them sporting injuries even more gruesome than my own. They ignored my presence, flocking toward the corner of the room, where a blurry form stood over what looked to be a body. I focused my eyes, but while the people around me were in sharp focus, I couldn't even make out this mysterious form's face or clothing, nor anything around them.

Curiosity pulled me closer. I bumped into one of the crowd, a young man who was missing an arm and a large chunk of flesh from his torso.

"You..." he hissed.

A chill crept over my shoulders, down into the depths of my chest. I recognized him. I'd seen him in my nightmares, relived my last dance with him in death.

"You did this!" he screeched. "You murdered me!" With his remaining arm, he gathered the front of my emann and yanked me forward.

I opened my mouth to speak, but an unseen force pulled me from his grasp. He screamed after me, climbing over others to try and reach for me as I was dragged further and further away. Despite his anger, I found myself desperately reaching for him, but the force pulling me was too strong, and I slammed hard into darkness.

The first sensation to come to me was a deep ache in my chest, a strange hunger for….something.

Air, that was it. I needed air. I gasped, forcing air into my lungs, gulping it down so quickly that I thought I might vomit.

I couldn't see. I reached a hand to my face and felt for my eyes.

Oh. They were closed.

I opened them to find Weiran's face, less than a foot from mine. His cheeks were rosy, but his eyes were rimmed so black I might have thought he'd been punched. His lips were tinged blue, and he violently shivered. His arm shot out beside me as he tried to steady himself, and gentle hands pulled him away.

The Priest. His face was a mask, but there was anger—no, *fury*—in his eyes, though I didn't understand why.

I tried to push myself up, but there was no strength in my arms, and I just collapsed with a groan.

I had the sense that I should be angry, or perhaps happy to be breathing once more. But I felt nothing. The Priest's doing, I realized.

"I am going to release you," he murmured, grasping my hand. His voice was gentler than ever I'd heard it. "Take things slowly. I know this is unsettling."

Unsettling? I didn't feel unsettled. I felt...fine.

He squeezed my hand, and emotion began to creep into the edges of my consciousness. I focused on what I was feeling, trying to identify it. It seemed foreign, these emotions. Like I hadn't felt them in years. But as the seconds wore on, the sense of betrayal became undeniable.

Weiran killed me. He murdered me, in front of a crowd. The Priest and Tsavi…they helped him. These people who had fooled me into believing they were friends of mine.

It hurt, so badly I felt it in my muscles and bones.

And then there was the anger, the indignation. How *dare* they? How *could* they?

I yanked my hand free and pushed myself up, weakness be damned.

The Priest, to his credit, did not move his gaze, and he did not try to calm me. Somehow, this made me even angrier. Did he think I was so meek, so powerless, that I would allow this?

Zentouran stirred in my chest. Good. Without a second thought, I released him into the room. He filled the space, growling and pacing at Weiran and the Priest.

Weiran, to my satisfaction, fidgeted nervously as he backed against the wall. It would be easy to take my revenge. Zentouran could kill him, easily.

"Kita," the Priest said in a still voice that would have been easy enough to calm me before.

Not now.

I looked to Zentouran. He stood poised, his muscles bunched and ready to pounce. He was angry for me.

Zentouran. Please protect. Protect, not slaughter. He didn't want to be the murderous beast he was at his birth. And despite how I felt about Weiran and the Priest in that moment, I didn't want that either.

I exhaled, and Zentouran lay down at the foot of my bed, watching, waiting, but not killing.

"Kita, this will exhaust you," the Priest said, glancing at Zentouran. "Release him, so that you may rest."

I stared at him, his words seeming somehow nonsensical. How could Zentouran exhaust me? He was my child. And then I realized something else—the gossamer thread that had always bound us into a strange parasitic relationship was gone. The thought brought a smile to my face.

But there was another sensation, something stranger even than the nothingness and everything of death. I felt as though my very skin was a loosely fitted emann, and with one wrong move, I would slip free, back into death, intertwined with Zentouran for eternity. In the moment, there was nothing that seemed more enticing. This life was difficult and painful, and death was easy.

I fixed my gaze on Weiran—the one who ripped me from my skin in the first place and then forced me back in when I had outgrown it. Why had he done any of it? I couldn't make sense of it.

He stared at me, his eyes wild and defiant.

"You will leave me now," I said, my voice steeled with a sternness I hadn't had since before I left the palace. It was false authority, of course. He'd seized control of the city, and he had powerful people like Tsavi and the Priest on his side. And I wouldn't ask Zentouran to kill for me, though Weiran had no way of knowing that.

For a moment, he held my gaze, his mouth pressed into a thin line, and for a moment I thought he might argue. But eventually, he just sighed and left me alone with the Priest.

The sat next to me on the bed, resting his elbows on his knees. He paused for a moment, considering what to say.

"Things have changed," he finally said, his voice quiet and almost melancholy.

"You murdered me," I seethed.

"Weiran did," he said. "I didn't know."

"You could have stopped him. You could have—"

"I…I know. I didn't know what to do, I-I-" he stopped, swallowing hard. It was strange to see him so flustered, wringing his hands as he stumbled over his words.

It was almost funny.

"Believe me, " he said, "I know what it's like. Dying, I mean. Being clawed back. I don't wish it on anyone. Weiran and his...his goddess-scorned plans!"

I watched as he got up and started pacing. My anger was quickly cooling, replaced by a deep sense of pity.

His head snapped back to me. "Death has changed you," he noted, his voice already returning to its monotonous timbre.

"Yes, I suppose so," I replied. His eyes flit to Zentouran.

"You've gotten stronger."

"I've learned about myself."

He nodded slowly and returned to my bedside. As he sank to one knee, he asked, "what did death teach you?"

"I just saw my life," I said simply. "Everything that was and could have been. Death didn't teach me how to free Zentouran from my grasp; that just became self-evident."

"Zentouran?"

This is my name, Zentouran cut in, his voice deep and velvety.

The Priest blinked his surprise.

"We all deserve names," I said softly, reaching out for his hand. "Yours was taken from you. Perhaps you should reclaim it."

He just looked at my hand, as though he couldn't comprehend anything I was saying.

"We who serve the goddesses give up our names for them," he muttered.

"I saw no goddesses in death."

He barked a laugh. "And who gave you these images?"

I shrugged. Perhaps he was right. I could have argued further—he had been a toddler when his name was stolen. He'd had no choice in the matter. But it didn't matter. A name was simply unimportant to him. Not having one, though...

"And you? Is this what you saw, when you died?"

"At first," he said. "Some of what I saw came to pass, eventually. Perhaps some of it will yet. The first time, I struggled to understand it all. I fought, parsing every image I saw. Perhaps it is as you say; my ability's strength became self-evident. As I dug through my memories, of my life to be, of my possibilities, I just felt more because of course I could." He shrugged.

"Death stole from you," I said gently. "Tsavi, too."

The Priest nodded, solemnly.

"Nothing like that happened to me," I said. I admit to feeling a strange sense of superiority as I said it, but this was quickly dashed.

"So I thought, at first,"the Priest replied. "You must remember; I went through this process four times. I didn't notice what it was doing to me until the second or third. But it began earlier. Looking back, I see signs even the first time I was returned to this body."

I looked down at my hands. It would be a falsehood to say that I didn't feel different. All the revelations, the sense that my spirit would, at any moment, slip free from my body, it was all new. But I didn't feel that anything was missing.

He watched me with an unreadable expression. Despite my annoyance, I felt myself shrinking under his gaze. After an uncomfortably long moment, he sighed and pat my hand.

"Get some rest. You lost a great deal of blood. The healers fixed the most pressing damage, but your body still has work to do. Sleep. I'll come and see you tomorrow."

"He's mad, you know," I muttered as he turned to the door.

The Priest stopped. Without turning, he said, "he's troubled. But he's not wrong."

"And when he decides that you'd serve him better in death?"

My words hung heavy in the air. He'd thought about it, I realized. He'd wondered whether all his suffering—the dying, returning to life, dying again, the loss of his own emotions, the peace of eternity, only to be dragged back to the pain of reality—had been because it furthered Weiran's cause.

But it didn't matter. The Priest had stayed. Had helped him. There was not going to be any revelation; he'd already had it. He'd made his choice. It was clear to me then. As close as I felt we had become, as much as I had come to like him, I could not trust him. Even if he didn't know Weiran's plans, even if he apologized over and over again, it did not matter.

"I'll make sure food is brought to you this evening. Sleep well," he said, and he disappeared through the door before I could say anything else.

* * *

I woke to the sound of Zentouran bounding through the courtyard just outside my window. The moon was full and bright overhead as he ripped plants from their roots, tossing them into the air and shaking his head as they rained down upon him.

Though I was cold and weak from blood loss, the sight warmed me.

For a moment, I felt guilty. Had Weiran's sister planted those flowers? Had she taken the time to cultivate the garden?

Then I remembered what Weiran had done to me, and I suddenly wished Zentouran would destroy it all.

"My princess," someone whispered. Warm breath on the back of my neck raised gooseflesh. Zentouran was quick, bounding through the window as quickly as I could turn around.

We both relaxed as we realized who it was.

"Di…ditan?"I asked, my voice breaking as tears welled in my eyes. Without thinking, I pulled him into an embrace. He tensed against me, but I held fast to him, pushing my face into his chest to avoid crying.

All the tension melted away from him and he wrapped his arms around me, his heart beat strong and loud against my throat.

"How are you here?"I mumbled into his torso. "I…I thought…"

He pulled away and fixed me with a worried stare.

"We've been looking for you," he replied. "The prince and I."

Ran. So Ditan was with him, hunting me down?

As though sensing my hesitation, he said, "He wanted so badly to find you. To bring you home. The emperor has promised mercy."

The emperor. I was not keen to experience his idea of mercy, not after what he had done under the guise of teaching me.

I grasped Ditan's face, searching his night-blue eyes.

"He's not a merciful man," I said. "Ran is a fool if he thinks otherwise."

"The prince is a good man," Ditan replied. "He cares deeply for you. As do I." He pat my hand and smiled sadly.

"How did you find me here?" I asked.

Zentouran walked over and laid down at my feet, staring up with huge black eyes.

Ditan eyed him somewhat suspiciously, but chose not to comment.

"They have a shadowwalker. I followed when she brought you here and waited. My princess, they've taken the prince."

"What?"

"In the chaos of…" he paused, trying to find the right words, "in the chaos of what they did to you, their shadowwalker took him. I failed to protect him."

I blinked. I saw him. I had almost thought it was a strange hallucination, fed to me by a dying brain. But it was real. They took him. Was this their plan the whole time? Was this why they took me with them in the first place? Everything Weiran had ever done, every decision he made seemed suspicious.

"You can't blame yourself. These people have been planning things for months. Maybe years. If they killed me publicly, I imagine they'll have an unpleasant fate in mind for Ran."

"He's not here in the palace. I've searched. My princess, I fear that they're keeping him in *Telombraj*."

"Then you can find him, right?"

He shook his head. "If I don't know where they put him, I could look for an eternity and never find him. Time and space work differently there."

I sighed and sat on the bed, suddenly feeling very tired again.

Ditan watched with a mix of worry and desperation. He couldn't afford to return to the Capital without Ran.

And I didn't plan to let him.

"Weiran never mentioned your presence," I said. "He knew Ran was here, but he didn't say anything about you. Is it possible he doesn't know you're here?"

Ditan shrugged. "I guarded the prince primarily from *Telombraj*," he said. "He thought it best to appear as though he were alone. We rode together on the road, but in the city? If that's the only place they laid eyes upon him, then perhaps."

I nodded. An idea was quickly forming in my mind.

I just had to convince an empath that I wasn't lying to him. Simple.

"We'll get him back," I said, trying to sound more confident than I felt.

I turned to Zentouran. He sat up and arched his back, stretching like a cat just awoken from a nap.

"Can you fetch me the Priest?"

27

Ran

Ran had hoped that he could pick one voice out of the cacophony and hold fast to it like a line in the sea. He had thought that, perhaps, by focusing in on just one voice, he could keep the rest from pulling him under.

But sound didn't work the same there as in the daylight. The voices writhed and curled in on each other like a ball of snakes. They burrowed deep into his mind until he could not focus on anything but the whispers.

He had walked so long that a dull ache pulsed up his legs and into his hips, and yet Ran was no closer to the obsidian city. How long had it been? A day? Maybe more? He wasn't hungry or thirsty, though he was certain that enough time had passed that he should have been.

How did Ditan and the other shadowwalkers find solace in this place?

He groaned, trying to push the voices from his mind, but as he took a step, his foot slipped through the slick stone ground, sending him sprawling. Pain laced through his ribs as he took ragged breaths, dragging his foot free.

It had been a long time since he'd lost control of his affinity like that.

Why had that happened?

He wound his hands into his hair, trying to calm himself. His mother would have known what to do. She always seemed to. But she was gone, bones picked clean by carrion long ago.

He curled into himself. He'd cracked a rib in the fall, he was fairly certain, but he didn't care. The whispering voices tormented him, but he could do nothing about that. He couldn't seem to move away from where he was. All he could do was wait and be ready to fight. Yet, fighting, too, seemed impossible.

"You tried to leave," someone said, their voice clear and bright.

Ran tried to turn and face it, but found that he couldn't move. He strained, but his muscles refused to obey.

He realized that there was another noise low in the back of his mind. It was a low, droning note that seemed to envelop him despite the low volume, rooting him to the spot. His eyes darted around as he strained to see through his hair.

"So this is the famed Prince Ranjali," a new voice—lightly accented and dripping with malice—said. "Hmm. A little pathetic, isn't he?"

Footsteps echoed off the slick stone floor and a hand roughly grasped his chin, jerking Ran's head up.

Ran recognized the figure at once—the man who had killed Kita. Wrath bubbled within him, but he could do nothing.

"I dreamed of this, you know. Staring you in the eye as you realize that your empire will fall. Because it will. It's begun already; you just haven't been paying attention. Now, Avestsut is free from your grasp. The rest of the continent will follow. Especially once the emperor's heir is…removed."

The terrorist smiled, his eyes blazing, and abruptly dropped Ran's head.

Ran yelped in pain as his chin hit the ground. He had to do something. He couldn't move, but maybe…

He reached out with his affinity, feeling the cool stone against his face. Straining against the siren's note, he liquefied the ground as far as he could.

The terrorist screeched an Avetsi word as he sank calf-deep into the ground, but before Ran could swallow him completely, the note holding him to the ground changed, and though he struggled to maintain his hold on the ground beneath him, it was wrenched from him.

The terrorist pulled himself free. He released a string of what Ran assumed were obscenities and kicked hard at Ran's chest. He heard the ribs snap before he felt it, but the pain was quick to follow. He bit his tongue to stop from crying out, but each new breath brought a fresh wave of agony.

"The cost for this will be high," Ran hissed through shallow breaths.

The terrorist launched another kick, this time at his face. His nose and cheekbone cracked, and, unable to move his head, blood spilled down his throat, choking him as he struggled.

"Don't you speak of costs to me," the terrorist muttered bitterly as he knelt in front of Ran's crumpled form. "I have paid them all. Enjoy your time here. It'll be the last place you see before you die."

Ran managed to move his head just enough to see the shadowwalker fade from view, the terrorist and another man—presumably the siren—held tight in her arms.

As the siren disappeared, so too did his song. Its strange echoes—and the hold it had over him—abruptly receded. It was as though ropes had held him fast and were suddenly cut. It took a moment for the feeling to return to his limbs, and he was left with a dull ache all over his body. He leaned over and fell into a fit of coughing, sending blood spraying across the floor. He gingerly touched his nose, hissing at the pain. It was crooked.

Ran took three quick breaths and wrenched it, doing his best to straighten it as much as he cool. Tears welled to his eyes as a sharp pain laced through his face.

He flexed his fingers and realized that he had pulled a chunk of hair from his scalp. As sharp needles of pain radiated through his scalp, he started to sob.

"It's alright," he heard. It was his mother's voice, though whether he was hearing or remembering it, he couldn't say. "You are doing well." As always, she was patient, without a hint of condescension.

How different might life had been if she had not died?

He wanted to get up, to keep going. But what was the point? All his walking had amounted to nothing; he had gone nowhere.

He felt himself slipping through the stone. He should have been panicking; he should have been struggling. Yet, he didn't fight it. He was content to slide off into nothingness. Perhaps he would suffocate, but that seemed better, somehow, than facing these terrorists again.

"Ran?" someone called. A hallucination, he supposed.

"Mother," he replied, his voice dreamy.

"What? No. Ran, it's me!"

He blinked and turned as he pulled himself free from the ground.

Kita. Beside her was a tall, broad shouldered man. Ran recognized him from the public audience—another one of the terrorists.

This place was driving him mad.

"Kita, I failed you," he muttered, tears welling in his eyes again. "I'm sorry."

Kita sighed and kneeled before him. There was a faint scar across her neck. He'd never noticed that before.

He found himself reaching toward her, his fingers brushing her neck.

He recoiled.

"I don't understand," he said. "I don't…"

She pulled him into an embrace.

"What did they do to you?" she breathed.

"Be quick, Kita. Weiran will be expecting me."

Kita sighed in frustration as she turned to the man beside her. By the way he was dressed, Ran guessed he was a priest, though he couldn't understand why a holy man would be working with terrorists to rebel against the empire.

"I just had to see you," Kita muttered. "They're planning to kill you."

Her words were like a knife to the heart. There was so much about this that just

"I don't understand," he muttered again.

Kita straightened. "I'm here to say goodbye," she said. "I'm alive. I wanted you to know that. And I wanted you to know…that I'm sorry."

He wanted to ask her what she meant, but a now familiar figure shimmered into view. The same female shadowwalker from before. He instinctively raised a hand, but saw the fear in her face and dropped it.

"Be strong," Kita said, her voice suddenly forceful. She held his gaze as the shadowwalker took her arm. There was something she was trying to communicate to him, but he couldn't understand what.

And then, she, the shadowwalker, and the priest were gone, leaving him alone once more.

The cacophony of voices burrowed into his head once more, and he screamed, so loud it tore at his vocal cords.

"My prince, we must go," a familiar voice said firmly.

Ran turned to find…Ditan?

"Wh-what?"

"We must be swift, my prince. Let us go before they return."

He nodded and took Ditan's hand.

Light pierced through Ran's eyelids, so bright it made him nauseous. He clenched his teeth, waiting for the feeling to pass.

Finally, he allowed himself to open his eyes.

To his surprise, the room was small and dark, with only a thin, high window for light. The air was damp and smelled of earth. And yet, it was such a stark contrast to the creeping darkness of Telombraj that he kneeled down and dug his fingers into the dirt floor. He could smell the salt on the air; they were back in Avetsut. He moaned softly as he took in the sights, smells, and feel of the room around him.

"You found me," he said, but Ditan was gone. He was alone. Dread crept in as he realized that he had no idea where in the city he was, and that—if what the terrorists had said was true—he was now in hostile territory.

Someone laid a hand on his shoulder, but their fingers phased through as Ran instinctively used his affinity to protect himself.

"Ran," Kita said calmly, lowering herself to his level. "You're shaking."

He glanced up. Ditan stood behind her, a wry smile on his face.

She was right. He was shivering as hard as he ever had, despite the warmth of the room.

"Y-you...you're alive?" he managed to say. "B-but I s-saw..."

She fixed him with a sad smile.

"Don't doubt your eyes. I was murdered full view of the entire city. But Weiran's a deathseeker."

A deathseeker? He'd never heard of anyone having that ability, except for in the old stories. He's assumed they were a myth.

Were the goddesses real as well?

"My prince, are you alright?" Ditan asked.

Ran found that he couldn't look the guard in the eye. He hadn't done anything wrong, but Ran couldn't help but associate him with that place, the cold darkness and maddening voices.

"I...I..." He wanted to reassure them both, but he couldn't.

"Ran, I don't know what you need. Tell me how to help you," Kita said. Her voice was soft, like his mother's.

But Kita was real. Kita was alive.

"We must go," Ran said softly. "Leave this place, return to the palace. Things will be fine once we get home."

Kita sighed and sat before him.

He knew it was a futile suggestion when he'd said it, but her face confirmed it.

"I can't go back there," she said. "He'd kill me. You know he would."

"No! He promised mercy. He swore it."

"And what do you imagine his mercy would look like, Ran?" She took his hands in hers, and this time, they remained solid. "You've been fortunate. You haven't crossed him. He hasn't felt the need to punish you. And in any case, I've seen so much since I've left the palace. I can't be a part of this empire anymore."

Her eyes bore into his, pleading. She wasn't asking him to let her go, he realized. She was asking for something else. His understanding, perhaps.

"You know," she said, "they told me you were coming to kill me. I almost died at the temple. I didn't know who to trust. I must admit that they had me confused, but I could never shake my belief in you. I know you. You're a true optimist. You have this strange ability to always see the best in everyone, even Grandfather. I don't want you to lose that, but I want you to see, really see. He's not a good man, Ran. He's just not. Under his control, this empire is not good. You'll be better, I know it. But I can't be here to watch it. Let him think I'm dead, please."

He stared down at the ground. He couldn't let her go, not after everything he'd done to find her. It had been a long journey, and now that he was so close, he had to see it through.

But...

She gave his hands a squeeze and let them drop, straightening herself and turning her attention to Ditan. Ran watched as the pair exchanged a longing look.

"I love you, Ran," she said, turning back to him. "You are my family, and you always will be. But I think this is it. We both need to leave the city. I think you know that."

He looked away. He couldn't admit it out loud, but he'd made his decision.

He nodded once, curtly, and could almost feel the energy in the room shift. She knelt before him once more and pulled him into an embrace.

He broke down, then, sobbing into her shoulder as all his emotions came flooding out. Without her in the palace, there would be no light, no relief from his father's expectations. And though he wanted to believe his father's words, he knew, somehow, that she was right. His mercy would inevitably be cruel.

They held each other for a long time, and he realized that she was crying too. He wiped his tears and then hers as they broke apart, and he shakily got to his feet.

"I'll let Isa know," he said.

She smiled, rubbing her now-puffy eyes.

"Thank you," came her reply, and then she and Ditan both were gone.

The room took on a strange energy. At once, it was both a comfort— a warm, damp cave to hide away from the upheaval of the city—and a torture—walls moving in to constrict and crush him.

The sound of the door opening roused him from his panic. Aka strode in, a smile stretched across her face.

"Lovely prince!" she said, her voice a sort of whispery shout. As large as she was, she seemed to fill the space, and her energy was bright and warm.

Too much. He shrank away, and her smile faded.

"I am glad the shadow boy was able to find you," she said. "Are you well?"

"Y-yes," he lied. He had to regain some bit of authority, some sense of himself. He was the crown prince.

But he just couldn't.

"The city is a dangerous place now," she said. "I will bring you back to the capital. You will not come to harm, I swear it."

"No!" he snapped. He couldn't bear it. He'd grown to like Aka well enough over their travels, with her tales of growing up on the savannah. But the thought of returning home with a beserker in tow, like some sort of chaperone, was not acceptable.

Besides, he had promised her leave.

"Lovely prince, do not be stubborn. The city is baying for blood just now. Yours would do quite nicely."

"I know, I just…" he swallowed hard. "Go and visit your children. You have done enough for me."

"These things do not work like that," she complained, her voice tinged with annoyance. "I am bound to your family. I cannot leave you in danger, any more than I could sprout wings and take to the sky. I simply cannot."

Right. Whatever compulsion his long dead ancestor had forced upon her family was evidently stronger than he'd imagined.

But there was another option.

"Go with Kita," he said. Before Aka could open her mouth to protest, he continued, "she is of my blood. She is traveling south. I do not know where. But protecting her would get you closer to your family."

Aka shifted her weight from side to side, her yellow eyes unreadable. He half-expected her to protest, but she didn't. Instead, she nodded.

"First, I will ensure your safe passage from the city," she began, "and then I will meet the lady Kitania at the border. She'll have to pass there if she is to travel south."

Ran smiled, trying to muster as much warmth as he could. Aka returned a tight-lipped grin and disappeared back through the door.

28

Kita

When Ditan and I returned to my chamber, Zentouran had occupied himself by rolling on the ground. To the servants' credit, his black fur was completely clear of dust.

I suddenly found myself feeling nervous. I didn't want Ditan to leave, and part of me wanted to ask him to stay, to accompany me to the south.

But having seen what had happened to Ran, I couldn't ask that of him.

I worried for Ran, for the man he was becoming. He was good. I knew that, despite everything Weiran had tried to get me to believe. But the empire was a complex, living creature that I feared he wouldn't be able to wrangle.

Locking eyes with Ditan helped me to push those thoughts from my mind, for the moment.

I didn't quite know what to say. I wished things could be different. But even if the ball had never happened, a true relationship could never have been. My grandfather had made his opinion on that matter abundantly clear.

Thinking back to the memory of those illusions made me tremble.

Perhaps all thoughts of Ditan would now be tainted. Perhaps my grandfather had at least won that victory.

I cursed the evilness of the man.

Zentouran, catching on to my thoughts and perhaps thinking I deserved a moment's privacy, hopped through the window, ripping up flowers and racing back and forth through the garden.

"You will take care of him, won't you?" I finally asked.

He blinked and frowned. "Of course," came the reply. "It is my duty."

Sighing, I took his hand and gave it a squeeze. "I wish things were different," I said, softly.

His gaze shifted down to his feet. I wished he would say something.

"I don't just mean you being his guard," I muttered. "Ran and my mother don't get along. He doesn't have allies in the palace. I think, perhaps, he'll need them in the days to come."

"What can I do?" Ditan asked, his voice strained with anguish. "I have no power in the palace."

I scoffed. "You have the ear of the crown prince. That's power enough. On top of that, you're a shadowwalker. Your kind are revered—"

"My kind are feared," he corrected. "Assassins. Spies. That's what they think of us."

"Even better," I pointed out. "My grandfather is adept at using fear to his advantage. Perhaps you and Ran could do the same."

"I'm not sure what you're implying," he said, slowly.

I flinched. I wasn't trying to imply anything, not really. At the same time, denying it seemed dishonest too.

"Just...just take care of him," I settled on.

Ditan locked eyes with me. His eyebrows furrowed, and I could tell there was something he wanted to say.

Instead, he leaned in and kissed me. He was hesitant at first. Perhaps a little bit unsure, but we quickly melted into each others arms, desperate to make the moment last. If we parted, that would be it. He would leave, returning to Ran's side, and I wouldn't see him again. I couldn't bear the thought.

But we couldn't leave Ran alone. Weiran would learn what had happened soon enough, and given all his ridiculous planning and what had already shown himself to be capable of, it seemed fairly obvious that he would rage and claw through the city, searching for his escaped prisoner.

Against my better judgment, I pulled away, resting my forehead on his chest. I closed my eyes, listening to the thud of his heart.

"Go, then," I whispered.

I wanted him to refuse. I wanted him to stay, but he simply kissed me once more, gently, and I found myself holding nothing as he dissolved into shadow.

I clasped my hands together, cracking my knuckles.

Zentouran poked his head through the window, his tongue lolling as he watched me.

There is much to do before we leave the city, he said, his thoughts rumbling loud in my head. *Weiran and the others will be displeased. We should go.*

"Of course," I said. "We should find Tesyel, Kordritse, and Malen. I think we'll need them."

He clambered back through the window, shaking himself like a dog before crossing the room and yanking the door open. I followed behind.

Servants gasped and yelped as we roamed the halls, and Zentouran did nothing to alleviate their fears. He stared hard, baring gleaming black teeth if anyone dared approach.

I found myself holding my head just a bit higher.

I turned a corner and ran directly into Tsavi. Immediately, Zentouran positioned himself between us, snapping his jaws in warning.

Wisely, Tsavi backed up, though he didn't seem particularly afraid.

"Kita," he said, looking down at his feet.

"Excuse us," I said, brushing past him.

"Wait!"

I turned, resting a hand on Zentouran's shoulder as he let out a low growl.

Tsavi ran a hand through his hair.

"Look, I didn't know," he muttered.

I let out a chuckle. He didn't know. What did *that* matter?

"Weiran didn't tell us he was going to do that. I swear it. If he had, I—"

"You'd what? Do nothing, as you did when you realized what was happening? You speak Avetsi. You heard his words, and you stood there like a dutiful soldier. Simply following your commander's orders. You could have stopped him, easily. You know it. He only has dominion over the dead, and you're perhaps the most powerful person I have ever met."

"You don't understand," he muttered, shifting his weight from side to side.

"Of course I do. At the end of the day, we're all pieces in Weiran's grand plans. Perhaps you have accepted your role. Maybe you're grateful that he brought you back from death—"

"I am *not* grateful," he hissed, his eyes suddenly full of the same fire I normally saw in Weiran's, despite the clouding. "But we are all pieces. That much is true. I gave my life for this revolution long before I died."

This drew another laugh. "A revolution, is it? We'll see. You're still a tiny group of terrorists going up against the might of the empire. What chance do you have, really?"

"Well, we took this city. That's a start, isn't it?"

"And will you keep it, once the people realize they've been manipulated by a siren's call?"

"I did *not* manipulate them!" he snapped. "Opened their hearts to what was happening, perhaps, but never manipulation."

I regarded him carefully. He was getting riled now, stepping closer even with Zentouran in his way.

"I liked the façade you wore when we first met," I said. "That man was kind. Take care of yourself. And, perhaps, be a bit more critical of Weiran in the future. Maybe people will call for your head one day."

"Why would they? I'm nobody. An orphan Vayan boy with no family name."

Was he really this dense? Had someone convinced him of this? Or was he really that unaware of his own power?

I didn't have the time or, honestly, the will, to continue to converse with him, and I turned to leave.

"Kita, wait. One more thing."

"What?"

He glanced over his shoulder and squeezed past Zentouran (who, annoyingly, let him do so) so that he could whisper directly in my ear. I started to protest, expecting him to use his affinity for something nefarious, but he just whispered, "Your creature has no song to me. I can hear nothing of him. Do you understand what I mean?"

I searched his eyes, clouded though they were. No song? He'd talked about songs before, but I hadn't paid much attention. This seemed important though. His eyes pled with me, begging me to understand.

"I...I think so," I replied. I had a guess, at least.

"You're wrong when you say I'm the most powerful person you know. Very wrong." He held my gaze for a moment and then walked past Zentouran again, disappearing around the corridor corner.

I pushed his words from my mind as I flagged down a wide-eyed servant girl.

"Can you find Tesyel, Kodritse, and Malen?" I asked as she slowly backed away.

"A-alright!" she squeaked before turning and running down the hall.

When they saw me, their eyes went wide and they rushed forward, crushing me in a hug. The girls chattered in Avetsi. Tesyel didn't bother to translate as he sobbed into my clothing.

"My lady, w-we thought you were dead!" he cried.

I rubbed his back; he seemed so small.

"You weren't at the public audience, were you?" I asked gently.

"N-no, but some of the others were. They told us…"

I knelt down and wiped his tears.

"I'm alive," I said gently, wrapping my arms around him, "but I have to leave the city. It's time for me to move on. I had hoped the three of you would help me."

"Of course, my lady! Whatever we can do, we will!" he said. Once he translated for Kodritse and Malen, they nodded enthusiastically.

I ran my fingers through the ends of my hair. Everyone thought I was dead. Perhaps I didn't need to be completely unrecognizable.

They finally seemed to realize that Zentouran was there. Kodritse yelped, and Malen tripped. Tesyel stood without speaking, his eyes darting from Zentouran to me and back.

"This is Zentouran," I said evenly. "He will not harm you."

This I swear, he agreed. In an apparent effort to disarm them, he opened his mouth, his tongue lolling as he panted like a dog.

* * *

A few moments later, we were back in my quarters, chunks of hair falling to the floor as Kodritse and Malen did their work. With the curls went the last vestiges of my life. I was no longer Kitania sa Isali Melyora, third in line to the Imperial Throne. If I was honest with myself, that aspect of me had died the moment I fled the palace.

But somehow, it never felt real until my hair was cut, when I became just…Kita.

I didn't bother to look in the mirror afterward. I knew it would look good; the girls were deft with their hands, after all. But it was too hard to face myself.

Malen, Kodritse, and Tesyel stood back, pressing themselves against the wall to avoid getting too close to Zentouran, as they waited for me to speak. I flashed them a weak smile.

"I'm leaving the empire," I began. "I would hope that you can come along."

The three of them huddled together, whispering amongst themselves. I waited as patiently as I could, tapping my foot as they talked.

Finally, Tesyel turned toward me. "Kodritse and Malen…they cannot leave this place. They have family here. They do not speak the languages of the south. They feel they would be more a hindrance than a help."

"I see."

"But they're my only family here, and I know they'll be safe. I can't do much, but I could at least translate for you as you traveled south."

I flashed him a warm smile and pulled him into an embrace.

"Besides," he mumbled into my shoulder, "I've always wanted to roam!"

"Good!" I said, pulling away from him. "Get your things. Pack light."

He nodded and bounced out of the room, the girls close behind.

"Now," I said, tapping my chin as I turned to Zentouran, "how are we going to make you in any way inconspicuous?"

In response, a ripple raced down his fur, and the beast was gone, replaced by the naked, long-haired man I'd seen in my dream. He was far too tall, his skin, eyes, hair, and nails all as black as his fur had been. But perhaps, once he was clothed, people would mistake him for a beserker of some kind.

"Is there anything here you could...you know, cover yourself with?"

He shrugged and smirked, holding himself with a carefree ease that told me he'd happily go naked.

29

Kita

Tesyel led me once more through the Bazaar. I had expected it to be similar to the last time he'd taken me, but the air was abuzz with an energy that set me on edge.

I tried to push away the hushed whispers and sideways glances. They didn't suspect me. Why would they? Even if someone thought they recognized me, I was dead. As far as they knew, deathseekers didn't exist. I was safe.

But the knot in my stomach refused to loosen.

Zentouran loped behind me, his presence a small comfort. We'd hastily wrapped him in bedsheets, styled as best we could to look like an emann, but this was a temporary solution that would attract almost as much attention as he would have had he just gone nude.

"Do not worry," Tesyel reassured us with a wide grin. "I know somewhere that has clothes for *anyone!*"

He darted through the crowd, weaving his way so expertly it was almost as though this fluid movement was his affinity, and not his gift of tongues.

Zentouran and I barely kept up.

Finally, we found ourselves at a small stall. A young woman—barely out of her teens, by the look of her—sat behind the little counter, leaning against her arm with a bored expression plastered across her face.

As Tesyel jabbered away in Avetsi, she slowly glanced his way, paying Zentouran and me no mind at all. It wasn't until the boy jerked a thumb in Zentouran's direction that she seemed to notice we were there, and even then, she barely gave him a second glance.

Finally, she nodded and spoke back to him. Whatever she said, he shook his head violently and launched into speech again.

"Ugh," the girl said, rolling her eyes as she spoke. Her response, this time, was more acceptable, and Tesyel turned to me.

"She can dress him. I even got you a discount!" His smile was so wide that his eyes were nothing more than slits.

"Oh, good," I said, dipping my hand into the pouch at my hip. "How much?"

He shifted his weight from side to side, rubbing his hands together. "Just a single gem!" he said, "And on top of that, she'll change some of the gems for you. That way, you can buy things at the other shops."

"Oh," I said. "Will the other shops not take them?"

"Some may not," he said. "Best to have coin. But don't change it all; when we leave the city, I don't know if they'll take Avetsi or imperial coin."

"Okay, how many then?"

He turned to her and repeated the question in Avetsi.

She stared at me with big brown eyes and held up 3 fingers.

Obediently, I unearthed three gems and dropped them onto the counter.

Almost instantly, they were gone, swept into a bag on the other side of the table. She disappeared behind the counter, rummaging through her things for several minutes before popping up, a stack of clothing in hand. She squinted at Zentouran, mentally sizing him up before nodding and pushing the stack of clothes toward them.

"You try on," she said in a thick Avetsi accent, as she jerked her head toward a small stall nearby that had sheets pinned to all the sides.

Zentouran grunted and took the clothing from her, fluidly entering the stall without so much as a noise. He was so tall that he could peek out over the top.

It seemed almost more lewd to watch him that way than if he had changed in front of us all, so I looked away.

"Here," the woman said, producing another stack of carefully folded garments. On top, she dropped a pile of gold coins.

Tesyel darted forward, shoveling the coins into his own pack before neatly packing the clothing away.

"We should consider hiring a guide," Tesyel muttered.

"Yes, I know," I replied. Even with whatever information he had managed to get, the deserts to the south were immense, and I had never spent even a moment in such an environment. It would be impossible without someone to lead us.

"Besides that, what do we need?" he asked, his eyes darting around the bazaar.

"Food, new bedrolls, horses." I scratched the back of my head, missing the weight of my hair. "Could I trust you to buy our supplies, and then meet me at the stables?"

"Oh, yes!" he said, nodding repeatedly as he bounced on the balls of his feet. "The stables are just there," he said, straining to his tiptoes and pointing as best he could over the crowd.

"Good," I said, a warm smile spreading across my face. "Off you go."

He gave one last curt nod before slipping into the crowd.

"Is this sufficient?" Zentouran asked, his deep voice rumbling through my chest.

I do not know how the girl at the stall produced clothing that fit him, but it was as though it was all custom made for him. He wore billowing linen pants the color of sand, with a white linen shirt that fell exactly at his wrists and hips. The white scarf, he'd tied around his neck.

The girl at the stall looked over and flashed a satisfied smile, but when he returned it, his teeth gleaming black, her face drained of color.

I rushed forward and grabbed him by the wrist, pulling him away.

"Thank you!" I called over my shoulder, dragging him behind me before she could respond.

We had to be careful, but before I could verbalize it, he heard my thoughts.

I know, he spoke directly into my mind. *I am sorry.*

"Come on," I said, letting him go. "To the stables."

The stables stood in the shade of the cliffs; the smell of straw and horse manure mingled with the sea air as we approached.

I was just about to walk into the small wooden building beside the paddock when the crowd around us shifted.

"Get back!" a loud voice called. The air grew thick. Zentouran lunged forward and grasped the back of my shirt as a gust of wind blew towards us, throwing some of the people in the crowd to the floor. I tried to brace myself, but I, too, was lifted into the air. If not for Zentouran, I would have been sent flying.

"I said back!" the voice screamed once more.

The gale subsided. I turned to see the crowd dispersing, people yelling as others hushed them.

And as the sea of people parted, a small group of soldiers marched forward.

I tried to pull Zentouran away, but before I could, the soldiers stopped, their company parting to reveal Weiran and the Priest.

I opened my mouth to speak, but Weiran's expression stopped me. The fiery wrath in his eyes made me forget, for the moment, that he had no offensive abilities to speak up.

But the Priest did, and the soldiers as well, so I had the good sense to shut my mouth.

"What. Did. You. Do?" Weiran demanded, each word punctuated with a step.

The Priest didn't meet my eyes.

Zentouran pulled me aside, stepping between me and Weiran.

Even this did not temper his rage.

But Zentouran's presence was a comfort to me, so I gathered enough courage to reply, "what are you talking about?"

"Don't play with me!" he snapped. His voice was strained, his accent thick. "After all I have done for you, this is the way you repay me? Are you acting against me?"

This was too much. All he had done? What *had* he done for me, exactly?

"Excuse me?" I replied. "You *murdered* me, less we forget!"

"I FREED YOU!" he roared. "I gave you the chance to live without having to look over your shoulder. I freed you of the notion that this empire was a just one. You have no idea how much planning this took, how much work."

"No, I don't," I retorted, "because your plans are all secretive and nebulous. I was sympathetic to you, Weiran! I was! But you...you murdered me! You murdered the princes and the generals, all in cold blood."

"What, was I supposed to be honorable about it? Kill them all in the field of battle? Would that have made you feel better? And with all the casualties that would have resulted, would that have been better?"

His stare, still angry, still fiery, had something else too. He *wanted* me to agree with him. I couldn't understand why, when I was almost free of Avetsut and the empire, why he would care, but he did, badly.

"This...this is a betrayal," he said quietly.

I laid a hand on Zentouran's arm, gently nudging him out of the way. I wanted to look Weiran in the eye.

"A betrayal?" I repeated. "Do you hear yourself? You stole from me, do you realize that? You killed me. That was bad enough. But you brought me back, and that was worse."

He sighed and threw his hands in the air. "Dying is so bad, but living again is worse?"

"Weiran," the Priest warned, but Weiran shrugged him off.

"Death will come eventually for you. For us all. I have given you another chance at life. You should be thanking me. You should be groveling!"

"Is the Priest groveling? Is Tsavi? You have no idea what death is. You have no idea what it is to feel as though you'll slip from your skin, back into the void. To feel as though your entire life was nothing and everything. There is nothing I could say that would make you understand, so don't pretend that you do just because you are a deathseeker."

He stared, hard, his jaw working. "You freed my hostage," he finally said.

"I freed my family," I corrected. "If you thought I would allow you to execute him, then you never knew me at all."

"He hunted you. He was there at the temple. He followed you all the way here, and still you defend him."

"And what did happen at the temple? Because it's been bothering me for some time. It made no sense for the emperor to destroy a mutually beneficial relationship. So why?"

He narrowed his eyes, but said nothing.

"And you?" I asked, turning to the Priest. "You just allowed him to work his plans? To massacre your sisters?"

The Priest's face remained stoic, and that hurt more than anything. When Weiran had murdered me, the Priest had begged forgiveness.

But for this, he had nothing to say.

"I'm leaving," I explained. "I want nothing to do with any of you, or any of this."

"You think that's still an option?" he asked. "You have shown that you're willing to work against us. You can't be allowed to leave now." He turned to his soldiers and barked an order in Avetsi, but before any of them could raise a hand against us, Zentouran jumped forward, slipping free of his shirt and kicking off his trousers. They all stared, some wide-eyed, some slack-jawed, and some confused, as his skin rippled and his beastly form emerged.

He loomed large, so huge that he was fully capable of swallowing any of the soldiers whole. His wet black teeth gleamed as he snarled a growl, saliva dripping into the dirt.

"Stop that creature!" Weiran yelled, pulling the Priest forward.

The Priest looked up, his eyes widening as he and I both realized that his affinity was, for the moment, useless. He could control my emotions, but not Zentouran's.

"You will tell your men to stand down," I shouted over the din. "Or Zenoutran will kill you."

The fire in Weiran's eyes quickly shifted to uncertainty before hardening.

"Kill this beast!" he screeched.

I sighed.

A few of the soldiers collected themselves and attacked, launching fire and air at him. All their attacks glanced off. Another soldier—a metalurgist—jumped forward, a sword of liquid metal materializing from his hip as he slashed.

Zentouran waited, absorbing every blow. The sword left no mark. Another soldier—this one barely out of boyhood—raised his hands, whipping the wind once more. I grasped Zentouran's tail just in time for him to push forward, the gale ripping at Zentouran's fur and lifting me off my feet.

"This is pointless, Weiran. Live to fight another day!" I yelled as the wind died, the boy soldier looking positively exhausted.

Weiran stared, jaw clenched, as his soldiers tried to land a blow.

Nothing harmed Zentouran, who stood, tail wagging menacingly, and waited.

I wasn't going to ask him to kill. But Weiran did not know that.

In the corner of my vision, there was a flash of movement. I turned just in time to see the Priest upon me, his elbow driving the breath out of me.

I stumbled back. Zentouran turned his great head, growling.

No! I thought to him. *Focus on them.*

He obeyed, rearing up on his hind legs, his full height casting shadow down the street.

The Priest hooked an arm under my armpits and dragged me back, my feet scrabbling against the dirt.

"Stand down, Kita," he grunted. "Don't make me take your emotions. Please."

I bit down hard on his arm, but he didn't react.

Zentouran crashed down, flinging soldiers aside as easily as he might swat a fly.

A thought occurred. He wasn't draining my energy reserves. There was no reason I couldn't create another.

I drew in my breath, holding an image in my mind. Exhaling, I released it, and one of my warriors stood before me, the gossamer thread connecting us once more. He did not hesitate, leaping into the Priest. The three of us fell in a tangled heap.

The Priest was the first pull to himself free. He drew his twin blades and slashed. With no weapons, all my warrior could do was leap back, but one of the swords caught him in the shoulder. I hissed in pain, sinking into myself.

For a second, the Priest and I locked eyes. He wiped his face and threw himself forward, swinging his second sword.

I thought I had gotten a good sense of his fighting abilities. First at the temple, when he and Weiran sparred, and then again when we trained together. But now, it was abundantly obvious that I hadn't ever seen his true skill.

He moved in a twisted dance of violence, easily avoiding any of my warrior's movements. He was like a cat, dancing around his prey and pouncing when he found and opening. He was toying with my creation, who could do nothing but roar and try to grapple.

The Priest stabbed at him, burying a sword in his chest. A moan escaped my warrior's lips as he stumbled forward, driving the blade deeper. It was as though he was carving my heart free.

Don't give up, I pressed to him. *Keep fighting.*

My warrior gripped the blade, spat black blood onto the Priest's face, and headbutted him, forcing him to release the grip. With a pained moan, he pulled the sword free and swung it at the Priest, cutting deep into his shoulder.

But the Priest was not done. He caught his balance and swept his opponent's legs, sending the warrior crashing bodily to the ground. Kneeling over him, he took one last glance at me and swiped the blade cleanly across my warrior's throat. The cut was so deep, so vicious that only a bit of skin and muscle kept the head from rolling away.

Bile rose in my throat. The pain was paralyzing, so deep and sharp that I heaved the contents of my stomach onto the street. I tasted blood, but it was not my own.

As my warrior lay dying, the Priest turned to me, his stoicism suddenly dark.

"Stop!" a voice rang out.

Weak and trembling, I pushed myself up to find Zentouran, his snarling maw mere inches from Weiran's face. He'd cleared the way and held Weiran under his paw, thick saliva dropping onto his prey's face. Weiran turned his head away from the great creature as Zentouran inched closer.

The Priest ran to Weiran's side, slashing futilely at Zentouran's paws, but my boy—my protector—did not move.

"Stop. You win. Call your creature off and leave. Just go," Weiran spat.

The soldiers, who'd been easily scattered, approached gingerly, trying to reach their new prince—or whatever he was now—without getting too close.

"Zentouran, leave him. We have business elsewhere."

He sniffed at Weiran's form once more and backed off, releasing Weiran from his grasp.

As Zentouran walked toward me, flopping down and resting his great head on mine, the Priest helped Weiran to his feet. Neither of them took their eyes away from us.

"If you come back here, I will have you killed," he warned. There were no teeth behind it, and we both knew it.

"Go back to your palace and leave me be," I replied.

For several long seconds, we locked eyes, as though each of us were waiting for the other to fold.

Weiran blinked first.

"I sincerely hope I never see you again," he said. Before I could think of a retort, his soldiers ushered him away.

I sighed and looked around. Zentouran's clothes had been scattered by the wind; his scarf was nowhere to be found, but I was able to locate both his shirt and trousers; they were dusty, but unharmed.

"Thanks for saving the clothes," I muttered as I shoved the garments in his direction. I couldn't keep my hands still.

He rumbled a laugh as his fur rippled and he stood in his humanoid form. His voice was a comfort, and I found myself able to breathe a bit more easily.

"I'll go and see about those horses," I said, looking away as he pulled his pants on.

* * *

Tesyel gasped and clung to me.

"We're fine, I promise!" I reassured, patting him on the head. I almost regretted mentioning the incident to him.

"Are you sure? The city guard?"

"Everything is fine. We're leaving them all behind."

He looked unconvinced, and given how that fight had gone, I felt about as unsure as he did.

"They cannot harm us," Zentouran said, his deep voice vibrating through my chest.

Tesyel peeked at Zentouran, but didn't say anything.

"You've done well to get our supplies," I said, changing the subject. The boy brightened, flashing me a bright smile. "Any word on a guide?" He shook his head, turning his attention to the spotted horse we'd purchased. He buried his hands in its mane, stroking the rather disinterested mare.

"We'll go to the border," he said. "There will be lots of people traveling south; with luck, there will be tribesmen that can take us exactly where we need to go."

"What's the likelihood of that?"

The boy shrugged. "If not, someone will be heading in that direction."

I couldn't help but smile at his earnestness.

The border to the south was about a mile outside the city proper, where the earth narrowed. A thick stone wall well over a hundred feet tall blocked any path south, stretching from coast to coast.

The only way south by land was the border crossing.

"They're supposed to open the gate today," Tesyel explained as we approached the gate. He rode the horse, while Zentouran and I walked on either side.

"And then I'll be free of all this," I replied. It was a comforting thought, but terrifying. I had no idea what lay beyond. Was I really prepared to cross?

Ultimately, it didn't matter. There was no other option that I could see.

A small crowd had assembled near the gate, each grouped into small traveling parties. Most of them didn't seem to be Avetsi. They mostly wore white and tan linens, unlike the brightly dyed colors I'd seen in the city. Many of them spoke tongues I'd never heard, though Tesyel's ears perked as we passed each new language.

I was suddenly overjoyed to have him along.

Off to the side was a gorgeous horse with a coat like molten gold. As it pawed at the ground, the light seemed to glitter off its flank.

Its rider noticed my interest and dismounted.

They were covered from head to toe in white linens, with a white scarf wrapped around their head so that only their eyes peeked out.

"Toi lamn?" a bright feminine voice said.

"Uh…" I replied, looking to Tesyel for help.

Before he could open his mouth, she realized I didn't speak her tongue and switched, first to Avetsi and then to the imperial tongue.

"Do you like?" she asked, stroking the horse's neck.

"It's a beautiful animal," I said, relieved that Tesyel would not have to translate the entire conversation.

"Yes, yes. Bred especially for desert travel. She's a good girl." The rider's accent was thick, but her voice was clear.

"Do you journey into the desert often?" I asked, trying not to sound too desperate.

"Oh, yes. My people trade with the Empire quite often, though it seems that we may need to adjust our policies now."

"Right," I muttered.

"This is your first time traveling south, isn't it?" the rider asked, raising an eyebrow.

Guard your tongue, Zentouran spoke into my mind. *I do not trust this woman.*

It was a fair thought, and after my experience with Weiran, I wasn't eager to trust anyone either. But we needed someone to help us.

"Yes," I admitted. "I'm meeting someone."

"Ah, where do you travel?" the rider asked. "Perhaps we could ride together. It is always nice to have a companion on the road."

Tesyel and I exchanged a look. I didn't know what to say.

"I'm meeting with a member of the Notasi tribes," I finally said.

The riders eyes brightened.

"Ah, yes! The Notasi!"

"You know them?"

"Yes, of course, of course. A strong people, they are. I trade with them often. They are nomadic by nature, of course, but most of them travel in and out of Oryn-tal with some frequency. I don't believe I will be traveling quite that far, but I can journey with you for a while, at least."

I do not like this, Zentouran said.

I agreed. There was something about this woman's eagerness that was off-putting. We would need to be careful.

Still, we needed her, at least for the moment.

"It would be lovely to travel with you," I said with a smile. I waited for her to ask my name, but she just mounted her horse and nodded.

A loud scraping noise signaled the opening of the gate. The crowd pushed forward, swelling against the slowly swinging stone.

The four of us waited to the side until the others all passed through.

I mounted my horse, Tesyel sitting in front of me as Zentouran walked beside, a newly acquired scarf concealing most of his face.

The woman mounted up and clicked her tongue, gently prodding her horse along. City watch eyed each of us with suspicion as we crossed the border, but they did not stop us.

Nothing seemed different on the other side of the border. The cool sea air still wafted, salty and brisk. To the south, there was nothing but green land and the small groups spreading across as the earth widened toward the horizon.

And yet, everything had changed. The city and all its noise was behind us. The Empire was behind us.

And ahead?

30

Ran

"There is no way that this is the stealthiest option available," Ran muttered, tugging at his shirt.

Aka frowned. "Lovely prince, this is the fashion of the city. No one will question it." She was almost unrecognizable in her own Avetsi garb, having traded her animal skins for an orange linen dress. With her hair tied back with a matching scarf, she really did look Avetsi.

Ditan stood in the corner, arms crossed, and said nothing, though he did—rather annoyingly—lift an eyebrow.

She was right, of course. He'd seen more bright, ostentatious colors since arriving in Avetsut than he had ever imagined. So, he really shouldn't have been surprised when she brought him linens in blues the color of the sea, and of pinks the color of the sunrise.

That didn't mean he had to like it.

"My prince, I must protest this plan," Ditan said. "It would be a far easier escape to take you myself, and—"

"No!" Ran snapped. "No," he said again, more softly this time, as he worked his fingers. He couldn't go back to that place, even to save his own life. He just couldn't.

"Yes, my prince," Ditan murmured.

A pang of guilt ran through Ran's stomach. He wished Ditan hadn't been dragged through all this. He was a good man.

Something else to add to his guilt.

"Well then, lovely boys," Aka boomed, raising her arms. "Let us go. Cover of night is upon us. The horses await outside the city. If we can slip away unseen, you may just make it back to your father."

Ran's expression soured. He wanted nothing less than to discuss his father.

He exchanged a look with Ditan, nodding curtly. The guard returned the expression and faded into the shadow.

Somehow, Ran expected that his first step outside of the little room in which he'd been holed up would result in his capture, that the first person to see him would pounce upon him, dragging him back to the torment that was Telombraj.

Nothing of the sort happened. The streets were sparse. The Bazaar and docks saw only a few merchants and fishers left, cleaning stalls and sweeping as the moon made its ascent.

Ran allowed himself to relax slightly, until Aka hooked an arm around his and pulled him forward. It took everything in him not to phase away from her.

"Ahhh!" she called, her voice echoing through the empty streets. "A beautiful night, yes?"

"Yes, I suppose so," he muttered, his voice rough and tense.

The dark of the night jangled Ran's nerves; with the moon bright and swollen overhead, the sky was too similar in color to the lonely Telombraj landscape. He found himself wishing they'd left during the day. Even if it meant more eyes upon them, at least this nagging dread would subside.

With the docks at their backs, they pushed forward through the Bazaar with ease and started the arduous climb up the cliffs.

He felt it before he saw it, the tickling brush of static electricity that stood the hairs on his arm on edge. Then, a hand appearing from the darkness, reaching for him.

On instinct, he solidified the air in front of him, pushing the wall of solid atmosphere outward.

The female shadowwalker stumbled back, yelping as she met Ditan's newly materialized form behind her.

He did not speak, nor did he hesitate. His dagger flashed in the moonlight as he slid it between her ribs, so deep that the tip poked through her chest, spreading a bloom of red across the white of her shirt.

Ditan spun her, locking eyes with her as she gasped for air, trying in vain to grab at the blade. He closed the distance, his face—cold and stony—mere inches from hers.

Her face was twisted, not in pain, but confusion, as she struggled to form words.

Ditan pulled his knife free, and she gasped. He caught her as she fell, still holding her gaze as she blinked, and her mouth gaped.

Aka tightened her grip on Ran's arms as the light in the girl's eyes flickered.

Still, Ditan held her, waiting until the last of the fire was gone from her gaze before whispering something unintelligble into her ears and lying her tenderly on the ground.

"What did you do?" Ran hissed, breaking Ditan's reverie.

The guard was at Ran's side at once, roughly gripping him by the shoulder.

"No!" Ran screamed, but Ditan did not listen, and an instant later, there was a strange flash of dark, and the three of them stood atop the cliffs, their horses whinnying and rearing at the sudden appearance.

Ran's heart pounded, drumming loud and almost painful against his ribs. He phased himself free, took two steps, and vomited, heaving until there was nothing left in him.

He collapsed, digging his fingers into the grass and turning it to liquid in his hands.

"Breathe," he muttered to himself, trying to calm his quick, gasping breaths.

"My prince," Ditan said, his voice full of concern.

"Don't!" Ran snapped. "Just...don't." He knelt there for several moments, and slowly—very slowly—his heart rate calmed.

"My prince, we should not stay," Ditan said, kneeling beside him.

"I know, I know," Ran replied, swallowing hard. "You killed her," he said. As soon as the words left his lips, he was struck by the obviousness of the statement.

"Yes, my prince," Ditan replied. He wore a concerned expression, but didn't seem bothered by what he'd done.

"You killed her!" Ran repeated, his voice thin. He felt as though he were on the edge of breaking, shattering into hundreds of pieces that could never be reassembled.

"They wanted to execute you," Ditan said. "I could not let that happen. You are under my charge."

He was right; of course he was right. That girl—no, woman, Ran reminded himself—had cast her lot with terrorists. This was a natural consequence.

But still, to watch the cold efficiency with which Ditan had performed his duty was too much.

Ran staggered to his feet. If there had been anything left in his stomach, he would have vomited again.

"Let's go," he said, his voice raw and cracked.

* * *

The Temple of Hope sat in a shattered stone heap. Rocks and boulders had tumbled down the ziggurat, and in the months that Ran and Ditan

RAN

had been gone, no one had cleared them away.

The sun was bright overhead. The market district should have been buzzing with activity.

There was none.

All the market stalls were unmanned. As they approached the bridge that led into the Capital, the only people they saw were city guards.

"Halt!" a stern voice called. Ran looked up with weary eyes to see one of the guards approaching them, his hand raised.

"You will let your prince pass," Ditan hissed, a hand on his dagger.

The guard's gaze slid to Ran, and his eyes widened.

"Prince Ranjali?" he asked. "Is that—"

"Allow us to pass, or you will explain to my father why you've delayed me," Ran snapped.

The city guardsman swallowed and hurried to the side, dipping his head as the pair rode on.

"What is going on?" Ran called to Ditan as they cleared the first gate. "Where is everyone?"

Ditan just shrugged.

As the gate closed behind them, they paused, staring at the destruction before them.

The entire Silk District had been burned to the ground, the majority of the houses and building nothing but burnt husks.

Ran and Ditan exchanged a look and carried on toward the palace.

Of all Yor-a, the palace seemed to be the only thing that was the same as we left it. It stood, imposing and grand, over the ruined city.

When they reached the stables, they dismounted. Ran rested his forehead against the stubborn white horse's. It affectionately nibbled on his hair, and he had to gently pull away before he lost even more.

The walk to the palace doors filled him with a strange anxiety, a twisting knot in his gut that tightened the closer he got.

Ditan followed, ever dutiful and silent behind.

Ran knew that most people at the palace had no idea where he'd been. As quiet as the emperor would have wanted things kept, he would have ensured utter secrecy.

But there were so many eyes on him that he couldn't help but think that they knew of his failure.

They watch because you are the crown prince, he reminded himself. *That is all.* But he couldn't shake the feeling.

Ran found his father exactly where he assumed he would, watching the gutted city from the rooftop gardens. He waited quietly, hands folded, eyes cast down, as he waited for the emperor to speak.

The emperor did not.

Unable to bear the silence, Ran said, "Father, I—"

"What would possess you to speak right now, boy?" The emperor's voice was so even that Ran debated, for the moment, whether he would rather return to the shadows than stand there and listen.

The emperor turned to face his son, eyes narrowed, brow furrowed, and he said, "All you had to do was retrieve the girl and bring her back to this palace. A simple matter. It should have been done in a day or so. Had I sent my guard to do it, it would have been done. The matter would have been dealt with and we would move on."

"Would you have killed her?"

"Do not speak, boy!" the emperor roared, spittle flying from his mouth.

There was something in the emperor's eyes that finally, *finally* told Ran what Kita and Isa had always known. He had been too stubborn, too awed by his father to believe it.

He met his father's gaze. His defiance seemed to anger the emperor further, but he didn't care.

"You disappear for months. You anger one of my most trusted commandants, destabilizing the leadership of the Eastern Fort. You reappear in Avetsut just in time for the city and the region to declare

310

its independence by rather publicly killing a member of the royal family—"

"You were going to kill her," Ran interjected. He did not drop his gaze.

"Quietly!" the emperor yelled. The look in his eyes had turned murderous, and Ran thought he might be beaten while servants and guards alike watched. Even Ditan, loyal as he had been, would be forced to do nothing, or even carry out the act himself, if the emperor deemed it so.

Ran no longer cared.

"And what happened here, while I was gone? What have you done to our city?"

The emperor breathed a deep sigh and ran a hand through his hair.

"After terrorists attacked the temple, they turned the people against us. A false flag operation, designed to sew discord. The Middle Gates were battered down. There were riots in the Silk District; nobility were forced from their homes. It took a great deal of military force to quell. I am told there are similar concerns coming from the north. It's all a mess that I have to contend with, alongside all the headache you've caused me."

The emperor turned his back to his son and resumed gazing out over the city.

"You will return to your quarters," he said, his voice suddenly very still. "You will remain there until I have decided what will be done with you. Do not assume this matter is settled."

"Yes, Father," Ran said, spinning on his heels. There was a sour taste in his mouth, but he knew better than to push the matter.

He was halfway to his apartments when he stopped.

"Ditan," he said, glancing over his shoulder.

The young shadowwalker, still following close behind, paused, and quickly dipped his head.

"I'm going to speak with my sister. Please make sure that I'm not followed."

"Yes, my prince," Ditan said, and then he was gone.

Isa's chambers were guarded by a pair of guards that Ditan did not recognize. They looked rather bored as they stood, shifting their weight from leg to leg as they quietly waited.

"Leave," Ran said.

The guards glanced at each other.

"We are under strict orders. We cannot leave our post!"

Before Ran could reply, Ditan was between them, dagger drawn against one of their throats.

"You speak to the crown prince," he hissed, "You would do well to follow his command."

"M-my apologies!" the other guard stuttered, raising his hands. "We weren't…we were just—"

"Be gone, and quickly," Ran muttered, crossing his arms.

Ditan released his prey and the pair of them were off, nearly tripping as they scurried away.

"She won't be happy to see me,"Ran said quietly as he walked to the door, pressing his hands against the beautifully carved wood.

"Shall I accompany you?" Ditan asked, but Ran simply shook his head and pushed the great wood doors open.

He had expected to walk into Isa's receiving room. That is not what he found. Instead, he was back in Avetsut.

It wasn't the same as he remembered. There was the sea, with its reed sailing boats dotting the bay. There was the amphitheater, though it was much broader and deeper than it had been. Everything was still—the birds overhead. The waves out near the docks. Even the amphitheater. It was packed with people, each of them sneering toward the stage. He turned his head to the stage and there was Kita, hands bound and mouth gagged. She was frozen in a silent scream, tears streaming down her face, mixing with blood as a large ornamental sword kissed her throat.

A large, laughing man held the sword, nothing at all like the slender, angry-eyed youth that had been there.

And at Kita's feet, as though to catch her as she fell, knelt Isa. Isa didn't cry, she didn't scream, though there must have been a great deal of that when reports of Kita's death first reached her. Instead, she just stared up at her daughter's face.

Ran opened his mouth to speak, but couldn't find the words.

Finally, Isa noticed that he had walked in. Suddenly, all of the figures' faces snapped to him, burying him under their accusatory stares. Worst of all was Kita, staring hard with her throat gaping.

"Leave me," Isa growled. Her voice was hoarse and gravely.

Ran did not move. He knew what he was seeing wasn't real, wasn't even what happened, not really. But it broke his heart anyway.

"Go," she said.

"Isa, I—"

"What is there to say? I asked you, Ran. I begged you to let her go. And now this. Because of you." Her words stung him. "When she was born, Father wanted her sent away. Given to one of the noble families. Did you know that?"

He blinked. He didn't know that.

"I begged him. I got down on my knees, still bleeding from childbirth as healers frantically stood over me, and I pleaded with him not to take my child from me. And do you know what he did? He smiled. It was like he had been waiting for the opportunity. And he gave me a choice—my crown, or my baby. That was the first choice I had to make. It wasn't hard; I never wanted to rule. It was almost a relief. But then...then, it was my husband."

Husband? He'd never known that Isa had been married.

As though reading his mind, she said, "Kyr and I thought if we were married by the temple, he wouldn't interfere." She snorted a humorless laugh. "It didn't stop him. He simply said he would have Kyr killed. So I begged again, and again, he smiled. And so my husband was sent away. But at least I had my baby. At least I had Kita. Now?" She stood, and her illusion faded, leaving him face to face with his sister, an angry mother with nothing left. She grasped his chin and roughly jerked his face toward her, pulling him so close that he see her pupils contract. He resisted the urge to push her away.

"Isa, calm now. There is something you need to know."

"I am going to make you wish for death," she hissed at him. "Every horrific nightmare that I can imagine will be your reality, from hence forth. I will make you question the nature of reality so thoroughly that you won't be able to trust your own senses. You'd better fucking kill me."

Despite himself, despite the seriousness of the moment, he barked a laugh. For all her posturing about how much she hated him and their father, Ran couldn't help but to see the similarities in the three of them.

"Enough of this," he said, phasing out of her grasp and stepping back. "Torture me if you wish. You would not be the first. But before you do, you should know that Kita lives."

"Liar!"

"I saw her myself, after I watched her blood spilled. This hell that you've imagined for yourself, I've lived. But Kita is alive."

"If you saw her die, then how could you say that?"

"They've got a deathseeker," he said, his voice low.

"They don't exist," she muttered, but he could tell from the tone of her voice she was beginning to doubt herself.

"At least one does, and for whatever reason, he saw fit to return her to us."

Isa glared at him, searching for some hint of whether he was truthful.

"She saved me from falling into the hands of these conspirators. If not for her, I would myself be dead, no doubt."

Isa took a step back, and then another. She wanted to believe him, he could see it in her eyes. She wanted to grasp at the line he had tossed her.

"Then where is she now?"she asked quietly.

"Seeking her father," he said simply. "Perhaps, by now, she's found him."

"This cannot be true," Isa replied, shaking her head slowly. "Please, Ranjali. Do not get my hopes up."

"I know my word means little to you," he replied, "but I swear to you that she lives. You, Ditan, and I are the only ones that know, and it is in Kita's best interest for the secret to remain between us. I don't know what Father will do if he finds out."

Ran could see the thoughts flowing through her head. Whatever she was thinking, she did not share. Instead, she absently pat his shoulder. Then, she pulled him into a tight embrace. He was so shocked that it took him a moment to return her hug, but when he did, he found that he needed it, perhaps as much as she did.

They stood together, brother and sister, for a long moment, until finally, wordlessly, she broke away and crossed the room. She didn't say anything more.

And really, what more was there to say?

31

Epilogue

The sun had begun to set over the ocean, casting the yellow palace in a soft, pinkish orange glow.

Weiran lowered himself onto the edge of the cliff, taking a swig from his goblet.

Keep going!

MURDERER!

I want my mother, I want my—

Why do you just sit? Avenge us, by all the goddesses!

We know you can hear us—

Why? Why? Why?!

He squeezed his eyes shut. His head throbbed from the noise, but that was nothing new.

There was a hand on his shoulder. He knew from the touch that it was the Priest. His priest.

"Nokinan's remains have been brought to the Temple of Wrath," he said, his voice cool and even.

Weiran nodded and asked, "has someone sent word to her nephews?"

"Yes."

"Good. She was a good woman, and they are good boys. Let's send some gold for them. "

"As you wish."

Weiran leaned against him, breathing in his scent.

"What troubles you?" the Priest asked.

Weiran shrugged. "The usual. Do you have any herbs?"

The Priest rummaged through his pack and produced a few leaves.

"This is all for now. The rest needs to be rationed until we can find more. I'll go walk the bazaars tomorrow."

Weiran frowned, but took the leaves and stuffed them into his mouth, chewing frantically. The voices did not completely quiet, but they dimmed somewhat.

He allowed himself to breathe.

"I thought you would be happier," the Prince noted.

Weiran sighed. He'd thought so too. "I suppose there's still a lot to be done. We freed one city. There's an empire left. And with no sign of the spoiled prince, I worry we've tipped our hand too soon."

The Priest was silent, as he often was.

"We adapt," Weiran said, trying to sound resolute. "Our plans are solid. I'm told the Imperial Army marches south as we speak. Are we ready to move?"

The Priest hesitated.

"What?" Weiran asked, snapping his attention to his lover. "Something troubling you?"

"This is your home," the Priest said simply. "Do you truly wish to abandon it?"

Weiran allowed his gaze to wander back to the city. This was a view he'd cherished as a child. He'd always loved this place—the freedom he'd always felt, even among his servitude. The bright colors, the ocean, the bazaar—it all meant something to him. He'd always hold it in his memory.

But some things were more important.

317

"If we could garrison, we would. But I'd rather lose Avetsut and win the war. The forces we leave will do their jobs."

"And do those forces know you're sacrificing them?"

Weiran locked eyes with the Priest. As usual, he was annoyingly stoic; his eyes betrayed nothing.

"It's best they don't," he said.

"Best for you? Or for them?"

"Best for us all."

Murderer!

Fiend!

Fuck the empire!

Fuck you!

He chewed harder, willing the herbs to take the edge away. He could already tell that sleep would not come easily that night.

"Do you doubt me?" Weiran asked.

The Priest squeezed his hand, resting his chin on the top of Weiran's head.

"I believe your plan is solid," he replied.

"But?"

"There is no 'but.' I promised you when we met that I would follow you until the end. And even after returning from several ends...here I am."

"And you resent me for it," Weiran whispered.

"I resent no one. I don't believe myself to be capable of it anymore."

Weiran recoiled. That stung almost more than if the Priest had cursed him.

Weiran sighed. "I'm sorry," he murmured. "I know you hate me for bringing you back, but I can't do this without you. I can't let you just become another ghost."

"I know you can't," the Priest replied, and his voice, once more, betrayed nothing. "And I don't hate you."

Somehow, that was worse.

Weiran buried his head in his hands.

The Priest ran his hands through Weiran's hair, but the motion was mechanical. He'd been this way since the second or third time he'd been dragged away from death.

So why couldn't Weiran just let him go?

"What is the mood down there?" he asked. "Can you tell?"

"Hmmm," the Priest replied, turning his attention to the bustling bazaar below. "With so many people, it's hard to detect changes. Some have that nervous excitement that comes with change. Some resent. Some accept. Others are no different at all. It's the nature of a city, I suppose."

"And it doesn't bother you? Feeling all those emotions at once?"

"No, it doesn't."

Weiran let out another exasperated sigh and swung his legs up and away from the ledge. Climbing to his feet, he asked, "and Tsavi?"

"He is a ball of emotion still. Confused. Still grieving the death he could have had. I know the feeling."

Weiran ground his teeth. "I should not have allowed Kita to cloud my judgment. It was a mistake."

The Priest shrugged. "Tsavi is still committed. Do not dwell upon it."

"How can I not?" Weiran demanded, whirling around. "All I've done is make mistakes!"

The Priest stared, hard. "You've liberated this city. Your plans move ever forward. Yes, you've made mistakes; so have we all. We move forward."

"I don't understand you. You don't even believe in this cause."

The Priest paused before rising and pulling Weiran into an embrace. Weiran didn't fight it, and he allowed himself to melt into the Priest's arms.

319

"To tell you the truth, I didn't believe the deathseekers were real. Throughout my training, I always thought them to be a myth; a lesson to be learned. Then I met you. You dragged me from the comforting embrace of death. And yes, death was a comfort to me; I spent four eternities in the bosom of the goddesses. But...I got to be a part of something else. Something mythical. That isn't so bad, is it? And though my emotions have dulled....I don't know. I still love you. So...if it gives you purpose, it gives me purpose. I am with you."

The tears came then.

9 798989 926213